Peter Watt has spent time as a soldier, articled clerk, prawn trawler deckhand, builder's labourer, pipe layer, real estate salesman, private investigator, police sergeant, surveyor's chainman and advisor to the Royal Papua New Guinea Constabulary. He speaks, reads and writes Vietnamese and Pidgin. He now lives at Maclean on the Clarence River in northern New South Wales. He has volunteered with the Volunteer Rescue Association, Queensland Ambulance Service and currently with the Rural Fire Service. Fishing and the vast open spaces of outback Queensland are his main interests in life.

Peter Watt can be contacted at www.peterwatt.com.

Author Photo: Shawn Peene

Also by Peter Watt

The Duffy/Macintosh Series
Cry of the Curlew
Shadow of the Osprey
Flight of the Eagle
To Chase the Storm
To Touch the Clouds
To Ride the Wind
Beyond the Horizon
War Clouds Gather
And Fire Falls
Beneath a Rising Sun
While the Moon Burns
From the Stars Above

The Papua Series
Papua
Eden
The Pacific

The Silent Frontier
The Stone Dragon
The Frozen Circle

Excerpts from emails sent to Peter Watt

'I have been enthralled with your books since I was given a copy of *Cry of the Curlew*; your storytelling comes alive in my mind when I read your books. Thank you for taking me on amazing adventures.'

'I have, with a saddened heart, just finished the last of the Duffy/ Macintosh saga. I cannot express how I have loved this series. I waited and waited for the last one . . . Please tell me you are going to write another historical family saga! Thank you for the many hours of reading pleasure and please keep writing.'

'Thank you for the hours of taking me back to our early history. You are a master storyteller.'

'Have just finished *From the Stars Above*. Brilliant. Couldn't put it down . . . what an ending!'

'Bugger! It's over. I have just finished reading *From the Stars Above*. It seems I have been reading your books forever . . . the only problem, as some of your other readers have said, is that once you start it's hard to put them down to do other things . . . Thank you for the hours of enjoyment reading all your books. I look forward to your new characters in the next book.'

'You have obviously done your research well, particularly in the various theatres of battle. You are also able to throw in a lot of hope and Australian humour throughout some of the sadness, which is life itself. Thank you and keep writing.'

'Just to let you know that we are still reading your books and love them all . . . Keep them coming.'

'I have just read *Beneath a Rising Sun* and I am in tears. My uncle was a coast watcher during the Second World War in the Pacific and was shot twice. I only found out at his funeral. When I was a child, we used to play games in the bush . . . I only realised that he was teaching me jungle warfare when I was in the Infantry during the Vietnam War. I will be reading more of your books. I have had my cataracts done so I can start reading again.'

'I have just finished *While the Moon Burns*. Another excellent read. My wife gave me the book last Christmas and I deliberately resisted reading it until now, knowing it's almost at the end.'

'Well, Pete, I finished *From the Stars Above* at 3.20 am this morning . . . curse you. It was a great read and a fitting end to the saga.'

'Every Christmas I buy books to place under the Christmas tree. Many years ago, I placed *Cry of the Curlew* there for my husband as to me it sounded like a good read. All these years later we have all of Peter's books. Looking forward to the next book.'

'Once I get started on your books I just can't put them down. They are so entertaining and full of Australian history. Please keep writing.'

The Queen's COLONIAL

PETER WATT

PAN
Pan Macmillan Australia

First published 2018 in Macmillan by Pan Macmillan Australia Pty Ltd
This Pan edition published 2019 by Pan Macmillan Australia Pty Ltd
1 Market Street, Sydney, New South Wales, Australia, 2000

Map on pages pvi-vii taken from *The Cambridge Modern History Atlas* by Sir A. William Ward, G.W. Prothero. Sir S. M. Leathes & E.A. Benians, 1912, copyright Cambridge University Press, reproduced with permission.

Cataloguing-in-Publication entry is available
from the National Library of Australia
http://catalogue.nla.gov.au

Typeset in Bembo by Post Pre-press Group
Printed by IVE

For my beloved wife, Naomi.

THE
BLACK SEA
THE CRIMEAN WAR
English Miles

Reference
Territory restored by Russia to Turkey in 1856.
" " " " " Moldavia in 1856.

R U

R. Bug

R. Dniester

Bessarabia

R. Pruth

Nikolaief

Ocholso

Odessa

Kinburn

Kher

Moldavia

Jassy

Akkerman

Po

AUSTRIA

Galatz

Ismail

Kilia Mouth

Sulina Mouth

S.ᵗ George Mouth

Wallachia

R. Aluta

Buckarest

Dobrudja

Kala

Sevas

C. Kherso

Bu

R. Danube

Silistria

Bulgaria

B L A

Isker

Shumla

Varna

Mᵗˢ

Maritsa R.

Burgas

Adrianople

Maritsa R.

Bosphorus

Constantinople

Skutari

Kulah

S. OF MARMORA

R. Sakaria

O

M

N

Mᵗ Athos

Gallipoli

Dardanelles

ÆGEAN

SEA

mbridge University. Press.

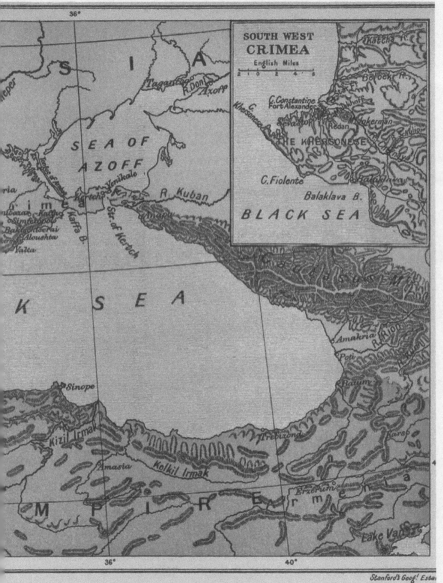

PROLOGUE

Puketutu
The Colony of New Zealand

May, 1845

Eighteen-year-old Second Lieutenant Samuel Forbes wanted to run away. But it was the duty of the junior officer to give courage to the red-coated soldiers. He held the regimental colours aloft, knowing that he must stand firm.

The field was covered in thick gun smoke, the Congreve rockets being fired by the blue-jacketed rocketeers only yards away adding to the confusion of the battlefield on rolling green plains surrounded by heavily forested hills. In many ways, the countryside reminded Samuel of his family estate in England.

Men screamed in pain as the Maori musket balls ripped holes in the British army ranks, and the fortified wooden fortress the Maoris called a *pa* did not look as if it could ever be breached. No sooner did the weakening ranks of half-naked Maori warriors — with their fearsome tattooed faces – fall back than an attack would be launched from the rear of the British force.

Samuel Forbes had never wanted to be a soldier. His father had purchased a commission in an infantry unit and left him at the gates of the regiment in England when he had just turned sixteen. Military life did not appeal to the young man, who had always dreamed of a career as a poet, extolling the romantic beauty of life. His father had told his second-born son that he was far too sensitive to be a member of the Forbes family, and army life would teach his dreamer son the lessons to face reality in life.

Now, all he could see was the savagery of war and he knew – as much as the lowliest soldiers surrounding him – that they were losing, against an enemy they had severely underestimated.

Beside him, a soldier fell screaming as a musket ball tore through his groin. Samuel wanted to be sick as he glanced down at the red-coated soldier writhing in pain at his feet, blood rapidly spreading on the white trousers. Samuel could feel his hands shaking uncontrollably as he attempted to stand firm, holding the regiment's colours, wondering when the bugler would call to either advance or withdraw.

'Fall back!' a voice called in the din of musket volleys, exploding rockets and men yelling in pain and fear. Samuel recognised the command coming from Captain Larkin, his commanding officer. Samuel glanced around him and could see the men withdrawing, carrying and dragging their wounded comrades, joining the survivors of the original four hundred and twenty sent to teach the impudent natives a lesson about the might of the British Empire. The redcoats, their white cross belts over their jackets, took up a defensive position to repel any counterattack, the wall of shining steel bayonets a deterrent to the bravest of Maori warriors facing them.

'Well done, Mr Forbes,' Captain Larkin said when Samuel joined him in the line. 'I fear we will have to give the ground to these rascals today.' He sighed, and the order was passed along for the regiment to withdraw back to the coast.

As Samuel marched with his men, he could not get out of his mind the sights and sounds of his first battlefield. He knew that they would haunt his dreams, and he also knew that this first clash with the Maori warriors would be his last.

A Village outside Sydney Town
The Colony of New South Wales

May, 1845

Eighteen-year-old Ian Steele closed the cover of Thucydides' *History of the Peloponnesian War*. The flickering candle on the wooden table beside his bed cast a dim light over his tiny room. With loving care, he placed the book beside the candle before blowing it out. In the darkness of the room, he lay back on his bed and stared at the ceiling, pondering the tactics he had read in the precious book, the last gift his father had given him before he died a year earlier. He had idolised his father who, as a young soldier, had fought at Waterloo before his regiment had been sent on garrison duties to the British colony of New South Wales. Here he had met, fallen in love with, and eventually married a young Scottish girl, Mary, who had been transported as a convict and served her seven years for committing the crime of fraud. Colour Sergeant Malcolm Steele had taken his discharge in Sydney, and invested his pension money in a small farm on the outskirts, in the shadow of the Great Dividing Range that had once hemmed in expansion of the rapidly growing population of Sydney Town.

Ian had been born after his mother had lost two children in their infancy, and he had survived to become their only child. Both his parents shared a passion for learning, and his mother was one of those rare women who could read and write. When Ian had returned from his schooling, she would ensure that he studied beyond what was expected, and the boy had excelled in his class. He grew to love learning and read every book he could get his hands on, from Greek mythology to books concerning military matters.

Ian remembered the times his father would take him to the garrison in Sydney, meeting with his old comrades. He would sit and listen attentively amidst the smoke of their long, clay tobacco pipes as they reminisced on past campaigns in exotic lands, and from an early age had been captivated by their stories. Oh, but to be able to march with them, and face the fierce enemies of the Queen!

But reality was early in the morning he would saddle his pony and ride to the blacksmith shop, working the day away forging and bending steel for horseshoes, wagon wheels and ploughs. It was a long way from the ambitions of a colonial boy who dreamed of fame and fortune in a society that had also transported its class system from the British Isles. He was the son of a lowly, former non-commissioned officer and former convict woman. But at least the colonies, these new lands used as a dumping ground for England's unwanted, had seen many of low birth rise to positions of power and wealth. All one needed was intelligence and ambition to struggle up the social ladder.

Little did Ian know that fate was conspiring to change his life forever on a faraway obscure battlefield in the colony of New Zealand.

Part One

Sons of the Empire

The Colony of
New South Wales

1852

ONE

I an Steele stood in front of the entrance of his blacksmith shop, watching the trickle of gold seekers pass by. They journeyed on horseback, in drays and on foot, pushing wheelbarrows as they marched west across the nearby range of hills known as the Blue Mountains. They were still heading for the fields near Bathurst after the discovery the previous year, and Ian knew that the same sight could also be seen in the colony of Victoria further south, where the hopefuls streamed off ships from every part of the globe, heading for the Ballarat goldfields in search of the valuable yellow metal.

The Australian colonies were already seeing a dramatic change in its importance to Mother England, and a population explosion for the continent.

'Bloody fools,' Francis Sweeney said.

Ian nodded, agreeing with his sixteen-year-old apprentice. The boy had a good head on his shoulders, and had not deserted Ian when the word spread as fast as the bushfires in the Sydney district in summer. Ian had trouble keeping up with the demand for the shovels and picks he now churned out of his business, and he'd been able to apprentice the young man.

At twenty-five years of age, Ian was prospering from the demand created by gold. He had to admit to himself, he had been tempted to join the steady throng heading west over the hills a year earlier, but was smart enough to know that gold and iron were partners; iron tools are needed to scrape out the gold nuggets. His foresight proved right, as he was strategically located on the main route west. Already he had accumulated a lot of money, and now considered he might be ready to court the eligible ladies of the district. He knew he was attractive, with his plain but appealing face and muscled body honed by hard work. He was clean-shaven and had a thick mop of hair. He stood at a respectable five foot ten inches. But it was his grey eyes that held the appeal for the fairer sex, and his ability to make a good living.

Ian turned his back and walked back into the shop. The heat from the ever-burning fires of the forge was uncomfortable, but over the years Ian had grown used to it, and in winter it was pleasant. But this was mid-summer, and when a customer occasionally stopped by to purchase from the piles of shovels and picks stacked outside, the foray outside the shop was welcomed.

'It is time for you boys to eat.'

Ian broke into a broad smile as his mother entered the shop carrying a basket of bread, cold meat and chutney.

'Frankie, take a break,' Ian said, placing the heavy hammer he had been using to flatten a plate of iron on a solid bench.

The young apprentice gratefully removed his leather apron, joining his boss and Mrs Steele outside under the shade of a great gum tree that had stood since well before the appearance of European settlers in this region. For the moment, the countryside around Ian's shop was still a panorama of rolling fields, dotted with bark huts marking small farms, and copses of tall trees.

Ian had built a table and bench under the shadow cast by the tall gum, and his still-growing apprentice was eager to partake of the midday meal. It would be washed down with a mug of sweetened tea, to the lazy caws of crows in the trees around them.

Francis waited patiently as Mary Steele said a short grace, and then pulled aside the tea towel to reveal a loaf of freshly baked bread and a haunch of cold beef. The chutney had been purchased at the store, and she carved the meat for the two men as they prepared their bread and chutney.

'Thanks, Ma,' Ian said, biting into the meal.

'Thanks, Mrs Steele,' Francis grunted, reaching for his mug of steaming tea, poured from the blackened billy can.

Mary Steele shared the gossip she had heard at the local store, and Ian listened with love in his heart for this frail but tough little woman who had lavished him with love throughout his quarter century on earth. It had been she, and his father, who had insisted on him continuing his learning through the scarce books they had spent small fortunes on to obtain for his library.

'I met Isabel MacHugh at the store today,' Mary said, catching Ian's attention. She was a pretty young lady of eighteen years of age, who Ian had admired from afar.

'Her family are Methodists,' Ian said. 'And own half of the land around here. I doubt that she would consider a blacksmith a worthy catch.'

'You have prospered, and you well know that your father was a Catholic, and I was born Presbyterian,' his mother countered. 'In the colonies, such unions are possible between people of different Christian beliefs.'

'Yes, but you had to promise the priest that I would be baptised Catholic,' Ian reminded his mother, and she fell silent. His father had not been a religious man, whereas his mother was devout in her beliefs. Ian remembered how his father would philosophise on how on the battlefield dying men did not call out to the Lord, but for their mothers. Mary Steele had despaired that her son held any Christian beliefs – but at least he believed in the Ten Commandments.

'Hey, it looks like we have a customer,' Francis said, interrupting Ian's thoughts about Isabel MacHugh.

Ian glanced up to see a horseman approaching on a very fine steed, dust rising in puffs from the hooves. The rider drew close and pulled up his mount a few yards from the table. Ian could see that he was a young man about his own age, clean-shaven with long dark hair and very pale skin.

'Good afternoon to you,' he said from astride his mount. 'I wish to purchase a set of shoes for my horse.'

Ian rose from the bench, wiping his greasy hands on the sides of his trousers.

'I can do that,' he said, eyeing the stranger with curiosity.

'I should introduce myself,' the stranger said with a wan smile. 'I am Samuel Forbes. My uncle owns the Wallaroo estate not far from here and recommends your products. He says they are of the highest quality.'

'Sir George Forbes,' Ian said. 'Your uncle is a good man – well respected in the district. You must be the man who writes poetry I have heard talk about.'

Samuel looked surprised at Ian's comment. 'I was not aware that I held such a reputation.'

Ian grinned. 'I just also happen to love good poetry,' he said. 'I am fortunate to have a copy of John Donne. *I wonder, by my troth, what thou and I did . . .'*

'*Till we loved? Were we not weaned then?* Good God, man,' Samuel said, dismounting with practised ease. 'You are very surprising. I would not have imagined in my wildest dreams that a blacksmith could quote "The Good-Morrow".' Samuel extended his hand to Ian and the grip between them was strong. Ian introduced his mother and Francis. Mary made a small curtsey as she knew of the aristocratic Forbes family in the district.

'Would you join us for a simple meal, sir?' Mary asked, brushing down her dress.

'I would be delighted,' Samuel replied, removing the broad-brimmed hat when he stepped into the shade of the gum's branches. He sat down at the bench beside Francis, facing Ian and his mother.

The conversation under the gum tree flowed almost exclusively between Ian and Samuel, once they established that they both had a love for the arts. Samuel laughed when he pointed out that Ian, with his brawny build, looked nothing like a lover of the arts. The midday meal extended a little longer than normal for Ian, as the two immersed themselves in conversation on common ground despite between worlds apart socially. Both men instinctively recognised the basis of a friendship.

'I will have the horseshoes ready by tomorrow morning,' Ian finally said, reluctantly breaking the mood but recognising he had to be back at work at his forge.

Samuel rose and shook Ian's hand. 'I shall have one of the servants pick them up,' he said. 'Thank you, Mrs Steele, for your generous hospitality, and wonderful food.' He made a small tilt of his head to her, which made her flush in appreciation.

Francis had already gone inside to resume his work leaving Mary and her son alone.

'You have a queer expression, Ma,' Ian said, noticing his mother watching the departing horseman.

'It is as if you and Sir George's nephew could almost be twins,' Mary said quietly. 'You even look remarkably alike in the face.'

'Ma, he is highborn. How could we look alike?' Ian chuckled.

'Call it a silly mother's intuition, but I feel you were two souls born to meet one day.' Mary said quietly. 'Why? God only knows the answer to that question.'

Ian stopped smiling as his mother turned to return to their two-storeyed stone house a half mile down the dusty road towards the gently flowing river that meandered through the district. Ian watched her depart in the heated haze of the day, wondering at her statement. He and Samuel Forbes were so different, he mused. He was the son of a well-known aristocratic English family, and Ian was a simple blacksmith born of a convict mother and British soldier. They were at least both learned men, albeit Ian was more self-taught then formally educated.

He shook his head and walked towards the open doors of the forge. It was Sunday on the morrow and a time of rest. The good people of the district would attend their various churches, and in the afternoon, take time to reflect on the grace of God over a roast meal.

Ian knew that there would be a gathering on the banks of the river in the late afternoon, as young couples had the opportunity to stroll together in the shade of the great gums under the watchful eyes of parents and guardians. Ian also knew that Isabel MacHugh liked to go to the river on Sunday afternoons with her brother acting as chaperone. What did he have to lose? Ian sighed. He would dress in his best Sunday clothes, and go to the river.

*

The late Sunday afternoon proved to be more temperate than hot, and Ian stood nervously, gazing at the small parties of families sharing a picnic basket amongst the boulders and spaces at the river's edge. He nodded to many who passed him, recognising them from his business dealings, and even to the gang of five young Irishmen who at different times could be friend or enemy. Ian knew them all as childhood friends but had avoided joining them as he grew because they were considered yahoos – young men without much ambition, except to bring attention from the constabulary for their anti-social behaviour. Most were the children of former convicts and the district was divided in its view of loyalty to the Crown.

As the Irish boys passed him, Ian sensed from their swagger they were looking for trouble. Ian glanced around, seeking Isabel, but could not see her. He was about to return home when he noticed the gang at the edge of the river surrounding two well-dressed men and a pretty young woman. It was obvious that the Irish boys were harassing them, and as Ian watched, he realised it was Isabel with her brother, and Samuel Forbes.

The leader of the gang, a big man of around the same age as Ian, was pushing Samuel in the chest, attempting to provoke him to fight.

Ian walked quickly towards the gathering.

'Hey! Conan, leave Mr Forbes alone,' Ian said in a loud voice, immediately attracting the attention of the gang.

Conan Curry desisted, turning to confront Ian. 'Is this fancy man a friend of yours, Steele?' Curry asked. Growing up, Conan had once been Ian's best friend, and they had been inseparable. But later in life, they had taken different roads to adulthood.

'He is,' Ian replied, stopping a couple of paces from the bully. 'So are Miss MacHugh, and Master Edward.' Ian made the statement confidently, even though he hardly knew the trio.

'So, what are you going to do about it?' Conan Curry asked. Ian quickly made an assessment of the situation, seeing that Isabel was trembling.

Without a word, he swung a right-hand hook that caught Conan unawares on the jaw, snapping his head to the side, causing him to stumble backwards. The blow would have felled most men but the Irish boy was tough, and quickly recovered. He rushed Ian with his head down. That was a mistake. Ian grabbed the back of his head and brought his knee up into his opponent's face, smashing his nose. Curry went down, bleeding profusely. He lay groaning at Ian's feet while the others looked on, a mix of awe and fear in their expressions.

'Who wishes to be next?' Ian asked, glaring at the four remaining members of Conan Curry's gang. None seemed to be keen to take on Ian, who had grown up in the rough and tumble of the colony and whose reputation as a street fighter was well-known to them.

'We meant no harm,' one of the others said. 'We was just having a joke.'

Ian recognised the gang member as Conan's younger brother, Kevin. They had always disliked each other. 'Get your brother home,' Ian said. 'No one is laughing at your joke.'

The remaining members helped Conan to his feet. He was holding his broken nose and turned to Ian. 'I'll see you again, Steele,' he said. 'Next time, I'll be ready for you. You're a traitor to your faith, sticking up for these damned English Protestants.'

Ian watched warily as the gang stumbled away.

'Good God, man,' Edward said. 'You certainly gave those ruffians a lesson.'

'I feel that such a forceful application of violence was not called for,' Isabel said, and Ian turned to stare at her. He was smitten by her pretty pale face, framed by curling locks of golden hair, and big, blue eyes. She was truly a beauty, but she was wrong in this case.

'I mostly acted on behalf of Mr Forbes,' he said with a touch of anger.

'Well, I appreciate your intervention, Mr Steele,' Samuel said. 'I have seen enough violence in my life.'

Edward thrust out his hand. 'Ignore my sister, Mr Steele. I thought Samuel and I might have found ourselves a little outnumbered. I know the reputation of the Curry brothers for mischief.'

Ian accepted the handshake and glanced at Isabel, who he noticed was gazing at Samuel with an expression of fondness.

'Mr Forbes was about to read one of his latest poems to Edward and me when those hooligans so rudely accosted us.'

'Mr Steele appreciates poetry,' Samuel said.

'Oh!' Isabel exclaimed, looking at Ian with surprise. 'I did not think a common blacksmith would have any appreciation of the finer things in life.'

Her comment stung Ian, and he suddenly felt out of place in the company of the three aristocrats.

'Mr Forbes and I were discussing our appreciation of the poetry of that great bard, John Donne,' Ian said.

'Please, Mr Steele, my friends call me Sam,' Samuel said with a warm smile. 'I think your generous action here this afternoon has warranted such informality between us.' He held out his hand and Ian could feel a strong grip of friendship.

'A pleasure . . . Sam. Alas, Ian cannot be abbreviated. Now I think we are able to hear your poetry in the tranquillity of the river and the soothing shade of its mighty gum trees.'

Samuel, Edward and his sister sat down on a blanket they had brought with them, whilst Ian remained standing in case the Curry gang returned. Samuel removed a small notebook from the pocket of his waistcoat and thumbed it open. He began to recite that which he had written, and Ian noticed gloomily how Isabel fixed upon him with adoring attention. When Samuel finished his recitation Edward said, 'Bravo, old chap. Well done.'

Isabel clapped daintily with gloved hands, and Ian nodded his head, appreciating the high quality of Sam's poem.

'It will be getting dark soon, so I think I should take my sister home,' Edward said, rising from the blanket. 'It has been a very queer day today.'

Samuel reached out to assist Isabel from the blanket and Ian noticed how their hands remained together for a short time upon her standing.

'I would like you to be my guest at my uncle's house this Wednesday evening,' Samuel said to Ian. 'He stocks a fine port, and I am sure it may go some way towards thanking you for your timely intervention this afternoon.'

'I would be honoured,' Ian said. He had come to acknowledge that Isabel MacHugh was beyond his charms and station in life, but he felt a strange kind of bond with this colonial aristocrat.

*

That evening, Ian returned to the stone cottage he shared with his mother. She noticed that he was strangely silent as he dined with her on a roast leg of mutton, served with baked potatoes, gravy and garden peas.

'Something has happened today,' she said as Ian toyed with the peas on his plate. 'You have a strange air about you.'

'I met Samuel Forbes again this afternoon,' Ian said. 'I think we formed a friendship.'

Mary stared at her son. 'I had a dream last night that you and he would form a bond that will take you into another world, away from me, far across the sea,' she said sadly. 'I tried to call to you in my dream, but you were in a terrible place of fire and death.'

Ian looked sharply at his mother. His father would often tell him of how uncanny his mother's dreams were. It was said that in his mother's Scottish family, the women were renowned as fortune tellers, so much so, that many years before, one of Ian's great-great-grandmothers had been hanged as a witch.

'I think you just had a nightmare,' Ian said, but felt his skin crawl with nervous fear. It was the utter conviction in his mother's words that made him uneasy. How could it be that he could ever leave the shores of the colony to travel across the sea? His world was restricted to the forge at his blacksmith shop. He may have dreamed of soldiering for the Queen when he was younger and following in the footsteps of his beloved father, but the only army in New South Wales was a British regiment on garrison duties. The last time a British regiment had left the colony was to fight the ferocious Maoris in New Zealand when he was about eighteen years of age.

Ian shook his head as his mother rose from the table to take her plate to a large basin of washing water. This time his mother was wrong, Ian convinced himself.

TWO

Ian left early, putting the blacksmith shop in the care of his apprentice. He rode his pony home, quickly washed, changed into his best suit of clothes, and rode to the Forbes estate, about an hour away from the little village that was Ian's home.

He rode up a long well-maintained road to the large house surrounded by lesser buildings housing convict labour, and sheds for storing bales of wool before they were transported to the Sydney docks for the voyage to the English mills.

He passed by men in shabby clothes chipping at weeds along the road, and could see other men working in gardens, where European trees were being planted. It was as if Sir George Forbes was attempting to turn the harsh Australian landscape into that of the English countryside, with its evergreen trees and shrubs.

The house was constructed of sandstone carried from the quarries around the harbour and had a wide veranda encircling it. A couple of majestic chimneys stood tall at either end of the house. The afternoon was very warm, and Ian could feel sweat trickling down his chest under his starched shirt.

He reached the front of the house and hitched his pony to a rail provided for such a purpose.

A well-dressed older man stepped from the house to greet him. Ian knew that this was not Sir George, but one of his many servants.

'You must be Master Steele,' he said with an accent that revealed he was not colonial-born. 'Sir George and Mr Forbes are expecting you.'

As Ian stepped up onto the sandstone-paved veranda, Samuel appeared to greet him.

'I am pleased to see that you were able to join us this evening,' he said.

'Nice to be entering your house through the front door, and not the servant's entrance at the rear,' Ian said, accepting the handshake. In the past, he had been greeted with grunts due to a mere servant.

'Ah, yes, standards must be retained – even in the colonies,' Samuel said with just a hint of embarrassment. Ian followed him into the house and was surprised that it was just a little cooler than the outside. The house was relatively large with luxurious wallpaper and fine furniture. Paintings adorned the walls; portraitures of family members beside rural scenes of an English countryside, and fox hunts filled with horses, dogs and riders in red jackets.

A young girl wearing the dress of a servant dusted a dining room cabinet. She smiled shyly when Ian passed her. Sir George rose from a great leather armchair when Ian and

Samuel entered a room with a billiard table at its centre. Ian reflected on how much Samuel and his uncle looked alike, and it struck him that, as his mother had noted, he too shared similar features to the English aristocrats.

'Sir George, this is the man I spoke of, Mr Ian Steele,' Samuel said. Sir George walked towards Ian but did not proffer his hand. Ian felt like he was being appraised, as one would a fine horse.

'My nephew has spoken of nothing else since you and he first made acquaintance,' the English aristocrat said. 'I welcome you to my home, Mr Steele, and pray that you enjoy yourself.' Ian did not bother to say that he had met George Forbes earlier when he had delivered goods to the estate. He had simply been the local blacksmith then, and not an honoured guest, and easily forgotten.

'Dinner will be served at six o'clock sharp,' Sir George said, returning to his comfortable chair to continue reading the Sydney newspaper.

Samuel turned to Ian. 'I think that we should go out to the garden for some fresh air,' Samuel suggested, and Ian followed him through the front door to a gazebo covered in a grapevine. There was a bench encircling the inner part of the structure, and the men sat down facing one another. The servant girl delivered a jug of water with sliced lemon, pouring two glasses before departing.

Ian was thirsty and quickly swallowed down his drink before pouring another. The summer sun was setting but the heat was still in the air.

'I am pleased that you were able to join us for supper tonight.' Samuel said. 'I should learn more about a man I may deem as a dear friend in the future. It is obvious that you are both learned and courageous.'

'I am a mere blacksmith,' Ian replied. 'My father was

a soldier for the Empire, and my mother, who you have met, was born in Scotland. She despairs of me ever being a church-going person.'

'Ah, we have that in common,' Samuel smiled. 'I fear that I prefer to write poetry on Sunday mornings than attend our church. My absence has raised the eyebrows of God-fearing people in the district. But I have noticed that you colonials are less religious than those I remember from my early days in England. I am afraid that I have been exposed to Charles Lyell's geological works on the great age of the earth, which disputes religious thought on the matter. I think science may be able to explain many things our rather ignorant religious leaders profess to be irrefutable dogma.'

'I am of the same mind,' Ian agreed. 'The answer to many questions can be found in books.'

'You view the world with a questioning eye,' Samuel said. 'My impressions of you are that, had you not been born to the lowly state of a working man, you might have been able to mix in the world that I was born to.'

'Ah, but this is the place in the British Empire where a man such as myself may aspire to fame and fortune,' Ian said.

'Do you wish to aspire to fame and fortune?' Samuel asked.

'Does not every man?' Ian countered. 'It appears we are only held back by the circumstances of our birth. You have been very fortunate in life. You have been born into wealth and privilege.'

Ian saw a dark shadow cross his friend's face at his last statement.

'Before I was sixteen years of age my father took me against my wishes to a barracks in London, where I was commissioned as an officer,' Samuel said stiffly. 'He cared little for my feelings. I found army life tedious and rough.

Eventually, I was sent to New South Wales with my regiment on garrison duties and was fortunate to have my uncle living here after his exile from England by the family. I have grown very fond of my uncle, who is not like the rest of my family in England. But I was shipped to New Zealand, and what I had always dreaded eventuated. I found myself holding the regimental colours on some damned piece of ground fighting in a battle for the Queen against her enemies. We lost that day against the noble Maori warriors, and soon after I fell ill. My regimental commanding officer gave me leave to return to my uncle's estate until I was well enough to resume my duties with the regiment. That was a few years ago now and I have since resigned my commission.'

'You fought in a battle?' Ian asked with a note of awe, feeling a new respect for his friend. 'I would not have believed that you would be such a man.'

'I had no choice,' Samuel replied bitterly. 'My memory of those hours was of noise, fear and young men dying horrible deaths from musket-ball wounds. As for my courage . . . well, I was shaking so badly, I thought I would drop our colours. I never want to return to the regiment.'

'I know that I may be naive but all I have ever wanted to do is serve regimental colours for the Queen. I have read every book I could get my hands on about tactics and strategy. I expect fear and carnage will be the experience of a soldier, but I have a need to find out myself. Alas, being a colonial gives little opportunity to be commissioned into a British regiment.'

'Beware of what you desire, my friend. It might come true,' Samuel said as the manservant called them to supper. As they walked towards the house, Ian pondered Samuel's mysterious warning.

At supper, Ian felt ill at ease. Servants carried dishes of rich food to the table, with its fine linen cloth and silver cutlery. Ian closely watched to see what Samuel did, and quickly picked up the etiquette of dining amongst the privileged. They sat at the end of the table, with Sir George occupying the top end.

Conversation was polite. The hot weather, the fortunes of those seeking gold, and Sir George even complimented Ian on his enterprise, supplying the eager prospectors.

'Do you intend to remain with your trade?' Sir George asked, sipping from his bowl of kangaroo-tail soup.

'I have little choice,' Ian admitted. 'I have prospered well of late.'

'What if you had a choice in life?' Sir George asked. 'What might you do?'

Ian paused. 'My father was a soldier. I always dreamed of following in his footsteps.' Ian also noted the exchange of knowing looks between uncle and nephew.

'That is a lowly aspiration, to be a mere soldier,' Sir George said. 'They are recruited from the scum of the British Isles. But to be an officer in the Queen's army is a privilege.'

'A privilege only a gentleman can afford,' Ian said. 'It requires a great deal of money to purchase a commission.'

The subject was dropped, and the three men finished their supper. Ian had never partaken before of such fine food, but it was time to return as he would need to be at his forge before sunrise. He bid his guests a good evening and mounted his pony to return in the dark to the village.

★

Sir George and Samuel retired to the billiard room to smoke cigars and share fine brandy. Samuel stood by the billiard table, idly rolling the ivory coloured balls across the smooth surface.

'I must agree that there is something in what you told me after you met Mr Steele,' Sir George said. 'He and you have an uncanny likeness, albeit Mr Steele is more robust in appearance.'

'Ian is highly intelligent, even better educated than most of my former fellow officers,' Samuel said. 'He even dreams of soldiering, which I cannot comprehend. But that is his dream, although I am at odds to wonder why.'

'Your dearly departed grandfather wrote before his death to say if you served out at least ten years in his old regiment, he would consider you worthy of a substantial inheritance of the Forbes' estates in England, even in your position as second son. Otherwise, you receive only a pittance of the estate,' Sir George paused. 'I understand why you do not wish to resume your commission in the army, and sympathise. Your father, as my older brother, was quick to have me exiled to this land, with barely enough capital to establish my sheep farm. I suspect that he is rather annoyed that I was able to become wealthy by my own means. Wool has been good for this colony, thanks to Captain MacArthur and his wife's nurturing of the industry.' He glanced up at Samuel. 'I must admit, I have grown very fond of you, as one would a son.'

Samuel met his uncle's gaze. 'And I of you,' he said with genuine conviction. His uncle had proved more a father than his own, who had so cruelly condemned him to a life on the battlefields of Queen Victoria's many small wars around the globe.

'I think we share a mutual ambition to take our revenge on the family,' George said, taking a long swallow of his brandy. 'One that has a vast financial benefit for you.'

Samuel nodded. Fate had brought a man into his life who appeared more than capable of showering the family name with honour, and establishing a guaranteed comfortable future for himself to pursue a life as the next poet laureate of the Queen. Such a dream was easy – plotting the next step would not be. First, he must get to know his friend better. Samuel also had an ulterior motive – a need for revenge against the man who had dealt him his unwanted life as a soldier.

★

Ian was not surprised to see Samuel visit his place of work within the week.

Samuel dismounted and met Ian at the entrance to the blacksmith shop, presenting him with a bundle of books.

'I thought these might be of interest to you,' Samuel said. 'I know your interest in military history, and my uncle agreed that you be allowed to borrow them.'

Ian looked with greedy eyes on the titles of the leather-bound books. 'Please pass on my gratitude to Sir George,' Ian said, wiping his hands on his leather apron before accepting the small pile.

'Besides the books, I have also come to invite you to travel with me to Sydney next week. My uncle has business in the town, and I am sure you may also be able to find an excuse to accompany me.'

'That is far too generous. Besides, I have much to do here.'

'You have told me your apprentice is very competent, and he can look after your shop for a few days.'

Ian glanced down at the books in his hands and then at Francis, and was overcome with a sense of spontaneity. 'As it stands, I do have some business in Sydney.'

'Good. I will be taking my uncle's gig. It will be less arduous than riding mounts,' Samuel said with a smile. 'I am looking forward to us sharing good conversation, and we have comfortable accommodation in Sydney Town with a dear friend of mine. We depart early tomorrow morning.'

Samuel remounted his horse and rode away, leaving Ian with the gift of the books. Ian walked back into the shop and informed Francis of his plan. Francis was delighted to be left with the responsibility of minding the business while Ian was gone. After work, Ian went home, informed his mother that he would be going to Sydney and his mother simply nodded with an expression Ian could not fathom. He packed a few items in a roll of canvas.

As promised, Samuel arrived early the next day driving a horse-drawn gig.

Ian slid his rope-tied canvas package into the gig and pulled himself up next to Samuel.

'A Stanhope,' Ian said. 'Very impressive, but not the best for our journey along the track to Sydney.'

'My uncle had it imported,' Samuel replied, nudging the horse to step off. 'I agree that it is too lightly sprung for the colonial roads, but if I take it carefully, it will get us to our destination.'

For the first hour or so, the road was well-formed but they soon came across a rough and winding track through dense eucalypt forest. Ian had been dozing for a short time when he was awoken by the gig coming to a stop.

'What is it?' Ian asked, forcing himself fully alert.

'I thought I saw movement off the track up ahead, in the shadow of the trees,' Samuel said quietly. 'Call it an instinct, but I suspect someone is waiting ahead for reasons I fear may be nefarious.'

Ian knew that his friend's fears were well-founded. Bushrangers haunted the roads to Sydney, waylaying gold prospectors returning with money in their pockets. The appearance of an expensive gig would attract unwanted attention from such criminals.

As if on cue, a man wearing a bandana over his face stepped from the trees just paces away, and Ian could see that he was not alone. Two similarly disguised men wearing the rough garb of bushmen joined him. They were armed with wooden clubs.

'Stand and deliver,' came the command from the first man, brandishing an antiquated musket.

Ian noticed that Samuel had slipped his hand into his coat pocket, and now produced a small Colt 31 revolver, which he whipped up to point at the man holding the musket on them, much to the surprise of both Ian and the bushrangers.

'Sir, I suggest that you point that unreliable gun away from us, or I may shoot you.'

The startled bushranger blinked at the sight of the cap and ball revolver pointed at him, but did not comply with Samuel's order.

'Do I have a need to explain that the revolver in my hand contains six balls to the one in your musket?' Samuel said calmly. 'That is more than enough to shoot you and your two companions, even if I miss thrice. We do not carry a large sum of money or gold, and I am sure that you would prefer to go home for supper this night.'

Ian looked into the eyes of the bushranger and, even with his disguise, recognised him immediately.

'Conan Curry, what the devil are you up to?' Ian asked harshly. 'Is that Kevin with you?'

The man under Samuel's gun lowered his weapon

reluctantly. 'Steele, what are you doing on the track?' Curry countered.

'Just trying to go about my business in peace,' Ian replied.

There was a tense pause. 'Pass by then,' Conan said miserably, waving his musket towards the direction of Sydney.

Ian took the reins while Samuel cradled the small revolver until they created a safe distance between themselves and the would-be bushrangers.

'So, it was those ruffians who caused the mischief at the river,' Samuel said. 'I heard that highwaymen were known to haunt this road, and you can see I came prepared.'

'Bloody good that you did,' Ian said with a grin, remembering the stricken expression in Curry's eyes when he was confronted with the multi-shot weapon. 'I always wondered where they were getting their money to spend in the village tavern on Saturday nights.'

'I will report them to the district magistrate to have the constables arrest them,' Samuel said.

'I was impressed by the way you handled them,' Ian said. 'They might have been tempted to do us some harm.'

'They were nowhere near as fearsome as the Maori warriors I faced in New Zealand.' Samuel grinned.

'I know that Miss MacHugh will be impressed when I relate how you faced down a gang of bushrangers,' Ian said. 'I couldn't help but notice how smitten she is with you.'

'She is a wonderful young lady,' Samuel replied. 'My uncle thinks that we should plan to wed. Her dowry would be quite substantial.'

It was not the answer Ian wanted to hear but he had a need to see where he stood in the eyes of the very desirable young woman. It seemed he was hardly noticeable in her life.

The journey continued without incident, and just before the sun set on the very warm day, they came to clusters of well-kept stone cottages at the edge of Sydney Town. Samuel reined their dust-covered carriage to a halt and climbed down stiffly. He had hardly touched the ground when a well-dressed young man of about the same age stepped from the cottage to greet them.

'Dear Samuel, it is good to see you after such a long time,' the young man said, before noticing Ian. 'I can see that you have brought company.'

Ian dismounted, recognising the other man's accent as North American.

'James, this is the man whom I wrote to you about, Master Ian Steele. Ian, this is my dear friend, James Thorpe,' Samuel said. Ian thrust out his hand in greeting. He could feel that the other man's hand was soft and smooth, indicating that he did not indulge in manual labour to make his living.

'Mr Thorpe,' Ian said. 'It is a pleasure to meet a friend to Samuel.'

'Please call me James,' the young man said with a smile. When Ian glanced at Samuel, he could see that he was pleased.

'Did you have a good journey this day?' James asked, gesturing for them to follow him behind the white picket fence, through the attempt at a garden and inside the neatly laid out cottage.

Ian glanced at Samuel, who discreetly shook his head with a frown. It was obvious that Samuel did not want to mention the incident along the track with the Curry gang.

James produced tea and cake for his guests, and that evening prepared a meal of roast lamb with vegetables. This was followed by rum and cigars outside under the stars to alleviate the heat of the day inside the cottage, which was cluttered with books, on shelves and in wooden crates.

It was a pleasant evening of talk about colonial politics and literature. Ian was able to glean from James that he had crossed the Pacific in search of gold purely for the adventure, as he came from a wealthy family in New York. He had met Samuel at a gentlemen's club in Sydney the year before and they had become firm friends, in such a way that now made Ian feel as if he was an outsider. But it was even more than that, something he couldn't quite name. Under the light of the stars and influence of the rum, Ian tried to dismiss his feeling of unease.

THREE

The tavern was filled with a rowdy crowd of revellers on the outskirts of Ian's village, a place condemned by the God-fearing citizens of the district. A violin screeched and played out a popular tune, hardly heard in the din of raised voices lubricated by cheap rum and gin.

The Curry boys had their own table and four of the brothers were joined by young Francis, Ian's apprentice. It was not as if he'd had much choice, as two of the Curry gang sat him down with a promise of a free drink. Francis knew the reputations of the men whose company he reluctantly shared.

'You lookin' after the business while the boss is away?' Conan asked, leaning towards Francis, breathing alcoholic fumes in his face.

'Yeah, that's right,' Francis said.

'We saw your boss today in the company of that English

nob, Samuel Forbes,' Conan said. 'Has Master Steele got ideas about joining the ruling class?'

Francis felt the tankard of rum thrust into his hand by Kevin Curry. He took a sip. 'Mr Steele is just friends with Master Forbes – that's all,' Francis said.

'So, you are lookin' after the shop and takin' the money from the customers,' Conan said, leaning back in his chair. 'Where do you keep the money when Steele is away?'

Francis was wary of the question, but felt intimidated by the crush of the tough men around him.

'The money is kept safe at his house,' he replied, and immediately wished he could have thought of something else to say, disguising the whereabouts of the blacksmith shop's substantial takings. But he also knew it did not pay to attempt any lies to the notorious louts, whose violence was well known to all.

'He don't seem to spend his money hereabouts,' Kevin said, leaning into Francis, who now regretted his visit to the tavern on this hot night.

'He buys books,' Francis said, realising that not all the sweat trickling down his face was from the oppressive heat of the summer's eve. 'He don't have much money.'

'Frankie, you are a pal,' Conan said. 'Take your rum and leave us.'

Gratefully, Francis rose from his chair and departed into the smoke-filled air of the tavern, packed with layabouts, farmers and the village tradesmen. The rum had lost its appeal and Francis exited the tavern guilt-ridden for disclosing the financial matters of his boss. He tried to convince himself that the questions from the Curry boys was little more than simple curiosity.

When Francis had departed, Conan leaned forward to the members of his gang. 'Steele deserves to get his comeuppance,' he growled. 'Me and Kevin will take his money so quietly, he'll never know until he goes to count his takings. It will be simple, stealing while his ma sleeps. No harm is to come to Mary Steele, she has been good to us when we were kids.'

★

It was the barking of the village dogs that caused Mary Steele to come awake, then she thought that she heard a sound in the kitchen. Mary rose, lit a candle and armed herself with a metal fire poker, descending the narrow wooden stairs with great caution. Afraid as she was, Mary Steele had faced dangerous situations as a young convict girl, and had learned to deal with her fear. She was sure that an uninvited intruder was rummaging around in the small kitchen.

Her suspicions were confirmed when she heard a muffled voice exclaim. 'Begorah! I found it, Conan!'

Mary stepped from the stair into the dark kitchen, the flame from her candle immediately alerting the two intruders.

'What are you doing in my house Conan Curry?' she demanded fearlessly, causing Conan and Kevin Curry to stop in their tracks. Mary glanced down at the small leather bag Conan was holding in his hand, knowing what was inside. 'What are you doing with my son's money?'

Kevin glanced panic-stricken at his brother.

'It's our money, Mrs Steele,' Conan brazenly lied. 'It's money he owes us.'

'Well, you will return the pouch, and take up your claim when my son returns,' Mary said, focusing her attention on Conan, who was in the process of replacing the bag where he found it in the cupboard. She did not notice Kevin step behind her, or when he slid a heavy wooden club from his shirtsleeve. Conan saw what his brother was about to do and screamed, 'No!' but his warning came too late. His brother brought the hardwood club down at the back of Mary's skull with a sickening crunch, causing her to crumple to the floor of the kitchen. A heavy pool of blood immediately began to form around her head.

'God almighty!' Conan said in shock. 'Why did you go and do that, Kevin? We will surely hang if we are caught. Mrs Steele was a good woman and did not deserve to be slain. You are a bloody fool.'

'She knew who we were,' Kevin said, staring blankly at the lifeless body of the woman at his feet. 'We have to get out of here.'

'It won't be long before someone discovers we killed Mary Steele,' Conan said.

'No one saw us do it,' Kevin said, snatching up the bag.

'We was askin' Frankie 'bout where Steele kept his money,' Conan said. 'It won't take the magistrate long to send the road patrol after us. We have to get out of the district.'

Kevin retrieved the pouch and ran his hand through the substantial pile of silver coins he found inside. 'We have enough here to get out of the colony,' he said. 'We still have our cousins back in dear old Erin. We could use the amount we have 'ere to set us up.'

Conan looked to the leather pouch his brother held in his hand. 'Not such a stupid idea,' he said. 'We take Mrs Steele out the back and hide her under the woodpile. It will give us time to get to Sydney and take a boat out of the colony before the traps are onto us.'

Kevin nodded. To be caught would surely mean hanging from the gallows at the Darlinghurst gaol in Sydney Town.

The two men lifted the slightly built woman and carried her to the backyard. In the dark, they piled cut logs of timber on her body until it was concealed, but in their panic, they did not return to the cottage, leaving the immediate evidence of the terrible crime.

The following morning Kevin and Conan Curry took the track to Sydney. Conan had always lived with his brother's cruelty and protected him, but the murder of a woman he had truly liked and admired was beyond anything he had done before. Conan rued the plan to commit the burglary and its terrible consequence yet time only moved forward, and life could not be replayed.

★

Mary Steele was not in her pew at church for Sunday service, and Mrs Amelia Barton was concerned that her lifelong friend may have been unwell. She was aware that Mary's son, Ian, had travelled to Sydney with Mr Forbes, and Mary may have come down with an illness. The Steele cottage was on her way home, and she stopped to knock on the front door. There was no answer and Mrs Barton walked to the backyard in the rising heat of the summer's day. The back door was open and she went inside, immediately seeing the large pool of blood on the kitchen floor.

'Oh, my dear Lord!' she exclaimed.

When she looked down, she could see that the blood trail led out the back door. In her confusion, the elderly lady considered that her friend may have had an accident, and turned to follow the heavy blood droplets leading into the yard to the woodpile. It was then that she could see the cloud of flies buzzing in and around the piled logs. She gasped in horror when she saw a bare foot protruding from under the wood heap.

'Oh my God!' she screamed, tottering away from the horror she imagined beneath the timber.

Within the half hour, the district magistrate, Captain Henry Dyer, accompanied by a police constable, had uncovered the body of Mary Steele.

'She has been slain,' the constable said, seeing the terrible crushing blow to the back of Mary's blood-encrusted head. 'Her neighbours said they saw her in the early evening, so she must have been murdered last night or early this morning. Whoever did this attempted to cover their bloody work.'

'Her son is the blacksmith, Ian Steele?' the magistrate said, bending to examine the fatal wound.

'That is correct, sir,' the constable said. 'But I know he has been away since early yesterday morning. I was informed that he was on his way with Mr Samuel Forbes, long before this could have happened.'

'We will have to get news to Mr Steele concerning the untimely demise of his mother,' Dyer said, rising to his feet. Already, concerned citizens were gathering at the front of the house as the news spread like bush fire through the village. 'Do you have any idea who may have done this wicked deed?'

'Not at this moment, but I will be asking questions of the locals,' he replied. 'Someone has to know something of this affair.'

'Arrange to have the body taken to her room,' the magistrate said. 'In this heat, we need to make arrangements to place her in the ground as soon as possible before corruption sets in.'

The constable nodded and turned to another police officer, who had hurried to the village from his own station a couple of miles away when he was informed he was needed to assist in a murder investigation. He was not alone when he joined the magistrate and his fellow policeman; Francis Sweeney was with him.

'Sir, this young man may have some information on what has happened here,' the second constable said.

Francis stepped forward and looked with horror at the body of Mary covered in flies. For a moment he was speechless.

'What can you tell us?' the magistrate prompted.

'Last night I was at the tavern and the Curry brothers were there,' Francis said, continuing to stare at the lifeless body. 'They were asking me about where Master Steele kept the takings from the blacksmith shop.'

'Did you tell them?' Dyer asked accusingly.

Francis hung his head in shame, and the magistrate looked away in disgust.

'With all respect, sir,' the first constable said. 'I know of the Curry gang, and I also know that they are very prone to violence. I've suspected them to be involved in a number of matters but I have never been able to detain them, as people around here are frightened of retribution from the family. In my opinion, any of the Curry boys are capable of doing this. And it is well known that they have a strong dislike for the slain woman's son.'

'I suggest that you continue with your duties, constable,' the magistrate said. 'Question the family as soon as possible.'

The constable did, and learned that Kevin and Conan had departed hours earlier. Their mother, a tough former convict, informed the village constable that her sons had told her they were heading south to the goldfields of Ballarat, in the colony of Victoria.

The constable informed the mounted police of her statement, and they rode the track in search of the suspects. The lie they had left with the family worked, as the two brothers made their way towards Sydney Town, carrying the stolen money. It was enough to pay for berths aboard a ship heading for the British Isles, and then on to Ireland.

*

Monday found Ian at a warehouse on the city harbour, purchasing iron ingots for his blacksmith shop. Samuel and James had chosen to spend time together at the cottage and Ian loaded the heavy metal bars aboard a dray he had hired to transport the cargo back to his village.

When the loading was over, Ian stopped to wipe the sweat from his face and gaze at the forest of ships' masts laying at anchor on the inviting blue waters. All around him, the commerce of the bustling port went on. Cargoes of supplies needed for the growing population of the colony, bolstered by the gold now pouring out of the hinterland discoveries, piled up. The wharf resounded to the multitude of languages being spoken by the visitors. Ian could see the numerous Chinese immigrants, with their long pigtails and exotic clothes, Europeans with the dress of their nations. He reflected how each would contribute to the face of the continent. So many people with so many languages, he thought as he gazed at the mass of humanity coming ashore around him.

He pulled himself aboard the dray and flicked his big draught horse into moving away from the harbour. He would stop over that evening at James' cottage, and leave early next morning for the trip back to the foot of the Blue Mountains.

Just after midday, he reached the cottage and was pleased to see Samuel and James were at home. He was welcomed with a glass of crushed lemons in water which proved to be refreshing, and he could smell the inviting aroma of a beef stew cooking on the stove.

Samuel pulled Ian aside and led him to the backyard to sit under a trellis overgrown with a grapevine to provide shade against the blistering hot sun while dinner was being prepared.

Both men sat with glasses of lemon water.

'I suspect that you may be curious as to why I suggested that you and I travel together to Sydney,' Samuel said. 'I know that you have a business to run at your village, and time away is a possible loss of profits.'

'I have used this opportunity to purchase supplies for the business,' Ian replied. 'Besides, I enjoy your company.'

Samuel smiled at the compliment. 'I suppose that you have noticed that we look so much alike, albeit you are of a much more robust physique. But in all other appearances, we could almost pass as brothers.'

'That has been mentioned by my mother,' Ian said, taking a sip of his drink. For a moment, Samuel looked away at the rolling plain behind the cottage, to the distant line of great gum trees.

'Would you consider being me?' he asked quietly.

Ian frowned at the strange question. 'What do you mean by that?'

'Just what I said,' Samuel replied. 'Would you ever consider taking my place as Samuel Forbes?'

Ian did not know if he should laugh or scoff at the lunatic suggestion. 'I think you should elaborate,' he said.

'I would request that you assume the role of myself for the next ten years or so,' Samuel said, leaning forward. 'You see, it would be very financially beneficial for both of us if you pretended to be me. My uncle has already given his blessing – and is a part of the conspiracy – if you should agree. I know I may sound as if I should be incarcerated in Bedlam but I also have great faith that you are the one man who could carry out this mission on behalf of us both. For you to do so would mean your dream of being a commissioned officer in a British regiment, a generous stipend from my family in England, and the once-in-a-lifetime opportunity to amass enough money for you to be able to retire as a wealthy country squire back here in the colonies, if not an even higher station in the mother country. Please consider my offer.'

The opportunity to be an officer was all that Ian had dreamed of, but the offer was ludicrous. Wasn't it? 'And what benefit would this exchange of roles do for you?' Ian asked.

Samuel sighed. 'I would be able to leave this lie I live,' he said. 'James and I could sail for America and start a life together. James is a man of independent means, but I do not wish to be a burden on him in the years to come. There is a condition imposed by my grandfather that if I serve honourably for a period of ten years in the army, I will inherit a substantial portion of the estate. Its income will be my retirement fund and give me financial independence in the future.'

'Then why not simply return to your regiment and serve out the ten years?' Ian asked.

'Because I would lose James from my life, and I love him. I doubt you will be able to comprehend that.'

Stunned, Ian almost dropped his glass. He wondered if he had heard correctly. For a moment, he had trouble absorbing just what was implied.

'What about Miss MacHugh?' Ian asked feebly, and Samuel smiled sadly.

'Miss MacHugh will always remain a fond memory,' Samuel said. 'But I cannot love her as I do James. I do not expect you to condone – nor even understand – but if you accept the offer I have made to switch places I, as Samuel Forbes, will not blacken the family reputation as a sodomite.'

'God almighty!' Ian exclaimed, shaking his head, still trying to come to grips with Samuel's explosive confession. 'Do you really think that I could ever fool your family?'

Ian watched as the smile returned to his friend's face. 'So, despite what I have confessed to you, you are considering taking on this adventure?'

'Adventure,' Ian repeated. 'Maybe a dank gaol cell in England if I am uncovered for the impersonation.'

'My uncle will brief you on every aspect of the family, and being a Forbes, when you return to the village,' Samuel said. 'By the time you eventually meet my family, you will know more about me than I know. Meeting you was like an answer from heaven.'

'But why is your uncle going to help?' Ian asked, ensuring that no stone was left unturned.

'My father, my uncle's elder brother, had him exiled to the Australian colonies many years ago for an indiscretion. But, as they were blood, he also had to ensure my uncle had enough financial support to establish himself here. As it was, my uncle went into wool and has well and truly made his own fortune.'

'What was the indiscretion, may I ask?' Ian questioned.

'Sir George was deeply in love with my mother,' Samuel said. 'So he was banished to this convict colony. He will do anything to strike back against my father now my mother has passed away. We Forbes are a cold and vengeful family of vipers but I suspect that you are more than capable of dealing with snakes.'

Ian stood slowly and gazed westwards towards the sun on the horizon. 'Your proposal has much adventure attached,' Ian sighed. 'But I could never leave my mother to pursue the dream I have always harboured to serve the Queen and the Empire. I thank you for trusting your secret and confidence in me – but I must decline.'

Samuel stood and offered his hand. 'James and I are booked on berths for San Francisco in a couple of weeks. We will meet again as I know you have to return the dray. You might think on my offer, and if you still decide not to take it up, I will always consider you a dear friend. I pray that you do change your mind. I feel my venture would be of great advantage to us both.'

Ian accepted the gesture of friendship, putting out of mind what he now knew about Samuel Forbes. He preferred to remember Samuel as a friend and nothing more. In the eyes of the law his friend was a criminal but Ian had only known an intelligent, gentle and courageous man. His confession had not changed the nature of Samuel, and Ian was confused.

That evening, the three men drank good rum and played cards. The next morning Ian set out to return to his village to resume his life as a country blacksmith. The silver lining to his return was that Isabel MacHugh was a truly single woman who would need consoling when Samuel sailed for the Americas.

FOUR

I an sensed that something was different about the village as he pushed his dray across the dusty track towards the outskirts of the town. His suspicion was confirmed when he saw two horsemen in the uniform of the Mounted Police ride towards him. He pulled his dray to a stop to await them.

'Are you Mr Ian Steele, the blacksmith?' one of the constables asked.

'I am,' Ian replied. 'Why do you ask?'

The constable cleared his throat. 'I am sorry to say Mr Steele that your mother, Mary Steele, has been slain by a murderer early Sunday morning past. Her body has been laid out at your home.'

For a moment, the news seemed unreal. He had only kissed his mother goodbye days earlier. How could she be dead?

Ian flicked the reins and the big cart horse hurried forward into the village as fast as the big horse could. As he approached his house, he could see Francis and a neighbour standing outside the picket fence. They saw him approach and Francis walked quickly towards him.

'I am sorry, Master Steele,' Francis said. 'We had no way of sending you the tragic news any earlier. I told the magistrate that you said you would return by this evening from Sydney.'

Ian alighted from the dray. 'How could this happen?'

'The police have a strong suspicion that Kevin and Conan Curry might have killed Mrs Steele,' Francis said. 'It appears that they have fled south to Victoria.'

Ian brushed down the dust from his trousers and strode away towards the cottage, where he saw more neighbours inside the house. They greeted him with grim faces and condolences. Ian climbed the stairs to his mother's room, where he saw a grey-haired, elderly lady sitting in a chair by the bed. Mrs Barton was holding a perfumed handkerchief to her nose to help disguise the sickly stench of decomposition in the hot air of the room.

'Ian,' she said, looking up at him. 'I cannot find words for the foul deed committed against your mother.'

'Thank you, Mrs Barton,' Ian replied, taking steps towards his mother's body laid out in her best Sunday dress on top of the mattress. He gazed down at her face, and thought that she looked as if she was asleep.

'I hope you do not mind but I have arranged for Mary to be buried tomorrow morning,' Amelia said. Ian nodded his agreement. In the heat of the summer, bodies began to decompose very quickly.

Amelia rose from her chair to exit the room, leaving Ian privacy to mourn his mother.

*

Many attended the funeral from the district as Mary Steele had been well-liked and respected, despite the fact she had once been a convict. The sun blazed down on those who attended, and amongst the mourners was Isabel MacHugh and her parents.

The wooden coffin was lowered into the grave while the pastor droned on about the grace of God. Ian stood with his head bowed, forcing back the tears. They would come when he was alone. In the distance, a crow cawed its lazy call across a plain of desiccated grass. Oh, how he wished that he had listened more to his mother's stories about her life as a young girl in the Scottish Lowlands, he reflected as he stood by the grave. Now part of his soul was gone forever.

Many of the villagers murmured their condolences in his ear as they passed by out of the tiny cemetery. At the centre of the land for the dead was a giant gum tree, a reminder that the inhabitants now lay for eternity in a foreign land, far from home in the British Isles.

'I am sorry for your loss, Mr Steele,' Isabel said, touching him on the arm with a gloved hand. 'I knew of your mother's charitable work in the district.'

Ian turned to Isabel, whose pretty face held sincerity in her condolences.

'Thank you, Miss MacHugh,' Ian replied. 'I appreciate your kind thoughts.' In that moment, Ian felt that this was the woman he should be with for the rest of his life. Isabel walked away to her parents and their fine carriage drawn by two horses, and he was reminded that she was far above his station. He watched her helped into the carriage by the driver and realised that he was alone.

*

Mrs Barton had arranged a respectful wake at Ian's cottage and only a few from Mary's church attended.

Tea was served with a few dainty cakes, but Ian felt out of place amongst the elderly friends of his mother. He hardly spoke with the guests but stood holding his cup of tea, reflecting on a future without his beloved mother. The cottage would be his, and he owned his forge. Life ahead would be spent in the village until he eventually found a wife more suitable to a lowly blacksmith, and eventually, he too, would join his mother and father in the cemetery at the outskirts of the village. The likes of Isabel MacHugh were not within his reach, and his dreams of adventure before he died would be that only.

With these thoughts, Ian made a decision.

Francis attended the wake and stood quietly at the back of the small dining room holding a cup of tea. Ian went to him. 'You have proven to be an excellent apprentice, Frankie,' Ian said. 'I know that your family are good people and struggle to earn an income. I have a proposal for you. How would you and your family like to move into my mother's cottage, and pay a small rent?'

'But where would you live?' Francis asked in his surprise at the generous offer. He and his family lived in a bark hut outside of town, where his father struggled to eke out a living on the small agricultural holding.

'You might say I will be living in a mansion,' Ian said with a smile. 'I will also sign off your papers, and make you a qualified blacksmith, and hand over the shop as a business partner. I trust you to bank ten percent of the profits in my name.'

'Master Steele, I am at a loss for words at your generous offer,' Francis replied, his thoughts reeling at Ian's sudden and life-changing offer. 'I can promise you on my family's name I will honour your offer, and my family will be forever in your debt. May I ask, what are your plans for the future?'

'I may travel and see some of the world while I am still young,' Ian answered. 'Or maybe go seek my fortune as a gold prospector.' Ian felt uneasy to be lying to his apprentice but it was necessary if he was to accept Samuel Forbes' proposal. There was a lot to be done.

Time was of the essence and Ian knew that when he took the dray back to Sydney, he would be cutting things short. Samuel and James were close to departing the shores of New South Wales for America.

When the last guest departed the house, Ian sat down at the kitchen table with a bottle of good Irish whisky that his father had kept in a cupboard. Ian knew his mother's puritan view of alcohol meant that Ian was not to drink under her roof, but now she was gone, and he poured the contents into a glass tumbler.

'To the finest mother and father a man could have,' he said softly, raising his glass as a toast. 'I hope you will forgive me for what I am to venture in the future.'

That night, Ian got truly drunk for the first time in his life.

He remained for a couple of days to ensure all the loose ends of his life were secured. His mother's will had left him the cottage, and Ian welcomed Francis' family into his house. They were grateful and thanked him profusely for what he had done for their son and themselves.

By the weekend, Ian gathered together a few valuables and hitched up the dray to return to Sydney. Only Francis saw him off.

Before sunset, Ian was outside the cottage that James and Samuel shared. As they greeted him, Ian was fully aware that there was no turning back to his predictable life as a village blacksmith. He was not sure what lay ahead, but it was his one and only chance to be a soldier for the Queen, and to carve out his place amongst the aristocracy of the Empire.

★

'My uncle will send a letter to my older brother explaining how I . . . you have changed with a robust life in the colonies. That will explain why I . . . you have broad shoulders and muscle, whereas I left England a callow youth,' Samuel said with a grin as he sat with Ian under the shade of the grapevine covered trellis. 'I will brief you on anything about the family I remember before being shipped to the colony. By the time we are finished, you will know who each person in my family is and the peculiarities of my life in England. You will have to know something about my military service, and the main characters of the regiment. By the time we part, you will know more about my life than even my dear James. My uncle will be your main support when I am gone, and will provide any other information you require to pass as me.'

Ian nodded. There was much to learn but he was determined to be a successful student. His new life depended upon it. 'Your uncle must be very fond of you to provide support for the pretence.'

'You have actually touched on the real reason my father hates my uncle . . . and me,' Samuel said, his voice cracking. 'Sir George is my real father, not the man who had me exiled to the army. My mother wrote to George many years ago to say they had a son who she named Samuel. My father also suspected the infidelity and has always resented my existence. He would disinherit me if he could, but the secret remains between the two brothers, and now you and I.

It was important that you share the secret because when you return to England, you will understand the animosity from my father.'

'Sir George Forbes . . .' Ian echoed. 'God almighty, you have an interesting pedigree.'

'It is your heritage now,' Samuel said with a shrug. 'I think that you will be able to deal with my family much better than I would have. And at the end of ten years, both you and I will be beneficiaries to a small fortune.'

'That fortune will be yours alone,' Ian said. 'I seek fame as much as fortune.'

'I pray that we both succeed in realising our dreams,' Samuel added. 'I have a small gift for you.' He reached into the pocket of his coat and produced the small Colt revolver. 'I would like you to have this,' he said, handing the pistol to Ian. 'If you ever encounter the likes of the Curry brothers, I would think that this could be needed.'

Ian took the pistol. 'Fate is a strange thing,' he said, holding the gun. 'You and I met in such an insignificant part of the world, and here we are. Who is to say that I never meet once again with Kevin and Conan Curry?'

'From the little I experienced in your mother's company, I sensed a truly warm and loving woman,' Samuel said. 'You have been a very fortunate son. I never really knew my mother. My life was in the hands of a governess and servants.'

Ian recognised the sadness in Samuel's eyes and realised one very important aspect of his life compared to that of his new friend; Ian had known the love of wonderful parents.

Samuel continued, 'But, what we must now do is have my uncle polish your education to become a good member of the English upper classes. He will teach you the manners desired of a gentleman, and you will have to learn to alter your accent, although your accent may be excused because of my long time in the colonies.'

The two continued to discuss matters relevant to Ian assuming the life of an English aristocrat until the sun began its descent on the horizon.

That evening, Ian stayed and the three men indulged in port and cigars after a delicious meal of fish cooked in oyster sauce served with garden vegetables, accompanied by home-baked bread. Ian had to admit that James was a fine cook, although he was not altogether comfortable having learned of the true relationship between James and Samuel. He tried to put the matter out of mind, and in the morning bid the two men the best of fortune, before returning to his village.

Ian had returned the dray to the Sydney wharves and now took the lightly sprung carriage back to Sir George's estate, where arrangements had been made for him to learn the mores and manners of a gentleman.

As Ian travelled along the rough and dusty track between the stands of eucalyptus trees and wattle bushes, he had time to think about the great adventure he was about to embark on. With the death of his mother, he no longer had any ties to the colony, and ahead was the chance to further himself as a soldier of the Queen. No doubt his departed father might have been sympathetic to his aspirations, but he had told his son of the horrors of the battlefield. The stories did not seem real to a young boy, who had a need to learn from his own experience.

In his coat pocket he could feel the small pistol, and wondered if he would ever catch up with the Curry brothers. He knew the chances of that were sadly about nil. But he also knew that if he did meet them, he would kill them.

*

The wharf was crowded with passengers awaiting the order to board the ship returning to England. Two tough-looking men stood apart from the well-dressed passengers booked in first class, looking about furtively to see if they had drawn any attention from the authorities. Conan had purchased their fares for the journey in steerage – the cheapest fare. He had explained to his brother that they needed to ration the money they had stolen, as it would have to last until they reached Ireland. The slim clipper ship they were boarding was known as the greyhound of the oceans. It was a ship with a lot of sail and, if the winds prevailed, they could be in England within a couple of months.

'Time to go aboard,' Conan said, hoisting the canvas bag containing the stolen money on his shoulder.

'Do you think Steele will be looking for us?' Kevin asked.

'If he is, he will be heading south to Victoria,' Conan replied, walking up the gangway. 'The hope of him meeting us in this lifetime are as good as you and I being knighted by the Queen.' As Conan stepped forward, he did so with the image of Mary Steele's body at his feet, fighting back the haunting memory with the knowledge that he could not turn back time. He had a blood loyalty to his brother, and this had led them to the clipper ship bound for England, with no hope of return to New South Wales.

FIVE

Sir George Forbes was expecting him. He and Ian sat in the billiard room which was the most private place in the sprawling sandstone-built house, surrounded by well-kept gardens watered from a nearby creek that still had pools of water. Tea had been brought to them by a young servant girl.

'Samuel has instructed me to divide his allowance with you,' Sir George said. 'That way you will be able to sustain yourself without the usual income you would have received from your blacksmith shop.'

'That was very thoughtful of Samuel,' Ian said, sipping his tea.

'When he first proposed his venture to me after meeting you, I must admit that I had reservations. But the more I have grown to know you, I feel his scheme might just work. I pray that it does, because Samuel deserves a new start in life, away from my brother. It is his hatred for me that put the poor boy in his current situation.'

Ian was not sure if he should mention that he knew that the man sitting opposite him was in fact Samuel's real father.

'I love my nephew as I would love a son,' Sir George said, and that decided it for Ian; he would not reveal what Samuel had confided in him.

'In the next few weeks, you will keep up appearances as a full-time blacksmith, working for me,' Sir George said. 'We will have ample time for me to brief you on all those in the family, as well as boyhood friends that Samuel knew in England. By the time you leave here, you will be Samuel Forbes, and in the years ahead secure my nephew's inheritance. I suspect that in doing so, a young man like yourself will profit greatly as well. Samuel has told me of your desire to serve in the Queen's army. A smart officer has the opportunity to take advantage of situations to enhance his reputation and fortunes.'

For the next month, Ian was instructed in how he should act in the company of the rich and powerful. Ian could relate the who's who of the family as well as close friends. Knowing all this did not alleviate the uneasy feeling that he might strike a situation that could reveal him as an imposter. But he balanced that against what he could also gain within the Forbes family circle. Ian was instructed in the etiquette of social occasions and who deserved deference in meetings and provided a profile of those influential within the family's circle of friends and acquaintances. Ian learned that the family fortune had its roots originally in slavery and then the good fortune of investing in the East India Company, but the astute ancestors had also diversified into manufacturing, mining and shipping. Although a vast fortune had accumulated in the family coffers, the Forbes family had not been able to achieve a higher social standing in the rigid class system of the English aristocracy. They were not completely seen as outsiders, and George's brother plotted to ensure that the right marriages within the family might establish closer links with that old aristocracy.

He warned Ian that the two most dangerous men he would face were Samuel's older brother, Charles, and father, Sir Archibald Forbes. By the time Sir George was satisfied that Ian had passed his tests to become a real member of the Forbes family, Ian felt confident enough to walk into any manor in England, and pass as one who had been born into great wealth.

In the meantime, Sir George had despatched a letter to his brother, narrating how Samuel had thrived in the colony. He was no longer the callow youth left at the gates of the regiment, but a robust and confident young man. He also made mention that Samuel would be returning to join their grandfather's old regiment as a commissioned officer. Sir George knew that this would keep Ian away from those who might have known Samuel in his old regiment.

The day came for Ian to journey to Sydney and onto England aboard a clipper.

'You have first class passage, befitting a Forbes,' Sir George said. 'As you can see, you have only the finest of clothes that can be obtained in the colony, and even the pistol you carry has Samuel's initials engraved on it.'

'Sir George, I cannot think of a way to express my thanks for all that you have done for me,' Ian said.

'Thank Samuel,' Sir George said with a smile. 'I am sure that you and he will one day meet again. I must admit that in our time together, I have had to rethink my thoughts that gentlemen are born and not made. Seeing the way you have borne yourself, I must admit it is possible to shift from the lower classes to a station where one would call you a gentleman. Be always on your guard and, God willing, your life will be filled with fame and fortune. I have a package of letters and papers for you that may assist proving your identity.' Sir George held out his hand and a thick but small leather satchel. Ian accepted the gesture with gratitude.

'The carriage is waiting outside to take you to Sydney,' Sir George said, and Ian thought that he saw just a hint of tears in the nobleman's eyes as he turned away.

A convict servant assisted Ian with his baggage to the horse-drawn carriage, and in the heat and dust of the summer under a blazing sun, Ian's journey as Samuel Forbes began.

As Ian sat next to the driver, he gazed at the fields of desiccated grass and tall gum trees, wondering if he would remember the smell of the sun-baked plains, and the acrid scent of the bushfires that raged this time of the year. But the closer they came to Sydney, the more Ian looked to the unknown future, and what it might hold for him. Soon, he stood at the gangplank of the sleek ship while his baggage was being loaded aboard.

For just a moment, Ian looked around him, and then down at the wharf. This was the colonial land of a continent where Britain had sent her unwanted for their crimes committed mostly due to dire poverty. His own mother was one of those who had in desperation forged a document to obtain five shillings. That amount had cost her a fare to the other side of the earth, where she had met a good and sturdy British soldier. Ian's father had been a gentle and intelligent man who had been self-educated. He had despised the class system of England and took his discharge in the colony where men of ambition could rise to make a good life. Ian had loved his father, who never used violence to punish him. A mere sad look of disapproval had been enough to bring Ian to heel. It had been his feisty mother who had inflicted any corporal punishment with the wooden mixing spoon – but not severely. Ian had been born under the Southern Cross, and now he was returning to the bosom of the mother country as a gentleman, albeit in disguise as another man.

A whistle blew, and a voice boomed, 'All going aboard, go aboard.'

Ian stepped onto the gangplank.

*

They could hear the shrieks of women, and the cries of men from the married section of the ship. Conan and Kevin Curry gripped the edge of the wooden table at the centre of their steerage single quarters aboard the clipper ship. The storm raging in the English Channel had caused all hatches to be closed down, and in the near pitch-blackness of the cramped and unhygienic quarters, the voyage was hell. From the outset, the normally fast clipper ship had been delayed in its journey by storms and failing winds. The journey had taken weeks more than the skipper had anticipated.

'We should have spent some of that money on first class,' Kevin groaned, feeling the nausea welling up inside once again as sea sickness racked his body.

'Couldn't attract attention to ourselves,' Conan said, breathing in the stench of the remnants of the midday meal of pickled pork, dried peas and bread spread across the now slippery deck of steerage.

The stink was enough to make a man sick, and Conan's only consolation was that the captain had declared they would be in the Thames River the next day.

They shared their quarters with many other single men, some of as dubious character as their own. Others had once been prosperous until they squandered their savings in a fruitless search for the elusive gold of the Australian colonies, and now returned as poor men to the homes they had left behind in the British Isles.

'Have you got the money on you?' Conan asked his brother.

'No, it's safe enough under my bunk,' Kevin groaned, caring little for the leather pouch when all he wanted to do was die and rid himself of the terrible torment of sea sickness. The sleeping arrangements consisted of rows of bunks along either side of the hull with the tables down the centre. The ship was infested with rats, and the food with weevils. The barrels of water were filled from dirty streams when the ship was in port, and algae often flourished in what was meant as drinking water. Both men were aware of that illness known as cholera which took passenger lives on such voyages, but the need to escape the possibility of the hangman's noose back in New South Wales had motivated them into facing this danger.

By early morning, the storm seemed to be abating and Kevin retired to his bunk. He had complained before the storm that he was feeling ill, and Conan could see that his brother was running a fever. The nausea and vomiting had not helped his condition.

Conan also went to his bunk and was awoken with the flood of fresh air when the hatches were finally opened. The stench of vomit prevailed but Conan could also smell the brine saturating the air. His bunk was next to his brother's, and he slipped out to wake him as someone shouted, 'London is off the portside bow!'

Some of the steerage passengers were already clambering up the stairs, joining others on deck to see the first sight of the world's most important city.

'Kevin, get up, you lazy bastard,' Conan said. He bent to shake his brother by the shoulder and froze. His brother's eyes were open, his pale skin a deathly pallor. But what was most obvious was that Kevin's throat had been cut to the spine. His brother was well and truly dead – murdered in the darkness of the night. Without much further thought, Conan slid his hand under his brother's meagre mattress to feel for the money. To his horror, the leather pouch was gone. Just as they had reached London on their way to Ireland, Kevin Curry had been robbed and slain. When Conan looked around, he could see that all those in steerage had departed, leaving him alone with the body of his brother.

Conan groaned his despair. He was now alone and penniless, hours from landing in a foreign city in the land of the hated English.

Already the ship's crew were swabbing down steerage with vinegar, removing the remnants of the night before, and the ship's doctor attended to declare Kevin dead. He scribbled that the cause of his death was foul play.

'I regret to say that the chances of arresting your brother's murderer are slim to none,' the doctor said sympathetically. 'You should report the matter to the police.'

Conan nodded, knowing that he would not be doing so. He could not afford to draw the attention of the law.

Conan watched as a couple of men wrapped his brother's body in a sheet and carried it up to the deck for removal from the ship.

'Where are you going to take him?' Conan asked.

'Do you have any money to give him a proper burial?' one of the men asked, and Conan said he did not.

'He will get a pauper's grave,' the man replied, taking away the body to a cart waiting on the wharf.

Conan left the ship with only the clothes he was wearing, and a few pennies in his pocket. He did not take anything that belonged to his dead brother. The stench rising from the polluted river caught Conan unawares, and the haze of smog over the city burned his eyes. Summer was coming to the northern hemisphere and Conan was in a state of despair.

He walked from the Thames dockside into the bustling city until he found a pub. He went inside, took the last few coins he had, and ordered an ale in an attempt to drown his sorrows. The bar was crowded with working men who ignored the stranger amongst them.

Conan took his ale, swallowed it down, and glanced around him. His eye caught sight of a soldier wearing the colourful red jacket so well-known to the world. On his sleeve, Conan could see the chevrons of a sergeant. The sergeant caught his eye.

'Hey, stranger, I will buy you another ale,' he said.

The army sergeant was a big man, wearing a medal for some campaign he had fought on the edges of the British Empire. He called across to the publican for another ale, flashing silver coins when he did. He had an Irish accent, and Conan joined him at his table.

'I thank you, sergeant,' Conan said, sitting down, accepting the tankard of brown liquid placed in front of him. 'But I cannot repay the offer.'

'I can hear from your voice that you hail from the Emerald Isle,' the sergeant said. 'But I can also tell you have lived in the Australian colonies. I once did service in New South Wales. Are you just off a boat?'

'I am,' Conan said, taking a sip from his tankard in the smoke-filled bar. 'Just disembarked a few hours ago.'

The sergeant leaned forward. 'Are you lookin' for a job?'

'I am,' Conan replied. 'I kind of lost my savings when my brother died just outside London on our voyage.'

'You look to me like a big, strappin' young man, ideal for the British army. I can sign you up. I sign up a lot of lads in this pub for a life of adventure, where the army gives you a uniform, a square meal a day and travel to exotic lands to do the Queen's good work. I am Colour Sergeant Leslie and authorised to sign you up.'

'I'm not an admirer of the British,' Conan said. 'Why should I fight for them?'

'There are a lot of the lads in my regiment,' Leslie said. 'You don't have to like the Queen. We Irish like a good scrap, and we aren't fighting other Irishmen. If you take the Queen's shilling, you will have a secure job for the rest of your life. What is your name?'

'Conan Curry.'

'Ah, Conan, with a good Irish name like that you would make a fine soldier,' the sergeant said, and Conan sensed that the army sergeant must be a recruiter, finding his enlistees in pubs such as this one close to the disembarkation points along the Thames wharves. No wonder he initially called him stranger. It was obvious that he was a shrewd man who had the ability to draw in those down-and-outs as fodder for the British army.

Conan swallowed the last of his ale, placed the tankard on the rough, wooden table and stood. 'I would be thanking you, sergeant for your hospitality and will be thinking upon your offer.'

'You know where to find me,' the sergeant said with a shrug.

With two ales in his stomach and nothing in his pocket, Conan exited the pub. Fortunately, the weather was mild and he began to walk aimlessly amongst the better-dressed citizens of the city, hoping to hear the accents of fellow Irishmen who might be charitable enough to aid him in finding work and a place to put his head down. For now, he knew that he was truly alone in a place where he could not see the open plains, or smell the eucalypt trees.

*

The two-storeyed brick house off the leafy fringes of Hyde Park was one of a few select homes for the rich. The butler took the letter delivered to the front door, placed it on a silver platter and walked towards the drawing room, adorned with painted portraitures of men and women past and present, where a tall man in his late fifties sat with a newspaper.

'A letter for you, Sir Archibald,' the butler said.

'Thank you, Gilston,' Sir Archibald Forbes said, taking the correspondence. He could see that the letter had travelled from the colony of New South Wales, and also recognised his estranged brother's handwriting. He frowned as he opened the letter.

Archibald read slowly, taking in each spider-like word on the fine paper. When he had finished, he reached for the bell to summon his butler.

'Please inform my son that I wish to speak with him,' Sir Archibald commanded.

The butler disappeared, and minutes later, Charles Forbes appeared in the drawing room. Although he was married, he and his wife, Louise, were estranged and Charles resided at the family home in London.

'Is something the matter?' the lean man in his late twenties asked, seeing the concern written across his father's face.

'I have received a letter from your uncle in New South Wales, writing to say that we can expect your brother will be returning to us very soon.'

'Samuel,' Charles said. 'This is rather unexpected. I thought that my brother was enjoying life in the wretched colonies.'

'From what George has written, it appears your brother has a desire to return to his grandfather's regiment, and not the one that I selected for him. He wishes to complete his service to the Queen as an officer in the army. You do know what that means for your future.'

Charles sat down in an ornate chair opposite his father. 'It means that after ten years, my worthless brother will be entitled to a third of the Forbes estate, in accordance with the wishes of your father.'

'That is a substantial inheritance. It could weaken what we have,' Sir Archibald said. 'I had hoped that a dangerous life on the imperial frontier might have solved that problem for us. It was not to be when your brother resigned his commission, but still, I was pleased he did so because he had not satisfied the conditions of his inheritance. Now he may do so, if he takes up a commission in your grandfather's old regiment. I feel this change of circumstances will be yours to rectify.'

Charles looked hard at his father. He was aware of the bitterness he held towards Samuel, who he believed was not his son, but the product of betrayal by his wife with his brother. While Samuel was in his father's presence, he was always reminded that the boy was another man's offspring. If he'd had his way, the boy would have been smothered at birth. It was obvious what his father was saying, and although Charles held little love for his brother, the suggestion made him uncomfortable. While he was pondering the return of Samuel, a young lady of around eighteen years entered the room. She had blonde hair and an appealing face. Not beautiful but attractive to the opposite sex.

'Gilston has told me the news that a letter has arrived from New South Wales,' she said, excitement lighting her beautiful eyes. 'Is there news about brother Samuel?'

'Alice, my dear,' Sir Archibald said to his daughter. 'It is indeed a letter from your uncle George with news of your brother. It seems we may expect a visit from him very soon.'

'Oh! How wonderful,' Alice said, clapping her hands together. 'It has been so long since I last saw him. I was a mere child, and he was always so kind to me. I remember how Sam would read stories to me when mother was ill and I was frightened.'

'You may not recognise him now,' Sir Archibald said. 'Your uncle has said life in the colonies has made him more robust.'

'I will recognise him,' Alice said, beaming. 'Do we know when he will arrive in London?'

'It is hard to say. It will depend on the speed of the ship that brings him back to us.'

'I will pray that his journey will be safe,' Alice said, not noticing the dark exchange of looks between her oldest brother and father.

SIX

Night arrived in London and Conan Curry felt the pangs of hunger gnawing at his stomach. He had drifted into the poverty-stricken neighbourhoods of the city, where narrow and filthy cobblestoned streets were filled with young and old whose faces reflected their poverty. Raucous prostitutes plied their age-old trade, and urchins in rags stared with blank eyes at all passing by. The air stank of rotting garbage and human waste. It was the size and dangerous demeanour of Conan that kept the beggars and gathering of thugs from confronting him for any valuables they thought he might have had upon his person.

Still, Conan felt vulnerable. A couple of ales earlier in the day was no substitute for a good portion of beef or mutton.

'Hey, you, stranger.' A man's voice called to Conan from the gloom of an adjacent alley. Conan turned to see a couple of young men step from the dark. 'We haven't seen your face down here before. Where you from?'

Conan sized up both men, whose dress appeared as if they might be a little more prosperous than those around them. The man who called to him had a Welsh accent and Conan was alert to any movements that may indicate a threat. He wished that he had at least a knife to protect himself.

'What business is it to you?' Conan asked.

'You look like you could handle yourself, Paddy,' the larger of the two men said, detecting Conan's Irish accent. Conan did not sense any menace in his statement. It was more like an enquiry.

'Do you want to find out?' Conan countered, and the man asking the questions smiled.

'No, but I need another man for a quick job around here. You look like you could do with some friends hereabouts. Are you interested? The job will give you a place to flop tonight, and some bread and grog in your guts.'

'What have you got in mind?' Conan asked.

'In the next street, there is a man of some means going from house to house. He looks like he might have a shilling or two on him. Me and my brother also think he might give them to us with a little friendly persuasion. You get what I mean?'

Conan knew exactly what they meant. How ironic, he thought. He had fled from New South Wales because of a heinous crime, only to fall in with men of his own ilk on the other side of the world. It was almost like criminality recognised its own.

'Is this generous man armed?' Conan asked, and saw the two thugs look at each other.

'Don't know,' the obvious leader said. 'But the three of

us could easily take him on in these streets. It sounds like you know what you are doing.'

'We split three ways,' Conan said. 'Fair is fair.'

For a moment, the other two men hesitated. It was obvious they had considered their offer to join them meant Conan was only to receive a small portion of the robbery. But they also sensed that the man they had picked was not new to this kind of craft.

'Third shares it is,' the leader of the two said with some reluctance. 'About time we got to work.' The two men had not offered their names, nor did Conan. If anything went wrong, no names could be offered up to the police. But in this part of the city, the sight of uniformed Metropolitan Police was rare. It was not a safe place for anyone at this time of night.

The three men made their way through the night, and emerged from a side street of rundown terrace housing.

'We wait here,' the leader said, taking up a position out of the fever-like light cast by a gaslight lamp. Conan stood by his newly acquainted companions, wondering who they were about to rob, and saw a door open. A tall, well-dressed man stepped out with a black bag in his hand.

'That's him,' the leader hissed and stepped forward to intercept the man. Conan followed, pushing his way through the people wandering the garbage-strewn street. The man they had targeted glanced up at the three who had suddenly appeared blocking his path.

'Give us your money and bag,' the leader growled in the startled man's face, and Conan could see a long knife had been produced to back up the threat.

'This is outrageous,' the victim protested. Conan thought his accent was North American, perhaps Canadian. 'I protest this nefarious act.'

'Just give up all your valuables, and I won't slit your gut,' the leader said, pressing the blade into the victim's stomach. 'Take everything you can,' he continued, looking at Conan, who plunged his hand into a trouser pocket to produce a small leather bag of coins. Meanwhile, the leader's companion had retrieved the bag and a fob watch from the waistcoat the man wore. The robbery had caught the attention of some of the people in the street.

'Robbery!' someone yelled, turning all attention to the three men surrounding their victim.

'Got to get out of here,' the leader said, turning on his heel, and running down the street, followed by Conan and the other man who had the black bag. They knocked down anyone who dared to attempt to block their path, and ran hard until the leader ducked into a narrow alley, clambering up the rickety stairs of a tenement house, and bashed on a wooden door.

The door opened, and the three men fell into a dingy room lit by a single candle held by a young woman with a pinched face, wearing an old threadbare dress.

Conan was gasping after the desperate escape, breathing in air that smelled of rotting cabbage and human sweat. The young woman, barely more than a girl, cast Conan a questioning glance.

'We got some goodies, Molly,' the second-in-command said, holding up the bag victoriously. 'We done good.'

'Who's this, Edwin?' she asked, staring curiously at Conan. Conan noted the names.

'Just a Paddy we found wandering the street looking for a meal, and somewhere to put his head down. We needed another man to pull off the job.'

'What's your name?' she asked, turning to Conan, who could see that she was very attractive under the grime.

'Conan,' he answered.

'Conan. And where are you from?' she asked, appraising him with eyes that spoke of some admiration for what she saw.

Conan considered lying, but thought it was not necessary in the company of people like himself. 'I just got off a ship from New South Wales, and was fortunate to meet Ed and obviously his brother.'

'That is Owen,' Molly said. 'He's my brother, and so is Edwin. What you got in your hand?'

'I got this,' Conan said, opening the leather bag, spilling a handful of shillings on a battered wooden table in the tiny room. The siblings' eyes lit up with appreciation. Molly quickly counted the small fortune.

'There's two guineas here,' she said. 'What's in the black bag?'

Edwin opened the bag and stared inside. From the disappointed expression on his face, the other three could see that there was not much. Edwin reached in the bag and removed what looked like a flat spoon. 'It looks like the thing a surgeon has,' he said in disgust.

'Well, we can sell them things to the right person,' Molly said hopefully. 'They should bring in a penny or two.'

'So we robbed a medical man,' Conan said. 'No wonder your locals were a bit upset.'

'Don't matter,' Owen said with a shrug. 'He can spare the money for us poor folks. Toffs like him have plenty of money.'

'I cooked a stew,' Molly said. 'The Paddy looks like he could use a feed.'

Conan nodded his appreciation and Molly went to a corner of the room to remove a pot from a small coal stove. She set three bowls and spoons on the table next to the small pile of silver coins. The stew of cabbage, mutton and a few carrots was ladled out, and Molly brought over a loaf of bread, cutting it into thick slabs to accompany the stew.

The three men sat down at the table and tucked in. Molly sat with them, and they ate in silence, eyeing the coins at the centre of the table.

'Paddy here says he will have a third of our takings,' Owen said, wiping the gravy from his chin with the back of his shirtsleeve.

'If he wants another meal and place to sleep, he will have to pay rent,' Molly said. 'His share will get him a couple of weeks under my roof. He will have to earn his keep if he is going to stay with us.'

Conan looked at the young woman with just a touch of respect for her quick thinking.

He shrugged. 'Suits me fine. Where do I put my head down?'

'You sleep out here on the floor,' Molly said. 'I have my own room, and don't get no ideas of sharing it with me, Paddy. My brothers have the other room.'

Conan nodded, hoping he might get a blanket or two to soften the hard wooden surface. At least he had somewhere to stay and a meal in his belly.

Conan remained at the table when the two brothers retired for the evening to sleep. Molly remained with him, sewing a dress in the dim light of the few candles in the room. She had made a pot of tea and Conan sipped the black liquid sweetened by a small portion of sugar from a cracked cup.

'Were you a convict?' Molly asked while she sewed.

'No, I was freeborn, but my father was, and so was my ma,' Conan said.

'So, why have you come to England?' she asked without taking her attention from her task of stitching.

'My brother and me had some trouble and had to get out of New South Wales. My brother died of the cholera on the ship just as we got here,' Conan lied. 'And our savings was stolen.'

Molly glanced up from her task with an expression of compassion. 'I am sorry for your loss. Me and my brothers lost our parents last year in Wales from the cholera. We had nothing, so we came to London to make our fortunes. It has not happened yet.'

'I can see you have a little way to go,' Conan said with a smile. He liked this Welsh girl the more he got to know her. 'I am hoping to get to Ireland where I can find my relatives in Dublin. I just need to make a bit of money for a fare.'

'It's not much better there,' Molly said. 'At least in London, there's always a chance to make money off the rich toffs. You could do well with my brothers. You're a big man and look as if you can handle yourself.'

'Would you like me to stay?' Conan asked.

'Only if you want,' she replied casually without looking at him. Conan sensed that she was attracted to him.

'I will think about it,' he said, finishing his mug of tea.

'I will get you a blanket and something to put your head on,' Molly said, rising from the chair.

Molly brought the blanket and a pillow stuffed with horsehair. She laid it out for him and retired to her tiny room, leaving the colonial Irishman with his thoughts.

Conan stared at the darkness around him as he lay on the hard floor; his thoughts drifted through the last twenty-four hours, and to the past, to Mary Steele lying dead at his feet. Oh, if only he could turn back time and still have the kind woman alive. Her untimely death haunted him and he cursed his dead brother for his stupid and foolish act of killing her. Kevin had paid the price for his crime and Conan felt sadness for his death. Sleep came to his troubled mind and the world faded from his consciousness.

*

Dr Peter Campbell cradled the goblet of brandy as he sat on a divan in the Forbes London residence. He was still shaken by the bare-faced robbery he'd endured on his charitable rounds in the London slums.

'That is the thanks you get for helping those wretched people,' Alice said, sitting opposite him with her hands folded in her lap. 'We have attempted to warn you that it is dangerous to go into those areas. The poor people there have no gratitude for your selfless service.'

'My dear,' Peter said. 'This unfortunate incident has not deterred me. I shall resume my assistance to them when I am able to replace my medical bag. I have reported the matter to the police, and from my description of my assailants, a detective thinks it might be the work of a couple of Welsh brothers they have had their eye on for some time. The third person is a mystery I am sure they will solve.'

'Oh, Peter,' Alice said, exasperated by the surgeon's humanitarian attitude. 'What would become of me if something horrible ever befell you. I think that I would simply die of grief.'

He smiled. 'I grew up on the Canadian frontier. These men were not half as scary as a grizzly bear on the rampage.' Seeing she did not share his humour, Peter put down his brandy and knelt before her, taking her hands in his own. 'The best thing that has ever happened in my life was the fortune of meeting you. I promise that I will also make enough money to win the approval of your father for a chance to have you become my wife. I know he currently disapproves of a colonial wedding his only daughter, but I think I can eventually win him over.'

Alice looked down into his face, tears in her eyes as she gripped his hands.

'I do love you so,' she said. 'You are so different to all those stuffy young men my father would have court me. They may be rich and respectable, but they are not you. I know that when my brother, Samuel, arrives home, he will like you and help persuade father of your good intentions.'

The Canadian doctor had heard Alice continuously prattle on about her beloved brother who was, amongst many things, a war hero who had faced the savage natives of the British colony of New Zealand, holding the regimental colours against the Maori onslaught. Peter hoped she was right. He needed more allies within the Forbes family if he was to win her hand in marriage. He knew he had Alice's younger brother, Herbert, who had just turned sixteen on his side. The boy admired the doctor, who told him stories about the wild frontier of Canada. At least for now, he could see the love in her eyes for him and hope for the future.

*

The seas were calm and only a few fluffy clouds lay on the horizon. A gentle breeze filled the sails of the clipper conveying Ian Steele to London. He stood at the rails, gazing out over the English Channel at seagulls whirling over a shoal of small fish off the starboard. The captain had announced they should be docking in the early morning, and the young colonial felt both excitement and trepidation for what lay before him.

His first test had come only a week out of Sydney when one of the passengers learned who he was – at least, who

Samuel Forbes was. The man, a banker from London in his late fifties, had approached Ian one evening on deck and introduced himself as a friend of the family. He said that he only remembered Samuel as a young boy of five when they first met, and then said that he, Samuel, had grown to be a fine young man.

Ian casually asked if the meeting had been at their London residence near Hyde Park or at the country estate in Kent.

The banker said that it had been at the London residence, where he had been a dinner guest, and noticed him with a book in his hand, which made an impression on him. Ian was nervous, but he also noticed his ability to put into practice the background stories he had been taught by both Sir George Forbes and Samuel himself, and appeared to fool the man into believing that Ian was in fact, Samuel Forbes.

On the occasions that Ian was in the man's company, he was able to keep up the pretence with practised ease, to the extent that the banker said he would enjoy having Ian dine with his family when they reached England.

'Land ahoy!' a crewman cried from the sails above, and Ian quickly crossed the polished deck to see the faint outline of land.

'From this distance, that would be either the Isle of Wight or Dover we can see,' an older passenger mentioned from behind Ian. 'Either way, we are almost home.'

Home, Ian mused. Not if he was unveiled as an imposter. Then, home might mean being returned to the Australian colonies as an imposter in chains. A dread filled him, but he knew now there was no turning back. From herein, he must become Samuel Forbes, and forget he was ever the son of a convict woman and a former British soldier.

★

It was the heavy, hurried tramp of boots on the narrow staircase to Molly's dingy residence that alerted Conan. He came awake and leapt to his feet.

'Open in the name of the Queen,' a voice boomed, as fists crashed against the solid wooden door.

'Quick, this way,' Molly hissed to Conan, who was still shaking off the sleep. It was dark and, he guessed, in the very early hours of the morning.

Molly slid back a wall panel and gestured for Conan to slip through. He cast around him but could not see Edwin or Owen. Without hesitating, Conan entered the stuffy space as Molly slipped the panel back. Conan could see a sliver of light and realised that there was an exit into an adjacent hallway of the tenement. He felt around with his fingers to find that he could slide the panel and crawled out into the vacant hallway. Through the flimsy walls, he could hear the raised voices of police demanding that Molly inform them of the whereabouts of her brothers and the other man associated with them.

As Conan made his way cautiously down the steps of the hallway, her protests of innocence faded, and he opened the door to the street, peering carefully to see a uniformed policeman wearing his top hat and blue, swallow-tailed coat standing outside the front entrance of Molly's residence with short wooden truncheons in his hand. Conan could see that he was staring into the building, and that the sun was not above the horizon.

Very carefully, Conan stepped from the tenement, walking softly away along the virtually deserted street. He had not had time to grab his boots and, though shoeless, he attempted to appear inconspicuous. So far, so good. There was a street corner where he could turn to be out of sight of the police.

To his surprise, he saw Edwin and Owen walking towards him, with Owen carrying a bag. They stopped when they saw Conan.

'What are you doing here?' Edwin asked.

'Don't go back to your sister,' Conan warned. 'The traps are there looking for you.'

'Traps?' Owen queried.

'Police,' Conan corrected himself. Traps was not a word the Welsh brothers were familiar with.

'We had better make ourselves scarce,' Edwin said, tossing the bag of what Conan guessed was the result of a burglary that night.

'I'm going on my own.' Conan said. 'I don't think they know who I am. Do you have my share of the money we took yesterday?'

'We do,' Edwin replied. 'But it is not a good time to dole out your share with the peelers not far away. It looks like they have caught onto us.'

'Then we had better get out of London,' Conan suggested.

'Where do we go? The peelers must know who we are to come to Molly's place and if we are caught, it will be all over for us,' Owen said.

'I have an idea,' Conan said. 'I know how I will disappear, where the traps won't find us.'

SEVEN

Conan led his newly found friends in the direction of the Thames docks. He remembered the pub where he had met the recruiting sergeant, arriving as it was opening. Sure enough, he sighted the uniformed Irish sergeant standing outside.

Conan turned to his confused companions.

'If you want to keep out of the clutches of the peelers, your only choice is to enlist in the army,' he said.

'The army!' Owen exclaimed. 'That does not sound like a good idea. I would rather take my chances with the peelers.'

'Prison has bars, and at least with the army we still have our freedom,' Conan responded. 'The army might mean being posted to the colonies, and I can tell you it is far better than being in this cesspool.'

'Maybe the Paddy has a good idea,' Edwin said. 'The peelers

will not look for us in the army and later, we can leave quietly when the heat is off us.'

'What about Molly?' Owen asked. 'The peelers are sure to find the doctor's bag.'

'Molly is smart,' Edwin said half-heartedly. 'She will give the peelers the slip. Molly will be safe, and we can contact her after we go into the army when we get leave.'

Conan caught the eye of Colour Sergeant Leslie, who was preparing to enter the pub. 'Sergeant, would you be looking to recruit three for the regiment?' he asked.

Colour Sergeant Leslie stood appraising the three men. 'Was it not you I spoke to only yesterday in the pub?' he asked Conan.

'It was, sergeant,' Conan replied. 'I thought upon your words and have convinced these two Welshmen of the bounties the army has to offer three, healthy and future loyal soldiers of the Queen. Besides, I've heard it said that the Welsh were the Irish, who couldn't swim to Ireland.'

Colour Sergeant Leslie broke into a grin.

'You men, come with me to the barracks,' the British army, senior non-commissioned officer said, and the three followed him to the gates of the regiment a short distance away. Conan was sure that he had made the right decision. He suspected that if the Welsh brothers had been picked up by the police, it would only be a matter of time before he was implicated in their gang. Enlisting in the army gave him breathing space to consider options, and to eventually reach Ireland. He would be signing on for ten years of service, but he had no intention of remaining a soldier of the Queen, and desertion was in his future.

*

The hansom cab that brought Ian to the impressive house just off Hyde Park came to a halt. Ian sat for a brief moment, wondering if he should have the driver turn around and take him back to the docks.

'Would you like me to assist you with your luggage, sir?' the driver asked.

'No, I can manage,' Ian replied, as he only had one bag of essentials. He alighted with his bag in hand, paid the driver, and took a deep breath as the horse-drawn cab clattered away. It was mid-morning, and the sun was a feeble light in perfectly blue skies.

Ian stepped forward to walk up the short flight of steps to the main door where he rang a bell, waiting for the entrance to open to his future.

The door opened and a serious-faced older man answered. Panic gripped Ian. Was this man his supposed father?

'Yes, sir, is there anything I can do for you?' the well-dressed man asked. Ian struggled in his memory to remember all that he had been briefed by Samuel and Sir George.

'Yes, I am Master Samuel Forbes. I believe that my father has been expecting me,' Ian finally replied, calculating that the man standing before him would have to be a valet or butler.

'Master Forbes, I will inform your father that you have arrived,' the older man said. 'Please come inside.'

He stood aside, and Ian stepped into the foyer of the Forbes London residence. He was immediately impressed by the obvious display of wealth in the relatively spacious room, adorned with paintings and Chinese vases on stands.

Ian was standing alone as the butler went to fetch Sir Archibald Forbes. He was taken by surprise when a very attractive young woman burst into the foyer, followed by a gangly young man in his mid-teens.

'Sam!' the young woman said, hugging him to her. 'You have certainly changed in your time away from us.' Ian knew this must be his sister, Alice, and the young man standing shyly behind her the younger brother, Herbert who Sir George briefed him had been a mere boy when Samuel had left England.

'Alice, your warm reception has made the long and difficult voyage worthwhile,' Ian said.

'How delightful! It is so good to have you return to us,' Alice said, overjoyed at the reunion with her older brother.

'Herbert, you've certainly grown since our last meeting,' Ian said, extending his hand to the slim, good-looking young man who had stepped forward, accepting the outstretched hand. It was a firm grip from Herbert, who had not uttered a word. Ian could see that the youngest brother appeared in awe of this meeting.

Two men entered the foyer, and Ian could see that they were obviously father and son. This had to be his father, and eldest brother.

'Father, Charles, I pray that you received the letter from Sir George,' Ian said. He could see the coldness in both men's faces. There would be no warm reception from either.

'Samuel, I hope your voyage to return home was pleasant,' Sir Archibald said without offering his hand. 'I can see that your time with my brother in the colonies has changed you very much.'

Ian could feel the dryness in his mouth as his supposed father appraised him. This was the ultimate test of the impersonation he had assumed. 'It is good to be back with my family.'

'We should have a welcome home dinner party for Sam,' Alice said. 'I can arrange the guest list. I only wish mother was with us to celebrate this joyous moment.'

Ian noticed Sir Archibald cast his daughter a disapproving glance.

'We shall see,' Sir Archibald said. 'But first, I think I should speak alone with Samuel before we make any arrangements. Samuel, if you will come with me to the library.'

Ian nodded and followed the tall man down a long hallway and up an elegant staircase to a room lit by gaslight. He entered, casting around at the walls filled with books. Samuel had briefed him that this was his favourite room in the London house.

Sir Archibald closed the door behind them and stood at the centre of the room, hands behind his back.

'Sir, you are not my son. I wonder why you should pretend to be so,' he said.

'You are correct, I am not your son,' Ian answered, his heart pounding with fear. 'George Forbes is my real father.'

The blood drained from Sir Archibald's face.

'I am not sure if anyone else is aware of this, and I am sure that it is not something you would like for your friends to know. After all, I am still Samuel Forbes.'

'Has my brother acknowledged you as his son?' Archibald asked quietly.

'He only intimated that I was,' Ian said. 'He is aware that to do so would gravely damage your reputation in London society, and to the memory of my mother. I have always been aware of your resentment towards me, and why you were so hasty to have me sent away with the regiment. If it is any consolation, I have only returned to be commissioned into my grandfather's old regiment, and expect that you will arrange for that to occur. I am sure that you will be pleased to see the back of me.'

Ian could see that his unexpected declaration of not actually being Archibald's true son had taken him unawares. Ian could see some of the doubt about his being Samuel Forbes had drained from the other man – but not completely.

'My brother wrote to me that you had changed somewhat from the boy I last saw. You even appear to have a touch of a colonial accent.'

'I was not aware of that,' Ian said, growing more confident in his impersonation. 'I suspect that was inevitable, mixing with the colonials of New South Wales for so many years.'

'I think that we should rejoin the rest of the family,' Archibald said and walked stiffly out of the room.

Ian followed him to the drawing room where the family had gathered. Sir Archibald walked over to Charles and spoke quietly to him. Charles glanced at Ian with a frown as Alice took Ian's hand and led him to a sofa. Most of the dryness in Ian's mouth had gone, but he also knew that his place in the family was not completely cemented. His revelation concerning his parentage had put Sir Archibald off-foot. It was obvious that he did not wish to have it known that Samuel was his brother's son. For the moment, he felt secure that he was being perceived as the prodigal son, returning to the bosom of the family, albeit still a tentative situation. The sooner he could join a regiment, the better.

*

'He is not Samuel,' Charles said to his father in the privacy of the library. 'I could not even bring myself to greet him.'

Sir Archibald poured whisky in a crystal glass and slumped down in a big leather chair.

'I had my doubts, until Samuel raised an issue that only he could have known about,' he said, swishing the liquid around the tumbler. 'We have to accept he has changed considerably since we last saw him.'

'Did he mention that he is only my half-brother?' Charles asked, standing with his arms behind his back.

'Yes,' Archibald replied and took a swallow of the golden liquid. 'Until otherwise can be proven. We both know what will happen if he serves his ten years with your grandfather's old regiment. His claim to our estate will considerably weaken it.'

'But, according to your father's wishes, if he does not survive his ten years, his share is forfeit to the estate. As Alice relies on our generosity with little share left to her, that would mean that your true sons, Herbert and I, inherit the family estates.'

Archibald rose from his chair and walked over to his son, placing both hands on his shoulders.

'You are my firstborn, and the treachery of your mother cannot be rewarded. Herbert has expressed his desire for a career in the army as a commissioned officer and has completed his training as a gentleman cadet. Only you are worthy to be the lord of the estates.'

'Thank you, Father,' Charles said with genuine gratitude in his reply. 'I will always be by your side.'

'I know,' Archibald sighed. 'Until the time the good Lord summons me to His breast.'

'What should we do?' Charles asked.

'I arrange for his commission into the regiment, and we wait to see what may occur after that. If the situation does not go the way we like, then we make other plans to ensure your half-brother does not serve out his time.'

Charles knew that his father meant only one thing. The family had always had a reputation for being ruthless in business and life. They had taken their place in English society as one of the wealthiest and most influential families of their time and nothing would stand in the way of Charles to go even further in the ranks of the rich and powerful of the Empire.

*

A single bed, washbasin and dank stone walls. This was Molly's world in the female prison. The police had found the doctor's bag, and she was arrested for being in possession of stolen property.

Arrested and conveyed to prison, Molly knew that she would be found guilty. She had often heard stories in the slums that transportation to the colonies was as good as being sent to the moon. But she also had heard that the colonies no longer wanted convicts, which was only a partial relief. To be sent to the other side of the world had terrified her. However, a sentence in an English prison was of little consolation. All she could ponder in the silence of her cell was the fate of her two brothers and the Irishman she had found attractive.

Molly could hear the hob-nailed boots of the prison warder come down the corridor, and stop outside her cell. The door clanked open, and she heard her name called. 'Prisoner Molly Williams. You are to come with me.'

Molly was shackled and led down the corridor. She knew it was to appear before the judge and hear her sentence.

An hour later, Molly was escorted back to her cell with the words, *'Sentenced to five years hard labour'* ringing in her ears. When the heavy door clanked behind her, Molly slumped on the small bed. She felt numb. She would be twenty-three years old when her prison sentence was up. All she could do was pray that her beloved brothers had escaped the clutches of the law. But would she ever see them – or the Irishman – again?

*

Under the English summer sun, Conan, Edwin and Owen drilled relentlessly on the open parade ground with thirty other recruits. The uniforms they wore were uncomfortable, and the boots barely fit. The bark of Colour Sergeant Leslie drilling them no longer had the softness of his Irish brogue. He was as English as the other senior NCOs, and officers of the infantry regiment. Conan questioned the wisdom of his choice to join the British army. Foot drill, never-ending cleaning of brass, belts and boots, standing to attention and the monotony of poor rations was the only life the three now knew. Even the shilling a day they were supposed to be paid dwindled when they were forced to pay for their rations and uniform. But they were in the company of men like themselves. Scum of the earth the great general Wellington once called his British troops. But it was the scum of society that built the British Empire in the far-flung places around the globe.

The training day came to an end and the three men lined up for their issue of rations at the other ranks' mess.

'I heard that Molly got caught and was sentenced to five years,' Edwin said. 'One of the other privates from Wales read it in the paper.'

'Bloody damnation!' Owen swore. 'We left her to the mercy of the peelers. We ran away like cowards.'

'There was nothing we could do,' Conan growled. 'I am sorry for your sister, but it could have been worse.'

'Worse!' Owen exclaimed.

'Your sister could have been transported to Botany Bay if the Brits still did that, and she would have been fortunate to have even got there. You don't know what the prison ships are like that send out prisoners. I know, because my father was transported, as was my mother. It is a living hell on those ships. The death rate is worse than the prisons in England.'

Despite his retort on the fortunes of Molly Williams, Conan was haunted by the thought of the young woman languishing in an English prison. Maybe if they were to be given leave, he might be able to visit her. That was his only consolation in the tough military world he had signed up to.

EIGHT

Entrée

   Cutlets of Lamb braised with Soubise sauce
   Salmi of young partridges a l'Espagnole
   Vol au Vent of Salt Fish a la maitre d'hotel
   Casserole of Rice with Puree of Game
   Saute of Fillets of Fowl a la Lucullus, with Truffles
   Fillets of Young Rabbits a la Orlies, white sharp sauce

Second Course Roasts

   Three Partridges
   Three Woodcocks

Six Entremets

   Spinach with Consomme, garnished with Fried Bread
   Whole Truffles with Champaign
   Lobster Salad a la Italienne

Jelly of Marasquino
Buisson of Gateau a la Polonaise
Alice of Apples with Apricot

Two Removes of Roast
Biscuit a la Crème
Fondus

Ian gazed in amazement at the menu in front of him on the long, highly polished dining table lit by a row of flickering candles in silver holders. Either side of the table sat the twenty, well-dressed guests of the Forbes family. At the head of the table sat Sir Archibald Forbes and to his right, Charles. Ian was aware that both men were watching him with an intense scrutiny. Ian glanced down at the menu and wondered what half the dishes were. He knew from his training with Sir George in Australia that he must never let on any ignorance of what the rich and powerful took for granted. At least he identified the meal would consist of rabbits and fish – both he knew well from growing up in the colonies.

The dinner had been arranged by Alice to welcome her brother home to England, and as such, Ian had not been in her company for any long periods of time as she fussed with the catering and guest lists.

Instead, Ian had been shadowed by his young brother, Herbert, who was obviously smitten by his older brother's adventures in the colonies. The few letters that did find their way back to England from Samuel had described how different the colonies of New Zealand and New South Wales were compared to England. Samuel had only mentioned in passing his experience fighting in New Zealand, but Herbert's hero worship translated his older brother's few words into a heroic stand against hordes of savage natives. Ian had sidestepped any descriptions of the skirmish by saying it was not something to talk about amongst men. Herbert had confided that he wished to be commissioned into his grandfather's regiment so that he could serve alongside Ian.

At least Ian had company when they took a ride on fine Forbes horses in Hyde Park and went for walks through the heart of the great city. At one stage, Ian strayed to the edge of the slums but Herbert plucked at his coat to warn him they should avoid going in. He explained how his sister's friend, Dr Peter Campbell had been robbed at knifepoint by three brutish men when he was providing medical assistance to the impoverished people of the slums.

Ian listened to him and that day purchased a copy of Mr Charles Dickens' just-released novel, *Bleak House*. The gift delighted Alice. Reading was a shared passion of Samuel and Alice.

Now he sat opposite Alice and a gentleman she introduced as Dr Peter Campbell. The two men had shaken hands prior to moving into the dining room cluttered with servants and guests. It was obvious that his sister had only eyes for the tall, good-looking Canadian surgeon.

A servant leaned over Ian's shoulder and poured him an expensive Spanish red wine. Ian raised his glass to Alice and Peter. 'To your health, and my thanks for this truly magnificent feast,' he said quietly. Alice smiled, and Peter raised his wine glass.

'To you, old chap,' he said. 'Your return has brought light into Alice's life once again.'

The evening wore on with trivial chatter and gossip between the guests. The ladies wore their finest jewellery that sparkled in the candlelight, whilst the gentlemen the most expensive of suits. Ian was courteous to the gentleman on his right, and the matron on his left. He was glad that both preferred to chatter to those on their left and right leaving him to exchange the occasional word across the table to Peter and Alice. Ian learned that Peter had travelled extensively in Europe, spoke French fluently, and had studied in England at the Royal College of Surgeons. He had a moderately good income from his family in Canada, and was considered a colonial by the English. Ian thought that ironic as he was also being referred to in whispers as the 'colonial Forbes'. The rather sneering term from the British did not concern him. He was, after all, a patriotic member of the British Empire, regardless of their looking down upon those they called colonials. At least in the company of Peter, he felt more at home.

When the dinner was over, the gentlemen retired for port and cigars.

In the smoke-filled room, Peter struck up a conversation with Ian.

'I have been informed by your sister that you intend to take a commission in your grandfather's regiment,' he said.

'That has always been my ambition,' Ian replied. 'I hope to take up my commission within a fortnight.'

'From what I have read in the *Times* and from my travels in France, I believe that you may find yourself seeing action before you know it,' Peter said, puffing on his large cigar. 'The Muscovites have issued an ultimatum to the Ottomans and there is a rumour that the British and French fleets will be steaming to the Dardanelles very soon. It is the goddamn Papist Froggies stirring up all the trouble in that part of the world. Rather ironic, when you think that we were fighting the Napoleonic French a few years ago, and then the Russians were our allies.'

'What do you mean, the French are stirring up this possible war?' Ian asked.

'Some French monks were killed in Bethlehem fighting against Orthodox monks. The Papist Froggies don't get on with the Orthodox Church of the Russians. Needless to say, Tsar Nicholas blamed the Turks for not protecting the French monks. It appears that the Russians are attempting to expand their empire, and that cannot happen. I suspect that the Tsar will not back down on his move to declare war against the Ottoman Empire.'

'I am sure you are right in what you are saying,' Ian said. 'It seems I may be joining the regiment at the right time.'

'If we go to war with the Russians, I intend to volunteer my services as an army surgeon,' Peter said. 'War with the Russians will not be like any of the wars the British Empire has fought since Waterloo. We will be opposed by a European army of considerable military strength. I daresay casualties will be high, and my services required.'

'Hopefully the dead and wounded will be on the other side,' Ian said, taking a sip of his port. The news of a possible war had him in turmoil. The very reason he had taken on the risky impersonation of Samuel Forbes was to join the British army and serve as an officer. He had expected he might see service fighting the Queen's enemies armed with spears and antiquated muskets. Fighting the Russian army was another thing. He knew enough from his reading of military history the fearsome reputation of the Cossack cavalry men and the great size of their army.

'Alice has informed me that you, she and Herbert will be visiting your family's estate in Kent for a week before you join the regiment,' Peter said.

'Yes, I am looking forward to seeing the place that holds so many fond memories for me,' Ian lied.

'I hope to join you for a couple of days,' Peter said. 'It will be my first visit to the Forbes manor. I am sure you will be able to be my guide around the estate. I believe there will even be an opportunity to do a bit of hunting and fishing.'

'I will look forward to you joining us,' Ian said. 'My sister speaks very fondly of you.'

'I must say, old chap, it has been a pleasure meeting you. I need as many allies as I can gather within the folds of the Forbes family. Your father tends to see me as an upstart, colonial adventurer intent on marrying into their wealth. I can assure you that is not so. I would be happy just being with Alice in a log cabin in the backwoods of my country. I have no intentions on her inheritance.'

'That is good to hear,' Ian said. 'I sense that you are truly a gentleman of good character.'

Peter extended his hand. 'Thank you,' he said gripping Ian's hand. 'Your friendship has great meaning and importance to me. Your brother, Charles and Sir Archibald are not so warm.'

'I can identify with that,' Ian said with a grin, releasing the Canadian's firm grip. 'Neither have ever liked me very much.'

'Alice has told me of the animosity shown to you by Charles, and Sir Archibald, but does not know why it should be as such.'

'Nor do I,' Ian lied again. 'It may be because they perceived me as weak because of my love for book learning and poetry. The family history dictates that only the strong should rule.'

'Well, it is time that I must return to my club,' Peter said. 'I will be returning to my practice in the city to see patients. If I get time after that, I will resume my duties amongst the poor.'

'You are a good man, Peter,' Ian said. 'I will count you as a friend.'

Peter left to hail a hansom cab, leaving Ian feeling out of place amongst the guests of Sir Archibald. He quietly departed the room filled with pipe and cigar smoke to enter a hallway, where he saw Peter in a furtive embrace with Alice. Ian felt that he had intruded when Alice looked over Peter's shoulder to see him standing there.

Peter exited the building and Alice walked to where Ian stood.

'Dear brother, Peter told me how much he likes you,' she said, slipping her arm under his own. 'He has told me how he desires to offer his services as a surgeon in the army if it comes to war with Russia. I would pray that if that terrible situation arises, you would be there to protect him.'

'If war comes, I promise you that I would give my life to protect him.'

She leaned up and kissed him on the cheek. 'I do love you so, dear brother,' she said with a warm smile. 'You have grown to be such a handsome and dashing man. I know all of London society ladies will be standing in line to be in your company. I must retire, but tomorrow we will be travelling to Kent. It will be so good to visit all those places you and I knew on the estate and in the village.'

Ian watched her walk away. Her kiss on his cheek lingered.

*

It was an exceptionally hot summer's day. The clouds of smoke caused by the explosion of gunfire lingered in the still air.

'You soldiers are very fortunate men,' Colour Sergeant Leslie bellowed, holding a long rifle above his head so that the semi-circle of soldiers could see it. 'The Queen has been very generous in supplying us the very latest weapon of war. This is the point five-seven-seven calibre Enfield rifled musket. It is the best rifle the army has ever seen, and you will be issued one each for what I believe is a coming war between us and the Ivans. Today, you will be taught how to load and fire the Enfield out here on the range. You will also learn how you will look after it as you would any woman in your life. But you will also learn that the Enfield is different to women, because it will never let you down.'

Conan and the Williams brothers stood in the semi-circle, gazing with some interest at the rifle held above the instructor's head.

The Irish sergeant lowered the weapon, took a paper cartridge from a leather box on his belt, bit off one end of the cartridge, ramming it down the barrel with a rod slid from under the barrel, dropped a hollow-based, cylindrical lead projectile after the paper cartridge, also ramming it down. He replaced the ram rod under the barrel, cocked the hammer at the side and placed a small copper primer on the nipple above the powder-filled chamber. He slid the rear sight to a hundred yards, brought it to his shoulder and pulled the trigger. The rifle bit back into his shoulder, and a hundred yards away, a piece of wooden square peg splintered from the impact of the Minie bullet. The accuracy impressed the soldiers watching the demonstration. They knew the smooth bore was now replaced with the twisting grooves inside the barrel to ensure the projectile caught in the grooves as the explosion caused it to expand ensuring that the round flew straight and true at high velocity.

Pleased with himself, Colour Sergeant Leslie returned his attention to his recruits.

'You will now go through the drills of loading, aiming and firing the Enfield.'

By the end of the day, Private Conan Curry proved to be the fastest at reloading, and most accurate at hitting the target. The Irishman from the colony of New South Wales felt a strange euphoria of finding a home in England and its army. Even if it was amongst the traditional enemies of Ireland. He was able to console himself with the thought that he was not alone. There was a smattering of other Irishmen in the ranks of the regiment – along with Scots and Welsh. Army life was slowly seducing him.

*

Ian tried not to show his amazement at the three-storeyed, ivy-covered Forbes mansion at the end of the driveway as they approached in the carriage drawn by four fine horses. Beside him sat Alice with her parasol opened above her head against the bite of the summer sun. In the seat behind them was young Herbert, who looked bored.

'Oh, look Sam, the pond where you and I would catch tadpoles!' Alice exclaimed as the carriage passed a pond to one side of the carriageway to the regal house. Ian nodded and smiled as Samuel had not briefed him on the tadpole-catching incidents with his sister, but he pretended to remember.

When the carriage halted before the front entrance, they were met by the large staff. The men in dress coats and the ladies wearing white apron-like dresses.

'Welcome home, Miss Alice,' an elderly lady said, stepping from the line of servants. 'And you, Master Samuel. It is so good to see your face again after so many years.' Ian could see that there were tears in her eyes, and guessed from her warm greeting that she must be the nanny Samuel had told him about.

'Nanny Groves, it has been a long time,' he replied, stepping from the carriage. 'You have not changed in all the years that we have been apart.'

The elderly lady with her grey hair tied into a bun broke into a full flood of tears at being recognised, and Ian breathed a sigh of relief for playing his part. She impulsively hugged him, and Ian felt that if his supposed governess accepted him for being Samuel, he had passed a very important test.

A couple of manservants assisted with the luggage from the carriage and Ian was ushered inside the manor house, Alice and Herbert following closely behind.

Ian tried to recall the layout of the house as described by Sir George. This would be another test and he turned to his old governess.

'I would like to go to my old room,' he said.

'I will show you to your room,' Mrs Groves said.

'There is no need,' Ian replied. 'I know where it is.'

'Certainly, Master Samuel,' she replied, and Ian walked towards the large staircase in the ornate foyer to locate the room. He did not show his nervousness, but walked confidently up and turned left at the top to walk down a hallway until he felt he had located the room Samuel had once occupied. He opened the door and stepped inside. It smelled musty but he could see the rows of shelves stacked with books, and smiled. The more he was in the company of the family, the more he knew he was being accepted by the Forbes members. He felt that he was, in actual fact, Samuel Forbes, heir to the dynasty. As he stood at the centre of the room, he was aware that Alice had joined him.

'I insisted that your room be left as it was when you were taken to the regiment in London all those years ago,' she said. 'I do so remember how much fun we had here.'

Ian turned to look at Alice and could see from the expression on her face that she was totally convinced that she had her brother home. Now all he had to do was be commissioned into the regiment to join the circle of his future. What could go wrong now?

NINE

For their first day at the Forbes country manor, Ian had Alice's full attention. They spent the day riding the estate, and at night, played cards, with Herbert always hovering, eager to get Ian's attention. On the second day, Peter arrived, and Ian suddenly had less attention from his supposed sister.

On the third day, Charles arrived without his father, who had been called away on business, and the coldness that had started at their London meeting continued. Neither had spoken hardly a word to the other since Ian had arrived. Ian had noticed the doubt in Charles' eyes and realised that Sir George's warnings about his nephew and brother were well-founded.

But Peter's friendship warmed the air at the estate in the country.

'Alice has told me that you are a good rider,' Peter said one morning after breakfast.

'I did a lot of riding in the colonies,' Ian replied.

'Good, I have arranged to have a couple of mounts prepared for us,' Peter said and that morning, both men went to the stables where a couple of the Forbes' finest horses had been saddled.

The Canadian and the Australian mounted, riding down the grand driveway off the estate, and continued in a leisurely manner through avenues of shady oak trees until they found a winding, narrow road that took them to the edge of a country village.

'Well, old chap, time to find a pub and try a local ale,' Peter said as they trotted into the cobbled main street of the quaint village.

'No bark huts here,' Ian quipped when he looked down the street busy with the local population going about their daily chores. Ian could see that their arrival had caught the interest of the villagers, who stared with curiosity at the two well-dressed gentlemen riding fine steeds through their streets.

They came across a pub and dismounted, securing their horses to a railing by a water trough. When they went inside, the few patrons sitting at tables, paused to glance at the strangers entering.

Peter walked over to the bar and ordered two large ales, taking them to a table Ian had selected in one corner of the bar.

'To your health,' Peter said, raising his tankard.

'You too,' Ian responded, noticing that their appearance in the bar still caused interest to the other patrons, a few farmers and artisans from the district. He could see them whisper and cast the occasional curious glance in their direction.

'I thought that we might come here so you will be one of the first to know that I have been granted a position in the army as a surgeon in your regiment.'

'Congratulations,' Ian said, bumping his tankard against that of the Canadian doctor's. 'When do you commence your military duties?'

'As soon as I return to London at the end of the week,' Peter said. 'But I had another reason to get you alone today,' Peter said. 'I will be asking for Alice's hand in marriage and, as I am a colonial with few friends in this country, I am requesting that you be my best man at the wedding. I think you are the best choice, as I know how much Alice is fond of you as her brother.'

'Congratulations, old man,' Ian said, both flattered and mildly shocked at the announcement. 'When do you intend to ask for Alice's hand?'

'I hope to tonight,' Peter said with a touch of gloom in his answer. 'With Charles' blessing, if I can obtain it, in lieu of your father.'

'You don't sound all that optimistic,' Ian said.

'I know Alice feels the same way about me as I do about her, but your father considers me below her class and some kind of adventurer intent on getting my hands on a substantial dowry. I am afraid a medical doctor is not what he has planned for Alice's future.'

'If the family rejects your proposal, what will you do?' Ian asked.

'I don't know at this stage,' Peter replied. 'But if worse comes to worst, I would wish Alice to elope with me, after my service to the Queen as an army surgeon.'

'Let us hope that Charles sees sense and gives his blessing on behalf of the family,' Ian said. 'I think I would like to propose a toast to your success.'

Both men raised their tankards in silence. They finished the contents and exited the coolness of the bar into the warmth of the English summer. Ian could see dark rolling clouds gathering on the horizon and knew there would be a storm.

They had hardly made it back to the manor when the first fat droplets began to fall and the sky was rent by lightning.

The storm rolled on into the early hours of evening.

Ian had discovered a Charles Dickens' novel in the library and was absorbed reading it. The room was small with a comfortable divan and good gas lighting from the overhead chandelier. The evening meal was being prepared by the staff, and he expected the sound of the bell to tinkle on the wall calling him to supper. He did not expect the intrusion of Charles, storming into the room.

Ian closed the book as Charles towered over him, rage painted across his face.

'I have just come from a meeting with Dr Campbell. He has informed me that you support his desire to marry Alice.'

'That is right,' Ian replied. 'As a matter of fact, Dr Campbell has honoured me with his request for me to be his best man at the wedding.'

'There will be no wedding,' Charles snarled. 'He is not worthy of Alice's hand. I would have expected you to understand that matter. But you actually take his side. I feel that you have been too long in the colonies and have lost all respect for your station – *our* station – in society. You seem to have the manners of a colonial yourself.'

'In the colony of New South Wales, I noted that a man's standing in society is more based on his personal qualities, and not his birth into any privileged family. As a matter of fact, I have even witnessed former convicts become gentlemen of wealth and substance.'

'You sound like you admire those colonials who have risen above their station in life,' Charles spat. 'God has ordained that we rule. I have wondered from the first day I set eyes on you if you are really my brother, or an imposter.'

'I am as disappointed in our blood connection as you,' Ian replied. 'I should have told Mother about when you tried to push me under a moving wagon when we were little,' Ian countered, remembering the incident related to him by Samuel. 'It seems nothing has changed, brother Charles.' Ian was satisfied to see the expression of surprise on Charles' face.

'That was an accident,' he spluttered, and Ian knew he had the upper hand.

'It did not feel that way at the time,' he replied. 'I was fully aware of your hostility towards me,' Ian added. Charles stood to attention, his hands clasped behind his back.

'You should take care, Samuel,' he said quietly in a threatening manner. 'You've been away from England so long. Accidents like that happen all the time.'

'I will be careful,' Ian replied, remembering the revolver Samuel had given him.

Without any further discussion, Charles exited the room, leaving Ian with the copy of *David Copperfield* and his concern about the veiled threat. Was it possible that his own brother – half-brother – pretend brother – was capable of plotting to kill him? Ian shook his head. But still remembered the cap and ball revolver in his room.

The next morning, Ian read in the paper that the Russian army had crossed the Prith River into Moldavia. He knew that it meant war was almost inevitable with the Tsar, and that with luck, he would be in the thick of it, as he had always yearned to be in his little village on the other side of the world.

*

'They won't allow Molly any visitors,' Edwin said bitterly. 'She must be having sleepless nights, wondering where we are.'

'The prison might not allow any visitors, but I have been chatting with Colour Sergeant Leslie who told me that for a small fee, the guards will smuggle letters in and out of her gaol. We can at least get word to her,' Conan said.

Edwin and Owen paused in polishing their boots to stare at Conan.

'We can't read or write,' Owen said. 'But Molly can read and write good.'

'I can read and write,' Conan replied, examining the new shine on his polished boot. 'I can write a letter to Molly on your behalf, and Colour Sergeant Leslie can arrange to have it smuggled in.'

Owen and Edwin exchanged a look and nodded. 'We can get paper and pen,' Edwin said. 'Tonight, we write a letter to Molly.'

In the barracks that evening, the three men huddled together on Conan's bed to compose the words to their beloved sister. It was a strained effort by the brothers but the letter – filling two pages – described their life in the British army. When they were satisfied they had possibly eased their sister's concern for their welfare, they left Conan with the letter. Conan gazed at the ink on the pages, and impulsively pulled out another blank page, and began to write his own letter.

My dear Molly,

I wrote your brothers' words for them and now I write my own.

I am very saddened to learn of your miserable fate at the hand of the British justice. I will confess that when I met you for that short time I liked you a lot.

There is a rumour that we might be going to war with Russia very soon. I promise that I will look out for Owen and Edwin so that they might stay safe. I know that you were sentenced to five years, but I also promise to do everything I can to get you out of gaol. I will wait for that day no matter how long.

Conan pondered on the last sentence and put a thick ink cross through it to obliterate the sentence. With a piece of blotting paper, he dried the wet ink. He felt that it was possible his added words might give her hope and signed off the letter, carefully folded it and tucked it under his pillow. In the morning, he would approach the Irish sergeant with the few pennies he had to have the letter delivered via the corrupt guards of Molly's prison. He did not expect to receive a reply but before the week was out, Colour Sergeant Leslie slipped a letter into Conan's hand after an inspection parade. The colour sergeant had not asked payment from Molly, and Conan had a new appreciation of his fellow Irishman.

Conan felt his heart pounding when he hurried back to the barracks to read the reply.

On his bed, Conan unfolded the paper to discover there were two letters. One addressed to the three of them, and one written to him alone. He had hardly had time to read the letters when he was joined by the Welsh brothers.

'Is that a letter from Molly?' Owen asked eagerly, seeing the paper in Conan's hand.

'It is,' he answered. 'Our letter got to her.'

'What has she written?' Edwin asked eagerly.

Conan began to read the letter to them as they stood by his bed. It expressed how thrilled she was to have the message smuggled in to her and a special thank you to Conan for writing it. She also wrote of her yearning to be released and once again be back with her brothers. She explained that prison was harsh, but it was the loneliness that was worst.

Tears rolled down the cheeks of her brothers.

'Can I keep the letter?' Edwin asked, stretching out his hand.

'What for?' Owen said. 'You don't read, boyo.'

'Don't need to read to have it,' Edwin said, sniffing back his tears.

Conan passed the letter to him and he folded it with some reverence, as if it were a holy manuscript.

Both brothers departed, and Conan unfolded the letter addressed to him.

My dear Conan,

I thank you for your kind words which mean a lot to me in my time of joyless existence. I was able to discern the words you attempted to hide and was very touched by the feelings imparted by its meaning. Time will pass but I hope that the sentiment of your words remain.

Yours sincerely,

Molly

Conan felt a lump in his throat and reread the few words, his feelings in turmoil. Had he committed himself to this Welsh lass he hardly knew? What did the future hold for them?

A bugle sounded and called the men to their evening meal. With great care, Conan placed the letter inside his red jacket, over his heart. Edwin was not alone in his reverence for the written word.

*

The manor was in turmoil. The servants carefully avoided the family and guests as Peter's raised voice equalled that of Charles in the drawing room. Upstairs, Alice lay on her bed, sobbing inconsolably.

Ian and Herbert sat in a living room, exchanging

knowing looks. In the short time he had known him, Ian had grown very fond of the youngest Forbes brother.

'I think it is time for you and I to visit the local tavern,' Ian said to Herbert, whose face lit up.

'Charles has forbidden me to go to the village,' Herbert said.

'Well, I am your older brother, and I give you permission to accompany me.'

Herbert did not hesitate, and arrangements were made to have a couple of horses saddled. They rode to the village just on dusk and already, lights showed in the windows of the cottages of the village.

Both men dismounted, secured their horses and went inside to a rowdy, smoke-filled public house. The sound of a fiddle screeched in the corner, and men were singing old Kentish folk songs to the tune.

Their entrance was hardly noticed in the crowd, and the atmosphere reminded Ian of his own public house in his little village back in Australia.

Ian shouldered his way through the crowd to order a couple of tankards of ale and returned to Herbert, who he could see was entranced by the atmosphere of the public house.

Ian thrust the tankard in Herbert's hand, raising his own. 'Cheers.'

They stood and listened to the fiddler and the folk songs. Sweat rolled down most faces as the aftermath of the storm had left the night air humid in the crowded bar.

'It is grand!' Herbert said, his foot tapping to the rhythm of the songs. Ian could see that Herbert was already feeling the intoxicating ale and the music surge through his body.

Ian glanced around at the villagers enjoying this interlude from long, hard labour and felt his heart almost stop a beat when his eyes settled on those of a young woman only paces away. She had raven hair to her shoulders, emerald green eyes, and a complexion Ian immediately thought of as cream. In any world, she was an exceptional beauty. Ian was aware that she was appraising him, and he wondered if she was aware that he was staring at her.

'Hey, you just caused me to spill my ale,' an angry voice said from behind Ian, and his attention on the beautiful young woman was broken when he turned to see Herbert being cornered by a huge local lad.

Herbert appeared frightened by the larger man's menacing stance. Already, the confrontation was drawing attention immediately around them.

Ian stepped forward between Herbert and the local man. 'My apologies, sir,' he said. 'If my brother has caused you any grief, I will pay for another ale.'

The man turned his attention to Ian. They were eye to eye, and Ian could see a real threat in the man's expression. 'I don't just need another ale,' he snarled. 'I need an apology. And his boots.'

Ian realised that the man was a natural bully who used his size to impress his friends – if he had any.

Herbert tugged on his sleeve, saying, 'Samuel, he can have my boots, and an apology.'

'That will not happen,' Ian said.

'If there is going to be any trouble, you two can leave my premises,' the publican growled from behind the bar.

'Suits me,' Ian said casually, hiding his apprehension. The fiddle died away and the drunken patrons became aware that trouble was brewing.

It was the local bully who took up the offer and pushed his way to the entrance. Ian followed with Herbert in tow.

'Sam, it is not necessary to get into an altercation,' he pleaded. 'The man looks to be a dangerous brute.'

Ian ignored him as the patrons spilled out from the bar to witness the expected short, sharp defeat of the well-dressed stranger. From the corner of his eye, Ian could see the raven-haired girl join the ring of spectators, now around the circle of light from the village streetlamp, who were already cheering the local man Ian was facing. He had already removed his coat and Ian could see that he was a head taller than he but was intoxicated.

'Show him what's what, John,' a voice called as Ian passed his own coat to Herbert.

With a grin, the local champion charged at Ian, who stepped aside and swivelled to deliver a vicious punch to the kidney area of his opponent. It was delivered with the muscle of a blacksmith's arm, and his opponent doubled in pain. With a groan, he turned to resume his attack on Ian, who half-crouched. When the bigger man was within range Ian delivered a rapid rain of punches to his face and stomach that took the local thug off-guard. No one had ever stood up to him before. Ian was aware that he had to finish the fight fast, and grabbed the man behind the head, smashing his knee into his face, bursting open his opponent's nose. The local bully collapsed, but hefted himself on all fours. Ian did not hesitate but lashed out with his boot, catching the man in the face once again. The big man rolled on his back, clutching his badly damaged face with both hands. The crowd that had been calling for Ian's blood had fallen into a hush of shock. The show was over.

'Who are you?' a male spectator demanded.

'Samuel Forbes,' Ian replied as Herbert passed his coat. Already, a couple of the defeated man's friends were helping him to his feet, to take him inside the public house for an ale.

No other words were said as the crowd retreated to the bar, leaving Ian and Herbert alone. At least it seemed that way until Ian noticed the raven-haired girl step into the light before them.

'So, you are Samuel,' she said. 'We met a long time ago when we were both young at your family's manor. I know your brother, Charles.'

Ian frowned. 'May I ask your name?' he asked.

'I am Jane Wilberforce,' she replied with a sly smile. 'I am a seamstress, but many from here say that I am a witch. Traditional superstitions continue in this district, despite the church teaching that paganism is dead.'

Ian could feel the power of her beauty drawing him in, as she kept his eyes locked on her own.

'Sam, we must return to the manor,' Herbert said urgently, as if he believed Jane really was a witch.

'You said that you know my brother, Charles,' Ian queried. 'How do you know him?'

'That is none of your business,' she replied. She was close enough that he imagined he could smell wildflower scent surrounding her. 'But he was wrong when he described you as a weak man who is only interested in books and a world without war. I sense in you a true warrior, like those who once defended this country with sword and shield in days of yore. Your brother has badly underestimated you. It might be that you and I will meet again in the future, Samuel,' Jane said, and walked away into the darkness, leaving Ian with many questions swirling in his head about the mysterious young woman.

'I have never seen a real fight before,' Herbert said with a note of awe in his voice as he unsteadily attempted to put his foot in the stirrup, and swing onto his mount. 'You were magnificent, and I cannot thank you enough for standing up for me. Wait until I tell Alice of how you so easily defeated that brute.'

'Alice need not know of what happened here, tonight,' Ian said from astride his horse. 'You will need to know how to fight if you are going to be commissioned into the army. I will teach you.'

The two rode back to the manor under the light of a full moon that had risen above the sweep of green fields and copses of trees.

Ian could not get Jane's face out of his mind as they returned to the Forbes estate. He hoped that, as she had said, they would meet again one day.

TEN

The following day, Ian met Charles after breakfast in the manor's library for the discussion on the purchase of his commission into the infantry regiment. According to the conditions of the grandfather's will, money had been set aside for this purpose.

Charles assumed his usual stance of holding his hands behind his back as he offered a chair to Ian. Ian suspected that Charles felt that he had the high ground by looming over him.

'Father and I agreed that we will purchase you a second lieutenancy in the regiment,' he said without preamble.

'I want a captain's commission,' Ian countered.

'Good God, man!' Charles spluttered. 'That would cost the estate two thousand pounds!'

'I have earned a captain's commission,' Ian continued.

Charles remained silent for a moment, staring out the

window at the manicured lawns in front of the manor house. 'I agree to your request for a captain's commission,' he finally said, gritting his teeth.

'Thank you,' Ian said, rising from his chair.

'Word spreads very fast in the county,' Charles said. 'I have been informed that you were involved in a fracas at the village inn last night, with Herbert by your side.'

'Hardly a fracas,' Ian replied. 'Just a disagreement that was settled with fists and not duelling pistols.'

'When you join the regiment, you will have Herbert with you. It has been decided that we will purchase a lieutenant's commission for him. I trust you will be there to give him counsel and protection.'

'That is something we can agree on,' Ian said. 'If war comes, as many are saying it will, I will ensure that Herbert is safe.' Ian had to stop himself from saying, *as if he was my real brother.* He held out his hand to seal the promise, and Charles accepted the gesture of goodwill with a weak, limp grip. Without another word, Charles stormed from the library, leaving Ian amongst the shelves of precious books. His luck was holding out and his dream of serving the Queen a mere few days away. There was just one matter he felt he should attend to before he returned to London and that late summer's day, he hoped his luck would still remain.

*

Ian rode towards the village, passing farmers at work, stacking hay for the coming winter. It was warm, and Ian stopped to ask a group of labourers if they knew the whereabouts of Miss Jane Wilberforce. One farmer said that she was in the next field.

Ian continued and saw a solitary figure by a grove of ancient trees on a small hill. He immediately recognised the young woman with the long raven hair. Ian dismounted and left his horse to graze while he walked towards her.

She raised her hand to gaze at the figure emerging from the sun behind him.

'Master Samuel,' she said when he was a few paces away. 'What has brought you to me on this day?'

'I am due to return to London to take up my commission in the army, but did not want to leave until we met again,' Ian said.

'I knew we would meet again,' Jane said with a mysterious smile. 'I had a dream about you last night. Or should I say, a nightmare.'

'I would prefer you had a dream, and not a nightmare,' Ian said.

'Well, I dreamed that you were two people and marched with your men in a faraway world of ice and fire,' Jane said. 'It was not a nice place, and I saw the snow covered in blood. You were a warrior of great renown.'

Ian experienced a slight chill in the balmy sun. He remembered how his mother had once predicted the same thing for him, just before she was murdered. 'I suppose a soldier would live in a world of such things,' he replied.

'You were leading men,' she said with a frown. 'And one close to you could not be saved. I felt your pain in my dream.'

'But it was only a dream,' Ian said, trying to convince both of them.

'Yes, it was only a thing of the night.'

'Let us not dwell on things that are figments of our imagination,' Ian said. 'I would rather know something of you.'

'Come,' Jane said, taking Ian's hand. 'Follow me into the shade of the trees.'

It was like an electric shock through Ian's body when Jane took his hand, leading him into the grove of ancient trees. They walked a short distance to a small glade where Ian could see a ring of small moss-covered stones at its centre. It appeared to be very ancient.

'This is the place I come to be at peace,' Jane said, letting go of Ian's hand. 'It is the place where the Druids once came before Christianity chased them from the land. I only know what the old people of the village have told me about the Druids.'

Ian had read about the history of the Druids and knew it was a pagan time of mystical beings and human sacrifice that began to disappear when the Romans invaded. The stone ring fascinated him, and he felt that Jane was linked to this place.

'Do the people of the village know you come here?' Ian asked.

'They do,' Jane replied, gazing at the circle in an almost trance-like state. 'That is why they whisper behind my back that I am a witch.'

'I would think they call you a witch because you have the beauty that bewitches men,' Ian replied.

'Do I bewitch you?' Jane asked with a smile, turning to look into his eyes.

'Have you bewitched my brother, Charles?' Ian countered.

'He is not your brother,' Jane said. 'I sense that you are two people in one. You are not really Samuel Forbes.'

Her statement unsettled Ian. How could she know?

'I am Samuel Forbes,' he replied.

'You do not remember me,' Jane said. 'I would play with you and Alice when you came to stay at the manor. Even then, my charms had no effect on Samuel, who would prefer to play with dolls and not the soldier games his brother played. But now you have come to me as if we had never met before.'

Ian was troubled by the young woman's perceptiveness. 'What if you were right about me not being Samuel Forbes,' he said quietly. 'Would it matter?'

For a moment, Jane remained silent staring at him. 'Kiss me and I will know,' she said and Ian did not hesitate. They embraced, and Ian felt almost giddy when he tasted the sweetness of the lingering kiss that he wanted to go on forever. But she broke away and stepped into the centre of the ancient circle. Ian watched her as she raised her arms to the sky.

'On the sacred lore of the old ones, I swear I will never reveal that you are not the true Samuel Forbes,' she said before turning to Ian. 'Who are you? Is Samuel safe and well?'

Ian was entranced. 'Samuel is my friend, and is now probably living the life he wished for in the Americas. I am here to protect his future inheritance.'

Jane stepped from the circle of stones and drew close to him. 'I am pleased to know Samuel is well, as he was gentle and kind to me when we were children. We all have secrets. Mine is that I am the mistress of your brother, Charles.'

'Why?' Ian asked, stung by the revelation.

'Because he is very generous to a young woman who has no parents or prospects,' Jane replied. 'It is nothing more than that. He always desired me from those times I would go to the manor to be with Samuel and Alice. But, as a simple country girl, I am so far beneath his station, so he married a woman of the class acceptable to the Forbes dynasty.'

'Do you love Charles?' Ian asked.

For a moment, Jane gazed across the farming pastures shimmering under the sun. She turned her face to Ian.

'Love is not a word that has any place in what is between Charles and myself,' she said. 'It is a mutual convenience.'

'I understand,' Ian said. He had seen the dire poverty of London's slums and knew how hard it was for a single woman without family. It was possible if he was in Jane's shoes, he might have made the same choice.

'I think you do,' Jane said, and Ian could hear the sadness in her voice. 'For now, you must go from here.' She turned away from him. 'There is a long, dangerous journey ahead of you.'

'I will return in the future to be in your company,' Ian said. 'That must have been in your dream.'

Jane turned to gaze at Ian with a warm smile. 'I will dream of that tonight,' she said and touched his cheek with her fingers. 'Only the old ones of this place know what will happen in the future. There is another secret I may tell you when you return. But I would like to know who you really are before we depart.'

'My real name is Ian Steele and I am colonial born,' he replied, trusting this enigmatic woman with his secret despite the short time he had known her.

Ian reluctantly walked away to his horse grazing in the pasture. He forced himself not to look back, lest he weaken in his resolve to be a soldier. He felt as if he was actually part of a dream. Meeting her in such a short time and falling under her spell had seemed to happen in the blink of an eye. But each and every word spoken between them in the grove of the ancient circle of stones echoed in his memory. He knew that when he had the first opportunity, he would return to her.

*

Upon his return to London, Ian was outfitted with the uniforms he would require from a fashionable tailor to gentlemen. He was accompanied by Herbert, who was also fitted for his officer uniforms. In addition to the uniforms, both men purchased infantry swords to go with the kit required before joining the regiment. It was a costly enterprise, but Ian also knew it would have been even more expensive if he had joined one of the elite cavalry regiments as an officer.

Satisfied that they were outfitted, Herbert and Ian returned to the London home of the Forbes family, where Herbert immediately went to his room to change into the uniform of a young officer. When he had done so, he came downstairs to show off in front of his sister.

'Oh my!' Alice said. 'You look so dashing, Herbert. You will make young ladies swoon.'

Herbert beamed his gratitude for his sister's flattery.

Ian entered the room wearing his civilian dress, smiling when he saw Herbert preening in his colourful uniform. 'The uniform suits you,' he said. 'You are halfway to becoming an officer of Her Majesty.'

'I believe that we report to the regiment tomorrow,' Herbert said. 'I doubt that I will sleep tonight.'

'Charles has arranged everything,' Ian said. 'As a matter of fact, I believe we will be welcomed with a dining-in night at the officers' mess.'

'Oh, which uniform will I require?' Herbert asked.

'Your mess dress,' Ian answered. 'The really nice one you have.'

'That one,' Herbert said. 'I must go upstairs and ensure it will be in order.'

Herbert left Ian and Alice alone as he dashed up to his room to inspect his mess dress. He was like an excited schoolboy on Christmas Eve.

The smile on Alice's face had disappeared and Ian looked to her. 'Is something wrong?' he asked, and she turned to him.

'I fear that we will be involved in this war between the Ottomans and the Russians,' she said.

'If we are,' Ian said, 'I have already promised you that I will keep an eye on Herbert. From what Charles has told me, I will be assigned a company of foot, and will request that Herbert be assigned to my company. That way, he will remain close to me.'

'I trust that you will keep our little brother safe,' she said with a wan expression. 'I do not know how I would cope if anything terrible should happen to you or Herbert.'

'You know that Peter has said that he will act as a surgeon to the army if we go to war,' Ian said. 'I suppose I will also have to include him in the company that I am to watch over.'

'The three most precious men in my life will be together,' Alice said. 'Let us pray that the horrible affairs in the Orient come to nothing. My father has sided with Charles to oppose Peter and I being wed, but Peter has promised that when he returns, he will not let anything stand in our way. You must keep him safe.'

Ian did not reply. He was hoping that very soon he would see action leading his company in war. Alice's wish was the eternal one echoed down the ages by every mother, sister, sweetheart and wife across the world, when their men faced the possibility of armed conflict.

★

The Forbes carriage conveyed Ian and Herbert in their smart new uniforms to the gates of the regiment, where the sentries on duty saluted smartly.

A hansom cab pulled in beside the Forbes carriage, and Dr Peter Campbell alighted in his best suit, with a broad smile on his face.

'What are you doing here, Campbell?' Ian asked.

'I felt that I should be with you upon this auspicious day when you pass through the gates of the regiment,' he replied. 'Besides, I know one or two of your gentlemen officers from my club, and I'll take the opportunity to remind them that they owe gambling debts before they go off to war.'

Ian shook his hand and the three men stepped past the sentries at the gate, striding across the barrack grounds towards the regiment's headquarters building, passing by a group of soldiers being afforded a break from the hours of drilling with arms on the parade ground. A sergeant called his men to attention when he spotted the officers, and saluted. Ian returned the salute as senior officer. It felt good that he had been able to acknowledge the military gesture.

The group was only about ten paces away, but Ian had passed without really looking at them. He did not realise that his appearance had brought a look of shock to one private soldier.

'What is it, Paddy?' Owen asked when he noticed the stricken expression on the Irish soldier's face. 'You look like you've just seen a ghost.'

'Owen, boyo, look at that man with the two officers,' Edwin said. 'That's the man we robbed of his property. The one that must be a doctor.'

Owen looked away from Conan Curry to see the man his brother had identified, realising that Edwin was right.

'God blind me!' he swore under his breath, but also realised that the man who had been their victim was not likely to recognise a couple of soldiers amongst so many.

'You think the doctor is trouble,' Conan muttered. 'The real trouble is the captain with him.'

Both brothers glanced at Conan.

'What do you mean?' Owen asked.

'On your feet,' the voice of the drill sergeant roared, and the platoon of men immediately obeyed, cutting short for the moment any explanation by Conan of why he feared the captain who had come to the regiment. Conan tried to tell himself that he could be wrong, but something nagged him as his comrades drilling with rifles carried out the precise movements of shouldering arms, grounding arms and many other drill movements. As much as he tried, Conan knew he had just seen Ian Steele, former blacksmith and now a colonial officer in Her Majesty's army.

ELEVEN

That evening, Ian and Herbert were welcomed into the officers' mess by the president of the mess committee, and the commanding officer – a kindly older man in his late sixties, who also held considerable estates in the country.

Ian remembered all that Samuel had briefed him in mess etiquette, and easily passed the test that evening, passing the port and standing for the royal toast with his port raised to Queen Victoria.

When the dinner was over, Ian felt at home amongst his brother officers milling in the cigar smoke-filled anteroom. There was drunkenness and laughter as the various ranks of officers of the regiment mingled, and Ian was singled out by a fellow captain to recount his experience fighting in New Zealand. This was the only time that evening Ian felt uncomfortable as he recounted the skirmish from what he had been told by Samuel. He felt like a braggart but knew his identity must remain a secret at all costs. He wondered briefly if he was foolish to disclose to Jane that he was an imposter. But she had bewitched him, and since the kiss in the copse of trees, he had not been able to get her out of his mind.

'I say, old chap, I think we may be seeing more mischief from those Maori savages in the future,' said the fellow captain who had introduced himself as Miles Sinclair. He was well into his forties but had a professional air about him. His family were not as wealthy as those of his fellow officers, and had not been able to advance the captain's rank to major, but Ian sensed he was an officer who had seen much active service fighting in the small and almost forgotten campaigns overseas for the Queen and Empire.

'I have not had the pleasure of being posted to New Zealand,' he continued. 'But from what I have heard of the Maori, he is an intelligent and fierce warrior to be reckoned with. Mark my words, you may encounter him again one day. But first, we have to face the Muscovites from the way things are going over in the Crimea.'

The conversation was interrupted when Lieutenant Herbert Forbes joined them with a glass of port and glazed eyes. It was obvious the sixteen-year-old boy was having a hard time handling the consumption of alcohol. Ian excused himself and led Herbert aside.

'Tomorrow, you will be introduced to your men,' Ian said. 'You will need to have a clear head, so I suggest that you seek permission to leave the mess.'

'Who do I ask permission from?'

'The PMC,' Ian replied, remembering the protocol he had learned from Samuel. 'If he denies permission to leave, you go to the billiard room and find a quiet corner to kip in.'

'Thank you, Sam,' Herbert slurred. The foggy room was already spinning.

Ian decided to forget the PMC and assisted the young officer into the relatively quiet billiard room, sat him down in a big cane chair and let him doze off. Ian stepped back to gaze at the young man and experienced a pang of fraternal concern. It was obvious from all the rumours that in a short time, they might be at war with Russia, and Ian suspected this would not be like any of the small campaigns his regiment had fought. Memories of his father's stories about Waterloo echoed in Ian's thoughts, and he wondered if he could truly protect the boy sleeping in the cane chair.

*

He never tired of seeing Jane naked. Charles Forbes lay back against the clean, soft eiderdown pillows and watched her running the brush through her raven hair with her back to him.

'You're awake,' Jane said, watching his reflection in the big mirror she sat before.

Charles slid from the bed, naked, and padded across to her, standing with his hands on her bare shoulders.

'I must return to London tomorrow, so we should not waste time tonight,' he said. Jane pulled away from him.

'You're going back to your wife,' she said with a subtle tone of relief.

'Of course,' Charles said.

'I remember when we were young and played together. You said that you would one day wed me, and take me for your wife,' Jane said, staring at her reflection in the mirror.

'You know that was a preposterous promise,' Charles snorted. 'You have not the breeding for one of my station.'

'But enough breeding to take me to your bed whenever you wish,' Jane countered, turning to face him. 'Do you still sleep with your highborn wife?'

Charles walked back to the big double bed and slumped onto it. 'That is not your concern,' Charles replied.

'I had the good fortune of meeting Samuel when you were here last time,' Jane said. 'Your father sent away a timid boy, and a fine, strong and handsome man has returned.'

'When did you meet my brother?' Charles asked, sitting up straight on the bed.

'Oh, we met in the woods on farmer Clinton's place the morning after Samuel taught our village bully a lesson. I saw Samuel thrash John Melton outside the Goose & Gander. It was thrilling.'

'You are to stay away from Samuel,' Charles said menacingly, rising again. 'He is not what he seems.'

'I have no doubt about that,' Jane said. 'I remember you used to bully him when we played together as children. I do not think you will bully your brother ever again. Samuel has grown up.'

'Do I hear a certain amount of admiration for my brother?' Charles asked angrily. 'If you admire my brother, I can assure you he will not be around to see much of you in the future.'

'I am not your wife, so I see whoever I wish,' Jane said and was stunned by the back-handed blow to the side of her face, forcing her off the stool she was sitting on.

'I pay for you, and that makes you my property,' Charles said, standing over Jane. 'Now, get up and return to the bed.'

Jane slowly rose, holding her hand to her cheek stinging from the blow. She refused to let Charles see her pain and humiliation. Jane stood defiantly before him.

'You will one day come to regret that,' she said.

'You need the generous payment I give you for your services,' Charles scoffed, laying back on the bed. 'I know you, woman, and I know how much you dream of a life of wealth and recognition from those above you. No, it is not I who will ever regret what I do, but Samuel, and you if you ever cross me. Never forget that.'

Still smarting from the assault, Jane went to the bed, knowing that this cold and brutal man was her master. Her mind was divorced from her body in a place where a ring of stones had the magical power of the old gods who lived in the time before the Romans came to the English country-side. That night, when she had left the Forbes manor, she would go to the copse of trees and the ancient circle of stones. There, she would call on the gods of the past, to give her power over Charles – and the man who called himself Samuel Forbes.

*

The colonel sat astride his horse, the squares of brightly uniformed soldiers stood to attention in their ranks with rifles at the shoulder. Ian stood in front of his company with his sword held vertically before him. The parade had been scheduled for the morning after the officers' mess night, and Ian's head throbbed. He prayed that he would remember the sequence of orders, and his own role for the inspection by the commanding officer. Behind him, in a similar stance, was Lieutenant Herbert Forbes, standing at attention before his platoon of troops.

The regimental sergeant major was in his element as he bawled out orders. A spatter of raindrops fell on the men awaiting the regimental parade to be dismissed.

Eventually, it was Ian's turn to accompany the crusty regimental commander on an inspection of his company, with which Ian had not yet had the opportunity to acquaint himself. The regimental sergeant major followed a pace behind.

He strode along the ranks with the colonel, the senior officer occasionally halting, and talking to a soldier about his bearing and dress.

They came to Herbert's platoon, smartly turned out, and began the inspection. Ian hardly took any notice but when they came near the end file he glanced at a tall, well-built soldier, and their eyes met in mutual recognition. Ian felt as if he had been kicked in the stomach by a horse, and saw absolute fear in Conan Curry's eyes.

The colonel said something and Ian instinctively replied, 'Yes, sir.'

The colonel turned to Ian. 'Fine body of men, Captain Forbes,' he said, and Ian saluted his commanding officer by raising the hilt of his sword to his face, and then sweeping down the blade beside him to finish the salute. The colonel returned the salute and marched away with the RSM to join the next company commander. Ian was still reeling. He knew that, for the moment, he must concentrate on his parade drills until the order was given to be dismissed to their daily duties.

The order eventually came, and the rain began to fall as cold sheets gusting across the parade ground. Autumn was upon them and soon, it would be the vicious bite of winter.

Ian immediately went to his tiny office off the parade ground perimeter and was met by his corporal clerk with a smart salute.

'Corporal, we have not yet met, and I wish to know your name.'

The junior non-commissioned officer stood to attention whilst he was being addressed.

'Corporal Bingham, sir,' he smartly replied.

'Corporal Bingham, I wish to view the company roll,' Ian said, shaking off the rain from his uniform.

The corporal quickly retrieved the roll book and took it into Ian's small office, placing it on the desk before him. He stood back to throw a salute before Ian spoke. 'Once a day will do, corporal, when I arrive at my office.'

'Yes, sah!' Bingham replied, and exited the office.

Ian commenced turning over the pages, running his finger down the rows marked in ink of attendance. He was pleased to see that not many of his men were on sick parade or had gone absent from their place of parade.

Then his finger stopped moving when it rested on a very familiar name, Private Conan Curry. So it really was him. Ian sat back in his chair, staring at the name. His mind was in turmoil. Before him was the name of the man who was suspected of killing his mother in New South Wales, was now a soldier of the Queen. And yet, here he was, posing as Captain Samuel Forbes. Ian knew that he could not expose Conan Curry for his past crimes, as there was a good chance he would retaliate, informing the colonel that Ian was in fact a colonial imposter. It was a standoff, like two men duelling with pistols facing each other. Neither could shoot, lest they missed.

Ian sighed and closed the book. He stared at the wall opposite him with the portrait of a young Queen Victoria staring back at him.

*

Private Conan Curry was like a man in a daze. The odds of fleeing across the Indian Ocean to England, only to confront the son of the woman Conan's brother had killed, were almost beyond belief. At least Conan considered the fact that Captain Samuel Forbes was, in reality, Ian Steele, colonial blacksmith, and no doubt did not want to be exposed for the imposter he was. But Conan also knew there would be an eventual reckoning between them. How, where and when were the questions.

'Hey, Paddy!' Owen called across the barracks. 'It's official, we have a day's leave.'

'Good,' Conan replied without much enthusiasm. Owen joined him by his bed.

'I thought the news would be welcomed,' Owen said with a frown. 'You have been like a man sentenced to death since we came off parade. What's up?'

'Nothing of any great importance,' Conan replied, the recognition still haunting him and weighing like a haversack of iron cannonballs on his shoulders.

'I have come to know you, Paddy,' Owen said. 'Something has been troubling you since we returned to the barracks.'

Conan turned to his Welsh comrade. 'The company commander, Captain Forbes, is not what he seems,' he confided. 'And I will leave it at that.'

'I heard that he served in the colonies, and saw his first action in a battle against the Maoris in New Zealand with another regiment. A few of the lads say he is more colonial than English.'

'You could be right,' Conan said and fell silent as the dread slowly settled on him like a dark cloud. Somehow, he knew that one of them must die or the other would never be free.

TWELVE

Charles Forbes was haunted by the last conversation he'd had with Jane Wilberforce. There was something in her manner that made him feel that she was attracted to his brother. He left a meeting of the bank board to travel back to the luxurious house in London, thankful that his wife, Louise, was on holidays in France. It made it easier for him to visit Jane when she was absent.

Charles was met at the front door by the butler who took his hat and coat. After ordering a stiff drink, Charles made his way to the large living room where he found his father, Sir Archibald, already present in a chair, reading the newspaper with a drink at hand.

'Good afternoon, Father,' Charles greeted him. His father looked up from his newspaper.

'Your dark expression tells me that you have something bothering you,' Sir Archibald said. 'Did things go well at your board meeting?'

'Yes, yes,' Charles replied, slumping down into a comfortable leather chair opposite his father to wait for his port.

'Well, what is it?' his father asked.

'It is Samuel,' Charles said when a servant delivered his goblet of port wine. 'We paid a substantial amount for his commission, and that of Herbert. It bothers me that he suddenly appeared in our lives and cost us money from the family accounts. It would have been better if he had stayed with Uncle George in the colonies. At least then his inheritance would have been forfeit.'

'As I have intimated before, it is in your hands to ensure that never happens,' Archibald said. 'I do not trust the army to shorten his life. Samuel is the living reminder of treachery by your mother,' Sir Archibald said bitterly. 'He should have been strangled at birth. Not only is he not my son, but he is a blot on our good name. A blot to be eradicated.'

Charles stared at his father. There was no doubt that he meant that Samuel should die.

'It would be difficult to have his death arranged,' Charles mused. 'It would have to look like an accident.'

'I am sure the intelligent and cunning son that I have in you could think of something,' Sir Archibald said. 'Our country estate provides venues for many possible accidents – a fall from a horse and broken neck, accidental shooting whilst on a game hunt – it goes on. We would be beyond suspicion as he is a beloved member of our family. The police would not question any malice from us.'

Charles listened to his father's words but was not convinced. To arrange such an accident would require meticulous planning. There were easier ways with more certain outcomes. In some places of London's slums, life was cheap, and Charles remembered how Dr Peter Campbell had fallen victim to an armed robbery. It had been fortunate for the Canadian doctor that he survived the dangerous encounter.

'I have not seen Dr Campbell calling upon us lately,' Charles said causing his father to look at him sharply.

'You made the right decision, discouraging him calling on Alice,' Sir Archibald said.

'I have an idea to solve our problem of both Dr Campbell and Samuel,' Charles said. 'But you will have to trust me and allow Alice to continue seeing the Canadian.'

Sir Archibald frowned but could see the cunning in his favoured son's face. He was proud of the son who was so much like himself, and a worthy inheritor of the family estates. Charles was the epitome of what a Forbes man should be; ruthless, ambitious and without the constraints of morality. He was born to continue the family fortunes, and the existence of Samuel bothered Sir Archibald, who held the grain of concern that, somehow, it might be he who eventually came to rule the family. Whatever Charles was scheming, he had faith in it.

'I will send a message inviting Dr Campbell to dine with us,' Sir Archibald said. 'I am sure he will accept, if it means being in your sister's company.'

Charles smiled grimly, the plot to eliminate two unwanted people from the Forbes family set in motion.

*

Ian took a hansom cab into the centre of London, to the south of Pall Mall, where it stopped in front of a magnificent three-storey stone building. It was the Reform Club, open only to private members. The architects were inspired by the Palazzo Farnese in Rome, and when Ian entered, wearing the best of his civilian suits, he was immediately impressed by the airy spaciousness of the building. He informed one of the well-dressed doormen that he was a guest of Dr Campbell, who was also a resident of the club suites. Ian passed the man his card, and one of the doormen disappeared to fetch Peter, who appeared a couple of minutes later.

'Ah, Samuel,' he said with a broad smile. 'I am honoured that you would visit me at my humble abode.'

'How does a colonial get membership to such a fine establishment?' Ian asked as they walked along a wide corridor of columns.

'Well, one has to be friends with the founder, Edward Ellice, who made his fortune with the Hudson Bay Company, and who is a close family friend. The other way is to be a member of the House of Lords or Commons and have a substantial private income. I think you will like the coffee room, as we call it. It is in fact one of the finest eating places in London. I hope you are hungry.'

Peter led Ian into the dining room, where a few patrons sat at tables. Ian could see that no women were present in the gentleman's club, and guessed that he was looking at English politicians discussing matters of state over a fine piece of fish – or haunch of beef in rich gravies.

Peter signalled that he would like a table and the two were escorted to one in the corner of the restaurant. Next to them sat a man in his thirties, sporting mutton chop sideburns.

'I thought you might like to know that is the Duke of Marlborough,' Peter said quietly, leaning towards Ian. 'John Spencer-Churchill. From what Alice has told me about your interest in reading military history, I thought that you would like to know that we are in august company this afternoon. Besides being a duke, he is also a very conservative member of parliament.'

'I am impressed,' Ian said, carefully observing the layout of the cutlery on the table, remembering all the etiquette he had been taught by Sir George months earlier in New South Wales.

'I am about to upset our chef,' Peter said with a wry smile. 'I find the food here is not conducive to one's digestion, being too rich. If it would please you, I will order a clear gravy soup, followed by a roast haunch of mutton, sea kale and baked boiled potatoes. For the finishing course, rhubarb tart washed down by a fine claret.'

'That sounds fine to me,' Ian said. 'Why would that upset the chef?'

'Our chef considers my choice as too plain – the kind of menu the lower-class bank clerks and civil servants would eat at home with their families.'

'It's our stomachs – our choice,' Ian said as a waiter approached to take their order.

The order placed, both men settled back with the bottle of claret that had been brought to them by the waiter.

'Do you know that I have been invited to dine with your family this weekend,' Peter said across his crystal wine glass.

'Considering what happened at the country house, I am surprised to hear that,' Ian said. 'I have also been invited. If you ask me, it is rather peculiar as we are both *persona non grata* with Charles and my father.'

'I thought so too.' Peter frowned. 'But if it is my chance to see Alice, I will accept.'

'Then I should also accept,' Ian said. 'Who knows what Charles is scheming?'

Both men continued their meal, and eventually it was time for Ian to return to his regiment. Not that he had much to do with the training of his company or administration. That was in the hands of capable non-commissioned officers. Ian had been annoyed that he had little to do with his troops, but also consoled himself that also meant he had no real contact with Private Conan Curry. At least Curry had not exposed him, and the stalemate between them would continue until the opportunity presented itself for Ian to wreak revenge for the murder of his mother. The talk of war continued in the officers' mess with an eagerness to come to grips with the Russian Tsar's army. The whole Empire was affected. He had read that in his home colony of New South Wales – Sydney Harbour was being fortified with coastal gun batteries because of the threat of Russian invasion.

Ian considered the introduction of the new Enfield rifle could make the difference against the smooth bore Russian muskets, and this made him determined to have his company trained to a high level of marksmanship, to be able to decimate their foe at a greater range.

As the hansom cab conveyed him to the regimental barracks, he made a mental note to become involved in this aspect of training. Maybe he would identify his best riflemen and utilise them on the battlefield.

*

Charles Forbes had no contacts in the underworld of London, but he knew a man who might be able to assist him. One of the servants in the London house was known to have a shady past, and Charles summoned him to the library and closed the door.

'Andrews, I am aware that you have relatives who work on the Thames docks,' Charles said, pouring himself a glass of port wine. 'I believe they have reputations as persons of less than desirable character.'

The servant was a skinny man in his thirties with a pockmarked face but had proven to be a reliable worker around the London house.

'Sir, I have little to do with them,' Andrews protested, fearing for his job. Charles raised his hand to still the servant.

'It is because of their reputation that I have summoned you here,' he said. 'Your family's reputation for violence is what I desire for a very delicate task.'

A look of confusion clouded Andrews' face. 'As I said, sir, I have little to do with them.'

Charles reached into a desk drawer and produced a leather bag containing a substantial amount of silver coins. He spilled it on the desk in a dramatic display he knew would attract the attention of the man standing before him. The demonstration worked as the man's eyes almost popped out of his head as he viewed the money it would have taken him five years to earn.

'This could all be yours if you are able to satisfy a request I have. I should warn you that should you ever open your mouth to anyone about what I am going to propose, it would mean your neck stretched on the gallows.'

Charles could see Andrews licking his lips, staring at the pile of coins on the desk. He was like a man in a trance.

'What do I have to do, sir?' Andrews asked.

'First, you have to swear to me that this conversation between us never occurred. Do you understand me?'

Andrews, still staring at the small fortune, nodded his head.

'Say it,' Charles demanded angrily.

'Yes, sir, I understand,' he replied.

'Good,' Charles said, sipping his port. 'I need you to contact your relatives and give them the task of making two men disappear.'

'You mean . . . slay them?' Andrews questioned in a shocked voice.

'I did not say that. I will leave up to you how they

disappear,' Charles said. 'You realise that I do not wish to know how that task will be carried out. The amount will be split with whoever takes on the act of making the men disappear. I can arrange to have these men placed in a situation where you can do the rest.'

'I can do as you wish, sir.'

'You will get half of the payment now, and the rest when the task is carried out to my satisfaction,' Charles said, slipping half the pile into the bag. The servant stepped forward and pocketed the remaining coins. Charles knew that Andrews would be able to prove that the mission was real when his unsavoury relatives saw his good fortune.

A day later, the man reported to Charles that he had arranged for the gang operating on the docks to conduct the task, causing the two men to disappear in the murky waters of the great river. It was then that Charles revealed who he wished eliminated and how the scheme would be initiated. Charles was able to identify the approximate time it would happen, and Andrews knew the seamy back streets of the docks. London could be a very dangerous place; Charles was relying on it.

*

Both Peter and Ian arrived at the Forbes house early in the evening.

The butler opened the door to them and they were ushered inside. Ian was wearing a civilian suit and Peter was met by an elated Alice, who sparkled with joy and jewellery. Herbert stood behind his sister, wearing his officer's uniform, and looked the part of a dashing young man.

As spacious as the London house was, it was packed with guests wearing their best suits, and the ladies, their most valuable jewellery.

Charles cast a stiff smile that Ian could see was forced.

'Ah, Dr Campbell, Samuel. It is good that you could be with us tonight,' he said when they were in the dining room with the table set for a banquet. 'I thought it only fitting that we have all the family gather tonight.'

'It is good that you considered us,' Ian replied, but Peter remained silent. He was still puzzled as to why he should be included, when it had been made clear he was not to visit Alice ever again.

A servant mingled with the guests with flutes of champagne. He was joined by Herbert, who babbled on about affairs in the regiment. Ian hardly listened as he watched Charles amongst his well-dressed guests. It was obvious that he was not being introduced to Sir Archibald's friends, and had the feeling his invitation was not a gesture of reconciliation. So, why were he and his friend, Dr Campbell at this function?

Dinner was called, and the gentlemen escorted the ladies into the dining room. Peter had Alice's arm, whilst Ian and Herbert made their own way in. They found the places they were allocated at the table, and Ian found himself facing Peter and Alice across the table with Herbert at his side. Sir Archibald naturally sat at the top of the table, whilst Charles took up the opposite end.

The meal had hardly been served when Ian noticed a thin, pockmarked man slip behind Charles and whisper in his ear. Charles rose from the table and made his way down to Peter.

'My manservant has begged me for my help,' Charles said. 'He knows that you are a doctor, and has requested that I ask if you could help a member of his family, who is in need of urgent medical attention.'

'What sort of medical attention?' Peter asked.

'He has informed me that his cousin has been run over by a cart at the docks.'

'Damn!' Peter swore. 'Cannot he find someone else?'

'I am afraid the poor man is desperate,' Charles said. 'Otherwise, he would not have come to me at this time.'

Peter turned to Alice. 'My dear, would you mind if I accepted the poor wretch's plea for assistance?'

'I understand your need to help others,' Alice replied. 'Go, if you must, but hurry back.'

Charles looked across the table at Ian who was halfway through taking a spoonful of soup. 'It might be an idea if you escort Dr Campbell to his patient,' he said. 'He may require your assistance.'

'That is not necessary,' Peter protested.

'No, I will come with you,' Ian said, rising from his chair. 'I am sure we will not be too long away.'

Peter nodded and rose from his chair, taking Alice's hand and kissing it.

'I should also go,' Herbert said.

'No, that will not be necessary,' Charles hurried to say. 'Your bright uniform on the street might attract the wrong types.'

Herbert frowned.

'Charles is right,' Ian said. 'Mr Forbes, as your commanding officer, I am ordering you to remain here tonight as the representative of our regiment.' The order was given lightly, receiving a wry smile from Herbert.

Ian and Peter exited the dining room, and Peter went to the foyer, where his medical bag was located.

The bag retrieved, they were joined by the servant Peter knew from previous visits as Andrews. A Forbes carriage was waiting for them at the front entrance, and in the dimly lit streets of the fashionable suburb, it clattered away for its destination in the slum-like suburbs of the London docks of the East End.

Ian had a bad feeling as the better class of buildings were replaced with the dank streets leading to the River Thames. Somehow, he felt that it was connected to the unusual request for medical assistance. But it all made no sense, unless . . . it was an ambush. Was Charles capable of murder? Ian shook his head. The carriage clattered on and the echoes of the horse's hooves were the only sounds Ian could hear as they were conveyed deeper into the dark, dangerous streets of the docks.

THIRTEEN

Ian grew more uneasy as the coach took them into the narrow streets leading to the docks. On either side were darkened buildings, like stone valleys. He glanced at the servant, Andrews, and, in the dim light of the coach's lanterns, could see he also appeared extremely nervous. The only one who seemed calm was Peter, clutching his bag of medical equipment.

Ian reached into the pocket of his coat, reassuring himself the revolver was easily retrievable. It was not that he always carried it but his instincts had told him the invitation for dinner at the Forbes London house required protection.

'We are here,' Andrews said to the coachman when the carriage had reached a multi-storeyed warehouse overlooking the Thames River. Ian could see dim lights in some of the windows, and the noise of men at heavy manual work drifted to them.

All three men alighted from the carriage, and Andrews led the way in the half-light cast by a few fires burning in braziers, surrounded by men in rough garb huddled around them.

'I don't like this,' Ian said quietly to Peter. 'Something tells me we could be in danger.'

'I have grown familiar with such places in my work amongst the wretched poor of the slums,' Peter replied. 'This place is not unlike others I have visited.'

Ian was not convinced, slipping his hand back into his coat pocket to grip the pistol.

Andrews led them through a small door that opened up into a large storage room of goods awaiting shipment to the four corners of the globe, bales and boxes piled to the ceiling. Although there was lighting, the place was still dim, and the rows of stores cast long shadows.

'Where is your injured cousin?' Peter asked Andrews, who appeared to be on the verge of fleeing.

Before Andrews could reply, Ian noticed six men wearing handkerchiefs over the lower part of their faces step from between the mountains of stores. What Ian most noticed was the array of weapons they carried, ranging from axes to long knives.

'It's a trap!' Ian yelled to Peter. 'We have been lured into an ambush.'

Ian thought he could hear a noise behind him, swinging around to face three similarly dressed armed men approaching. The Colt revolver was in his hand, and the first assailant was only three paces away with an axe raised above his head when Ian fired. The lead ball took the man between the eyes. He crumpled, falling dead with the clatter of the axe ringing on the stone floor.

Ian was surprised to hear a shot behind him, and the yelp of a man hit by a ball. He was back to back with the Canadian surgeon, and when he glanced over his shoulder, he could see the outstretched arm of his friend, and in his hands a revolver, smoke curling from the barrel. Dr Campbell was also armed and had fired a shot. One of the men fell with a ball to his groin.

The sudden appearance of the firearms had thrown the would-be assailants off-guard, and they retreated into the shadows, dragging their wounded comrade with them.

'We have to get out of here,' Ian said as a musket discharged from the dark, and a lead ball slammed into a bale of imported cotton beside them.

Both men eased themselves towards the entrance, ensuring their pistols covered their retreat.

Outside, they saw the coachman holding a blunderbuss, but not pointed at them.

'Sirs, have you been harmed?' he yelled from the seat of the carriage.

Ian swung his pistol on the driver, now certain that his original concern had been confirmed. Andrews had disappeared.

'Lower the gun,' Ian called to the driver and he obeyed. It did not appear that he was privy to the mission to have them killed in the ambush.

Ian and Peter clattered aboard, ordering the driver to convey them back to the Forbes house.

'It appears that we killed one and wounded another,' Peter said, still holding his revolver in his lap. 'It will mean a police investigation.'

'Not if we don't report what has happened, as I am sure those responsible for attempting to kill us are not about to complain to the police. I suspect the man I killed is currently swimming in the river,' Ian replied.

'Charles and Sir Archibald had to be behind this ruse,'

Peter said bitterly as the coach trundled through the mean streets of London. 'The bastards want me dead.'

'If I am right, they wanted both of us dead,' Ian said. 'By the way, I would never have suspected that a medical doctor would carry a gun.'

'I grew up on the Canadian frontier,' Peter said. 'And after being robbed a few months ago, I reverted to my colonial past, and decided a pistol packed well in my medical bag. Maybe I should shove it in Charles' face when we return.'

'I understand your sentiments, but I have a better idea,' Ian said quietly. 'Just leave the discussion with Charles to me.'

By the time they returned to the house, the guests had departed. Alice met them at the door.

'I was worried for you both,' she said by way of greeting. 'After you left, Charles admitted to me that the place you were going to see your patient has a rather bad reputation for violent men. If I had known, I would never have let you go. Were you able to help Andrews' cousin?'

'I gave him a lead pill,' Peter answered with a twisted smile, glancing at Ian to see his grin.

'Is it a new medicine?' Alice asked naively, and Peter nodded as they entered the foyer.

'Has Charles retired for the evening?' Ian asked.

'No, he is in the billiard room with Father,' Alice answered.

'Good. I will speak with them before they retire,' Ian said, and brushed past Alice, leaving Peter with her.

He pushed open the door of the billiard room, seeing Sir Archibald and Charles seated with a decanter of port wine between them, and smoking cigars. They looked up at him in the entrance of the door, and Ian could see mixed expressions of shock and confusion.

'Father, brother,' Ian said casually, strolling into the

smoke-filled room and walking over to the table with the port bottle, pouring himself a glass then stepping back to stare at the two speechless men. 'As you can see, Dr Campbell and I survived our encounter with the ruffians at the docks,' he said, sipping from his drink.

'I do not understand what you are talking about,' Sir Archibald feigned. 'What do you mean, survived your encounter?'

'Charles knows what I mean,' Ian said, turning to stare at Charles. 'I doubt you will be seeing the servant Andrews in the near future.'

'Did you kill him?' Charles asked.

'No, he got away, but I suspect that if I report the matter of our encounter, the police will find him. He might have an interesting story to tell when he is faced with the evidence of an attempted murder of a prominent member of London society – if I may call myself that – and a surgeon who works amongst the poor of London's slums. I doubt that the police would be deterred from getting information about why Andrews should conspire with a third party to have Dr Campbell and myself murdered.'

Ian could see that his explanation had hit a nerve, as both men paled.

'I do not know what you are talking about,' Charles scoffed.

'Well, I think I had better report the matter to the police,' Ian said, taking a large gulp of the fine fortified wine.

'That might be a bit hasty,' Sir Archibald said. 'Such an incident would only attract unwanted attention from the newspapers. Knowing them as I do, they would attempt to include unwarranted innuendo and scandal into the police investigation. It is good to see that you were not harmed and, I presume, neither was Dr Campbell.'

'That is correct,' Ian said, finishing the rest of his drink. 'And because he was not harmed, I will make a proposition to you both.'

'What do you propose?' Charles asked suspiciously.

'I propose that you allow – even give your blessing to – Dr Campbell to continue to court Alice,' Ian said.

A short silence fell in the dimly lit room before Charles spoke. 'Anything to keep any scandal from the newspapers. Dr Campbell will have our blessing to visit with Alice. Anything else?'

Ian wished he could have thought of something else while he had Sir Archibald and Charles over a barrel. He could feel their guilt in the room although he knew they would not admit to conspiring to have he and Peter murdered. Then it came to him.

'I would like you, Charles, to break off any further contact with a Miss Jane Wilberforce.'

'You what!' Charles exploded, coming to his feet. 'How dare you tell me who I may or may not see.'

'Maybe your wife, Louise, is not aware of your meetings with Miss Wilberforce,' Ian said calmly. 'That should be good enough reason to break it off, before she returns from the continent.'

'Damn you!' Charles snarled. 'I think that is up to Miss Wilberforce to decide, and not you.'

'Well, that is what I ask,' Ian shrugged. 'I think it is better than a police investigation reported by Dr Campbell and myself.'

'I agree,' Charles grudgingly replied. 'I will not have any more contact with Miss Wilberforce.'

'Good,' Ian said, placing the empty glass on the billiard table and turning his back on the two angry men, he left.

He found Peter and Alice in a sitting room.

'Father and Charles have agreed to you and Dr Campbell stepping out together,' Ian said with a smug smile.

'Good God, old man!' Peter exclaimed. 'Did you hold a pistol to their heads?'

'Something like that,' Ian said.

'Whatever you did, you have earned our gratitude,' Peter said. 'I now have the opportunity to request Alice's hand in marriage from Sir Archibald.'

'That is another matter,' Ian cautioned. 'At least you and my sister have this time together.'

Alice slipped her hand into Peter's, and Ian could see the happiness in their faces. It was time for himself to seek the company of a woman who had entranced him.

*

War talk continued in the newspapers, the corridors of parliament and in the regimental officers' mess.

Ian devoted much of his time at the London barracks to managing his company of infantrymen. He was learning as he went, and studiously avoided contact with Private Curry. Ian had befriended Captain Miles Sinclair, whose military experience with the infantry regiment was recognised by all as the most competent of all the officers. Normally, officers left the running of the regiment to their senior non-commissioned officers and in many ways, the role of the officer was as a figurehead. But Miles Sinclair was different and actually involved himself in the welfare, training and leadership of his company. Ian relied on his new friend to teach him how to truly lead a rifle company, and Miles happily acted as his mentor.

On one morning, Ian summoned Herbert to his office.

'Who are the five best marksmen in your command?' Ian asked Herbert.

'My best marksman is Private Curry,' Herbert answered. 'He is outstanding.' He also provided the names of four other of his soldiers, including Private Owen Williams.

'If . . . when we go to war with the Russians, I want to use our best marksmen in a special detail to act as forward skirmishers for the company,' Ian said. 'Five from each platoon.'

'That will mean the men selected will be undertaking a dangerous mission,' Herbert replied.

'War is dangerous,' Ian reminded. 'But I see they would be in a position to identify enemy officers, and cause disruption before any attack can be launched. I have discussed the tactic with Captain Sinclair, who is also doing the same thing with his company. Captain Sinclair reminded me that sharpshooters using the Baker rifle were used successfully during the Napoleonic wars.'

'Private Curry is the best shot in the regiment, and is a colonial,' Herbert said. 'I feel that a word of encouragement from you would be appropriate.'

Ian was startled by the suggestion. 'I may do so, when I feel it should be done,' he said quickly. It felt as if fate was drawing the two men together, and Ian was not ready for that occasion. The meeting continued for a short time and Ian was pleased to see how dedicated young Herbert was towards the welfare of his men. Ian had observed that a couple of his other platoon commanders did not display the same concern for the soldiers under their command. But Colour Sergeant Leslie had gently guided Herbert in his duties.

When not at the barracks, Ian spent most of his time with Dr Peter Campbell at his club. Peter was now seeing Alice on a regular basis, and summoning the courage to once again approach Charles and Sir Archibald to ask for her hand in marriage.

The months passed. The leaves of autumn had blown away and the chill of winter came upon the British Isles as Christmas approached. Ian had leave and knew where he would go. Christmas was to be celebrated at the country estate, and Ian had sworn to himself that he would share it with the woman he hardly knew, but wanted to.

When Ian arrived at the house a driving, cold rain greeted him. He went inside to be greeted by Peter and Alice.

'Oh, it will be so wonderful sharing Christmas together,' Alice said, clapping her hands in delight. 'Herbert will arrive tomorrow, and the whole family will be gathered together.'

Ian smiled at Alice's happiness, and glanced at Peter.

'A brandy, old chap?' Peter offered and Ian accepted. Peter led him to the sitting room, where he poured them both a drink of the fiery liquid. A log fire was burning in a hearth and Ian was able to shake off the chill of the carriage ride from London.

Ian raised his tumbler. 'To Christmas, and the company of good friends,' he said. Peter also raised his brandy glass in response.

'The talk around the club is that we will be sending our regiments early next year to confront the Tsar's army,' Peter said. 'I presume you have read that our fleet is already in the Bosporus, and that the Ottomans defeated the Russian army at Oltenitza last month. No doubt you and I will be shoulder to shoulder in the fray. I find it ironic that we are allied to the Musulman against a Christian empire. I suppose one could say that the enemy of my enemy is my friend.'

'I hope you are right about seeing combat,' Ian said. 'My men are itching to get at the Muscovites.'

'I fear this war will be the biggest the British army has faced since Waterloo,' Peter said, warming his back against the log fire with his brandy in hand.

'My father fought at Waterloo,' Ian let slip, and felt a moment of panic for disclosing his real identity.

'I didn't think Sir Archibald ever served in the army.' Peter frowned. 'Do you mean your grandfather, old chap?'

Ian cursed himself for the slip of the tongue, but remembered that he had been briefed that Samuel's grandfather had also served at Waterloo.

'Yes, yes,' Ian hurried to correct. 'Just an error on my behalf.' Ian reminded himself that he was an imposter, and such slips could prove to be his undoing. Fortunately, it had been to Peter, and no one else.

'I am going to formally propose to Alice tonight,' Peter said.

'Have you permission from Sir Archibald and Charles?' Ian asked.

'You are family, and your approval is all I need,' Peter said. 'If necessary, Alice has agreed to defy her father, and marry me regardless.'

'Well, a second toast to wish you both happiness and good health for now, and into the many years ahead,' Ian said, once again raising his brandy glass.

'Thank you, old chap,' Peter said. 'Also wish me luck.'

'I must excuse myself,' Ian said, emptying the brandy glass. 'I have an appointment in the village before the light wanes.'

'It is a bitter day,' Peter said. 'Do you think it wise to return to the rain?'

'I suspect that when we meet the Russians on the battle-field, we will not be able to choose our weather.'

'You have a point there.'

Ian arranged for a horse to be saddled and mounted when that was done by a bemused stable hand, who considered anyone riding out in that late afternoon to be just a little mad.

Ian leaned into the rain, riding slowly towards the village.

The streets were deserted when Ian hitched his horse outside the tavern, from whence he could hear the sound of laughter and singing.

Ian stepped inside, and the appearance of the officer in his uniform caused many to cease in conversation to stare at him.

'Publican, drinks for everyone in the bar,' Ian said and saw the expression of pleasant surprise on the gathering of men and women. There was a rush to the bar, and Ian took the opportunity to cast about for Jane.

Their eyes met across the room, and Jane smiled warmly. Ian strode across to her.

'It has been a while, but you have always been in my thoughts,' he said.

'You have always been in my dreams,' Jane said. 'I knew that you would return.'

'I wish I could have earlier,' Ian said.

'You are soaking,' Jane said. 'I have a warm fire at my cottage. Should we leave the tavern?'

'I would like that,' Ian grinned.

That evening, in front of Jane's small fire, they made love.

FOURTEEN

Snow was falling gently outside the cottage as Jane lay in Ian's arms. The big bed had become the centre of his universe. The grey morning had arrived, and Ian realised that it was almost Christmas.

'Good morning, my love,' Jane murmured. 'The old gods guided you here to me.'

'What old gods?' Ian asked with a smile. 'My heart brought me here, and the spell you cast upon me.'

Jane sat up, drawing the blankets to her chin. The fire had gone out, and a chill filled the room. 'The ancient gods of Britain, before the Christian missionaries chased them back into the forests to hide.'

'Do you really believe that?' Ian asked, intrigued by her pagan views.

'Yes, I do,' Jane said. 'It is when I am in the stone circle that I see visions. I saw you before you first came to the village as a faceless presence. I knew from the moment I looked into your eyes that you were not Samuel Forbes, but one who I was destined to meet.'

'How could you know I was not Samuel, when even Sir Archibald and all the Forbes family accept me as the prodigal son returned?'

'Because I grew up with Samuel, and he was not like Charles. From when we were young, I knew Charles desired me, but when I once looked into Samuel's eyes, I could not see that same desire. He was a gentle and loving young man, but I could see his love was not for me. I know you have the physical appearance of Samuel, but when I looked into your eyes, I could see your desire for me, and that is when I knew you must be someone else.'

'You are the only person in England who knows that I am an imposter, but that was a pact I made with the real Samuel Forbes. We are friends, and what I am doing benefits us both. I have shared my secret with you only because I feel that you should know the real person who shares your bed. Ian Steele is a colonial, and now an officer in the Queen's army. I have always dreamed of doing it. Sharing my secret seals a pact between us. I suppose I am saying that from the moment I saw you, I knew you would be the one to travel with me on the road of life.'

Jane wrapped her arms around Ian, crushing him to her. He could feel her warm, naked flesh against his own, as if their bodies were fused as one.

'I would rather die than ever betray you, Ian Steele,' Jane said softly, her breath against his cheek.

Ian kissed her passionately, feeling his desire transport him to that wonderful world that he knew he could only share with Jane, when a heavy banging on the door shattered the moment.

'Jane, it is Charles. I know you are in there.' The raised voice boomed from the other side of the door.

'Bloody hell!' Ian cursed, slipping from the bed and grabbing his clothing. 'What does he want?' Ian quickly dressed in his shirt and trousers, while Jane began to dress at the side of the bed. It was Ian who opened the door when Jane was finished dressing, and Charles stormed past him to confront Jane.

'How dare you share your bed with my brother!' he snarled.

Ian stepped forward, grabbing Charles' shoulder. 'We made a deal that you were not to see Jane again,' he said angrily. 'Or have you forgotten?'

Charles turned to him. 'This woman is my property,' he said. 'I pay for the cottage and provide her with the money to survive. Without me, she would be in the poor house. If she chooses you over me, that is where she will find herself.'

Ian glanced at Jane who was staring at the floor, and knew what Charles was saying was true.

'Jane will come with me to London,' Ian retorted. 'I will look after her.'

'You!' Charles snorted. 'You will support Jane on a captain's pay?'

Ian glanced at Jane and could see tears welling in her eyes. 'I cannot go to London,' she said.

'Why not?' Ian asked in his surprise.

'I have seen the dreams of you soon to be in a world of fire, ice and blood,' she replied. 'I know you may think I am foolish with my beliefs about the old gods, but they have not been wrong before. There is one other who holds me to this village who I cannot tell you about. One who is also my kindred spirit.'

Ian wanted to say she was merely being superstitious, but something made him feel that the woman standing before him was very different to any other person he had ever known.

'We could still be together in London,' Ian said, and she shook her head.

'It would only be for a short time, and then you will be out of my life in a dangerous place,' she said. 'I must remain in the village where I was born. I do not expect you to understand.'

Ian turned to Charles, seeing the triumphant expression on his face. Confusion dominated Ian's thoughts.

'Dr Campbell and Alice are wondering where you are,' Charles said. 'It might be time for you to return to the manor.'

Ian looked back at Jane, who stood alone in her despair. Without a word further, Ian scooped up his cape, leaving the cottage to ride back to the Forbes manor in the light fall of snow drifting in the grey skies. This was the worst Christmas he could ever remember, and he suddenly felt a longing for the Christmas days spent in the baking heat of his home in New South Wales with his mother and father.

As he rode along the laneway of leafless trees, the snow concealed the rage in his face. He reached the manor and shook off the snow in the foyer of the house. His cape was taken by a servant and Ian knew where the liquor could be found. The sound of a woman wailing came from one of the rooms upstairs. He was met by a grim-faced Dr Peter Campbell.

'Is that Alice I hear?' Ian asked.

'It is,' Peter replied. 'I formally proposed and Alice accepted. Then I went to Sir Archibald, who outright refused to give away Alice's hand in marriage. He went one step further by demanding that I leave the estate before the sun goes down. Old chap, what in hell is going on?'

'Sir Archibald and Charles decided to renege on the deal I made with them just after the attempt on our lives,' Ian said, the rage gathering force. 'It is about time I confronted both of them.'

'Well, you have your chance with Charles, as he has just arrived here,' Peter said, gazing out a window to the courtyard below. A carriage had arrived and he saw Charles alight.

Ian immediately left the room and stormed to the front entrance, where a startled servant saw him fling open the door and walk towards Charles with murder in his eyes. A couple of paces from Charles, Ian stopped as the snow fell in ever increasing intensity. It was bitterly cold, but Ian did not feel it. He blocked Charles from entering the warmth of the house.

'You pledged to me that you were to break off all contact with Jane,' Ian said in a cold, steady voice. 'You and Sir Archibald also told me that Dr Campbell would have permission to continue seeing Alice. Both promises broken. I ought to give you a thrashing.'

Ian could see the rising fear in Charles' face.

'Father and I reconsidered our foolish acquiesce to your preposterous demands, and decided that we did not have to comply. I also know that you are only a half-brother to me, and that should be enough to disinherit you from any future claims on the Forbes estate. But, I admit, such proof is almost impossible to prove. Besides, Jane is little more than a whore who I pay for. You should step aside or I will call the servants to force you to do so.'

Ian did not budge, and Charles reached out to shove him in the chest. That was enough excuse for Ian to swing a punch that caught Charles in the face. Years of manual work had hardened Ian's body, and the punch split Charles' lip, splashing blood on the white snow at his feet. Adopting the stance of a bareknuckle fighter, Ian followed up with a barrage of blows. Charles reeled under the blows, unable to make any attempt to defend himself.

'Stop this now!' A voice roared from the steps behind Ian. The rage was dissipating when Ian saw his opponent sprawled on the snow at his feet, holding his gloved hand to his battered face. Ian turned to see Sir Archibald standing on the steps, flanked by two male servants. Sir Archibald hurried to his son, accompanied by the frightened servants.

'My son, do you need medical assistance?' Sir Archibald asked, kneeling beside Charles.

'I hope so,' Ian said calmly. 'Or I haven't done my job teaching the bastard a lesson.'

Archibald swung on Ian. 'I will arrange to have a carriage convey you and that Canadian colonial friend of yours back to London immediately. You are never again to return to the house, nor our London residence. Your brutal behaviour is not becoming of a gentleman of the Forbes name. Now, go and pack.'

Ian turned his back on Charles, who was being helped to his feet with blood flowing from his face. Ian felt good, the threat of being disposed from the Forbes properties not of great concern to him. Ian went inside the house and gathered together a few personal items. He was soon joined by a glum-faced Peter Campbell.

'It appears that I will be joining you on the trip back to London,' Peter said.

'What are you going to do about Alice?' Ian asked.

'Alice and I have made our own plans for marriage,' Peter said quietly with a grin. 'I did reluctantly examine

Charles on a request from Sir Archibald. You certainly did some facial damage that will leave a scar or two. Charles will be devastated; he's always considered himself as a pretty boy.'

The two men left the house to take the carriage journey back to London on Christmas Day. At least Ian felt the assault on Charles had been worth the cost to his place in the family. He had a family now, and it was the Queen's army. But Jane was not forgotten. Ian pondered on Jane's comment as to why she could not leave the village . . . *There is one other who holds me to this village who I cannot tell you about.* Who did she mean? Ian questioned himself as the carriage made its way through the gently falling snow.

*

Miles away in a London pub, four uniformed soldiers sat around a table in a smoke-filled bar. Privates Curry, Williams and Williams were joined by Colour Sergeant Leslie. The mood was festive and the ale and spirits flowed.

But Conan Curry was not in the mood to celebrate Christmas. He had in his pocket a letter from Molly, smuggled to him through the services of Colour Sergeant Leslie. The traffic of letters had cost in monetary terms, but well worth it to Conan, as a romance blossomed with each one. Colour Sergeant Leslie had taken a liking to the three men he had recruited, but did not let the friendship come between he and his duties as a senior NCO. The Christmas period was a time when a certain amount of fraternisation was allowed, and he shouted the three soldiers a round of ales before he would take his leave from their company.

'Cheer up, boyo,' he said to Conan, moping over his tankard of ale. 'It is a time of goodwill towards all men. I am sorry that you cannot be with your beloved.' It was no secret that the Irishman from the colonies had a great liking for the sister of the two Welshmen. 'But, with any luck, this time next year we will be fighting the Muscovites, and that will take your mind off tragic love.'

'Hear, hear,' Owen slurred, raising his tankard.

'To love and war,' Edwin said, sympathetic to Conan's growing love of his sister. 'Maybe Molly might get out early for good behaviour.'

'That is not likely,' Owen said. 'The bloody English don't like us Welsh much.'

'Or us Irish,' Leslie said. 'But they need us Celts to fight their wars.'

'We can't even visit our sister for Christmas. The peelers would pick us up if we did,' Owen said bitterly. 'Why do we fight for them?'

'Because, lad, it is a choice between joining your sister behind bars, or getting three meals a day, pay and a chance to travel to exotic lands to kill the enemies of the Queen,' Leslie said.

'Why did you join the regiment, Colour Sergeant?' Conan asked. Leslie paused for a moment, took a swig of his ale, and turned to Conan.

'I joined because it was the Queen's shilling – or possibly the hangman's noose. The same reasons many of the boys in the regiment are wearing red. That is all you need to know.'

The three soldiers stared at the man who had so much experience and had achieved rank in the British army.

'Would you have joined up, if you'd had another choice?' Conan asked.

'I would, lad,' the sergeant replied. 'There is something in a lot of Irishmen and Scotties that I know who are drawn to fighting.'

'And drinking!' Edwin added.

'And waxing lyrical with song,' Leslie continued. 'It is just in our souls to fight, and we don't care with who we do or for who we fight.'

'I knew a man like that back home in New South Wales,' Conan said quietly. 'Not of Irish blood, but a man who felt he was destined to fight under the colours. But as he was a colonial, that opportunity might never present itself.'

'Ah, his loss for being born a colonial,' Colour Sergeant Leslie said, sculling down the rest of his ale. 'It may be his fortune that he is on the other side of the sea, and away from what I think will be a hard-fought campaign against the Tsar and his army. The war coming is nothing like I knew fighting African natives armed with spears and shillalas. This war will mean bayonets and cannon.'

'The man I speak of is closer than you know,' Conan said. 'And I fear he harbours thoughts of killing me when he gets the opportunity.'

'You speak in riddles, Paddy,' Owen said with a frown. 'Who is this man you speak of?'

'Forget what I just said,' Conan answered, realising that the ale had loosened his tongue. 'Let's raise our tankards to Christmas 1853, and that this time next year we are facing Russian cannon as Colour Sergeant Leslie has promised us. It will mean a year closer to Molly doing her time.'

Silently, the four soldiers raised their tankards. They would return to the barracks that evening, as it was the only home they now knew and the only family they had.

Part Two

Soldiers of the Empire

The Dardanelles and Crimea

1854

FIFTEEN

The echo of drums and trumpets was long gone in the spring air of the Dardanelles Strait.

Captain Ian Steele stood at the railing of the troop ship as it steamed into the cluttered harbour of Gallipoli Village, so far from London. He remembered how, only weeks earlier, the crowds had cheered as they marched in slow time from the regimental barracks, passing Buckingham Palace, and the chaotic scenes at the wharves where women wept for departing husbands, inebriated soldiers sang raucous songs of the coming victory, and vital stores were haphazardly strewn about as senior naval and army non-commissioned officers countermanded each other's orders. Ian had noticed the chaos, and had a feeling the expedition to oust the Russians from the Crimean Peninsula did not bode well if this is how it had started. Now, he was gazing at the fortifications of medieval times bordering the shore as his ship approached.

Ian reflected on the months since Christmas, and felt a sadness that all his letters to Jane had not been replied to. He had been forced to spend many hours with his company back in the London barracks as they prepared for war, studiously avoiding contact with Private Curry, who in turn did the same.

Young Herbert was proving to be a good officer, caring for the welfare of his men under Ian's mentorship, and Colour Sergeant Paddie Leslie had been assigned the honour of standing with Lt Forbes and the regimental colours during the future battles they expected to fight. Ian was reassured, as he had faith in the Irish NCO's battle experience. The membership of the regiment had built a strong bond between he and Herbert, as that which existed between real brothers.

Ian remembered the face of Alice standing beside Peter Campbell as Ian raised his sword in a salute whilst leading his company, and taking the royal salute at Buckingham Palace. Alice had waved with tears in her eyes, and Peter nodded to him with a smile. But then it was time for the command, eyes front, and they were gone from his sight as the regiment continued to the wharves to board the troop ships.

The sun was warm in the cloudless sky, and within a couple of hours, they would disembark at the Ottoman village and march to their camp of white tents on the outskirts of the town, whose population of around thirty thousand Turks, Armenians, Greeks and Jews lived in relative harmony. Ian had read of the town's history of how it had been in many different hands since the Byzantine Empire. At the entrance to the Black Sea, it was a strategic naval base that controlled the gateway to the Mediterranean Sea. The combined Anglo-French force were to occupy and fortify the ancient defensive ruins, in case of the eventuality of the Russian navy attempting to break out into the seas beyond.

Gallipoli Village was the Ottoman foothold on the European continent after they had eventually defeated the Venetians to occupy the vital port city, now its own sea of ships' masts from England and France.

The ship was guided to a wharf and the soldiers of Ian's regiment assembled on the decks to disembark under the control of their company sergeant majors and junior officers. Ian ensured that his personal kit was in good hands of his batman and company clerk before stepping ashore to the sound of orders being bawled. It was a cluttered scene of stores being offloaded and troops attempting to assemble in their platoons and companies.

'Captain Forbes,' a voice called in the confusion, and Ian turned to see his friend, Peter Campbell, wearing the uniform of an officer without display of any commissioned rank, waving to him. Ian was surprised at seeing the face he last saw when they marched past Buckingham Palace. He pushed himself through the crowd of dockside workers slaving at piling the military stores.

The two men met with a warm handshake.

'How the devil did you arrive here before me?' Ian asked with a broad smile.

'The advantage of private resources enabled me to arrive before your cumbersome transport ships,' Peter said. 'It is good to see your smiling face again, old chap.'

'How long have you been in this town?' Ian asked, still a little stunned to see the Canadian.

'Just under a week. I have already come to learn that you can get drunk here for a few pence, and syphilis for a shilling. I am already contracted to your regiment as the surgeon. I even have a uniform of an officer but, as you can see, I hold no real rank. I have to warn you, cholera is rife here. We have already buried British and French soldiers who have suffered the scourge.'

'Well, all I can say is that it is grand meeting up with you again. Your support of my application for membership of your club gives me a place to stay in London. Needless to say, I billed all my expenses to a Canadian surgeon with the name of Peter Campbell.'

For a moment Peter blinked his surprise, and then burst into laughter at what he knew was a joke by his close friend. 'Is young Herbert with you?' Peter asked, taking Ian by the elbow to guide him from the wharf.

'Yes, I last saw him tearing his hair out in his attempts to keep his platoon together. We are to march to our encampment as soon as someone finds out where it is.'

'You are fortunate that I was able to acquire private quarters in the town, above a café,' Peter said. 'It will give you a place to go when the army food proves to be atrocious, as I have already seen being rationed out. On the other hand, the local seafood is quite appetising, but the local beverage a bit fiery for my tastes.'

'I will take you up on your invitation,' Ian said. 'Ah, I see my sergeant major requires me,' Ian said, noticing the company sergeant major waving to him. 'Just give me the address and if I am able to get time this evening, we will have a meal together.'

'Good chap,' Peter said, scribbling down an address and sketchy map. He handed it to Ian, who strode away to join his company.

Within the hour, the colonel had been briefed where he was to quarter his regiment, and the word was passed down to the company commanders. The soldiers were formed up and the band played a cheerful tune as they marched in formation to an area beyond the village, where they went about erecting orderly rows of white conical bell tents beside those of a regiment of French Dragoons. By nightfall, the task was complete, and the colonel had his officers assemble at the tent set out as the officers' mess.

'Gentlemen,' he said, perched on a wooden crate of tinned meat. 'Welcome to the Ottoman empire of our Muslim allies. With God's will, we should see action very soon. In the meantime, we have been assigned the task of assisting the engineers to reinforce the stone fortifications around the port in the eventuality that the Tsar takes a liking to the town. Training will continue with drill and small arms practice.' He continued with a few other matters and when his welcome speech was complete, invited his officers to join him in the mess that evening.

'Mr Forbes,' Ian said when he saw Herbert standing amongst the gathered officers. 'I require your services this evening.'

'What am I required for, sir?' he asked with a frown.

'You are required to accompany me to the town to gather intelligence on the local customs,' Ian said with a grin. 'So, we need to change into mufti and sneak away before our absence from the mess is noticed.'

Both men went to their respective tents and changed into civilian clothing. They met up and Ian glanced at the piece of paper Peter had given him that morning. Within the hour, both men were standing in front of a café where men of different nationalities sat drinking coffee and smoking from hookahs. Ian led the mystified young officer up a flight of stairs to a landing, where the wooden door was open into a small but airy room covered with a large colourful Persian rug. The room opened to a balcony above the café.

When Ian and Herbert entered, they were met by a beaming Peter Campbell.

'Dr Campbell!' Herbert exclaimed. 'It is good to see you. So you were the reason for my mysterious order from my brother to gather intelligence.'

'I suppose you could say that,' Peter replied. 'But I also wanted to introduce you to the cuisine of this part of the world. It is different, and I am acquiring a taste for the dishes they serve here. But first, a drink to celebrate our reunion. I brought with me a fine bottle of Scotch.'

Peter retrieved a bottle from a small cabinet in the room, pouring three glasses. He led them to his balcony overlooking the narrow street below, filled with traders peddling their wares to colourfully uniformed French soldiers.

The three sat in cane chairs on the balcony as the sun set on a balmy spring evening in the Dardanelles.

'To a safe return from this campaign,' Ian said, raising his glass.

'I suppose I should report to you both what I was privy to whilst at the Reform Club,' Peter said, gazing at the last rays of the sun over the tiled rooftops of the village. 'I have great concerns for the management of the coming battle with the Russians. From what I could gather, this has been a poorly planned campaign. The Commissariat has no idea what the army is doing, and without the logistics, no war can be won. The Froggies were allocated the best bivouac sites here, thanks to the incompetence of our own staff.'

'I noticed when we stopped off at Malta,' Ian said. 'It was a case of fending for ourselves.'

'The army has not any idea of dealing with the sick and wounded either,' Peter added. 'We may have the best rifles, but we need an efficient medical and supply system to ensure we win. It is as if we have blundered into this war rather than marched.'

'But we will beat the Tsar's army,' Herbert added optimistically. Neither Peter nor Ian replied.

That evening the three men ate from cracked plates a seafood meal of octopus, shellfish and fillets of fish cooked in olive oil and seasoned with local herbs. Unleavened flat bread was served to accompany the meal, which was followed by sweet and sticky pastry saturated with honey. The meal was washed down with a fiery clear spirit, and the talk turned to more mundane matters of gossip.

At the end of the evening, Ian and Herbert staggered their way back to their lines to sleep off the evening's meal and drink.

The bugle call to arise next morning was not welcomed by the two, who realised that the local drink had been more potent than they had anticipated. It was time to dress, make their way to the officers' mess, and partake of breakfast.

In the mess, Ian was approached by Captain Miles Sinclair.

'Captain Forbes, your absence last night was noted by the PMC,' he said, balancing a fine china cup of tea in his hand. 'Have you and Mr Forbes already discovered the haunts of the ladies of the night?'

'No, a man,' Ian replied, searching for the supply of tea for his hangover.

Sinclair raised his eyebrows. 'I did not take you for that kind of person,' he said with a smirk.

'A surgeon who is a friend from the Reform Club and will be joining the regiment soon,' Ian replied. 'He has some inside information on the strategy of this campaign, and we both agreed that it is not off to a good start.'

'Don't let those views find their way to the colonel, or he will have you on charges of sedition,' Sinclair quietly warned. 'Personally, I tend to agree with you. Even though we are prepared for the little luxuries of life for our mess, there still seems to be a shortage. It is not a good sign. But first, you must approach the PMC, and apologise for your absence. I expect he will also consider that Mr Forbes being your brother was under your influence when he was not here last night.'

Ian agreed with his friend and sought out the President of the Mess Committee to apologise with the excuse of visiting Dr Peter Campbell. It was fortunate for Ian that the PMC, a major, was also a member of the Reform Club, and knew the Canadian surgeon as a friend. Excuse and apology were accepted, with a caution not to repeat the absence from the mess in the future.

That day, Ian tended to his duties as a company commander and was pleased to see his clerk continued to be very efficient in administering the company needs. There was a visit from the quartermaster sergeant to complain that certain supplies he required for the soldiers of the company had not been met by the civilian suppliers. Ian knew why, but reassured the irate senior NCO that the matter would be rectified in time.

It was the fifth day of their encampment outside the village when the dreaded news of sickness within the regimental ranks reached Ian. It was Herbert who reported the matter.

'I have four of my men down with fever,' he said. 'And with the fever going through the ranks, the morale amongst the others is poor.'

'I will visit the medical tent and review the sick men,' Ian said, rising from behind the small wooden desk that the company clerk had been able to scavenge for his commanding officer. Ian grabbed his forage cap and sword to walk with Herbert to a large tent set aside for the sick. He was surprised to see Peter standing outside.

'Herbert, Sam,' he greeted them with a weary smile. 'I have just completed my rounds and can confirm that you have cholera raging through the regiment.'

'Bad air – miasma,' Herbert said.

'No, bad water,' Peter replied. 'But I cannot convince the soldiers treating their comrades that the water must be boiled before drinking. A friend of mine from the Royal College of Physicians, Dr John Snow, has done research through the Epidemiological Society of London he helped to establish with research into polluted water being the source of cholera. We have yet to understand what it is about tainted water that causes the sickness, but I believe if we ensure the troops have access to clean, boiled water, the incidence of the illness will decrease. I know my views are not accepted by most of my fellow practitioners, but I also know that Dr Snow is a brilliant physician. I trust his theory of the source of cholera.'

'If that is what you consider the cause, I will post an order that all drinking water for my company be boiled before consumption, under threat of military discipline if not complied with,' Ian said. 'The order will be posted this day.'

'Do you wish to visit the sick?' Herbert asked and turned to Peter. 'Is cholera contagious?'

Peter thought for the moment. 'I have treated many cases in London and have not yet been afflicted,' he said. 'But then, I do not drink polluted water.'

'Mostly wine and spirits,' Ian said with a grin. 'I don't think I have ever seen you partake of water.'

'Do you know something odd?' Peter said. 'Three of the men I examined look very much like the three who robbed me in London last year. I could be wrong as it was dark, and I was rather terrified. I would imagine that this is the last place one would expect to find the three ruffians who robbed me.'

'Which soldiers?' Ian asked.

'Privates Edwin and Owen Williams. The third is an Irish colonial, Private Curry.'

The mention of Curry did not come as a shock to Ian.

'What is their condition?' Ian asked.

'The two Welshmen may recover, but Private Curry is in a critical condition. The fever has him in its grip.'

Ian told Herbert to remain outside, and Ian stepped into the tent to be assailed by the stench of vomit and human excrement. Overflowing buckets were scattered amongst the men laying on the earth with only straw under them for their beds. Ian forced himself not to gag, and could see the soldier attendants wore handkerchiefs over their faces. It was a scene of misery, with many of the soldiers groaning in pain, racked by the constant vomiting and uncontrollable diarrhoea.

Ian squatted beside Conan, whose pain-filled face barely noticed the face above him. Ian could see the sunken eyes, wrinkled hands and clammy, pallid skin. But a spark of recognition lit Conan's eyes through the pain and fever.

'I know you, Ian Steele,' he croaked through parched lips.

Ian glanced around, ensuring that they would not be overheard.

'I am told that you are dying, Private Curry,' he said just above a whisper. 'You slew my mother, and are about to face your maker and answer for your sins.'

'I know that,' Conan said, tears appearing in his rheumy eyes. 'So, what I tell you is the truth. I did not slay your mother. It was my brother, Kevin, and he has already faced his maker. He had his throat slit on the ship we came out on. I liked your mother. She was always kind to us, and if I could go back in time, I would stop my brother from committing the foul act.'

With a great effort, Conan reached up to Ian with his hand. 'Please forgive me for what Kevin did. He was my brother and I had to protect him – regardless of the great crime he committed against a good woman.'

Ian frowned. 'I cannot forgive you, but possibly God will, in the next life, if what you tell me is true.'

'I swear it on my eternal soul, I had no hand in your mother's death. I would like a priest to be with me in the last moments. I swear what I know about you will die with me.'

Ian sensed that the dying man was telling the truth. He had once read that dying men are prone to confess the truth, as they have nothing left to lose.

'I cannot fetch a priest,' Ian said. 'I have also been informed by Dr Campbell that he believes you were in company with two of my soldiers in a robbery upon him. Is that true?'

Conan nodded weakly. 'Please tell him I am sorry for what we did,' he said. 'Here I am confessing to a bloody colonial imposter, and not a priest of the true faith.'

'You will pass on with my gratitude for keeping the secret of who I am, Conan,' Ian said with a note of softness in his voice. 'I pray that the Lord will be merciful towards you when you meet Him.'

Ian rose, confused at his change of feelings towards the man he had grown up with in New South Wales and, for a time, had been a close friend. He stepped outside the tent where Herbert and Peter were in a discussion.

'Ensure that the sick men are constantly given clean water with a dash of salt,' Peter said to Herbert. 'It may stave off the dehydration that cholera brings on.' He turned to Ian. 'Did you question the three men I think may have robbed me?' he asked.

'I questioned Private Curry, and he admitted that they were the same men,' Ian said. 'But from what you have told me, I don't think reporting them will matter much now, from the way they all looked to me.'

'This may be true,' Peter said. 'It is odd that I am now treating them in the possible last hours of their lives.'

'Everything considered,' Ian said. 'As soldiers in the service of the Queen, they may have just paid their earthly penance. God rest their souls.'

Ian walked away from the medical tent, his thoughts swirling. With the death of Conan Curry, the only real threat to his identity would be gone but, at the same time, he held admiration for the oath that Conan had sworn on his deathbed – to take that secret with him to the grave. In this, Ian had some regret for the soldier's imminent death.

Four days later, Ian was stunned to learn from his company clerk that Private Curry and the Williams brothers were recovering and returning to duty, thanks to the treatment Dr Campbell had suggested. The situation had dramatically changed.

SIXTEEN

There was blood on his hands, and also on his clothing. Charles Forbes stood trembling over the pregnant body of Jane Wilberforce in her cottage as the sun set across the Kentish fields. He dropped the knife and it clattered to the floor. The many stab wounds no longer bled into the large pool of blood surrounding her lifeless body. It was her fault that she had to die, he convinced himself. She had declared she was pregnant to his half-brother, enraging him, and his first strike with the long knife through her throat had prevented her from crying out for help. The other numerous wounds vented his rage until he was sure she was dead.

Charles could feel his body trembling as the rage drained away. He knew that under the law he had murdered Jane, and British justice meant that he would be executed by hanging if he was arrested.

Charles sat down on the edge of the bed, staring at Jane's bloody body. He knew that he would have to dispose of her, and required help to do so. He would need to confess to his father what he had done and implore him to help get rid of any evidence of the capital crime.

Charles gripped Jane's ankles, dragging her out of sight under the bed. He found a wooden pail and went about washing away the large pool of blood off the floor. When he glanced around the room, he noticed blood had sprayed onto the walls, and scrubbed away the most obvious traces. Satisfied that he had cleaned up enough to rid the cottage of obvious signs, he dropped the cloths he had used in a wooden pail.

But when he caught his reflection in a tiny mirror, he saw that he was still covered in Jane's blood. As nightfall was upon the village, he felt that the blood would not be seen, and made his way to his horse in the dark. The street was deserted, and Charles rode to the country estate to seek help.

When he arrived at the Forbes country manor, he led his horse into the stables, careful to keep an eye out for the stable hands. They were not in sight, and Charles stripped off his blood-soaked coat, burying it under a pile of hay.

Satisfied, Charles made his way to the house, and was met by the butler who cast his master a curious glance at his dishevelled appearance, but did not question him.

Charles pushed past him, going directly to the drawing room where he knew he would find his father reading *The Times* and smoking his pipe, with a glass of sherry on hand. Charles stepped into the room. Sir Archibald looked surprised at his unkempt appearance.

'You have blood on your trousers,' Sir Archibald said, placing his newspaper on his lap. 'What has happened?'

Charles picked up the sherry decanter, pouring himself a generous amount. 'I killed someone,' he said. 'It was an accident.'

'Good God, man!' Sir Archibald exclaimed, rising from his chair. 'Who did you kill?'

'A village girl,' Charles replied, swallowing the full contents of his glass.

'Not that Wilberforce girl?' his father asked, standing at the centre of the room. Charles nodded, pouring himself another sherry. 'Does anyone know of what you have done?'

'Not that I know of,' Charles answered. 'Her body is still in the cottage we rented to her in the village.'

'We must dispose of it before the act is discovered,' Sir Archibald said. 'It must disappear. You were always a fool to be involved with her. Your wife was aware of the affair, you know.'

'I suspected that Louise's indifference to me was due to her probable knowledge of the affair,' Charles said. 'Well, I can honestly tell her that I am no longer seeing Miss Wilberforce,' he added with a bitter laugh. 'How do I rid us of the evidence?'

Sir Archibald thought for a moment. 'You take a carriage to the cottage in the early hours of this morning and retrieve the body. I am sure that you are strong enough to carry her to the carriage. You then take the body to the grove of trees where the old circle of stones is located and bury her there. No one disturbs the stones. The folk here have a deeply rooted superstition about that place. You do this alone, and ensure that you are not seen by anyone.'

'Is that the best plan you can think of?' Charles asked.

Sir Archibald shot his son a frosty glare. 'Can you think of any other plan that does not involve others who might talk?'

'No,' Charles sighed, placing the empty sherry glass on a small wooden sideboard.

'I strongly suggest that you go about the task now, and have it done before the sun rises,' Sir Archibald said. 'You need to destroy the clothing you wore as well. The amount of blood will raise questions.'

'I will do that,' Charles replied, rubbing his forehead with his bloody hand.

'Go now,' Sir Archibald said. Charles first went to his room, where he stripped off his blood-stained clothing, changing into clothing he usually wore when inspecting the estate. He went to the stables and was startled to see a stable boy waiting for him.

'What are you doing here?' Charles demanded of the young boy.

'I heard you return a while ago, Master Forbes, and thought that you might need my help putting away your horse.'

'That is not necessary,' Charles snapped. 'I am capable of doing that myself. You are dismissed.'

Confused, the stable boy stumbled away, leaving Charles alone. He waited until the boy had exited, feeling his heart beating hard in his chest. It was the little unexpected things that could undo him, Charles thought. Satisfied he was alone, he found a shovel, and went about preparing a one-horse carriage for his journey back to the village.

It was in the early hours of the morning that he reached the village. An owl hooted and some dogs barked. Charles waited in the carriage at the edge of the village to see if there was any reaction to the barking dogs, but no lanterns appeared in doorways. He proceeded as quietly as he could to Jane's cottage, and went inside the darkened residence. Groping around under the bed, he secured her ankles, pulling Jane's slight body out. He knelt down and slung her body over his shoulders. She was not heavy and, with little effort, he was able to take her to the carriage. The task done, Charles directed the carriage out of the sleeping town.

It was a new moon and the relative darkness concealed his exit from the village. He continued until he came to the fields where he knew the circle of stones existed on the hill. He halted the carriage and removed Jane along with a shovel and staggered across the fields until he came to the copse of ancient trees. A large owl flapped over his head, causing Charles to drop Jane's body in his fright. He had heard the old stories about the circle of stones being a sacred place of the Druids, and that they had even practised human sacrifice. Well, he had a sacrificial victim for them, he reassured himself.

Charles entered the stand of trees and could see the dim outline of the stones. He stepped into the centre and began digging. The ground was relatively soft, and within an hour, he had made a grave deep and large enough to accommodate Jane's body.

Charles placed her face up in the grave and carefully covered her with dirt. He groped around to find leaves and twigs to conceal the evidence of freshly dug earth. Satisfied, he stepped back to gaze at the resting place of Jane Wilberforce. Now he would spread the story that she had come to him with a request to leave the village for the bright lights of London.

Charles was about to walk back to the carriage when a terrible thought crossed his mind. His half-brother would eventually return to England, and no doubt search for Jane. Charles had discovered the pile of letters Ian had written to Jane, and ascertained that Samuel had intended to marry Jane at the first opportunity. Charles had come to appreciate that the meek and mild boy who had been exiled with the army to the colonies had returned a tough and dangerous man. Charles felt a shudder when he considered the possibility – as remote as it was – of Samuel discovering the murder and linking it to him. He did not doubt that Samuel would kill him. What was it that his grandfather would say about the art of war? The best defence was one of offence. Charles contemplated what he must do. He had failed once in eliminating his half-brother, but he would not fail a second time, especially now he had more at stake.

Charles left the place of the stones, walking back to the waiting carriage with the irrational feeling that Jane rested in a place of her own choosing, not his. There was a time that she may have been hanged as a witch, he mused. But that fear was one step behind him as the sun rose across a misty landscape filled with angels and demons.

*

Captain Ian Steele was not a happy man. Ian stood in the shade of a gnarled olive tree on top of a small hill, watching his company drill under a warm sun. They fired their volleys in well-formed ranks, and then charged at straw dummies with long fixed bayonets.

'You appear to be in deep thought, Samuel,' Miles Sinclair said when he walked over.

Ian frowned. Miles Sinclair had grown to be a close friend as well as a fellow company commander.

'You would think that there must be another way of fighting a war than just simply lining up, firing a volley, and then charging the enemy ranks,' Ian said, observing the cloud of gun smoke drifting on the slight breeze of the day.

'It worked at Waterloo,' Miles said with a shrug.

'That was over forty years ago,' Ian replied. 'We are now armed with a rifled musket that can fire at an enemy at a greater distance – and with greater accuracy. Why do we still form ranks, exposing ourselves to a volley at close range?'

'You would need to convince the colonel that we should employ different tactics, if you have any in mind. Alas, I doubt he will listen. He was a young officer at Waterloo.'

'I know. It is just an idea, but what if we had sections firing while the other sections advanced, like the children's game of leap frog.'

'We would lose the concentration of firepower the formed ranks provide,' Miles said. 'But we have a rifle that fires further, so maybe we will be able to pour in enough musket balls before the Muscovites can close with us.'

'I concede your point,' Ian replied. 'But I think we are throwing away the advantage our Enfields have over the Russian smoothbore muskets.'

'When you are a colonel, you can write your own rules on battlefield tactics,' Miles said. 'Until then, as commissioned officers of the Queen, we just follow orders. It is as simple as that. Well, I had better join my company, and review their training.'

Ian watched his friend walk down the opposite side of the hill to join his junior officers. Ian sighed, and did the same with his company.

That evening, back in the British lines, Ian went to his tent and saw a letter on the small table in one corner. He picked it up and noticed the English postmark. Very carefully, Ian opened the letter of very thin paper. His hands trembled as he read the words so finely written in beautiful copperplate.

My Dearest,

I have not replied to the letters you have sent me until I was sure that the voice from the stone circle had told me of our fates. The spirits of the ancient ones have blessed us. I carry your child within my body.

I do not know if you welcome this news. I do know that I love you with my heart and soul but do not expect anything from you other than that you also love me.

My wish is that when you return to England that you may hold in your arms the result of the union of you and I.

I promise that I will reply to all your correspondence from this day on and pray that you may remain safe in the world of blood and ice that the ancient ones from the other world have given me the vision to see when we were together.

I am counting the days, hours and minutes before you return.

With all the love in my heart and soul,

Jane

Ian read the letter three times. Each time lingering on words and phrases. He carefully folded the letter and placed it on the table, as if it were an offering on a church altar. So that was it! He was now to be a father. When Ian stepped from his tent to join his fellow officers in the mess, he felt as if he was walking on air. He also felt exasperated that he could not tell Jane this very moment how happy he was. It would take a letter and many weeks before one would reach her. At least then she would know how thrilled he was about her pregnancy.

New tactics were forgotten as all he thought about was whether he would be the father to a boy or girl.

Even as Ian revelled in his new status, a stable boy found a blood-stained jacket under a pile of straw. He lifted the jacket and, in his horror, recognised it as belonging to Master Charles. It terrified him, and he did not know if he should tell Master Charles of the discovery. Something told him that option was not a good one. The boy wrapped the jacket in a hessian cloth bag and found a place in the stables where he knew some planks were loose. The boy peeled away a plank, placed the bag in a space between the walls, and sealed it again.

That night, Charles came awake in a cold sweat in his bed. The coat! He had forgotten to retrieve it from under the straw in the stables. He quickly dressed, and went with a lantern to the stables, but when he searched for the incriminating evidence, it was gone!

Charles knelt by the pile of straw with the lantern, scratching amongst the dry stalks. It was obvious that someone had found the jacket, but he knew if he asked too many questions, it would draw attention to its existence. In the distance, an owl hooted, as if mocking him. Charles felt a chill of fear. It only took one thing to go wrong to reveal his role in Jane's murder, and that only reinforced the urgency to have his half-brother eliminated before he could ever find out about Charles' treachery.

That night, Charles tossed and turned, his dreams filled with the image of the stone circle's magic, and its curse upon him, as Jane reached up to claw him into the earth with her and her unborn child.

SEVENTEEN

Ian wrote religiously each week to Jane, but there was no reply to his letters. Ian was confused, because she had informed him of her pregnancy and how she would keep in contact by mail. In desperation, Ian wrote to Alice, and in her reply, she said that she was informed by Charles that Jane had moved to London and her whereabouts unknown.

The information concerned Ian as she had been quite adamant she had to stay in the village of her birth. The dark hole the silence created drew Ian into despair.

To alleviate his despair, Ian threw himself into personally supervising the training of his company. His involvement was noted by his fellow officers, who remarked to him that the senior NCOs were the best people to run the day to day administration of the regiment. Their job as officers was simply to lead their men into battle. Ian did not agree; he had the opinion that the men must have a personal respect for their leaders and, as such, should be seen as much as possible amongst them. He encouraged his young lieutenants to follow his example. The old timers of the regiment wondered what was happening. However, the men who had not seen military campaigns yet, appreciated the concern shown by their officers. All young officers in his company attempted to practise this new kind of leadership, but one junior officer made it known the company commander was breaking the natural order of military protocol. Lieutenant Jenkins made his concern known to Herbert, knowing that he was the brother of their company commander. Jenkins was a handsome officer in his mid-twenties and the only son whose very wealthy family was well-known, with a social pedigree in the best aristocratic circles of London. He was lazy and arrogant to boot, and saw the campaign as a temporary measure to enhance his reputation before one day taking his seat in the House of Lords when his father passed. The army was only a stepping stone to his future aspirations in politics.

Ian would ensure that he visited the sick at the old Turkish barracks, now used as a hospital, and encouraged his officers to make a habit of learning about each and every man under their command. When Ian learned of his junior officer's contempt for him, he offered a transfer to another company, but the colonel refused Ian's request. Ian was stuck with Jenkins. Under duress, Jenkins reluctantly accepted Ian's authority, for the moment. For the young English nobleman, war was simply a game – like fox hunting with the hounds.

Private Curry was a member of Herbert's command, and Ian was forced to come in contact with him as he supervised the training of the company. Whenever this situation occurred, Conan made no sign that he personally knew Ian, and the oath he swore when he thought he was dying seemed to be holding. It was an uneasy truce between soldier and officer.

The illness that racked the British and French soldiers followed them when the regiment was shipped to the Black Sea coastal town of Varna, Bulgaria. After disembarking from their ships, the regiment was marched eight miles inland to camp on the shores of the picturesque lake at Alladyn.

At first, Dr Campbell had hoped the change from Gallipoli might act to improve the health of the soldiers, as the location near the lake appeared clean. But at night, the mist could be seen rising from the lake, and soon he was treating soldiers for severe diarrhoea. Soldiers appeared to be feeling constant nausea and lassitude. The tent he had set up as his place of treatment was overcrowded, with men laying on the earthen floor.

Then a hot wind from the west blew a white dust of eroded limestone over the camp, covering food, and the men, with a fine white powder. Cholera returned with a vengeance, first to the French army and, a few days later, to the British. Moving the camp did not help with the climbing rate of serious illness.

Ian noted how those he saw around the camp appeared languid, gloomy and very pale under the fierce, summer sun. Even Lord Raglan was not in much better condition, and it was said that the quartermaster-general, Lord de Ros, was a complete wreck.

Ian had observed Dr Campbell's suggestion that he boil any drinking water, and Ian enforced the rule on his company with the threat of fifty lashes for breaking it. The rate of sickness fell amongst his troops compared to the other companies of the regiment.

Ian walked the rows of white tents, observing the dire conditions both officers and men were subjected to. Flies, gnats and brown beetles swarmed the camp, settling on scraps of meat discarded by soldiers too weak to eat, and the stench of human waste pervaded the hot dry air as latrines overflowed. The rotting corpses of animals added to the hellish conditions, and adding to the misery was the appearance of lice and very big rats.

'Sir, may I speak with you?' It was Colour Sergeant Leslie.

'Yes, Colour Sergeant,' Ian replied.

'Mr Herbert has been taken to the hospital. I fear that he has the cholera.'

'Thank you, Colour Sergeant,' Ian said and went quickly to the makeshift hospital, packed with both British and French soldiers. The old veterans paid to be ambulance attendants were in no better condition than the men they were supposed to convey to the hospital. As many did not come out of the hospital alive, many of the troops preferred to hide their symptoms.

Ian arrived to see the carts lined in rows with their deathly ill patients awaiting space inside the former Turkish barracks. It was a great rectangular building very much in disrepair, with a courtyard. Ian was assailed by the stench of suffering of the sick soldiers, and could hear the unending groans of the soldiers laying on the floor. He was met by Peter.

'Damned bad show,' Peter sighed when he saw Ian. 'You will find young Herbert just down the first row. I ensured that he has a comfortable mat of straw, and pray that his youth may help him survive.'

Ian found Herbert laying on his back, staring with feverish eyes at the ceiling. Ian knelt beside him and took his hand. It appeared that Herbert was not even aware of his presence.

'Hang on, old chap,' Ian said gently. 'You will get better.'

Herbert seemed to focus for a moment. 'It was not meant to be like this,' he said through parched lips. 'We are all dying, and I know this is not meant to be. War is not meant to be shitting yourself to death. A soldier dies facing his enemy. Oh, Sam, I want to go home.'

Ian secretly agreed with the young officer. Why was it that the British army was to be wasted by disease without even seeing the Russian army? The war was see-sawing. The Russians had been defeated at Giurgevo but, in turn, had defeated the Turks at Bayezid in Asia Minor. The British naval bombardment at Petropaulovsk had failed, and the war was now being lost to the unseen enemy of disease. From local knowledge, Ian had been able to learn that the hot, dry summers of this part of the world were followed by freezing cold and wet winters. It was now turning to autumn, and the British armies had yet to engage the enemy. As he knelt beside Herbert, Ian remembered his promise to Alice to keep her beloved young brother alive.

Ian turned to Peter, standing beside him. 'What can I do to help Herbert?' he pleaded.

'What would help is if you could find someone to sit with him,' Peter replied. 'One of his soldiers to ensure that Herbert receives clean water and sponging down when the fever is on him. I know his men have a respect and liking for him.'

Ian rose from beside Herbert. 'I will look to that matter directly,' he said as he left. He found Colour Sergeant Leslie hovering outside.

'Colour Sergeant, we will go to Mr Herbert's lines and request a volunteer – no – we will need three volunteers, if Mr Herbert is to be attended twenty-four hours a day, until he is well enough to leave that pestilent place.'

'Yes, sah,' Leslie replied, and the two men walked through the dusty camp site until they reached Herbert's platoon area. There they found three familiar soldiers sharing a large bottle of brandy. They rose unsteadily to their feet at Ian's approach, and Conan attempted a feeble salute.

'As you were,' Ian said, returning the salute. 'How much did that brandy cost you?' Ian asked the anxious-looking soldiers.

'Three shillings and sixpence, sir,' Conan replied. 'Some say brandy will ward off the cholera. The Froggies are coming down with the sickness because they drink their cheap wine.'

'I am not sure if Dr Campbell would agree,' Ian said with a wry smile. 'I will pay you each three shillings and sixpence if you are prepared to carry out a mission, sitting with Mr Herbert in the hospital.' Edwin, Owen and Conan looked at each other, and Ian knew the request was asking a lot of the men who had a dread of being counted amongst the sick.

'We will do it,' Conan answered firmly. 'But not for the money. Mr Herbert is a good officer, and we don't want to lose him.'

Ian was taken by surprise by Conan's refusal to take money for services rendered in the hell house. The two men exchanged looks, and Ian could see almost a plea to be allowed to redeem himself in Ian's eyes.

'Very well, Private Curry. Arrange amongst yourselves to divide the time into three so that you are by Mr Herbert's side for the complete day. Dr Campbell will give you orders on how to care for him. I am sure if anyone can keep him alive, it will be you three.'

'Yes, sir, we will,' Conan said.

'Very well, you men report now to the hospital,' Colour Sergeant Leslie said, taking command, as was his duty.

The three men were about to leave with the colour sergeant when Ian said, 'Private Curry, a word with you alone.'

Edwin and Owen glanced at each other and Conan. Ian walked away with Conan to a distance where they could not be overheard.

'Conan, if you can help Mr Herbert recover, I will be eternally grateful, and feel that what you told me when you thought you might die to be the truth about my mother's death at the hand of Kevin – and not you, I feel then that we can go on with our lives.'

'Sir, I swear even today that I would have stopped my brother if I could, and rue the day we stole your money. I wish I could turn back time, as your ma was a wonderful woman to all of us when we were growing up.'

'God will be your judge in the end,' Ian said.

'Mr Herbert is not your real brother, is he sir?' Conan said quietly.

'As you and I know, he is not, but he has grown to be as close as a brother I could have ever had, and I swore to protect him.'

Conan looked down at the ground. 'There is something else I should mention,' he said. 'As you know, me and the Williams brothers robbed Dr Campbell back before we signed up for the regiment.'

'Dr Campbell has already expressed his suspicions to me,' Ian said. 'That is a matter between you and he. But, knowing the doctor as I do, if you do a good job I am sure he will put the matter in the past.'

As the days went by, the three soldiers undertook to be by Herbert's side as he lay in the hospital, feeding him small amounts of water laced with sugar, per Dr Campbell's instructions. Eventually, Herbert showed signs of recovery, and it was while Conan was on his shift in the early hours of the morning that Peter Campbell joined him with a lantern.

'You three men have done an exemplary duty caring for Mr Herbert,' he said as the pale light of the lantern illuminated Herbert sleeping peacefully.

'Thank you, sir,' Conan said wearily. The harsh conditions were taking a toll on his health, and he remembered vividly his scrape with death back at the Gallipoli village. 'Sir, there is something I feel I must confess to you.'

'What is that, Private Curry?' Peter asked.

'It was me, Edwin and Owen who robbed you back in London.'

'I can also confess that I already knew that,' Peter said.

'How is it that you did not put us into the peelers?' Conan asked.

'Considering where we are, and what we have faced so far, I doubt the courts could have sentenced you to anything worse than this. In my opinion, what you have done for Mr Herbert more than compensates for your treatment of me in London. Your secret is safe with me.'

'Sir, if I may be bold enough to ask a great favour?' Conan said.

'What favour, Private Curry?'

'A certain lady was arrested in London for the crime we were responsible for, and sentenced to five years hard labour. Her name is Molly and she is a good girl, and sister to Edwin and Owen. I was wondering if you could put in a good word to the judges to have her released.'

'You are asking a lot for a matter I doubt I can influence,' Peter replied.

'Sir, I will pay every penny of my pay if that helps, and I am sure so will Edwin and Owen.'

'It is not the matter of the money,' Peter said. 'It is a matter of convincing the judicial system to contemplate a pardon.'

'You are a man of good breeding, even if you are a

Canadian. I am sure the judges would listen to you,' Conan pleaded.

'I will consider what you have asked, Private Curry,' Peter said. 'In the meantime, you can resume caring for Mr Herbert, who I hope I will be able to discharge in the morning. I thank you for your fine service, and put it to you that you remain with me to assist other sick soldiers.'

'Sir, I thank you for your offer with humble gratitude, but I am an infantryman, and my duty is to fight the Russians alongside my comrades.'

'I thought you might say that,' Peter smiled. 'But the offer remains, if you change your mind. I am sure Mr Herbert would agree with me. You strike me as an intelligent man with a good soul, despite your past misdeeds.'

'Thank you, sir,' Conan replied, surprised that this man would be so forgiving.

The doctor left with his lantern, leaving Conan alone with a mere candle to light the dark night. Conan's thoughts were in turmoil. He had asked a great favour of the man he had once robbed at knifepoint, and yet the man had forgiven him and the Williams brothers. That would not have happened if they were civilians back in London and, for the first time, the colonial Irishman truly understood the meaning of brotherhood amongst soldiers. The robbery paled into insignificance when they all faced death from the unseen enemy of disease. They were already in hell, and only had each other to rely on if they were to survive. Lieutenant Herbert, who lay on the floor, was a living example of how the bond was stronger than all Conan had known before. Without the scum of the earth nursing him, the young man before Conan would not have lived. This was the way of soldiers.

EIGHTEEN

The hot wind continued to blow through the British encampment. Morale was low, and Ian could see the effect it was having on his fellow officers. A directive was issued that civilian clothing was not to be worn by officers, and orders were posted that any looting of the local population was a capital offence. Furthermore, no one was to stray further than a mile from camp. This offence was to be punished by flogging.

Ian adhered to the rules and ensured his company also did. He caught one of the junior lieutenants slouching around the officers' tents with his buttons undone on his jacket, and wearing a turban around his forage cap.

'Mr Jenkins, you are not regimentally dressed,' Ian said as the officer stood to attention before him. 'You will do up your buttons and remove that foreign headdress. It is up to you to set an example to your men.'

'With respect, do you know who you dare to speak to with such harsh words?' Jenkins said in a surly tone. 'I am not one of your private soldiers.'

'I know of your family connections, Mr Jenkins, and care not for them. At the moment, you are an officer of one of the finest regiments in the Queen's army, and will act as her officer.'

'It is said around the camp that you spent too much time in the colonies. The men call you the Queen's colonial,' Jenkins retorted. 'It is not your place to chastise me.'

Ian could hardly believe what he was hearing from this junior officer. It was outright insolence. However, he also realised the army carried with it a class system where gentlemen did not criticise other gentlemen. It was condoned to punish soldiers with severe discipline but not officers. Ian also accepted that if he reported the insolent young lieutenant's attitude to the regimental colonel, it would possibly be seen as his lack of command over his own officers.

'Maybe I should organise to meet with you tonight, just outside the lines, and have this conversation again,' Ian said, leaning forward into Jenkins' face with a menace that could not be mistaken.

'Are you offering me violence?' Jenkins asked in a frightened voice. He was aware how solidly built his superior officer was, and had heard a whispered rumour of how he and Dr Campbell had killed a man in London before the regiment steamed to the Dardanelles.

'More a lesson in discipline at the end of my fists,' Ian said quietly. 'Your choice.'

Jenkins immediately buttoned his jacket and removed the turban.

'Good,' Ian grunted. 'You are dismissed to your duties.'

Jenkins stepped back and saluted before scurrying away.

Ian watched the officer depart and sighed. If they remained any longer in the Varna region, they were all likely to die of disease. Ian found the harsh climate very much like that he knew in the peak of summer in New South Wales, but it was foreign to the bulk of the troops in the regiment.

In the first week of August, the hot weather broke, but the cholera continued claiming lives amongst French and British troops. In that same week, a fire on the docks at Varna destroyed thousands of pounds of critical military stores, and over one hundred and fifty tons of army biscuits. That same day, eighty men of the elite Coldstream guards died of cholera.

Herbert had rejoined his men, and the colour returned to his cheeks, which were showing the first signs of fuzz. He and Ian sat outside Ian's tent by a small fire, drinking tea from enamel mugs. They sat under a moonless night sky where the stars shimmered in the chilly air. It was a rare moment of peace away from the routine of the day in camp, where much time was spent assisting in the burial of soldiers who had succumbed to cholera from the regiment. Happily, not as many from Ian's company.

'Will we ever leave this accursed place, Sam?' Herbert asked.

Ian gazed into the night life of the camp, where lanterns burned to illuminate the men's tents. He could hear their subdued talk, and nearby, a fiddle screeched a melancholy tune.

'The bloody navy are the only ones seeing any action at the moment,' Ian said, sipping his sweet, black tea.

'I heard that they failed at Petropaulovsk,' Herbert said. 'That does not bode well.'

'We will get our turn to prove the might of the British Empire soon,' Ian said as a shooting star slashed the sky above. 'The colonel thinks we might be embarking for the Crimea as early as three weeks' time.'

'Anywhere has to be better than here,' Herbert sighed.

'Good evening, gentlemen.' The voice of Peter Campbell came from the dark as he approached. 'I brought some medicine for us.' Peter produced a silver flask and Ian could smell brandy, which was promptly poured into their now empty tea mugs. 'The troops swear it is the only thing to ward off cholera.'

'To our health,' Ian said, raising his mug in a toast, and Peter took a swig from his flask, settling down on a spare camp stool.

'What brings you to my humble abode?' Ian asked with a smile. The brandy was filling his veins with its fiery, magical glow.

'Oh, just on my rounds to visit former patients,' Peter said, staring into the flickering flames of the campfire. 'How are you feeling, Herbert?'

'Very well, Dr Campbell, thanks to you.'

'Thank the three soldiers of your unit who took turns nursing you back to health. I wish I had more like them to help me.'

'Ah, Private Curry and the Williams brothers,' Ian said. 'From what I have observed, they have shaped up to be damned good soldiers.'

'Rather ironic when you consider the three once held me at knifepoint,' Peter said. 'A matter in which I have informed Private Curry that I forgive them, considering the situation we are in here at Varna. I think just by being here they have paid their penance for past transgressions.'

Ian nodded.

'That Private Curry is a cheeky lad,' Peter continued. 'He has requested that I intervene to have a lady friend paroled or pardoned, who also happens to be the sister of the Williams brothers. It appears the police found her in possession of my medical bag when she was arrested. I cannot see how I can help her, even if I wanted to.'

'Do you want to comply with the request?' Ian asked.

'I would like to, old chap. I feel that what has happened in the past is a ghost of events. The men have proved themselves, and I feel they deserve some reward.'

'Did you not visit the tenements of the poor on your rounds?' Ian said. 'Is it possible that you mislaid your medical bag and later, being confused by the trauma of the previous robbery, forget you had left your bag in the lady's house?'

Peter stared at Ian and blinked. 'Your time in the colony of New South Wales has made you as devious as those that England sent there in chains,' he said. 'Would such a preposterous explanation gain the freedom of this poor woman?'

'If the request for her freedom was delivered to the right authorities, through Alice, who is your fiancée,' Herbert piped in. 'It would have to have some standing.'

'Herbert is right,' Ian agreed. 'You have nothing to lose, and I am sure your gesture would be greatly appreciated by the Williams brothers.'

'I suppose it is the least I can do,' Peter said. 'We will do it.'

A shower of shooting stars criss-crossed the night sky as the three men finished the remains of the Canadian doctor's supply of medicine.

*

'Dr Campbell would do this for us, sir?' Edwin asked as he and his brother stood before Herbert in his tent.

'He will, but I cannot promise he will be successful.'

'Sir, I cannot thank Dr Campbell enough,' Owen said. 'If there is anything we can do for the doctor?'

'Just promise never to rob him again,' Herbert said with a wry smile. 'And you can also be grateful to Captain Forbes. It is he who proposed a plan to free your sister.'

'Sir, we will,' Owen said.

'If there is nothing more, you are dismissed to your duties.'

The two soldiers provided the best salute they had ever presented before leaving the tent to hurry to Conan, who was washing his uniform clothing in a tub of lye soap in an attempt to kill the lice infesting it.

'Paddy, good news!' Owen said as they approached him. 'Doc Campbell is going to try and free Molly.'

Stripped to his waist, Conan looked up from his task. 'What do you mean?' he asked.

'Doc Campbell is going to write to the judge to ask for a release on the grounds that Molly was not in fact in receipt of stolen property. If it works, Molly will be out. Captain Forbes had a big hand in working out how they would free Molly.'

Conan rose from the wash tub and wiped his brow with the back of his hand. 'He's a good officer,' Conan said. 'I would follow him into hell if he ordered so.'

'We have a good officer in Mr Herbert, too,' Owen said, and Edwin nodded.

No matter how bad the conditions were in Varna, a small ray of hope penetrated the ever-present white dust that made life miserable. Molly's freedom meant everything to the three soldiers on the other side of Europe.

*

Ian's enemies were gathering.

'Old chap, I am not sure if you were aware that Mr Jenkins has approached me with a request to transfer to my company,' Miles said as the two men sat at a dining table in the officers' mess. Breakfast was over, and they were alone.

'That does not surprise me,' Ian said. 'I will gladly agree to his posting to your company.'

'I don't want him,' Sinclair said. 'He is an incompetent officer and should never have been commissioned. But, alas, his family connections make him a dangerous man. I have heard it rumoured that his family are about to pay for a captain's commission in the regiment.'

'God almighty! Why don't we have a commission system similar to the engineers and artillery, where a man is judged on his merit and not birthright to leadership positions?'

'Because men like you and I would not be where we are now, and families of social standing would be denied the God-given opportunity of ridding themselves of second sons,' Miles said. 'That was the situation in my family, as I know it was in your own.'

'At least it was something I desired,' Ian said. 'But, as we stagnate here, I wonder if I will ever get to prove myself.'

'Just keeping your company alive under the current conditions is the mark of a good officer, and from what I have seen of your men and heard around the campfires, you have succeeded in doing that. I would not doubt your ability to command what Wellington once called the scum of the earth. Having said that, you can keep Mr Jenkins, old chap.'

'I am aware that he spread word that I was not a fit and proper officer to be in the regiment,' Ian said. 'I am also aware he has complained of me directly to the colonel.'

'I was present at the meeting,' Miles said, drawing tobacco from a pouch and rolling it in some scrap paper. It was something new to the British troops, who smoked pipes or ready-prepared cigars. There was a new term for this item of tobacco rolled in paper – cigarette. 'When Jenkins left the meeting, the colonel asked my opinion, and I supported you. I am sure that you have the colonel's backing.'

'My gratitude for your speaking up for me,' Ian said.

'I suppose you know that you are known as the Queen's colonial in the lines,' Miles said, lighting up the end of the paper and drawing in the smoke.

'I have, and wondered why.'

'You still have your colonial accent, and there is something different about you in the way you treat your men. They actually feel an affinity to your style of command, as if you care for their wellbeing. Dare I say, they even think you could have been born of their class,' Miles said. 'From my experience, your men will serve well when we finally face the Muscovites on the battlefield, because they know you lead them. As a matter of fact, I heard a rumour in my company that a Private Curry gave one of Mr Jenkins' platoon a thrashing when the soldier complained about you. He said that you did not act like a proper officer.'

'He did!' Ian exclaimed, surprised, but pleased to hear the account.

'Ah, but that was to be expected when I also heard the Irishman was a former colonial from New South Wales,' Miles said with a smile. 'You colonials stick together. But it is about time I go and confer with my sergeant major as to the state of the company. It has been rather pleasant chatting with you, old boy.'

Captain Sinclair rose from the table, stubbed out his handmade cigarette and departed the officers' mess tent. Ian was left with thoughts about what was to come. It appeared his secret was safe with Conan Curry, and Ian hoped that Miles' company would be shoulder to shoulder with his own when the time came to face the might of the Russian army. What Ian had gleaned from many books on military strategy would be supplemented by learning from this British officer who had actually faced death on the Queen's far-flung battlefields. He just hoped that the same apparent dedication to professional soldiering was common to those generals under whose command the regiments of the British army lay. Ian would be bitterly disappointed in the months ahead.

NINETEEN

A secret reconnaissance had been carried out of the Crimean Peninsula by high-ranking British and French officers aboard the HMS *Fury*. The decision was to land troops at a place called Eupatoria, forty-five miles north of the target of the heavily fortified port of Sebastopol. But they also realised the army advancing on the Russian port would have to cross four rivers; the Alma, the Katscha, the Belbeck and the Tchernaya. Between the rivers lay four ranges of hills of varying heights and steepness.

*

'Is it true?' Herbert asked in his excitement. 'We are embarking from this damned valley of death for the Crimea?'

'It is,' Ian replied, packing a few belongings into a leather bag. 'Inform the company sergeant major to assemble the company, and inform them to pack, strike tents and be ready to board ship within the next twelve hours. We have been detailed to be amongst the first to leave.'

The excitement was apparent as the order was given and the troops realised that they just might be leaving the dreaded scourge of cholera behind them as they were shipped across the Black Sea to finally confront the Russian army.

Ian had a moment to reflect on what they would encounter when they finally confronted the Russian army. He sat on his bag, staring through the tent flap at one of the few soldier's wives organising to have her laundry tub loaded onto an ox cart. In his own company, he had only three soldier's wives permitted by a lottery to travel with their husbands. The wives faced the same hardships as the men they were married to, and made a small allowance acting as cooks, laundresses and occasionally nursing the sick. Whenever Ian came into contact with them, he was always kind, especially to Corporal Hunt's very pregnant wife. She somehow reminded him of Jane, who he had still not heard from. There was the possibility that Mary Hunt would have her baby delivered on some battlefield, as had been the lot of soldier's wives in past campaigns.

Within weeks, maybe even days, he would be leading his company into battle, and Ian suddenly experienced a chill of doubt. Despite his soldiers and fellow officers considering him a veteran from the New Zealand troubles, he had never actually faced the complexities of a real war. What if he allowed fear to dominate, and led his men poorly? What if he was incompetent and his men died for his stupidity? All he really had was a thorough academic learning of warfare; he had no practical experience, like Captain Miles Sinclair. He knew he was a fraud, but prayed that what was ahead might make him a man his father would have been proud of.

'Mr Herbert sent us to help you break camp, sir. Get your kit on one of the carts heading for the harbour.'

Private Edwin Williams' voice broke his inner thoughts and he rose to take the salute from the Welsh soldier, who was accompanied by his brother.

'Very good, Private Williams,' Ian said. 'Carry on.'

The two soldiers set about striking Ian's tent, loading all onto a nearby ox-drawn cart. It was time for Ian to walk amongst the men of his company, offering words of cheer and ensuring that they were in good spirits. In Ian's opinion, that was the job of an officer.

Ian was in the lines when he noticed a bearded man in civilian dress scribbling notes on a small pad.

'Who, may I ask, are you, sir?' Ian asked when he approached the man.

'Ah, you must be Captain Samuel Forbes who I have heard many good things about,' the civilian answered with a disarming smile. 'I am William Russell, special correspondent for *The Times*. I suppose you can say that I am a queer beast with the army.'

'I must say that I have also heard of you, Mr Russell,' Ian said. 'I have even read your dispatches in *The Times* and agree with your observations on the unreadiness of our army to fight this war.'

'It will only be the fortitude of these men around us who will overcome the disgrace of the political organisation – or, should I say, the lack of political support for our army. Very soon, we shall be facing the might of Tsar Nicholas and from what I have gleaned from talking to your men, I have great confidence that your company will acquit itself when that times comes.'

'Thank you, Mr Russell, for your confidence in my company, but I am sure the regiment will give an overall good showing when the time comes,' Ian said, pleased at hearing the war correspondent's praise for his leadership.

'Well, I feel I should amble off to the docks to observe the embarkations,' Russell said. 'We may bump into each other in Crimea.'

'I look forward to that eventuality, Mr Russell,' Ian said, and the journalist walked away to continue his notetaking, leaving Ian with a feeling that he had just met a man who might be useful for the future fortunes of the army.

*

Sir Archibald sat in his favourite leather chair in his London residence, with his favourite journal before him, *The Times*. The articles from the war correspondent were disparaging of the British government concerning its conduct in the campaign to date. Sir Archibald felt that the war correspondent was a traitor for his views, and should promptly be shot by the army.

'Good evening to you, Father,' Charles said when he entered the room. 'I trust that the board meeting at the bank went well?'

'Damned war is going to cost the country a lot of money,' Archibald growled.

Charles poured himself a cup of tea from the set laid out on an ornate sideboard. 'We are making a lot of money out of the war,' he said. 'Why should we bother how much it costs the country?'

'Yes, I suppose you are right,' his father agreed. 'I stopped by the club on the way home and had an interesting conversation with Lord Jenkins.'

'Jenkins?' Charles quizzed, sipping from his tea as he stood close to the open fire. The chill of winter was already settling on London.

'His son is an ensign in Samuel's company.'

'They are called lieutenants in the infantry regiments,' Charles corrected. 'But carry on.'

'It seems that his son has been corresponding from some place on the Black Sea that Samuel is proving to be a tyrannical and incompetent officer. Even offered violence to him.'

'Incompetency is not an unknown quality for many of our commissioned officers,' Charles said, balancing the delicate tea cup in his hand. 'But offering violence to a junior officer is something else. I always remembered Samuel as a meek and mild-mannered boy before he was sent to the colonies. Your brother, Sir George, has a lot to answer for, mentoring a brute such as Samuel.'

'I would be wary of Samuel's return if I were you, Charles,' Sir Archibald said. 'He is sure to go seeking the whereabouts of that wretched woman you were having an affair with.'

Charles paused, and despite the warmth of the billiard room, he felt a chill. His half-brother had already proved to be a resourceful and dangerous man. The greatest hope was that Samuel would be killed fighting the Russians, or taken by cholera. At least, as his father had informed him, Samuel was making enemies in his own camp. It was now essential that Samuel be eliminated from the family, no matter what it would cost. By the time Charles went to finish his cup of tea, it had gone very cold. But a thought came to him: the enemy of my enemy is my friend. The name Jenkins stayed with Charles.

*

September 1854, and the fleet transporting the British army to the Crimea steamed towards the shoreline of Calamita Bay. It was a beautiful sunny day and Ian Steele breathed in the fresh air from the deck of his ship. When he gazed at the coast he could see flocks of wildfowl, farmhouses and one or two farm carts on the narrow road. In the distance on the skyline Ian could vaguely make out mounted Cossacks watching them steam into the bay from their hilltop vantage point.

Beside them, the French fleet disembarked their troops first onto the beach. Bayonets shone in rows as the soldiers assembled on the busy beach, now being covered with military stores.

Ian watched as the NCOs barked orders to the men of the regiment as each climbed down into a navy row boat. Ian was in full regimental dress. He carried ration supplies in a haversack of four pounds of salt meat and biscuits. He also carried his greatcoat, fastened in a hoop around his body, a wooden canteen with his drinking water, and a small container of spirits. Ian also had his revolver strapped to his waist.

Before disembarking, Ian had ensured that every soldier was outfitted with the same amount of rations that he intended to last for three days. They also carried a greatcoat strapped into a knapsack. Each soldier also carried an item of the cooking utensils, and his armaments of firelock, bayonet and cartouche-box containing fifty rounds of cartridges of Minie bullets for their Enfield rifled muskets.

Dr Peter Campbell appeared alongside Ian. He was not armed and carried his medical bag. He greeted his friend. 'Damned good to not be eating salt pork and biscuits tonight. At least a change of diet to salt beef.'

'Do you see those Muscovites on the high ground?' Ian said. 'This is the first time we have even seen the enemy since we declared war against them six months ago. All we did was sit around and watch the regiment become severely depleted by bloody cholera while the politicians dithered about what we should do. The whole thing has been a shambles from the start.'

'Don't worry, old chap,' Peter said, patting Ian on the shoulder. 'You and your chaps will soon enough send them running using those fancy rifles you have been issued, while I will be using my surgical skills rather than nursing disease-ravaged men. We both get to use the talents we have been trained for.'

'Well, time to go ashore and admire the beauty of this place,' Ian said as the sailors in the rowboats beckoned to them. Ian was happy to be off the Royal Navy ship and going ashore to finally confront both his internal fears and the enemy. But as he did, he still experienced the nagging fear of the silence from Jane, supposedly in London, carrying their child. Ian knew that she must be close to giving birth. Meanwhile, his thoughts had to be for the welfare of the company of infantrymen he commanded. They too, had families, and it was his job to kill the enemy while keeping his own men alive.

It was with high spirits that Ian and his company landed on the Crimean beach, but Ian groaned in despair when his quartermaster informed him the tents had not been unloaded from the ships offshore. Cholera-ravaged soldiers lay in the open and, as night approached, the sky was filled with black clouds, and the wind picked up. Then came the rain in cold torrents, soaking the twenty-seven thousand British troops and their French allies, huddling in misery under their water-soaked greatcoats and blankets. Even the highest-ranking officers were forced to share the same miserable conditions as their men, and as Ian shivered in the cold, his doubts about the competency of how the campaign was being managed were reinforced. There was no fire to warm and dry them, nor was there a promise of breakfast under the current conditions. In the distance, Ian could hear the sound of the naval ships' bells, and quipped to Herbert beside him, 'We should have joined the bloody navy. At least they are out of this damned infernal rain. Even the bloody Froggies were sensible enough to land their tents. Even the Turks have shelter. If the Muscovites decide to attack us now, I suspect that for the promise of a tot of rum and a warm, dry bed, our men would surrender.'

Herbert did not reply to Ian's bitter statement but simply tried to stop shivering so violently. Peter stumbled through the torrential rain, looming out of the night to settle himself down beside Ian and Herbert. He wrapped himself in his heavy, water-sodden greatcoat.

'I just came from meeting a remarkable chap, Mr William Russell,' he said.

'I have already met our man from *The Times*,' Ian replied. 'Where is he?'

'He was sheltering under a horse cart with half the brigade staff,' Peter said. 'Mr Russell informed me that he will be reporting the conditions here to his readers as soon as he can have his communiques telegraphed out. I hope there are some in our old club who will be reading them, and possibly using their considerable influence to rectify this whole bungled war.'

Ian hoped his friend was right. 'Hope they feel moved enough to send us a crate of brandy.'

When the morning finally arrived, so did a searing sun, drying out the stores and men on the edge of the bay. But it also helped dry up the drinking water, of which there was already an acute shortage. Life for the army swung between extremes, and morale was low. For two days, while the confusion was being sorted out, the Russian Cossacks on the high ground above the beach simply noted the disposition of the Allied units, and number of troops.

At night, Ian and his men observed the glow of burning villages and crops beyond the beach. The Russian army was employing tactics they had used against Napoleon when he invaded their country almost a half century before. They were carrying out a scorched earth policy to meet the armies, who would surely begin an advance westwards, towards Sebastopol.

*

In London, Alice Forbes was surprised to find two letters arrive from the Eastern war front. She had been excited to recognise her beloved Dr Campbell's handwriting, and his letter overflowing of love and yearning, which ended in instructions for her to deliver the enclosed sealed letter to a learned judge he knew from the Reform Club. He had written that it was an attempt to free a woman from gaol who had been connected to the robbery upon him. Alice was puzzled, but personally delivered the letter as per the instructions the next day. It was handed to the doorman at the club, who promised to ensure the letter was personally handed to the judge. Alice departed in her carriage, wondering why Peter would plead for the release of a woman connected to the robbery upon him months earlier.

A week later, Alice received a visit from a law clerk who informed her that the matter Dr Campbell had raised concerning the innocence of one Molly Williams had been considered, and that the courts had decided to release her with a special pardon. The clerk added that the fine reputation of Dr Campbell, away serving with Her Majesty's army in the Crimean Peninsula, had helped in the consideration of releasing Molly Williams.

Alice immediately sat down and wrote the news to her fiancé. She was still mystified why he should go to such lengths to have a criminal released. It would take weeks for the letter to reach the frontlines of what was becoming a vicious war between the three big European powers of France, Britain and Russia, aided by the Ottoman Empire.

*

The days passed while Ian ensured that his company was drilled in tactics. Inspections of rifles and kit were conducted, and a few soldiers grumbled about the rigorous conditions set by their commander. But it all paid off when the word came down that the Russians were assembling a mere twelve miles away, at the Alma River.

At 3 o'clock in the morning, Ian had his company roused from their sleep to march on the enemy as a part of the regiment's battle order. As usual, Ian could see the confusion reign in the early hours of the morning as the commissariat officers vainly tried to meet the logistic requirements of moving support stores. However, the discipline Ian had installed in his company was paying off, as they assembled smartly with their battle kit in good order. The colonel addressed his regiment, and Ian knew that within the next few hours or days, he would learn if he had been born to battle.

TWENTY

In the early hours before dawn, Ian stood with his fellow officers of the regiment, listening to their colonel brief them on the order of march; the French divisions would be on one flank with six thousand Turkish infantry on the other. The warships would move along the coast to provide covering fire from their cannons.

As Ian listened to the briefing, he could see the numerous dots of campfires preparing the morning meals, and Ian hoped that it would not be the last meal of many of his men.

By the time the sun arose on a warm day, the regiments had been marshalled to march, but there was the usual delay as the transport units were in confusion. Ian stood in front of his company, behind him the men in lines ready to advance on Sebastopol across the Alma River. Ian had armed himself with his sword and revolver. Behind him, his men shouldered their rifles, tipped with bayonets ready for action. He stood alone, both excitement and fear washing through his thoughts. His forward position and personal weapons marked him as an officer, but it was essential in the long tradition of British officers to be seen by his men as the one who feared death the least. Up until now, he had enjoyed the fruits of being an officer, and now he was about to pay the price for those privileges.

A regimental runner came to him, informing Ian that the order was given.

'Company, advance!'

The wing of the British army moved forward at a steady pace on the undulating land of little forest and sparse grass. With each step forward, all men facing the possibility of their death or mutilation reflected on how they had come to this place at this time.

'When do you think we will see the Russians?' Private Edwin Williams asked Conan, marching just beside him.

'I don't know,' Conan answered. 'Ask Lord Raglan when you see him.'

A chuckle rose from those within hearing, and Edwin fell into silence when he realised that the Irishman was irritable because he was just as scared as he was. Edwin wondered if the Russian soldiers felt fear as he did.

'Whose stupid idea was it for us to sign up?' Owen asked as he marched behind Conan.

'Well, at least we are not doing time in some bloody British gaol,' Conan growled. 'You bloody Welshmen should have learned how to swim and get to dear old Ireland.' The age-old joke brought a grim smile to the faces of his two closest friends. 'At least we aren't carrying the regimental colours like poor old Mr Forbes up ahead. I heard that the Muscovites will target him when we get into a donnybrook with them. I feel a bit sorry for Colour Sergeant Leslie who has to stand with him when the fighting starts. Be thankful for small favours we aren't the ones in the colour party.'

After an hour, the huge mass of men marching forward were called to a halt for a fifty-minute rest on a ridge. They sat and lay on the earth, some smoking pipes and others rolling tobacco in sheets of paper. Then Lord Raglan and a large staff of British and French officers rode along the forward edge of the ranks. All men rose to their feet, rushing forward to give three rousing cheers for the British general. The sun shone on the metal of the rows of bayonets, and Ian watched with swelling pride for his role of leading his men into battle.

Then the order was given to once again advance down the ridge, even as carts took away soldiers who had succumbed to sickness or heat exhaustion.

Smoke rose from white-walled farm houses in their path, as the withdrawing Russians enforced their scorched earth tactic. The British army climbed a hill slope until they reached the top, and when Ian led his company onto the hilltop, they looked down over a sweeping plain, and beyond that, the sight took his breath away. He could see masses of Russian cavalry assembled to meet them.

When Ian looked to his left, he could see a large village in flames beside a small stream. He realised in this parched land, this stream was as valuable to his men as the Minie bullets they carried.

The army continued its advance to the point that Ian could make out the long lances the Cossack horsemen were armed with. A staff officer rode to Ian with orders, and Ian turned to signal Herbert and the other junior officers of his company to him.

Herbert hurried forward, accompanied by Colour Sergeant Leslie.

'We have the order to deploy our skirmishers forward,' Ian said. Herbert and the other lieutenants returned to their units to pass on the order.

Amongst Herbert's best marksmen were Conan and the Williams brothers, who put into practice their drill of moving forward quickly to a distance of around one hundred yards ahead of the army's front, at ten to twelve yards apart.

Conan took up a position in a slight depression, peering along the sights of his rifle at the rows of lances glittering in the sunshine, advancing towards him and the ranks of his comrades behind him. Conan was to attempt to locate any enemy who might look as if he was an officer and kill him, but all he could see were the grim faces of rough-looking men mounted on small, hardy mounts. So, this was what death looked like. Conan shuddered. His hands were wet with sweat, and he had to fight to control the urge to loosen his bowels, as he crouched with the rifle to his shoulder. To his left and right were Edwin and Owen, who he suspected were experiencing the same fear. Conan knew that they would be the first to receive the deadly tips of the lances through their bodies when the Cossacks decided to charge. The skirmishers felt very vulnerable in front of the regiment's ranks, as there was little hope of sprinting back to the relative safety of their company behind them when the fast-moving Russian cavalry advanced.

Now holding his sword in his right hand and the revolver in his left, Ian stared at the rows of Russian cavalry in the distance. He admitted to himself that he was terrified at the prospect of being skewered by a lance, but realised everything about an officer came down to showing no fear. He knew that the men he led looked to him to be the rock in an ocean pounded by the forces of death. When Ian glanced to his right, he expected to see Captain Sinclair standing in front of his company, sword raised and pistol in hand. But he was absent, and Ian wondered why.

Ian became aware that the cavalry was advancing slowly towards the British ranks, but suddenly, masses of Russian cavalry appeared from between the hills to their front. Ian quickly calculated that the Russian horsemen outnumbered their own cavalry by three to one, and the British would have to charge uphill. The odds were not good.

Lord Lucan stepped forward to wisely have his cavalry halt, and tasked them with escorting the forward skirmishers back to the lines of their regiments standing shoulder to shoulder with their Enfield rifled muskets ready.

A brightly dressed British cavalryman rode to Conan and the Williams brothers.

'I have orders to make sure you *sojers* return to your companies,' he said from aloft his big mount. Conan rose from his position, as did Edwin and Owen either side of him, and gratefully walked beside the cavalryman back to rejoin the ranks of his company.

Then the firing erupted from the Russian-fortified positions on the field, but they were inaccurate and still out of range.

Ian felt his heartbeat as he observed three large Russian infantry squares slowly descend the hills before them. Surely the battle would now begin. Why were they moving so slowly when they were advancing down the hill? Ian asked himself, and his question was answered when he noticed the centre formation advance in front of the other two to open its ranks, and the snouts of cannon could be seen. Ian remembered the stories from his father, who had told him how the solid cannonballs would bounce along the hard earth to rip off arms, legs, heads and disembowel soldiers in the packed ranks. One cannonball was capable of killing or maiming many men. It was deceptive to actually see the projectiles bouncing along the ground at high speed, and think that they held little fear at the end of their trajectory. It was only when they came to a complete stop that they lost their killing power.

It was the British cavalry in front of his infantry men who took the brunt of the Russian artillery.

Ian watched in horror as the white smoke erupted from the mouth of one cannon, and seconds later saw a splash of blood from a cavalryman's leg as the iron cannonball removed his foot from the ankle. More cannonballs bounced into the British lines, but were ineffective because of the long range they were fired at.

Ian was almost deafened when their own artillery opened up in a counter bombardment against the Russian squares. He watched as the Russians chose to retire out of range, on the reverse side of the row of hills to the British front.

Dr Peter Campbell had advanced with a small cart to carry his medical kit with the regiment. He had taken up a position behind the ranks and readied himself to treat battle casualties. His first patient was the cavalryman whose ankle had been shattered by the cannonball. The soldier was helped from his horse by one of the regimental clerks assisting Peter.

Peter laid him down on the grass and could see that the foot was dangling on just a strip of flesh. Blood was pumping from the severed artery.

'I just need a dressing,' the cavalryman said through gritted teeth. 'Then I will be able to rejoin my squadron.'

Peter had applied a tight tourniquet and could see that the foot would be required to come off back at a surgical station behind the lines. He wondered at the cool courage of the horse soldier lying on the earth. He signalled to a cart nearby intended to carry the first battle-wounded patient Peter had treated in this war. When the wounded man was being taken away, Peter wiped his bloody hands on his surgical apron.

The order came down the ranks that the army would bivouac in their current positions. Tots of rum and meat were consumed by the soldiers as they waited for the next orders. When supply barrels were emptied, they were broken up to provide wood for fires that night as the cold set in.

Ian found Captain Miles Sinclair sitting by a small fire with his company sergeant major.

'Join us, old chap,' Miles beckoned with a flask of his private stock of brandy. 'A bit different to facing those savage Maoris, I dare say.'

Ian felt a twinge of guilt, as he had never faced a real battle until this day, and it had not proved to be what he expected. It had been an anti-climax with the Russians retreating before them.

Ian squatted down beside his friend, taking the offered silver flask and swigging from it before returning the brandy to Miles.

'I noticed when we were facing the Muscovites, I could not see you out in front of your company,' Ian said.

'Ah, yes, old chap,' Miles replied as he handed the flask to his grizzled senior NCO. 'The men like to see us at the front, but when the shooting starts, I have found it wiser to keep my head down in the ranks. I would strongly suggest that you also follow my example, if you want to survive your first battle. Let the junior officers do all that heroic stuff of being up front. You and I are responsible to ensure that we stay alive to command and control our companies. The men do not perform well without leadership, and that is our prime responsibility. Any fool can make himself a target for their sharpshooters, but a smart army keeps its senior officers alive.'

Ian reflected on the advice of the seasoned officer, and had to admit it made sense. He sat for a while with the two men until he decided that he should seek out Herbert, and sit with him in the cold and damp night. At least it was not raining, and Ian found Herbert sitting with Colour Sergeant Leslie.

'I will be bidding you a good night, sir,' Leslie said when he saw Ian approach, leaving Herbert with Ian.

'What do you think will happen tomorrow?' Herbert asked Ian.

'I think the Russians simply felt us out today, and we can expect a full-scale battle when the sun comes up,' Ian said quietly. 'You need to try and get some sleep when you can.'

'I was terrified today,' Herbert blurted. 'And that was not even in the face of the Russians charging at us.'

'I have to admit that I was also frightened when I saw the Muscovite cavalry assembling in their formations,' Ian said, resting his hand on the young man's shoulder. 'I suspect that every man standing in the ranks felt the same as you and I. Fear is not reserved for the rank and file alone. We are allowed to experience what they feel, but not show it. That is why we are officers, and must set an example. I suspect that courage is the ability to overcome the natural order of fear, and we are expected to be good at that.'

'You have seen battle before,' Herbert reminded, and Ian once again felt a twinge of guilt. At least now, Ian had a better understanding of Samuel's distaste for war.

'Get some rest, Herbert,' Ian said, rising to now seek out his company sergeant major, and hopefully find sleep when his mind stopped racing.

*

Ian surprised himself when he did eventually fall asleep, but the pre-dawn chill came soon enough to wake him as men stirred around him.

The watch fires were being put out, and the day promised to be one too beautiful to die on. Ian looked across the valley at the peaceful meadows and vineyards. Bugle calls echoed in the hills as the men ate a hasty breakfast, looked to the maintenance of their rifles, and prepared for orders.

Ian stood on the high ground, surveying the hills to their front through a small telescope he carried. He calculated that the Russians would be covering the bridges and fords across the river with artillery guns. The enemy held the high ground, and it would be a good two-and-a-half-hour march to reach the base of the hills the Russians were entrenched upon. But when Ian turned to gaze at the men huddled under greatcoats – or standing around in small groups, he could see how exhausted they were from lack of sleep, and the continuing drama of cholera and dysentery. Added to this was heatstroke, which was beginning to plague the British soldiers, with drinking water almost non-existent.

'God help us,' Ian said quietly as both a prayer and statement of the condition of his men.

By mid-morning, the British army was advancing after moments of confusion and recriminations, and an almost carnival atmosphere existed amongst the troops. Ian took up his position at the front of the company, remembering the advice from Captain Sinclair. When the combat commenced, he would take cover amongst the ranks of his men to direct the fight.

After a while, the regiment halted to allow stragglers to catch up. Mail was distributed, and Peter was overjoyed to receive a letter from Alice. It had been posted weeks earlier, but that did not matter. What mattered was the love in each stroke of the pen to him from her.

Then the war truly commenced at the Alma River.

★

Russian artillery guns opened fire. The village before them suddenly burst into flames, and a gentle breeze carried the acrid smoke towards Ian's company. Round-shot tore through the ranks, and Ian could hear the screams of dying soldiers. He quickly glanced back to see Herbert holding the regimental flag aloft, and Colour Sergeant Leslie standing beside him. Many of the men had chosen to lay prone, attempting to avoid the heavy cannonballs coming towards them.

There was a vineyard close by, and Ian could see Russian skirmishers partly concealed amongst the rows of vines.

'Mr Forbes, your skirmishers to the vineyard yonder,' Ian screamed to be heard above the crash of heavy artillery guns. His order was received, and Ian saw ten riflemen advance from the ranks. Amongst them he could see Conan Curry and the two Williams brothers. They had bayonets fixed and grim expressions as they sprinted forward to engage the Russian sharpshooters. Ian could hear the sound of the cannonballs tear through the air, and the horrible thump as they landed amongst the packed ranks of the regiment. Smashed stone splinters and timber sprayed the air when the villas nearby were struck. Ian no longer felt the terrible gut-wrenching fear he experienced when they first formed up that morning. He was too busy considering the options he had to smash the Russian defenders.

All along the line of red-coated British soldiers came the order to advance towards the river, and Ian bellowed his orders for his company. He also realised that he had not taken his friend's advice to retire to the safety of the ranks, and was still a solitary figure waving a sword in front of the advancing company.

As he passed the vineyards, he saw from the corner of his eye three of his skirmishers emerge with bloodied bayonets. The roar of Russian artillery and musket fire was added to by the explosive crash of the British artillery guns firing in support of the advancing army. Already, smoke from the burning buildings was swelled by the acrid smoke of the guns, which stung Ian's eyes. He could see the white smoke trails of British rockets overhead as they sought out the Russian guns. He had not time to reflect on the fact he was now in a real war as he strode forward, his company following him into the gates of hell.

They reached the river and began wading across it under the constant roar of cannon and crackle of musketry firing from the heights above them. Herbert had already given the order to fire a volley up at the enemy, and this was followed by the other companies of the regiment doing the same. Spouts of water splashed around the soldiers in the river, and occasionally crimson pools appeared when a Russian shot found a target. Ian felt the chill of the water to his waist but held his pistol above it to ensure his powder cartridges were kept dry. Despite the lack of sleep, hunger and even thirst, the bulk of his men reached the other side, scrambling up the steep slope directly towards the Russians pouring fire into their ranks, killing and maiming many men.

A few mounted officers from other regiments splashed across the river with their men, and bellowed encouragement, as if on a fox hunt.

Ian could see the dark uniforms of his riflemen amongst the redcoats of other regiments. It was a desperate time, with British soldiers falling dead or badly wounded, and all Ian could do was continue leading his men up the slope, roaring profanities at the Russians, ignoring the death around him. His head throbbed, and his mouth was dry, but he experienced a strange red mist of determination to reach the entrenched enemy only yards away.

He was vaguely aware of a rifleman on his left having his jaw smashed away by a musket ball, and his blood splashed across Ian's face. Another soldier on his right screamed as a solid shot ripped away his leg, continuing on to take off a soldier's head behind him.

Then Ian could actually make out the bearded faces of the Russian infantrymen before him. He raised his pistol and fired point-blank into one of the enemy soldiers directly to his front, and saw him fall back. Ian was not alone, and was vaguely aware that Conan Curry and the two Williams brothers were either side, as if deciding to be his personal bodyguards. Ian was screaming ancient Gaelic slogans from the Scottish side of his Celtic blood, and the Williams boys did the same in Welsh. Atop the entrenchment filled with Russian soldiers, Ian slashed with his sword at the bayonet thrust at him. The sword and bayonet clashed but the Russian bayonet was diverted from Ian's stomach. Around him, similar scenes were being played out as men screamed curses, thrust with bayonets, and clubbed with rifle butts.

Ian leapt into the trench, scattering the enemy soldiers who turned to engage him. Ian was hardly aware of his predicament as the rest of his surviving company also fell upon the Russians. It was a tightly packed melee of men grunting, sweating and killing each other. Ian felt something sear along his arm, forcing him to reel back. The Russian withdrew his rifle to attempt another bayonet thrust, but Ian lunged forward with his sword, forcing it deep into the Russian musketeer's stomach. He was vaguely aware of the terror in the other man's eyes, and when Ian withdrew the sword blade, the Russian soldier fell to his knees, holding his stomach. A bullet from somewhere mercifully put the enemy soldier out of his agony. Again, Ian noticed the trio of his unofficial bodyguard stabbing and bludgeoning any Russians within reach.

Then Ian could see the remaining Russians scrambling out of the trench, retreating back to their secondary defences. But many still remained, determined to take as many British soldiers as possible into the arms of death before they forfeited their own lives.

Later, Ian hardly remembered being in the Russian trenches, shooting, stabbing and slashing with his sword. He did not know how many men he killed that day but in a slight lull, realised that it was his job to assess the situation, and best deploy his men. He screamed orders for the company to take up formation for a volley into the Russians being gradually pushed out of their defences. He was overjoyed to see young Herbert still alive, and standing firm with the regimental colours flapping in the breeze and shrouded by the clouds of gunpowder laying across the battlefield. Ian's order was passed down to his junior officers, and soon, Ian was pleased to hear the deadly controlled volleys pour the Minie bullets into the Russian defenders at close range.

As the smoke drifted, Ian could see that the volley had ripped apart the ranks of the Russian defenders on the ridge. Russian and British soldiers lay dead or wounded only a few paces from him, and it was then that he fully realised how outnumbered his regiment had been when attacking the heights.

'Charge!' Ian screamed and as one, his company thrust forward the long bayonets, running at the disorganised Russians, who now appeared to be fleeing down the slopes.

In hand-to-hand combat, Russian and Englishman sought to kill each other so close that they could smell the other man's breath, and see the terror in his eyes. The British riflemen also knew that they too must appear the same terrified way to the men they were attempting to kill. Curses in English and Russian mingled in a terrible form of personal war. The groans and moans of the badly wounded were a continuous whine under the noise of small arms and artillery fire.

Ian was once again fighting for his life as he clashed with a big Russian soldier who had turned to engage the advancing British officer. In desperation, Ian attempted to lift his sword arm to parry the Russian bayonet, and to his horror, realised that he had suffered a wound to his arm. He was certainly about to die when suddenly, he saw the big Russian soldier's head jerk back, a fine mist of blood left in the air. Ian turned to see Private Curry lowering his rifle with a grim smile. Ian nodded his gratitude.

The long hours passed, and the fighting continued as the Allied forces pushed the Russians back, but by 5 o'clock, it was assured the battle of the Alma River was over, with an Allied victory with a heavy butcher's bill.

A tremendous, ragged cheer rose from the throats of the soldiers who had survived, when the British generals rode by. It echoed in Ian's head as he sat on the earth atop the heights of the Alma River, surrounded by the bodies of British and Russian soldiers. His hands were shaking so badly that he could not reload his cap and ball pistol. Already his senior NCOs were carrying out a roll call of the company survivors, and Ian reflected on the last few hours of his life with an understanding of why Samuel had gladly exchanged places with him; dust, exhaustion, pain, sweat, smoke and the feeling of complete emptiness. Ian gazed at the cluster of men answering to the roll call and knew that he must find the strength to address them. His attention was distracted when he looked up at the smoke drifting across the battlefield to see flocks of birds flying in confusion through it.

'We did fine work this day.'

Ian glanced up to see the newspaper man standing a few paces away.

'I see that you are well, Mr Russell,' Ian said wearily.

'I am, but I am saddened to see the butcher's bill this great victory has brought us. I am not sure I know how to write the story.'

'It is one that needs to be told,' Ian said, pushing himself to his feet. 'If you will excuse me, Mr Russell, I should join my company.'

'I must compliment you on your bravery, Captain Forbes,' Russell said. 'I have spoken to a few of your lads, and they informed me how you led them up the hill without any sign of fear. Private Curry said that he and the lads would follow you into hell, if you so ordered.'

With those words, for the first time in his military career, Ian truly understood what it meant to be an officer of the Queen.

TWENTY-ONE

It was a cold, bleak day in London as the leaves began to fall in Hyde Park.

Molly Williams stood in front of the gates of the prison with only a small bag containing very little, other than the letters she had received from Conan. Molly took a deep breath, taking in the pungent smell of horse manure and smog of the factories spewing out their noxious fumes. At least it was the smell of freedom, and the click-clack hoofbeats of the big dray horses pulling wagons filled with barrels of ale passing by, the sounds of freedom.

Molly knew there was something that she must do before she sought a place to live and attempt to earn some small pittance to pay for food from her skills as a seamstress. She must find the lady who was responsible for her pardon.

Molly was an extremely intelligent young lady whose adoring father had taught her to read and write as a young girl. But these skills were not in demand for women in working-class life. More important to society was the dexterity of her fingers sewing the intricate needlework. Even that skill was being replaced by the great machines in factories, and she realised that without the support of her brothers in this uncaring city, she was very much alone. But she was at least free.

Molly set out on foot to find the woman who she had learned was her saviour.

Eventually, Molly came to the front entrance of the Forbes London residence, where she took a deep breath and walked up the stone stairs to the great door.

She rang a bell beside the door and waited until a gentleman opened it. She could see from his manner and dress that he was a servant.

'I wish to speak with the lady of the house, Miss Alice Forbes,' Molly said in a confident voice, realising that the servant was looking at her tattered clothing with disgust.

'I am sorry, but I do not think the lady of the house would have any interest in whatever you are peddling. Good day.'

Molly stepped forward and slipped her foot inside the door. 'Please tell Miss Alice that I come because of Dr Campbell. Please tell her that.'

The servant, a man in his middle age, had no time for the poor of the streets, and he could see that this pretty young woman looked very much like one of them coming to beg money.

'Please remain outside and I will inform the mistress that you have mentioned Dr Campbell's name.'

Molly withdrew her foot and the door closed. She waited a few minutes, wondering if the man had passed on her message.

The door opened and the servant stood before her. 'I have been instructed to escort you to the drawing room,' he said with a tone of obvious disapproval.

Molly followed the servant into the foyer, and then to the drawing room, where she saw a well-dressed, pretty lady with golden hair. She was sitting at a desk and rose when Molly entered the room.

'You may leave us,' Alice said, addressing the manservant, turning to Molly with a frown. 'May I ask, who you are, and how you know the name of my fiancé?'

'I am Molly Williams, and I have learned that your fiancé, Dr Campbell, wrote a letter to have me released, and you were the kind lady who delivered the letter. I only came to thank you, my lady for all that you and Dr Campbell have done for me.'

Alice's frown softened. 'Would you like to share tea and cakes with me, Miss Williams?' Alice asked, gesturing to Molly to take a seat.

'That would be very nice, Miss,' Molly said, looking to a divan. Alice rang a bell and a young girl in an apron appeared. Alice informed her what she wanted, and the servant girl disappeared to the kitchen.

'My brothers, Edwin and Owen, are serving with your brother, Mr Herbert, in the army,' Molly blurted, catching Alice's attention.

'Then they must be in Crimea,' Alice said. 'Dr Campbell and my other brother, Samuel, are also with Herbert over there. We have something in common, because I suspect that you must worry for the welfare of your brothers, as I do for my own brothers and my fiancé.'

'Yes, miss,' Molly said with her hands folded in her lap, perched at the edge of the divan. 'The man I feel very much for wrote letters to me on their behalf, as my brothers do not read nor write. But I do read and write. I fear for them when I read about the cholera.'

'My fiancé Dr Campbell also writes to me about the terrible conditions they are suffering, but has informed me that my brother Samuel's company suffer less because of his medical advice. Samuel commands the company your brothers belong to under my younger brother, Herbert.'

A tray with the teapot, cups and plates of cakes arrived and was placed on a small table. Alice rose and poured the tea, placing a cake on a small plate.

'Conan, the man I am very fond of, writes that they expect to go to war with the Russians very soon,' Molly said, accepting the cup of tea gratefully. The cake looked delicious, as Molly had been fed very little in prison, and her sunken eyes revealed her hunger. 'I pray that he is able to look after my brothers.'

Before they knew it, the two young women were exchanging news from the men who corresponded with them, and the morning passed quickly. Alice mentioned that Dr Campbell had a lot of respect for the three men who had robbed him in London, and the two women laughed at the absurdity of the situation, where the army seemed to be an institution where all that occurred before enlistment mattered little. The brotherhood of arms was the means of forgiveness against trespassers.

Lunch time grew closer, and Alice realised that she had an appointment, but was reluctant to break the bond that seemed to bind the two. Both had men they loved very much sharing the same regiment in the far-off place of death.

'Miss Williams, may I ask if you have employment?' Alice asked.

'Please, miss, call me Molly,' Molly replied. 'I do not have either a home or employment, for the moment.'

'Well, you will have both a home and employment if you wish to accept my offer to take a position at our country manor. We have employment for a resourceful woman who can read and write. We need someone to keep the ledgers for the management accounts. Are you able to do that?'

'Yes, miss. I once worked for Ikey Soloman the Jew, keeping his accounts in order. I know about ledger books and only lost my job when Ikey had to close his office for reasons of a dubious nature,' Molly answered enthusiastically. 'My father was a school teacher in Wales before he died of sickness when I was a young girl. I'd shown an interest in books, so he helped me learn to read and write, and I discovered that I had an ability to count numbers.'

'Good,' Alice said, rising to her feet just as Charles entered the room. He looked curiously at the pretty young woman in the tattered dress, holding a cup of tea in her lap.

'Who is this?' he asked in a cold voice. 'When did we start inviting vagabonds under our roof?'

'Miss Williams is not a vagabond, Charles, she is now an employee of the Forbes family,' Alice replied calmly. 'Miss Williams will be sent to our country manor to manage our accounts.'

'What!' Charles exploded. 'Look at her. She looks like she has slept in the gutters.'

'I am sure when Molly has the opportunity to bathe and be dressed in new clothes, you will not recognise the woman currently in our presence. Molly has told me of her experience managing accounts with another employer. I am sure Father would approve my choice.'

Charles glared at Molly sitting on the divan, appearing just a little cowed by him. Charles looked closer and had to admit that his sister was right. Cleaned up and in a new dress, this young woman would indeed be very attractive.

She might even be worth bedding, he mused in his darker thoughts.

'Very well,' Charles said. 'But you are responsible for her behaviour whilst she is under our roof.'

'Thank you, Charles,' Alice said as her brother turned to exit the drawing room. Molly stood unsteadily with tears of gratitude in her eyes.

'Thank you, my lady,' Molly said, her body trembling. Fortune was such a fickle thing. She had only come to thank Alice, but now she would leave with a future absent of hunger and cold, as winter approached the great city on the Thames.

*

The cries of the wounded for water and the lines of the slain being carried to a mass grave surrounded Ian as he stood on what had been the battlefield of Alma. Equipment from the dead soldiers lay in piles, and when Ian looked down at his feet, he could see a spent round-shot cannonball smeared with blood and brains.

Ian's arm throbbed from the bayonet wound he endured and had bound himself with a scarf. He knew that his company had fared better than their brother rifle regiments, and was prepared to march once again on the retreating Russians. But the order did not come. What Ian did not know was that a conference of the Allied generals had decided to take a long flanking march on the small Crimean seaport of Balaclava instead of a direct attack on the prime objective of Sebastopol.

'Good morning, Sam,' Herbert said as he joined Ian, who could see dried bloodstains on the young officer's field uniform. 'Do we encamp here on the heights for tonight?'

'I don't know,' Ian replied. 'I am just a lowly company

commander. If I had my way, we would have kept tight on the heels of the retreating Muscovites.'

'You are wounded,' Herbert observed. 'Your arm.'

'It is nothing.' Ian shrugged. 'A bloody Russian bayonet came a bit close. I will see Dr Campbell later today for a proper bandage. By the way, I must concede your terrible trio acquitted themselves well in the assault. I have been thinking that you should promote Private Curry to corporal. He has earned it.'

'A good choice,' Herbert agreed. 'All the men of my section look up to him. After today, I also feel that he should be promoted.'

'Make sure that our company gets as much as the spare kit from the dead we can,' Ian said. 'The way our commiseriate is operating on this campaign, we might possibly find ourselves short on ammunition.'

'I will do that,' Herbert said. 'But you must promise me to see Peter, and have your wound seen to.'

'I thought it was my duty to look after you.' Ian grinned. 'You are, after all, the little brother who I promised Alice I would keep safe.'

'I promised the same to Alice concerning your welfare,' Herbert confided. 'I was terrified during the battle. I felt that every Russian musket was aimed at me when I was holding the regimental colours. It was only the encouragement of Colour Sergeant Leslie that kept me from throwing down our colours and retreating.'

'You may be right about every Muscovite wanting to do away with you and seize our colours,' Ian said. 'I will suggest to the colonel that it is Mr Jenkins' turn to have the honour of carrying the colours into battle.'

'I don't think Mr Jenkins will like that,' Herbert said. 'I would prefer the honour be mine, and not Jenkins'.'

'You know you will be making yourself a target in the next battle we engage the Russians in,' Ian said.

'I am not a brave man, but I know my duty as a British officer,' Herbert replied. 'I would rather you write to our sister telling her how I fell holding the colours than retreat. Alice would be very proud of me if that happened.' Herbert paused before adding, 'The men of the company are boasting of the courage you displayed in the attack on the Russians today.'

'Bloody fools,' Ian growled. 'I was just too slow retiring into our ranks. Neither of us have a duty to die for those mutton-chop moustached, stiff-collared civil servants back in London, sipping their tea over the breakfast table, and safely reading the latest reports in *The Times*. It is not they who have to suffer as we do for imperial interests. Our only imperative is to lead our men wisely, stay alive, and kill as many of the enemy that we can. And as for Alice being proud of you being killed in action, I doubt that would be her reaction. She is a woman and be assured a woman does not have the same attitude to war that is thrust upon us. I think Alice would kill me if anything happened to you.'

'You sound like Captain Sinclair,' Herbert said. 'He often states that the British army should be led by men selected and then trained on their merit to command. His views are not popular amongst the others in the mess. And Alice would not blame you if anything untoward happens to me.'

'Captain Sinclair is the future of the British army,' Ian said. 'I have seen how men of lowly birth – even former convicts in the colony of New South Wales – rise to positions of power on their God-given natural abilities of leadership and enterprise. I think the realms of England could take a lesson from that.'

'You sound as if you admire the colonials,' Herbert said. 'It is no wonder the men of the company call you the Queen's colonial. I fear that you were too long away from the home of your birth.'

Ian looked at Herbert to see if he was accusing him or simply reflecting the attitude existing in his company. How ironic, Ian thought. How close to the truth his men were in their identification of him as a colonial. His life before England had been so strongly influenced by the growing attitude of all men being equal without class, although he had to admit, class still existed in his place of birth. There were still the wealthy landowners and others who were the hangovers of the class system from the Mother Country.

Then Ian was summoned to a meeting with the colonel after having his arm bandaged by Peter with all his fellow officers, and the orders were issued.

Dawn was a few hours away, heralded by the sound of the nearby French troops' drums and trumpets, rousing the armies into formation for the march on the Russian army.

Ian stirred under his greatcoat, covered in morning dew. The noise of an army rousing for war broke the nightmares of the sleeping hours when he tossed and turned, whimpering as the images of mutilated soldiers mixed with a strange flash of a circle of stones. None of it made sense, but somehow, he knew the circle of stones were those Jane had introduced him to. But now they were sinister in his dreams, mixed with memories of death. His small fire was still smouldering, and in the valley below, a heavy fog persisted where Ian could see the army gathering into formation.

He snatched a piece of cheese and stale bread, washed down with cold water from his canteen, and quickly gathered his kit together. Ian now had an Enfield rifle musket recovered from a dead soldier. Possessing it was a link to his men, and he slung it across his shoulder. He could see that the columns of French troops were on the move, disappearing into the fog of the valley below. When Ian glanced out to the sea, he observed the smoke trailing behind the funnels of the war ships as they weighed anchor and steamed south along the coast to accompany the advance.

Non-commissioned officers barked orders to fall in, and officers strode about to be seen by their men. Ian stumbled to his company, and was surprised to hear a ragged cheer for his arrival. He saluted his men in response to their touching gesture, and called for his subordinate officers for a briefing.

The sun was well up when the British army finally marched, with Ian at the head of his company. As they approached the valley floor, they were startled to see a carpet of grey-uniformed Russians covering the earth. The Russians had left their wounded behind in the retreat. The British army paused to assist the wounded Russian soldiers with food, water and medical help. Ian calculated over seven hundred Russian wounded, and it was decided that a surgeon from one of the regiments would remain behind with a servant to care for the Russian soldiers.

Then the army advanced into hilly, barren country covered in thistles. A small rutted track led through the hills marked by the wheel tracks of Russian artillery wagons. Ian knew as they marched that ahead lay yet another terrible battle, and the old feeling of apprehension returned. Would he be able to lead his men into hell again? Life was little more than the throw of the dice by the gods of war, deciding who would live and who would die.

TWENTY-TWO

It was with great pride that Corporal Conan Curry strutted amongst his section, displaying the broad white chevrons on his sleeve. A hurried job by one of the wives of the soldiers had completed the task of sewing them in place before the advance on Balaclava. The promotion carried with it an increase in his pay, and during a halt in the advance, Conan sat with the Williams brothers.

They sat on a ridge with the rest of the regiment looking over the Katscha Valley below. On the opposite ridge, they gazed at hills clad with shrubs here and there and pretty villas surrounded by white stone walls.

'Do you think that we might find some grog in those houses?' Edwin asked hopefully.

'I doubt it,' Conan answered. 'The Muscovites would have already looted them in their retreat.' Since his promotion, Conan had appeared to become wiser as a soldier.

He was proud of his recognition, and his promotion was accepted by Owen and Edwin, but not so much by the rest of the section Conan commanded. In their eyes, he had yet to prove himself.

'Do you think that the next time we meet the Muscovites it will be as bad as Alma?' Edwin continued to question like a curious child.

'I bloody well don't know. Only officers know the answer,' Conan replied, irritated at the stream of questions.

'Maybe you should ask Captain Forbes,' Owen said, resting on his elbows with his eyes closed. 'You seem to have some kind of bond with him. Is it because you are a colonial Irishman, and the captain is known as the colonial?'

Conan shifted uncomfortably. He carried the secret of who Captain Samuel Forbes really was, and had grown to truly like and respect his former friend from New South Wales. Captain Forbes' actions at Alma had given his company faith in his leadership. Prior to the battle, he had drilled his soldiers in tactics and marksmanship with the Enfield beyond the abilities of other companies. The soldiers of Ian's company had resented his insistence on perfection then, but now understood why he had been so harsh in their training.

'On yer feet. Form up!' The order was bawled by the company sergeant major, and the men rose, shouldered arms, and fell into their formations. Herbert was once again assigned to carry the regimental colours, and Colour Sergeant Leslie fell in beside him. The great mass of the British army began to roll down the ridge into the valley, and ascend the hills before them.

Dr Campbell marched beside Ian. He did not carry any arms but still wore a conspicuous military uniform similar to that of an officer in the rifle regiment. Ian had warned him that he was safer in the rear where he would carry out surgery, amputating arms and legs shattered by the heavy lead balls of Russian musket or cannon fire. But Peter felt comfortable in the company of his friend.

They chattered about life in London at the Reform Club, and yearned for the good meals they had taken for granted in that time of easy living. Eventually, they were on the top of the hills amongst the forest of shrubs and came across a villa of modest means with a veranda covered in honeysuckle, roses and clematis. The villa was also littered with broken music-stools, and chairs. The windows were smashed, and when Peter ducked inside, he returned to Ian to say, 'It appears that the home belonged to a Russian colleague, maybe a physician or surgeon.'

'Bloody senseless,' Ian grunted. They had become used to this scorched earth policy by their enemy, but the destruction of the pretty villas made little military sense.

That night, they camped at the little village of Eskel on the banks of the Katscha River. The village had also been vandalised by the retreating Russian army, smashing furniture and scattering personal possessions. A few of the residents returned, and the regiment was informed by them that the Russian army was demoralised by their defeat at Alma.

A mail delivery arrived, and Ian waited hopefully for a letter from Jane but was once again bitterly disappointed. There was absolutely no sense why she should not inform him of her condition. For all he knew, he might even be a father now. Never before had he felt so frustrated and helpless.

Peter and Herbert joined him in one of the deserted little houses for the night's bivouac. They recovered a small wooden table, lit a candle and sat around with a bottle of brandy Peter had been able to produce from his medical kit. As they had no glasses they shared the bottle, swigging from it in turn.

Ian gazed at Herbert, realising that the young man was barely seventeen years old, and yet his eyes were now those of an old man. He felt a wave of affection for the boy who was like a brother to him – if he only knew the truth . . .

'This country has its own charm,' Peter said, holding the bottle of brandy. 'The vineyards, flowers and forests. It is a shame to see it so destroyed by war.'

'I would rather be home,' Herbert slurred as the alcohol took hold.

'Ah, young Herbert, when you do return home, think of how all the pretty young ladies will be at your feet as you recount your heroic deeds,' Ian said, attempting to cheer the young man who he could see had been badly affected by the battle days before. 'Think how proud Alice will be of her little brother.'

'Alice has corresponded that she would rather have me back in London,' Herbert said, handing the bottle to Ian.

'Did she say the same for me?' Ian asked.

'No, she feels that Dr Campbell needs you to be at his side to protect him. You were born for war from what I have witnessed, and if that damned Jenkins continues to tell all who will listen what a bad officer you are, I will challenge him to a duel.'

'You will not challenge Mr Jenkins to a duel,' Ian said firmly. 'If he survives this war, I will.'

The three men spent the evening chatting about military matters, life at home and finally fell into sleep in the three beds they had found in the villa. The stuffing from the mattresses had been scattered but the weary men still slept fitfully in nightmares of exploding musketry and dying soldiers. During the evening, none had spoken of what lay ahead.

*

Despite the sleeting rain outside the window, Molly was warm, and well fed. She pored through the books of accounts, rectifying mistakes, and entering the expenditure and income. Whoever had been the previous bookkeeper had been sloppy, and Molly was actually finding spending that had not been accounted for.

She had been at the Forbes country estate for over a week, and was aware that her appointment was met with whispers from the staff of the kitchen to the servants in the front foyer. She was aware of the rumours because she had befriended a young stable boy who she had helped balance his pay with a few more pennies for his family. Molly was also aware that the boy had a crush on her, and she was pleased that she had at least one friend in the large staff of servants.

Molly had already written a letter to Conan, explaining her good fortune and praising the generosity of Miss Alice. Now she had a warm bed, clean clothes and employment that paid a better income than that of a seamstress. Molly knew that it would take a long time to receive a written reply and would sneak *The Times* paper whenever she could, to follow Mr Russell's accounts of the war in Crimea. There was not a night when Molly did not pray for the safety of Conan and her brothers.

On this bleak day, Molly worked studiously at the books and frowned. It appeared that Mr Charles was spending a lot of the estate's money, but dismissed her suspicions as she considered it was his right to do so.

As if conjuring the devil, she heard the door open to her small office, and turned to see who had entered without knocking. It was Charles. Immediately she could see that he was intoxicated as he stood in the doorway staring at her.

'I pray that you are happy in your work,' he slurred. 'Not every poor girl off the streets has been given your opportunities, although I have been informed by my sister you are much better than our last bookkeeper.'

'Thank you, sir,' Molly answered, uncomfortable in his presence. She sensed that the man standing in the doorway was leering at her. Charles walked over to Molly and placed his hands on her shoulders. Molly's body stiffened at his touch. She knew from experience that men such as Charles Forbes had the power to do as they wished. But she had a guardian angel when she heard the voice of Alice say, 'Charles, you must leave Miss Williams to do her work in peace.'

Charles withdrew his hands, and turning to his sister he said, 'I was just complimenting Miss Williams on the fine job she is doing.'

Alice hovered in the doorway until Charles brushed past her to return to his drinking.

'I hope my brother did not bother you,' Alice said gently, as if suspecting what had occurred before her timely inter-vention. 'He thinks he has a way with the ladies.'

'No, miss,' Molly lied, suspecting this would not be the last time she would be confronted by the master of the house. 'I can look after myself.'

'Good,' Alice said with a weak smile. Molly did not want to lose her wonderful job, but she was also not naive. What would she do if he came to her bed in the night, as she suspected he would?

*

The march south continued, and so did the dreaded shadow of cholera dogging the French and British armies. The regiment passed by beautiful snow-white stone cottages amongst the trees and vineyards. At one stage, Ian's company passed a chateau that obviously once belonged to a very wealthy person, and saw British soldiers from another regiment looting it. They appeared with armfuls of rich clothing, bronze art works and other items of value. Ian could see that his own men were eager to join the looting, but he roared his order not to break ranks. Ian did not believe in looting, and his men sullenly obeyed, watching an officer from a cavalry squadron ride away with a bronze statue. What was more valuable than loot lay ahead; a clear sparkling stream from which he ordered his company to fill their canteens before it was muddied by the passage of boots and hooves.

Then it was a struggle up yet another hill, but at least his men were not burdened by heavy looted prizes. In the early evening the army came to a halt, and Ian had orders passed down that he was to dispatch a section of riflemen to move forward as a protective party for Lord Raglan.

Eager to see what was ahead, Ian took command of ten riflemen from Herbert's platoon to follow Lord Raglan. They emerged from a wooded road into an open space, and were startled to encounter a large body of Russian infantry guarding a baggage train. Lord Raglan and his party of officers quickly spurred their horses back to the main body of the army, while Ian gave the order to his section to form a skirmish line. They were quickly joined by an artillery section, and a squadron of cavalry. As the guns were unlimbered, Ian gave the order to his section to fire on the retreating Russians. He was pleased to see around five of the enemy soldiers fall to his well-practised riflemen as the Russians fled out of sight, leaving their baggage train unguarded.

Ian saw a cavalry officer ride to the wagons and watched him begin to loot the legitimate spoils of war, and Ian turned to his own riflemen.

'Boys, take what you can,' he said and the men eagerly scrambled to take their place going through whatever stores they could in the wagons.

Ian decided he would also join them, and clambered into one of the wagons, whilst Conan and the Williams brothers did the same in another wagon, throwing expensive clothing over the side in search of more valuable, portable loot.

Ian found an ornate jewellery box which he flipped open. What he saw took his breath away; a heavy gold necklace with a diamond and blue sapphire attachment at its end. He also saw a pile of other valuable gold and precious stones in the box, which he snatched, and quickly pocketed. Ian knew what he had just found was a small fortune worth a king's ransom.

'Sir, look at this!' Conan yelled, triumphantly holding up a magnum of champagne. 'There's a lot more here.'

'Good show, corporal. Make sure you take as much as you can to share with the fellows in the company.'

Conan did not need encouragement and as he pulled away the stores in the wagon he found a sealed, wooden crate. Conan gasped when he was able to remove the lid, and saw wads of English pounds. Very quickly, he and the Williams brothers pocketed the glorious find, whilst the others of his section also made good discoveries of Russian coins and jewellery.

Ian returned his attention to the wagon he was scrounging through, finding even more precious jewellery, which he pocketed. Satisfied there was little else of portable value, he clambered from the wagon just as other soldiers arrived, hearing of the wonderful find. They too, joined in the pillaging that was sanctified under the rules of war.

Ian ordered his section to withdraw to the company lines, helping Conan and his section carry back as many bottles of champagne as they could. All the time, Ian's head was reeling from the knowledge of what was bulging in his pockets. It was his by right of war, and he understood why ancient armies would be distracted by such enemy baggage trains.

It was early evening when they returned, and Ian was joined by Herbert. Conan had insisted that Ian take two of the champagne bottles to celebrate their win.

'I would like you to find Dr Campbell and inform him that tonight, we wash down our salt pork and biscuits with champagne.'

Herbert grinned, and hurried away to the rear of the regiment in search of Peter, while Ian quietly made his way to a deserted section of the woods to carefully cache away his fortune in jewels. He tightly wrapped it all in a cotton cloth, and packed it into his haversack. Then he returned to the edge of the woods, where he met Peter and Herbert.

'Gentlemen, tonight we partake of good French wine, courtesy of our Russian foe.'

That night, Ian slept with his head beside his fortune with hopes of placing the beautiful gold necklace around Jane's throat. But all he dreamed of was the circle of stones and death.

TWENTY-THREE

Conan held the wad of pound notes he had counted. The three soldiers huddled away from their comrades in the chilly night, so they could not be seen.

'How much?' Owen asked.

'One thousand three hundred pounds,' Conan answered.

'What is that split three ways?' Edwin asked.

'We split it four ways,' Conan answered.

'Four ways?' Owen asked, puzzled at the maths.

'Yes,' Conan said. 'We include Molly in the split.'

The two brothers did not protest at their sister's inclusion, but Edwin asked, 'What if one of us gets killed?'

'Then we split it three ways,' Conan answered. 'I will hold Molly's share until we return home.'

'I heard that they recovered a chest of three thousand pounds,' Edwin said. 'Too bad we hadn't got to it first.'

Owen opened a magnum of champagne they had

recovered from the looted Russian baggage train, and the bottle was passed between the three to celebrate their windfall. But even as they swallowed down the fizzy alcoholic beverage, it was in each of their thoughts that they must survive whatever was ahead if they were to enjoy the financial fruits of their war.

★

It was a much happier army that marched the following day, as soldiers packed their kit with looted garments and trinkets. They marched through woods and along steep tracks without being harassed by the Russians, finally crossing the last river, the Tchernaya within a few short miles of Balaclava.

Ian stood with Captain Miles Sinclair gazing down at the tiny harbour of Balaclava.

'I'm no naval man, but it is obvious the harbour is too small to ride a fleet,' Miles said, and Ian agreed. He could see at least six British warships already in the harbour, acting as a blockade. Ian saw a crumbling ancient fort originally constructed well above the seashore, and mused that in its time, it would have been sufficient to protect the tiny port. Both men strode away from their high vantage point to rejoin their companies, as other officers took their place to observe the village of Balaclava on the coast. It was time to go down and occupy the little village unopposed, with its pretty villas and flower-covered gardens soon to be trampled under the boots of the British army.

Their entrance was met by the local Greek population with trays of fruit and flowers. Some had bread and salt, which was a traditional sign of submission.

Tents were landed by the navy, and the order was given to abandon the village which now was in a pitiful state due to the vast numbers of soldiers in it. The stench of cholera and dysentery pervaded, drowning the scent of flowers.

The tents were erected on the bleak heights overlooking the tiny harbour filled with warships and transports. Food and water became more plentiful, and Ian was given a large, spacious tent with a bed, table and a wood-burning heater to ward off the extreme chill of the approaching winter. He knew from the conferences he attended that there was a squabble between the two main allied armies of the French and British, as to how to take the main port of Sebastopol. The French favoured a siege, and the British an all-out assault on the Russian-held port city.

Ian knew that the inactivity of his company would lead to low morale, as his men shivered through the long nights and were confined to the regimental lines by day. Cholera still thinned the ranks of the soldiers, and Ian heard from a fellow officer that it was also raging in London. The medical theory of bad vapours causing the disease were scoffed at by Dr Campbell, who adhered to the theory it was a water-borne disease, so Ian ensured that all the water his men drank was first boiled. His rate of cholera patients was the lowest in the regiment. But the public in England still read of the appalling conditions of the sick and wounded in the Crimea. Not enough medical staff, medicines and even bandages. The pleas eventually stirred the civilian population in England, and a remarkable woman would offer her services to recruit women to travel to the war front to nurse the sick and wounded. Her name was Florence Nightingale.

*

Molly lay fully awake in her bed at the Forbes manor. First, she heard the creak on the stairs outside her bedroom. Then a short silence followed the sound of the door opening.

She tried to sit up in bed but felt the weight of Charles cover her. Molly fought, surprising Charles, who regained his feet.

'How dare you resist my advances!' he snarled. 'You have a choice between me bedding you, or packing your wretched belongings and leaving this house in the morning. It is your choice. A good job and me, or back on the streets.'

'I would prefer to return to the streets than let you have me,' Molly replied in a quavering voice.

'Then you have made your choice. I want you off the estate before mid-morning.'

Charles left the room, and Molly lay back against the pillow, shaking from the sobs that came easily. Her dreams of security shattered, and now she would have to return to the mean streets of London.

*

The chill of winter was becoming more apparent with each day in October. Ian sat beside Corporal Conan Curry in one of the trenches hewn out of the hard, stony earth with his telescope to his eye, watching the Russians in Sebastopol reinforcing their own earthworks. Ian could see an exposed Russian officer supervising the works to his front.

'Too far for a shot at that Muscovite officer,' Conan said, lowering his Enfield to rest on the edge of rocky earth of their trench.

'If you can't do it, no one can, Corporal Curry,' Ian said, and turned his back to lean against the side of the trench. Ian knew that morale was low in the regiment due to the inactivity. Whereas the adjoining French army had their military bands to play music each night, the British army had packed up its musical instruments, and assigned the bandsmen the duty of being stretcher bearers. The weather was growing colder by the day. He had hoped that his riflemen could at least take shots at the enemy within view, but they remained frustratingly out of range. Ian had an idea and sought out the colonel at his lunch. Ian proposed that he take a platoon of the best marksmen out during the night to close the range with the Russian defences.

The colonel agreed, but stipulated that Lieutenant Jenkins' platoon be the section to be used. Ian was not pleased with the choice, and argued the three best marksmen from Mr Forbes' platoon also accompany them. Chewing on the leg of a roasted chicken, the colonel finally agreed. At least Ian had been able to get a small concession, and did not tell his commanding officer that he, too, would go forward with the selected riflemen.

That evening, Ian briefed Jenkins and his men of the mission. None seemed very eager – especially Jenkins.

'What should happen if we are caught in the open by Russian cavalry?' Jenkins asked.

'I have Mr Forbes' men prepared to cover our withdrawal,' Ian replied. 'You are honoured with the opportunity to engage the enemy, Mr Jenkins.'

Jenkins did not appear to feel the honour. After dark, the riflemen moved forward after all loose uniform fittings were tested not to make any sound. The men used the lights of the Russian defences as a guide, and Ian moved quietly with Jenkins. Ian had been counting the paces until he was confident that the distance brought them within range of the forward defences.

'Pass the order for the men to deploy themselves to any cover they may find,' Ian whispered, and the word was passed down the line of advancing soldiers.

When they were halted, the men made the best of any concealment they could find in the dark and waited for the sun to rise.

Ian had carried his Enfield rifle and his pistol. He had left his cumbersome sword in his tent.

They watched and waited and, just after the sun was above the horizon, the first Russian soldiers appeared at their posts along the line, unaware of the British marksmen only two hundred yards out.

Beside Ian was Corporal Curry and the two Williams brothers. Ian had instructed them to seek out any obvious officers and senior NCOs they may be able to target.

'There!' Ian whispered, spotting an officer in his fancy uniform. 'There is your target.'

Conan carefully rested his rifle, took a breath and slowly released it, squeezing the trigger at the same time. The rifle fired and the officer dropped from sight. Conan's shot was followed by a volley from the other concealed British soldiers, and more exposed Russian soldiers fell from sight. The sudden sharpshooting from no man's land had caught the enemy by complete surprise.

Loading the rifled musket from the prone position was difficult and the riflemen were forced to kneel to do so. It was then that Ian could see how exposed they were on the plain between the lines, and wondered if he had made a terrible mistake. He had hardly chastised himself when Conan yelled, 'Sir! Cossacks!'

Ian swung his attention to their flank where he saw around fifty horsemen gathering to launch an attack on the outnumbered marksmen. They were a few hundred yards away, but it would not take long before their heavy swords would be sweeping down on the line of skirmishers.

'Mr Jenkins, give the order to fall back to our lines in an orderly manner,' Ian yelled to the officer a few yards away. Jenkins did not acknowledge, frozen by fear. Ian leapt to his feet and bellowed, 'Riflemen, to me.'

The terrified soldiers snapped from their fear at the sound of Ian's voice, and quickly ran to him. Already, musket balls filled the air from the Russian lines, and it would not be long before their artillery opened fire. Ian could hear the thundering of hooves on the plain as the Cossacks had assembled in an attack formation. He could see that the situation was desperate. Jenkins was cowering on his knees with his hands over his head.

'Form a line facing the enemy and move towards our own lines,' Ian said. He did not bother to order a square as it would have no use when caught with fire from the Russian lines, and the rapidly advancing cavalry. The single line with its face to the advancing Cossacks moved at a trot until Ian could see the sun glint on the raised sabres.

'Left turn and fire!' Ian yelled, raising his own rifle. The men obeyed and the rifle fire of their Enfields brought horses and Cossacks spilling on the grassy plain. But it did not deter them, and Ian knew that they would not have time to reload before the horsemen were on them. He glanced to his rear to see Jenkins still cowering and ordered Conan to grab the junior officer and drag him back to their lines. Conan sprinted to Jenkins, grabbed him by his jacket and hauled him to his feet, shouting in his ear to run. The situation was desperate until a withering fire of Enfields erupted on the Cossack flank from the red-coated riflemen rising from the concealment of the long, dry grass. The enfilading rifle fire smashed the attack as horsemen milled in confusion at the unseen enemy tearing their ranks apart. Ian exhorted his men to reload, whilst their officer, Lieutenant Jenkins, continued to crouch in the grass where Conan had dumped him. Jenkins had not even bothered to use his pistol.

Ian could see Herbert commanding his second row of men to fire as the first rank reloaded. The confused

Cossacks wheeled about, and retreated, leaving many dead and wounded on the plain. Wounded horses snorted pitifully, and Ian realised that his band of skirmishers were now out of musket range of the Russian frontline but not their artillery guns.

Ian ordered Jenkins' men to withdraw to their trenches in good order, and also realised with relief that none had been killed or wounded. Jenkins trailed along like a whipped dog, but raised his head when they were safely in their own lines. Herbert had withdrawn his men to the lines as well, and Ian sought him out with a broad smile. A cheer from adjoining regiments was heard along the line, welcoming the men home.

'Herbert, my gratitude for you disobeying my orders to remain in the lines.'

'I felt that we needed to be further forward to provide support for your mission,' Herbert said, basking in the success of his efforts. 'When you departed, I had my men move forward, and take up positions in the long grass behind you. I guess I have a good teacher in my company commander.'

'Sir, the colonel wishes to confer with you,' a breathless soldier said, approaching him along the trench.

Ian followed the soldier until they came to the colonel's tent, and Ian was partially surprised to see Lieutenant Jenkins in the company of the commanding officer. Ian saluted the colonel.

'Captain Forbes, it disturbs me when one of your own officers has levelled a charge of your reckless behaviour in the previous hours,' the colonel said. 'Mr Jenkins is a man of very high standing in London, and I must put stock in his allegation concerning your behaviour.'

Ian was stunned. After all, it had been the colonel who had sanctioned the mission, but Ian also knew it would not be tactful for him to remind the commanding officer of this.

'Sir, I acknowledge that there was some risk in what I planned, but that is the nature of warfare. We succeeded in inflicting heavy casualties on the Russians without the loss of one man in the regiment. It has been good for the morale of the men as this inactivity lays heavy on them.'

'That is not the point, Captain Forbes, the point is that Mr Jenkins feels you went beyond careful consideration of your plan. He has informed me that you were nearly wiped out when the Cossacks' cavalry intervened. It appears you had not calculated for that.'

'Mr Forbes was in position to counter their intervention,' Ian said.

'But you did not mention his part in your original plan to Mr Jenkins, and the men he commanded,' the colonel countered. 'I agree with Mr Jenkins that your brother's timely intervention was not something you had originally planned.' Ian knew what his commanding officer was saying was true. Ian had commanded Herbert to remain with his men in the trenches, but also remembered how Jenkins had lost control of his platoon in the retreat back to their lines. But this was not the time to raise that issue.

'Mr Forbes used his initiative,' Ian grudgingly agreed. 'I have since commended him for his foresight.'

'Then it is agreed that your actions were reckless,' the colonel said. 'Accept my reprimand, Captain Forbes, and apologise to Mr Jenkins for the danger you recklessly placed he and his men in.'

Ian was fuming. He was to apologise to the cowardly young man whose only claim to being an officer was that his family were a powerful force in London society. If Ian had his way, he would have charged him with cowardice.

But that did not seem to apply to officers – only the rank and file. Ian turned to Jenkins, who was smirking.

'My apologies, Mr Jenkins,' he grudgingly said, and the colonel smiled.

'Good show. I expect that you will take notice of any concerns Mr Jenkins may raise in the future concerning any operational missions you may plan. That is all. You are both dismissed.'

Ian glared at Jenkins, who still stood smirking at Ian's reprimand. Ian saluted the colonel and they exited the tent.

'Mr Jenkins,' Ian said when they were outside. 'Just remember that you are still under my command, and under military law you will still obey my orders.'

'That may not be for very long, Captain Forbes,' Jenkins said. 'Have I failed to mention that my family have just purchased me a majority? Oh, I must have forgotten. It should be gazetted by now. I have been granted leave to return to England, and when I return I shall be a major on Lord Raglan's staff.' Jenkins strolled away, leaving Ian in a state of near shock. If what he said was true, the incompetent and arrogant fool was about to be promoted to be Ian's superior officer.

TWENTY-FOUR

Molly had trudged the highway back to London. At the point of exhaustion on the cold bleak day, she had been fortunate to be given a carriage trip by a family of Quakers, who let her off not far from the bustling city centre.

Molly thanked them for their kindness. She knew that she must reach the Forbes London house to apologise to Miss Alice for resigning so suddenly from her employment. She did not want Alice to think that she had been ungrateful for the wonderful opportunity she had been afforded.

Alice was upset to see the young woman in such a state of dishevelment at her front door. She immediately had Molly ushered in, and a blanket placed over her shoulders while ordering hot tea and cake.

Molly's shivering ceased as the blanket and hot tea warmed her body.

'What has happened?' Alice asked. 'I can see that you have suffered hardship.'

'I have come to apologise for leaving your employment, miss,' Molly said. 'But my situation became intolerable.'

'Intolerable?' Alice queried with a frown.

'I do not wish to elaborate, but I was left with no other choice than to leave,' Molly replied. 'I wish it had been otherwise, as I am now destitute.'

'Was it Charles?' Alice asked in an angry voice. 'I know my brother's disposition towards serving girls.'

'If you may please, I do not wish to cause any embarrassment to you or your family,' Molly said, sipping from her cup of tea. 'I only wish my Conan and my brothers were here, safe from the battlefields.'

'I also wish my brothers and fiancé were here,' Alice echoed. 'From what I have read in the papers, the war is not going well for our men in the Crimea. Dr Campbell writes of the terrible conditions facing the sick and wounded. Herbert and Sam hardly write, but I know they must be in those terrible battles Mr Russell's dispatches describe.'

'I only wish if they cannot be with us, I could be with them,' Molly sighed, and Alice's face lit up.

'Do you think that you could tend to sick and wounded soldiers?' she asked.

Molly looked at Alice. 'I could,' she said. 'But I am confused as to what you mean.'

'I know a lady, Miss Florence Nightingale, who is currently calling for single ladies to go with her to the Eastern front. She has already assembled some Papist nuns, and will be leaving next week. I know if I spoke to her and introduced you, Miss Nightingale would surely consider you for her organisation. What do you say to that?'

'Oh, I would give anything to have the opportunity

to be near Conan, and my brothers!' Molly said, almost spilling her cup of tea in her excitement.

'From all that I have come to learn about you, Molly, I know that you have lived a harsh life, and that you are a caring and intelligent young woman who is hardy enough to endure the life I expect will require great fortitude and compassion. I am sure I will be able to convince Miss Nightingale to employ you. I will personally provide a reference.'

'Miss, if you are able to have me employed, I may even be able to seek out Dr Campbell, and thank him for having me released from prison. It would mean a lot to a poor, wretched girl as myself.'

'You may be poor but you are not wretched,' Alice said gently. 'Come, you are in need of a hot bath, and some new clothes.'

Molly rose from the seat, following Alice who was already ordering a hot bath to be prepared. As Molly followed Alice, she reflected on the goodness of this kind and gentle woman who shared the common bond of having men at the battlefront facing death on a daily basis. Divided by fortune and class, they were united in their fears for those they held most dear to them.

Within a day, Alice had been able to convince Miss Nightingale to employ Molly. She conveniently forgot to mention that Molly had been in prison, as only those of the most impeccable character were enlisted by Miss Nightingale.

The young Welshwoman prepared to steam with the contingent of nurses, headed for the battlefront of the Crimea, and Alice personally went to the docks to see Molly off.

★

A newly minted lieutenant, barely seventeen years old, was appointed to fill the vacancy left by Jenkins in the regiment. Ian met him at his tent, and was saddened to see how unprepared he was for the task of leading men in battle. Lieutenant William Sutton was awkward – as were many young men of his age – and stuttered. Ian felt sorry for him, and had also learned that he was a second son to a wealthy merchant family. Ian thought he was like a puppy, and took Herbert aside after he had dismissed the newly appointed officer.

'I want you to teach Mr Sutton as much as you can in the short time that we have before the next battle with the Russians.'

Herbert now had the brutal experience of a major battle, and Ian was proud of how Herbert had proved himself an excellent junior officer. The older soldiers under his command respected him, and Colour Sergeant Leslie was devoted to Herbert.

'I have heard that Mr Jenkins has departed for England,' Herbert said. 'I have also heard that his men lost all faith in him after that incident we had with the Cossacks. His men now accept your leadership as our company commander.'

'Nice to hear,' Ian said. 'But when the bastard returns, he will be appointed above you and I. I fear that his incompetence will have its influence on us.'

'You do know that Jenkins is distantly related to members of the Queen's court,' Herbert said.

'I was not aware of that,' Ian said, careful to cover his past by adding, 'I must have been too long in the colonies.'

As they chatted, the sound of artillery bombardment from both sides provided a constant background din. French, man-of-war naval ships fired from the sea at the formidable fortified town of Sebastopol, and on land, both Russian and allied guns were engaged in battery duels.

Suddenly, the ground shook under Ian and Herbert's feet, and the roar of an explosion, much louder even than when a magazine in the French lines exploded minutes earlier, shattered the day. Cheers rose from the throats of the British soldiers observing the artillery engagement. Both men stepped outside to see smoke rising from the centre of the besieged city.

'A direct hit on an ammunition magazine,' Herbert guessed, observing the huge pillar of smoke slowly rising above the town.

'But it has not slowed down the Russian batteries,' Ian added, as the cannons continued from within the fortifications of the city. 'I fear the only way to take the city is with the use of an infantry assault.' Both men fell silent, hoping that the massive allied artillery bombardments from land and sea on the stone walls of the city would finally cause the Russians to surrender.

A week passed of continuing artillery bombardment. Ian knew that his company were growing restless as the stench of rotting bodies filled the air. Disease had reduced the British army ranks, and although Russian deserters provided intelligence that the city was on the verge of collapse, the allied armies were too weak to attack.

Then everything changed towards the end of October, when the Russians began advancing towards Balaclava to break the Anglo–French siege. Rumours had persisted that they would attempt to do so, but when they did, the British army was caught off-guard.

'Stand to!' The order went down the lines of the regiment, and soldiers scrambled to grab their arms. Ian hurried from his tent, strapping on his sword and slinging his Enfield over his shoulder. He had been able to purchase a much heavier Colt Dragoon revolver from a trader who brought supplies from London, but also kept his gift from Samuel. Armed to the teeth, he glanced around to see that his senior NCOs were quickly assembling the soldiers for the fast march across the undulating, thistle-covered ground before the ridges ahead. Ian could see a distant mist of smoke rising from the opposite side of the rise before them, and clearly heard the roar of guns. He knew that the Turkish soldiers were appointed to hold the high ground, but to his dismay, he could see through his telescope the Turks leaving their redoubts as the Russian infantry poured over them.

As Ian advanced ahead of his company under clear, blue skies, he could see the other companies of the regiment doing the same. Ian noted Herbert was carrying the regimental colours, the flag fluttering in the slight breeze. As Ian advanced, he sensed that this was not going to be like Alma. It was the Russians who were on the attack and had already seized many of the defences on the ridges and hills ahead. Beyond was a valley. Ian wondered what they would see when they were able to gain the high ground, with his fears attempting to overcome him.

'C'mon lads!' Ian yelled, and the fear began to leave him. A buzzing in his ears made him aware that his blood was rising, and he no longer experienced the fear of death. This was his mission in life – to lead men in battle. On the regiment's right, Ian could see the Turkish soldiers being hunted down by squadrons of Cossacks, slashing with sabres, and cutting down the hapless Ottoman troops. He could hear the cries of the elated Russian cavalrymen, and the screams of the Turkish soldiers.

Ian could see their own heavy cavalry regiment wheeling into formation to counter the Russian breakthrough of the high ground before them. Ian was not aware that a Scottish highland regiment was already engaging the Russian forces on the other side of the hills, and had slowed down the overwhelming numbers of Russian infantry scrambling up the hillsides. With disciplined fire and sheer courage, the Scots met the lines of Russian soldiers.

The regiment came to a halt, and the men watched as the light and heavy cavalry squadrons of Scots and Irish, vastly outnumbered by their Russian counterparts, formed their ranks. Ian watched as the Russian horsemen descended the slope at the British cavalry. First at a slow canter, then at a trot. Ian heard the bugle call followed by a cheer from the British cavalry before they made their charge directly into the centre of the Russians. Sabres flashed in the sunlight, and the British squadrons smashed through the first line of Russian horsemen; the Scots and Irish numbers were reduced by the uneven ferocious attack, but they continued onwards to assault the second ranks of the Russian cavalry units, now charging at full strength against the surviving British cavalrymen.

Ian had now retired to the ranks of his rifle company, and stood by Herbert, holding the regimental flag.

'God help them,' Herbert said, and Ian nodded just as the remnants of the Scots and Irish horsemen broke through the final rank of Russians. In their wake, the British cavalry had left many Russians dead and mortally wounded on the bloody battleground, and the Russian lines were in disarray.

'Look!' Herbert said, and Ian turned to see the colourful uniforms of the Dragoons and Royals enter the fight, charging at the broken ranks of Russian cavalry, following up in the gaps created by the initial mad charge by the Scots and Irish cavalrymen. The unexpected second wave of British horsemen caused the Russian cavalry to break and run.

A mighty cheer went up from the riflemen observing the battle, and Ian was one of those who cheered loudest.

'By God, they have seen the Muscovites off,' Herbert said as the plain was now covered in dead and wounded men and horses of both sides. When the celebrating ceased, Ian realised that they could not conclude they had won the war – simply a battle – and ordered his skirmishers forward in the event of a counterattack.

On that same day, the light cavalry troopers were bitterly disappointed not to have been used in the decisive attack on their Russian counterparts. As Ian advanced with his regiment to the heights, the light cavalry was already forming up to charge down a valley at Russian artillery emplacements. Even Ian could see that it was a disastrous tactic, and later known as the ill-fated Charge of the Light Brigade. But, as an infantryman, Ian was more interested in keeping himself and his men alive, and less in the fate of the glamorous cavalrymen.

Ian's company found itself engaged in firing on the odd Russian or two they saw in the distance, but the range proved to be too far for any serious damage, although it was good for the British soldier's morale to be able to be a part of the fighting that day.

Towards dusk, the order was given to his regiment to fall back on Balaclava, as the Russians had successfully manned the heights and the valleys beyond. As they retreated, Ian could see how they had turned a victory into a defeat. Worse still, Ian realised, they had lost the main road for their supplies from the tiny port of Balaclava to their encampments.

'Sir, did we win a great battle today?' Private Owen Williams asked marching beside Ian.

'I don't think so, Private Williams,' Ian answered wearily. Not once that day had he drawn his sword, Ian thought. 'We will have to engage the Muscovites again to truly win this war.'

The men marched, their faces chilled by the coming winter.

★

It was warm inside the Brooks Club. Charles Forbes liked being a member because the club had a reputation for high-stakes gambling. The three-storeyed yellow brick and Portland stone building in St James Street, Westminster, was also close to the Forbes family offices. Inside the luxurious club, decorated in neo-classical style, Charles found himself sitting opposite Major Jenkins, resplendent in his ornate officer's uniform, and recently returned from the Crimea. Charles well knew the officer from past social events in London, and Charles envied the British officer's well-established social standing in London society. The two men were in partnership with others, and when Charles eyed his opponent in the four-man game, he could see a certain amount of cunning. Whist was the game, and the amount of money was set for the points won in the game.

Charles called for a French deck of fifty-two cards, and they were dealt to each player. Smoke from cigars and pipes filled the room, and the port wine flowed freely.

The game commenced, and the banter between gentlemen opened with Charles saying, 'Major Jenkins, I believe that you have recently returned to London from the Eastern front.'

'That is correct, sir,' Jenkins said, fanning his cards into suite order. 'I had the honour of serving with your grand-father's old regiment.'

'Ah, you must have met my brothers, Herbert and Samuel, whilst you served with the regiment,' Charles said, glancing up from his cards at Jenkins, puffing on a big cigar.

'I did,' Jenkins replied. 'Herbert was a fellow ensign, and your brother was my commanding officer. At least he was until my family generously purchased my majority.'

'What was your opinion of my brothers?' Charles asked.

'Herbert is a brave but misguided officer,' Jenkins said. 'I do not wish to dishonour your family name, but in my and many other's opinions, your brother Samuel is a dangerous fool who does not know how to act as an English officer. He is not a gentleman, and the soldiers call him the Queen's colonial behind his back, for his unprofessional behaviour. They say he is more colonial than a true English gentleman. I beg that you do not think that casts aspersions on you or your father, Sir Archibald.'

'Of course not.' Charles shrugged. 'The family have a similar opinion of my brother, Samuel. I must admit that we are not very close.'

The hands were being displayed for points and Charles and his partner on the other side of the round card table were scoring high, which Charles was thankful for. In the past, Charles had been forced to embezzle money from the family funds to secure his massive gambling losses at the club.

Near midnight, and much wine later, the games came to an end. The final scores were tallied and Charles triumphantly announced how much money was owed to he, and his card partner, by Major Jenkins and his partner. Jenkins looked uncomfortable when the result was announced by Charles.

'It seems that I must call on you as a gentleman to take my chit on what I owe you, sir,' Jenkins said across the table.

'I would like to do that, but the club rules say you must pay me now.'

Jenkins leaned back in his chair with his hands in his

pockets. 'Forbes, I do not have on hand the substantial amount I owe you at the present moment.'

'Are you returning to the Crimea per chance?' Charles asked, leaning forward across the table.

'I am,' Jenkins answered. 'I am to be posted to Lord Raglan's staff.'

'I think that I could forget this debt in return for a small favour. Perhaps we can discuss this somewhere more private?'

Both men rose from the table, and walked to a corner of the room where Charles knew they would not be overheard. He explained how the large gambling debt could be written off, and Major Jenkins readily agreed. After all, they both had the same enemy.

TWENTY-FIVE

It was a desperate time.

Fog and mist coupled with drizzling rain obscured the massive waves of Russians swarming out of Sebastopol in an attempt to break the siege at a village called Inkerman. The day saw the fog rent by the shells of the Russian artillery, cutting swathes through the British ranks advancing to meet the Russian infantry.

Ian led his company through scrubby bushes and thorns, his sword in one hand and the big Colt Dragoon revolver in the other. Over his shoulder was slung his Enfield. He could see that the terrain was causing his well-disciplined ranks to break up, and all the time they were not aware of the location of the enemy. And every now and then, a soldier would drop, as a musket ball or shrapnel found its mark.

To Ian's left, he could see the trio who now made it a point to be close to the company commander. Ian was about to bark an order for them to fall in with their platoon, but refrained. A strange bond had formed between the four of them.

Before Ian could get his bearing on the sound of musketry, the Russian infantry loomed out of the fog. They came forward yelling, bayonets levelled at British troops' stomachs.

Ian did not have to give the order to fire as he fell back to the first rank of his company, and realised that he was standing with Herbert holding the regimental colours, and Colour Sergeant Leslie standing steadily with the young lieutenant. The explosive ripping sound of the Enfields being discharged tore through the closely packed ranks of the advancing Russian infantry, and it was quickly followed by a second deadly volley from the ranks of the men behind the first, who were kneeling, desperately reloading their rifled muskets.

The Russian ranks faltered for a moment under the deadly fire of the British, but they quickly recovered, and came on through the mist with blood curdling roars of anger. There was around fifty yards between the two combatants, and Ian quickly realised that his company was outnumbered by at least two to one. He raised his pistol at arm's length, and knew he could not miss the closely packed Russian infantry. He fired rapidly until his revolver was empty, and prepared to meet the onslaught with his sword. He did not have to wait long; the enemy was on them with stabbing bayonets, met by his own riflemen with their own bayonets.

'On them, boys!' Ian yelled unnecessarily, lunging at a Russian with his sword. The soldier was quick, parrying Ian's lunge with the end of his rifle, but the Russian left himself open to a bayonet thrust from Corporal Curry. Ian raised his sword, but it was snatched from his hand by a Russian soldier. Ian had no weapon readily available to defend himself, and stumbled a couple of paces back. One of the Williams brothers stepped forward, engaging the Russian who had snatched Ian's sword, giving Ian time to unsling the rifle over his shoulder, which already had the bayonet fixed.

Now he fought as his men did, with rifle and bayonet.

The second rank of Ian's company quickly stepped into the gaps left by their dead and wounded comrades, holding tenaciously against the greater odds pitted against them.

The regimental flag continued to fly aloft in Herbert's hands, and men screamed for their mothers in two languages as death came to them, mingled with the sound of metal on metal. Grunting, cursing soldiers attempted to overpower their adversaries, while Ian's hearing rang with the noise of the occasional shot being fired nearby.

Nothing mattered as an officer except to stay alive like any other soldier. He turned his attention to his left, where he saw Corporal Curry attempting to ward off three Russians at once. Ian immediately pushed his way to him, and immediately lunged a feint at one of the corporal's adversaries. It worked, as the Russian swung his rifle barrel to deflect the tip of the bayonet which did not come as expected. He had exposed his body and Ian thrust again, the bayonet sinking into the other man's stomach. Ian twisted the bayonet to cause greater internal injury. It was not an immediate death strike but enough to disable the soldier, who now sank to his knees in agony, gripping the barrel of Ian's rifle in his futile desperation. Ian used all his strength to yank the bayonet out and was just in time to use the rifle butt as a club in the face of another bearded Russian, this one attempting to stab him with a sword. The edge slashed lightly across Ian's neck but his counter-blow caused the Russian to reel back. Ian was vaguely aware that his opponent must be an officer, but the sword was that of a cavalryman. The two squared off, and Ian sensed that his opponent was very good at using the sword. Eye to eye, the moment had arrived when one of them would be dead. Ian remembered that he had not yet fired his rifle, and pulled the trigger. The Minie bullet slammed into the Russian's chest, causing him to fall backwards. The bayonet against sabre duel was over. Ian saw Private Owen Williams bayoneted in the shoulder fall to the earth, a Russian soldier poised to deliver the fatal stab into his exposed body. Ian leapt at the Russian with his already blood-tipped bayonet, and thrust it into the enemy's armpit. Distracted, the Russian squirmed in agony, giving Owen time to recover his Enfield and thrust upwards, burying the bayonet in the wounded Russian's chest.

Ian withdrew his bayonet while Owen scrambled to his feet.

When Ian glanced over his shoulder, he could see a contingent of Russian soldiers desperately fighting towards the regimental colours. Herbert was using the staff to ward off the hands reaching for it, and Colour Sergeant Leslie was down on the ground choking the life out of a Russian. Without hesitating, Ian pushed his way towards the colour party, clubbing and stabbing as he did. A Russian had his back to Ian. Ian stabbed him in the back, feeling the bayonet hit bone, before sliding through the soldier's body to rip through his chest. When the Russian's body fell at Ian's feet, it jerked the rifle from his hands. Ian quickly recovered the only weapon he had left; the small calibre revolver Samuel had given him. He could see the desperate expression on Herbert's face as he continued to use the flag staff as a weapon, and was screaming incoherently as he did so. Ian was able to stand beside him, firing into the mass of enemy scrambling to capture the colours.

Then suddenly Corporal Curry and the Williams brothers stood with the besieged colour party. Their ferocious and desperate stand was telling on the Russians, who fell back. Ian was suddenly aware through the heavy mist of the day that the Russians were retreating. The company had held in the vicious melee of hand-to-hand combat.

But, as the mist began to dissolve, the full horror was revealed. Russian and British soldiers lay in jumbled heaps. The wounded of both sides attempted to crawl away, and the pitiful cries rose as a moaning wail. Unknown to the company was the intervention of French cavalry, slowly turning the tide of battle as the rain began to fall.

The order was given to retreat with what remained of the rifle brigades, and Ian's company stumbled back to form a new defensive line. Sergeant majors removed roll books, calling the names of their comrades. Many did not answer. As to who had won the battle of Inkerman, Ian did not know. His war had been measured in the yards around him and the regimental colours. But a passing staff officer informed Ian that the Russians had withdrawn, and that meant their overwhelming numbers had been defeated by the resolute defence of the British and French troops.

Ian could see that Herbert was trembling as he stood, still holding the bullet-riddled regimental flag. He also saw that blood oozed from a shoulder wound Private Owen Williams had received from a bayonet. Edwin was consoling him, and Ian also saw that Corporal Curry had been wounded. He sat on the wet earth in the rain, gripping his blood-soaked upper thigh. In the distance, Ian could hear the crash of artillery, and faint cries of wounded men from the sister companies of his regiment.

'Sarn't major,' Ian said to his senior NCO who had completed the butcher's bill of dead and wounded.

'Collect a party of litter bearers, and search the field for our wounded.'

'Sah,' the company sergeant major replied, standing to attention. He quickly found the bandsmen who were assigned to carry litters.

Ian turned to Conan holding his leg. 'Corporal Curry, report as wounded,' he commanded. 'And make sure that Private Williams is also tended to.'

Conan looked up at Ian. 'I only have a bit of a cut along my leg, sir,' he said. 'I just need a bandage, and I will be right to rejoin the fight with the lads.'

Ian could see the pain in the soldier's eyes, admiring his courage. Both men had come a long way from the dusty, dry plains, nestled at the bottom of the range of hills known as the Blue Mountains to this place of death.

'Conan,' Ian said quietly. 'Do as you are ordered, and if Dr Campbell gives you permission to return, then you will.'

Through pain-filled eyes, Conan looked up at Ian. The use of his first name in the familiar came as a surprise to the Irishman. 'I will, sir.' Ian helped him to his feet and towards two litter bearers who had joined the company.

'Sir, that fifty pounds me brother and I stole from you back home, I want to repay it,' Conan said in a quiet voice as they made their way to the litter.

'Where would you get fifty pounds?' Ian asked.

'We had a bit of luck back on that Muscovite baggage train,' Conan said. 'I would like to settle scores.'

'Keep it, Conan,' Ian said. 'You have more than earned the money since we arrived here. Nothing much matters more than surviving. Besides, I had some luck that day, too.'

'We are a couple of colonial bushrangers,' Conan chuckled, and Ian grinned.

★

That evening, Ian sat with Herbert around a small fire they had made. Ian passed Herbert a flask of brandy.

'Take a good drink,' he said. 'It will help settle your nerves.'

Herbert did. His whole body still trembled from the experiences of the savage hand-to-hand fighting. Ian secretly acknowledged that he could barely keep his own fears in check, and tried to block out the images that flashed in his mind of death at such close quarters. The rain had turned to drizzle, and the night was bitterly cold as they hunched over the barely flickering flames of the campfire.

'How much longer do you think our luck will hold out?' Herbert asked, staring intently at the flickering flames. 'So many of the company died today, and yet, we are still alive.'

'Only God can answer that question,' Ian replied, taking a long sip of the fiery liquid. 'Anyway, I promised Alice that I would take care of you. A promise is a promise.'

A figure loomed out of the night. Ian glanced up to see Corporal Curry standing over them, leaning on a length of stick.

'Dr Campbell bandaged the wound, and said I was fit for service, sir,' he said. 'But Private Owen Williams is being sent to some hospital away from the Crimea.'

'Join us, Corporal,' Ian said, waving the brandy flask in the air. 'We shall drink to our glorious victory today, and remember those who are unable to share our luck. To the brave lads of the regiment who fell here today,' Ian said, raising the flask, and passing it to Conan who, in turn, echoed the toast to the dead.

'Sir, I should go and tell Edwin about Owen's fate,' Conan said.

'You are excused, Corporal Curry, and I would add that you fought damn well today. You are a credit to us colonials.'

'Thank you, sir,' Conan said, standing up and gazing

into the darkness dotted by the many small fires of the night. 'We had good leaders.'

He walked away, leaving Ian and Herbert alone.

'I think I should return to my men,' Herbert said, and Ian nodded. When Herbert was gone, Ian felt the weariness overcome him. As desperately tired as he was, when he lay down on the earth under his greatcoat, he had trouble closing his eyes. Sleep finally came, and the nightmares returned. None cared when they heard the whimpering, for they were being echoed as the soldiers sought sleep in the night.

In his dreams Ian kept seeing the circle of stones, and now he associated them as a circle of death. The silence from Jane haunted him.

*

Molly stood outside the huge, former Turkish barracks located near the Ottoman capital of Constantinople. It stood at three levels and was designed as a massive rectangular building with an open parade ground. The British army had taken over the barracks and converted them into a hospital.

Molly was not alone. As they waited to enter the hospital, she was surrounded by fifteen Catholic nuns, wearing their habits, and a small group of young ladies Florence Nightingale had recruited in England.

Both trepidation and excitement buzzed amongst the party of women waiting to enter the hospital, and an army surgeon covered in blood greeted them.

Molly was close enough to hear the conversation that passed between Miss Nightingale, and the gruff, army surgeon. Florence was in her mid-thirties and wore her long dark hair in a tight bun, parted in the middle, as was the style of the day.

'I must be honest, Miss Nightingale,' the doctor said. 'We were informed that you were coming, but protested that an army hospital is not the appropriate place for women to act as nurses. You will be exposed to the horrors of war in such a place, and it is well known that ladies are of a delicate nature.'

Undaunted, Florence stood her ground. 'We will see, doctor,' she said firmly. 'I know how overwhelmed your staff is dealing with the sick and wounded. We have all read the reports in the newspapers at home. So, we will see how delicate my staff are when dealing with the fine soldiers of the Queen.'

Florence turned to her party, giving the order to enter the hospital.

Molly followed and the first thing that struck her was the terrible stench of putrefaction, vomit, and unwashed bodies.

Then she saw the men laying about on the floors in their own filth; bloody, dirty bandages wrapped around the stumps of amputated arms and legs. Men whimpered or moaned in pain as the women walked amongst them, some of the soon-to-be nurses holding handkerchiefs to their noses in an attempt to hide the foul stench of the over-crowded ward.

'One of our first tasks will be to scrub out the hospital,' Florence said to the accompanying army surgeon. 'Then we need to organise these men onto clean beds.' The doctor shrugged.

'You will have to find the items you need yourself,' he said. 'We are too busy dealing with the wounded.'

'I will,' Florence said. 'But first, I want to see where my nurses will be quartered.'

The doctor called to an orderly, an old man who had once been a soldier. 'Show Miss Nightingale her quarters,' he said and strode away to continue operating on the many wounded being shipped to them from the Crimea. The battle of Inkerman had placed his staff of surgeons under great stress, with the numbers of wounded flowing in, and, always, the cholera cases continuing to mount.

Molly was overwhelmed by the work ahead of her, and her nursing sisters.

She hardly had the heart to look at the many wounded and sick soldiers in their bloody uniforms, fighting back tears for their piteous plight.

'Molly?'

The barely whispered question came from a soldier sitting against one of the walls, and Molly turned to see who had called her name. She stared at the dirty and unshaven man, his uniform was covered in blood.

'Owen!' she gasped, stepping past other wounded men to reach him. When she did, she knelt beside her brother. 'Is it really you?'

Owen tried to reach up to touch his sister's face. 'I must be dead,' he said hoarsely. 'How is it possible that you are here in this hellhole?'

'It is a long story, but how are Conan and Edwin?' she asked, tears welling in her eyes.

'Last time I saw them, they were well. But that was many days ago,' Owen said. 'I got a Muscovite bayonet through the shoulder, and they sent me here. Oh, what a joy to see your face one more time before the grim reaper takes me.'

'You will not die, Owen Williams,' Molly said firmly. 'I have come to look after you, as you did for me when we were young.'

Tears streamed down both Molly's and Owen's faces as Molly gripped her brother's hands. 'What can I do for you?' she asked.

'Water,' Owen gasped.

'Miss Williams,' Florence said behind her. 'You must come along. There will be time later to talk to the soldiers.'

Molly rose obediently to her feet, reluctant to let go of her brother's hands. He smiled weakly and let go as Molly joined Florence.

'It is not a good idea to become familiar with the soldiers,' Florence said firmly.

'He is my brother,' Molly replied, wiping away her tears with the back of her hand as she stumbled through the rows of sick and wounded men.

Florence did not answer immediately. Then she said gently, 'They are all our brothers, sons, husbands and fathers.'

TWENTY-SIX

The days passed in a flurry of cleaning out the hospital, changing bandages, and scrounging for better food for the sick and wounded. Molly ensured that her brother received all the medical help she could plead from the medical staff. An old Turkish woman who sold treats to the soldiers noticed Molly with her brother, and could see the concern on the young woman's face. She shuffled over to Molly and Owen, who was now in a bed, looking down on the feverish soldier.

She said something which Molly did not understand until one of the nuns intervened.

'The old woman wishes to know what kind of wound the soldier has,' she said.

'You understand Turkish, sister?' Molly asked, surprised at the older nun's skill.

'Yes, my order has a convent in Constantinople and I

spent years here, and I learned the language,' she said. 'I have told her that the soldier is your brother, and he has a bayonet wound that went through his shoulder. She told me she has something to help fight any infection.'

'Tell her that I will try anything if it will help Owen,' Molly said, and the nun spoke with the Turkish woman, who produced a bulbous herb, cutting it into slices with a small knife, and handing the sliced, pungent smelling pieces to the nun.

'It is a herb called garlic,' the nun said. 'She says that it should be applied to the wounds.'

Molly took the strong-smelling garlic pieces and placed them over the entry and exit wounds. Molly than wrapped a clean bandage around the poultice. Owen squirmed as the garlic stung his exposed flesh. The old Turkish woman smiled knowingly.

'Ask the woman how much do I pay her?' Molly asked.

The nun translated, and turned to Molly. 'She said the treatment is free as she lost her son fighting the Russians. She also said that if your brother felt the stinging effect of the garlic, it means his flesh is still healthy.'

'Please thank the old lady,' Molly said. 'Tell her that I will say prayers for her son.'

The nun spoke and turned to Molly. 'She is grateful for your kind thoughts, but Allah is looking after her son, who died a martyr's death.'

The old Turkish lady nodded to Molly and shuffled away, selling her trinkets and fresh fruits to the sick and wounded in the ward that now smelled of antiseptic cleaner.

'Thank you, sister,' Molly said, and the nun resumed her duties tending the wounded.

When she was gone, Owen was alert enough to speak in a whisper. 'Molly, there is something I must tell you,' he said. 'Conan, Edwin and I came into some good fortune at Balaclava. As a result, we have been able to get our hands on a couple of hundred pounds each, and Conan insisted that you receive an equal share. He is holding it for you. It is more money than we have ever seen before.'

'Are you delirious, Owen Williams?' Molly asked, stunned at her brother's news.

'No, Molly,' he replied. 'It has come from a Russian baggage train we fell upon, and the money is a fortune of war. Even the officers took all they could. I know that the Irishman is sweet on you.'

Molly shook her head. What her brother was telling her was beyond her wildest dreams. Money to ward off poverty! But beyond all the money in the world, her first concern was that her wounded brother survive. No money fortune in her life could buy his life.

'I have proof of what I am telling you.' Owen said. 'Sewn inside my trousers is my share of the money. Do not let anyone take my trousers to be laundered. I would like you to retrieve my share for safekeeping.'

'I will do that,' Molly said, and later that night, returned with scissors. She was dumbfounded when she slit the trousers to discover the wad of notes which she quickly concealed in her skirt. It was indeed more money than she ever thought she would hold in her hands.

*

Winter had truly arrived in the Crimea, with a hurricane that tore away the bell tents of the enlisted men, and officers' tents. Rain, bitter cold, and then snow fell to add to the misery. It was at least a campaign where soldier and officer experienced the same hardships as they waited for the bloody war to continue at the siege of Sebastopol.

Ian stood in a trench of half-frozen slush, mud and patches of dirty snow, wearing his greatcoat and shivering like all the other soldiers manning the trench. It was a dark night and Ian knew that only a few meagre supplies would be brought up the five miles from the port of Balaclava. The group of soldiers standing guard in the trench were all new recruits. The previous months had decimated the regiment's ranks, and the fact that Private Edwin Williams and Corporal Curry remained made them battle-hardened veterans. Ian rarely saw his friend, Dr Peter Campbell, as his duties treating sick and wounded men were never-ending.

As many as possible were transported by ship to the hospital near Constantinople, and in return came a letter from Molly to Conan. It informed him and Edwin that she was a nurse with Miss Florence Nightingale's English contingent, and that Owen was recovering slowly from his wound. She also wrote of the present he had brought to her, imploring that he and Edwin take care of themselves.

Conan had been both stunned and overjoyed to read the letter, passing on the news to Edwin, who wept with joy.

It was now January and cholera continued to thin the ranks more than the occasional sniping Russian marksman. Ian had verified stories of the French soldiers swapping food items with the Russians, each side leaving the small gifts in places they knew their enemy would go. It was as if both sides recognised they were suffering because of the incompetence of their respective governments.

'A good evening to you, sir,' Ian turned to see Corporal Curry, and Private Edwin Williams standing beside him in the trench. Both soldiers shivered under their greatcoats.

'I wish it was a good evening, Corporal Curry,' Ian said. 'Just bloody cold, and wet.'

'At least the Muscovites are suffering the same as us out there,' Conan replied.

'But not in Sebastopol in their houses,' Ian said. 'That is where we should have been, if the French had listened to Raglan's advice to attack when we had the men to do so.'

Conan did not comment. He had little knowledge of the overall war strategy. All he was concerned about was just staying alive, and keeping the men of his section in the same state.

'I saw Major Jenkins at brigade headquarters today,' Edwin said. 'He is looking hale and hearty.'

This time, Ian kept his mouth shut. As much as he despised the man, it was a rule no officer spoke ill of another in front of the enlisted men, although he was aware of their low opinion of the former lieutenant.

'As a matter of fact, he recognised me, and said to pass on a message to you that he has grand plans for the company.'

Ian was puzzled by the message. Jenkins should have delivered it to him in person, as the company commander.

'Edwin, I want you to look to the lads of the section and make sure they are awake at their posts,' Conan said, and Edwin made his way down the trench, leaving Conan and Ian alone in the dark.

'Do you know that back home in Australia, it is summer, and we would all go down to the river to swim. That feels like a lifetime ago,' Conan said wistfully in the bitter chill of the night, and drizzling snowflakes falling around them.

'I remember,' Ian said. 'Maybe one day, we will again.'

'I never asked why you are pretending to be that Samuel Forbes person,' Conan blurted. 'You know I have sworn to go to my grave with your secret, but I would like to know why.'

'It is a long story, but a twist of fate gave me the chance to see what it was like to be an officer of the Queen,' Ian replied.

'There is not a day that I don't regret all that happened back in the village,' Conan said. 'I wish that I was still in the colony and could turn back time.'

'Right now, so do I,' Ian said with a bitter smile. 'This whole war has been nothing but a bloody mess. All we have to do is survive it.'

'Captain Forbes,' a voice called in the dark from down the trench. 'I am looking for Captain Forbes.'

'That is me,' Ian said when a well-dressed young lieutenant came close with a lantern held aloft.

'Begging your pardon, sir,' the officer said. 'But you are required at brigade HQ to meet with Major Jenkins just after first light in morning.'

'Inform Major Jenkins that I will report to him,' Ian said, and the staff officer made his way out of the forward trench, retreating to the relative warmth of the brigade HQ.

'It must be something to do with the grand plan Major Jenkins has for us, sir,' Conan said sarcastically as Edwin rejoined them to report all the section were alert at their posts.

'You can stand your section down, Corporal Curry,' Ian said. 'Mr Forbes is sending up a section to relieve you.'

'Thank you, sir,' Conan said, knowing they would find there a small campfire to eat their rations and smoke a pipe before badly needed sleep in the confines of a house that had been wrecked by artillery fire weeks earlier. It at least gave some protection against the biting winds of winter.

Ian remained in the trench, although he did not have to. He wanted his men to see that he was prepared to put up with the conditions of standing to against a possible surprise attack by the Russians from across no man's land. Before the sun was to rise across a bleak, winter's landscape, Ian made his way to Brigade HQ to meet with Major Jenkins. It was likely that the man who had once been his subordinate had nothing but ill will towards him, and that ill will could also affect the safety of his company.

Ian found Jenkins' tent, and entered without saluting. Jenkins was busy signing papers, glancing up at Ian.

'You will salute a superior officer, Captain Forbes,' Jenkins said coldly.

Ian gave a half-hearted salute, and grudgingly stood to attention. 'You may sit,' Jenkins said, gesturing to a wooden stool. Ian sat as Jenkins completed the signatures on the papers before him.

'I have a mission for your company,' Jenkins said. 'One suited to your previous demonstration of what I consider foolishness, but others feel was an act of bravado.'

'You mean going out in front of our lines to strike the Muscovites,' Ian said.

Jenkins rose from behind his table, walking over to a map of the region hanging on the wall of his tent.

'We have information that a high-ranking Russian officer in Sebastopol wishes to desert. We have smuggled in letters to say where we can meet with him at a speci-fied rendezvous point, and he insists that whoever does so must be a senior officer of the British army. Needless to say, I immediately thought that you would accept the honour of meeting with our Russian aristocrat, who will be able to provide us with invaluable intelligence on the state of the Muscovite forces within the defences of the city. You will select a party of no more than five men, including yourself, and I also suggest that you take your brother with you in case you are disabled in some way during the mission, so he can act as your second-in-command for the task. The meeting is to be here at first light tomorrow,' Jenkins said, pointing to a place on the map. 'It is a ruined, abandoned villa.'

Ian stared at the map, calculating the route there and back. It was a good distance from their own frontlines in no man's land, and he realised that the mission had a strong element of danger. Russian patrols of feared Cossack horsemen regularly scouted the area. 'We can do that,' Ian finally said after his appraisal of the map, and calculations in his head to the tactics he would use.

'Good, Captain Forbes,' Jenkins said. 'I expect to be drinking vodka with the Russian colonel for lunch tomorrow. I doubt that I have to inform you that this mission must be kept between us because of the sensitive nature of the man we wish to rescue. The only people who need to know will be the party you choose. I will emphasise the secrecy of what you do. If you have no questions, you are dismissed.'

Ian gave another half-hearted salute and exited the tent of the brigade staff officer. As he walked back to his company lines, he thought about the mission. Why would the man he despised and was despised by give him the opportunity to gain credit for bringing in the high-ranking Muscovite officer? As everything in this campaign was dangerous, the mission did not concern Ian as much as the motivations of the brigade officer he despised.

Ian found Herbert sitting by a small fire outside his tent and briefed him on the mission.

'Naturally, we will take Corporal Curry and Private Williams,' Herbert said. 'They are the most experienced and competent men under my command. It would not be wise to blood any of the new recruits with what is at stake. I will also include Private Cummings, he is another good soldier.'

'The matter is settled. We move out at last light,' Ian said. 'Get some sleep, and make sure the men selected also get some sleep. It will be a long twenty-four hours ahead of us – if we are to succeed.'

Early that evening, the five men assembled in the forward trench. They waited until it was dark, and a heavy downfall of snow helped them go over the top to trudge in the direction of the rendezvous point of the ruined villa. Ian used his compass to give them direction in the dark, feeling relatively secure as the falling snow would ensure any enemy scouting patrols would probably seek shelter for the night.

They trudged in silence throughout the night, greatcoat collars pulled up against the bitter, driving snow. In the early hours of the morning, just before sunrise, Ian spotted the silhouette of the bombed-out villa against the horizon of the rocky snow-covered plain, bordered by a thick forest of conifers. He signalled to the others to make their way towards the ruins, rifles in readiness against the eventuality that it was occupied by enemy picquets. Ian knew if there were enemy soldiers inside, his men had the element of surprise. He could not see any sign of light from a fire, and he cautiously entered the walls of the villa, with his big Colt revolver in one hand, and the smaller Colt in the other, his rifle was slung over his shoulder.

Satisfied that the villa was deserted, he gave the all-clear to the others to join him inside. The roof was mostly intact, although snow piled up in corners through a few holes in the tiles above. They hardly looked like British soldiers, as each man wore bits and pieces of clothing that had been scrounged for the most warmth. It had been noted that the only difference between officers and soldiers in the field in appearance was that the officers were ordered to wear their swords to distinguish their rank. Ian had been able to purchase a sheepskin jacket and a good pair of Russian boots that were fur-lined. The others of his party were similarly dressed. As scruffy as they appeared, each man's weapons were in immaculate condition.

'I know it goes against common sense, but I think we should light up a small fire out of sight of anyone in the countryside around us,' Ian said through chattering teeth. 'We need to warm our hands if we have to use our weapons.'

Herbert agreed, and the men scrounged loose pieces of timber boards from the house. They were able to break up a smashed table, and soon a small, warm glow heartened the chilled soldiers, who gathered around the flames to warm their gloved hands. Ian knew they only had a couple of hours before the dawn came to the white fields surrounding them. Now, all they had to do was wait.

*

'I am seeking Captain Forbes,' Major Jenkins said as he strode through the regimental lines. Captain Miles Sinclair stepped outside his tent flap to meet with the brigade major.

'One of my men reported this morning that Captain Forbes, his brother and three soldiers went over the top just after last light yesterday,' Miles said. 'I presume he is on a scouting mission.'

'Did he tell you or any of your men that he was on such a mission?' Jenkins asked.

'No, sir,' Miles answered. 'I have just presumed.'

'I have not authorised any mission to reconnoitre the enemy positions, Captain Sinclair,' Jenkins said. 'It sounds very much as if Captain Forbes and his brother have deserted to the enemy lines in search of a warm bed and bottle of vodka.'

'Sir, with all due respect, you know Captain Forbes would never entertain the thought of deserting,' Miles protested. 'I am sure that he is on a legitimate mission.'

'I am afraid all missions beyond our lines must first be authorised by me, and that is not so. I have already spoken with your colonel and he has informed me that he has not sanctioned any missions beyond our lines. I can only entertain the idea that the man is a traitor, and has taken other traitors with him. If for some reason we find him first, he is to be immediately arrested for desertion.'

'Sir,' Sinclair replied, not believing for a moment that his fellow company commander would ever desert. Miles Sinclair could only presume that whatever reason Ian had taken his party into no man's land the night before it must have been a damned good one.

Jenkins walked away, satisfied that his ruse would mean the death of Samuel Forbes, one way or another. Charles had also said he would be glad to be rid of his younger brother, Herbert, and would provide Jenkins a bonus when he returned to London.

There was no Russian deserter coming to rendezvous with Captain Forbes. Only a contingent of Russian soldiers tipped off from a letter left in the cleft of a stick where Jenkins knew Russian patrols passed. It was signed a friend of the Tsar, and Jenkins hoped that even now the Russians had deployed to the ruined villa, to capture or preferably kill the deserting British officer. Jenkins knew that when the Russians came for Samuel that his foolish reaction would be to stand and fight, not surrender. It was in the nature of the man and, as Jenkins was a gambler, he felt the odds were in his favour, this would be the outcome.

TWENTY-SEVEN

'I count around forty infantry, and an officer on a horse,' Herbert said, staring out of a window of the villa. 'I somehow think this is not the Russian officer we were supposed to meet with.'

Ian leaned with his elbows on the windowsill with his small telescope, observing the company of Russian infantry he calculated were half a mile away. 'It is too big for a scouting party. Besides, the Muscovites would have used cavalry for that. I have this feeling we were lured into a trap, and that bastard Jenkins is behind this treachery.'

'What are we to do. Surrender?' Herbert asked in desperation.

'Only as a last resort,' Ian said, lowering his telescope and turning to Conan. 'Corporal Curry, when do you think you can get a clear shot at that Russian officer on the horse?'

Conan peered through the window. 'I am sure I can get a good shot at him when he is about four hundred yards out,' Conan said, pulling his Enfield onto the windowsill, and sighting at the distant target.

'Good. I am going to gamble on your reputation as the finest shot in the regiment, Corporal Curry,' Ian said. 'I noticed a cluster of rocks about a hundred yards behind the villa. We will give them a hot time when they come about four hundred yards from us, then we will escape out the back door, and retreat to the rocky outcrop behind us, keeping out of their line of sight.' The rest of his party listened intently to Ian's desperate plan.

Ian lifted the telescope. 'I can see that their officer is assembling his company to advance on the villa,' he said. 'They are now advancing in two ranks. Boys, take up your positions, and deliver well-aimed shots. I will give the order for our retreat back to the rocks.'

They all found good firing positions and waited for Ian's order to open fire. Ian knew the odds were too great to survive a determined assault on the villa, and all he had on his side was fierce determination to make the enemy pay a high price before they were overwhelmed.

'Five hundred,' Conan muttered beside him as he observed the Russian troops advancing steadily at a marching pace, muskets tipped with the long bayonets at the shoulder. Their officer rode on the flank, and Ian frowned. It was as if the Russians were simply coming to meet them. They did not appear to be expecting trouble.

'Four-fifty,' Conan muttered once again, taking careful control of his breathing and weapon handling.

Then the rifle exploded into action, and a second later, the officer toppled from his horse. Immediately, the advancing infantry came to a halt, no longer shouldering their muskets.

'Get down!' Ian barked and a split second later the rattle of musket balls slammed into the stone walls of the villa. It was followed by a second volley from the second rank.

'Now!' Each soldier fired his Enfield, and so did Ian. Only Herbert was not armed with the long rifle, but he had his revolver and sword ready.

Conan had already reloaded in record time, and snapped off another shot, felling a Russian in the front rank. The two other riflemen also fired, bringing down another two Russian soldiers. Ian could see that the enemy infantry men appeared confused by the long-range accurate fire from the wrecked villa. Their officer was dead in the snow, and his mount already galloping across the plain.

'Look for anyone who looks like he might be giving orders – and kill him,' Ian said to Conan, who nodded, raising his loaded rifle musket. He could see a senior NCO exhorting the men to advance.

Conan took careful aim, fired and saw his target fall. The ranks of the enemy saw the leader die and fell back to get out of range of the deadly accurate fire coming from the villa. They knew it was an almost fortified position, and they would have to actually be on the villa before they could engage effectively with the unseen assassins by their sheer force of numbers.

'They are retreating,' Herbert said in an almost hushed voice. 'We have won the day.'

'Not really,' Ian said. 'I suspect that they are going to fetch their artillery guns and blast us out of our little fort. It is now that we give the fort up, and retreat to the rock outcrop. The building will shield us from view when we do.'

Ian gave the order, and his small party of men slipped out the back door to take up positions in the rocks behind the house. The Russians had not attempted to advance again, as Ian knew they were confident that their artillery guns would demolish what was left of the villa without exposing themselves to the long-range, deadly accurate small arms fire.

In the rocks, Ian examined the terrain around the villa. Another half a mile away was a large belt of densely packed trees covered in snow. The cavalry would not be able to hunt them down in such woodland, and he knew that this was where he and his party must reach to throw off any enemy pursuing them. But he also knew they could not make a rush towards the trees until dark, in the eventuality the Russians had cavalry in the near vicinity. Death under a swinging sabre did not appeal to Ian, and all he could do was pray for time. He hoped the heavy snow drifts on the plain would slow any artillery guns being dragged up to bombard the villa.

'We have to keep our heads down here, and not be seen by the Muscovites,' Ian briefed the men gathered around him in the maze of rocks. 'When it gets dark, we are going to make our way to that forest of trees yonder. From there, we will make our way back to our own lines.' The men voiced their agreement, although Ian could see the fear in their faces. Ian also knew it was a desperate plan where many things could go wrong. What if the Russian guns appeared in the next few hours? After the villa had been flattened, they were sure to advance with fixed bayonets, and even with the cover of the rocks, Ian knew he did not have enough men to stem their attack. Any attempt in daylight hours to flee across the snow towards the trees would be seen by their enemy only a half-mile away, and the good possibility that cavalry would ride them down. All they could do was wait until dark to make their escape.

The hours passed agonisingly slowly. Ian occasionally looked through his telescope at the mass of men on the horizon. Each time, he felt relief as the enemy had obviously taken the time to light fires and sit around them, as if waiting for reinforcements.

Just before the sun was to descend over a distant line of hills to the west, Ian heard the sound of horses neighing, and carefully made his way along the rocky outcrop. He observed two artillery guns being unlimbered. Ian also noticed that the Russians were using a combination of solid shot and the round gunpowder-filled shells that were fused to explode on impact.

The waiting troops remained resting as the Russian gunners went about the business of loading and firing the two guns.

The first ranging solid shot was a cloud of smoke, followed by the bang of the gun as the sound reached Ian. Seconds later, he could hear the solid shot smash through the front wall of the villa to the faint cheer of the Russian infantry watching beyond. It was followed by an explosive round that fell between the house and the rocks, exploding its iron fragments in all directions. Some rattled off the rocks, and the British soldiers hugged any space they could find.

The following solid and explosive artillery rounds smashed into the villa, and after an hour, the stone villa was levelled to the ground. This was the moment that Ian feared, as he huddled in their temporary place of their final stand facing the overwhelming forces arrayed against them.

'What do we do?' Herbert asked, fearfully.

'We wait until it is dark enough to make our escape to the woods,' he said, but noticed that the bleak sun was just touching the top of the distant hills. Only a miracle could save them now if the infantry once again advanced. Ian lifted the telescope and noticed that a small group of high-ranking officers had joined the Russian troops and were in a small group, as if discussing something.

The sun was now slowly sliding behind the ridges of the hills casting long shadows and when Ian looked back at the Russians, he could see that the lounging soldiers were now forming up in two ranks.

It was now twilight, but Ian knew they were still vulnerable. The Russians were advancing, but more slowly than the first time they attacked. It was now or never, and Ian turned to his men huddled in the rocks. They no longer had the outline of the villa to give them protection from being seen, but they had the rocky outcrop.

'We have to go now,' Ian said. 'Try to keep in a straight line for the trees with the rocks to your back. With any luck, we won't be spotted for the first moments of our escape. Run like the devil was chasing you.'

'He will be,' Conan said, and a chuckle broke the tension within the small party.

'Get to the trees, and when you feel that you are far enough in, turn east for our lines. Does anyone have any questions?'

None spoke. They all knew what they were about to do simply required them to run and hide. It was an act of desperation, but they had no other choice.

'Ready boys?' Ian said, half raising himself into a crouch. 'Go!'

The party scrambled from the rocky outcrop and began to force themselves through the soft snow as fast as they could. It was agonisingly slow, and a distant shout indicated to Ian that the Russians had spotted them. They had at least five-hundred yard start on the pursuing enemy, and were out of range of the smoothbore muskets.

Ian fell back behind the others fleeing to provide rear

protection, and in the distance, he heard the sound that he most dreaded. The muffled thunder of horses' hooves in the snow.

'Keep going!' he shouted when he saw the tree line only a hundred yards away.

Ian swung around to see half a dozen Cossacks charging, stirrup to stirrup, towards his men, waving their sabres and yelling triumphantly. They could see a helpless prey inviting them to cut them down with their slashing swords.

Ian raised his rifle, calculating the distance of the first horseman to be around two hundred yards, charging directly at him with his sabre raised. Ian fired, but missed. It was too late to reload so he snatched his twin pistols from his sash, standing his ground until the Cossacks were within range. He only hoped he would give time to his soldiers to reach the relative safety of the forest.

Two shots rang out behind Ian, and he saw two of the Cossacks pitch from their saddles. Ian instinctively knew it had to be Conan and Edwin who had fired the deadly shots. The odds were now down to four to one, as the surviving Cossacks continued their charge towards him.

Ian steadied himself, wondering why he was no longer afraid to die. His only fleeting regret was that he would never see Jane again or meet the child they had. When the first horseman was fifty yards away, Ian could see his bearded face, and raised his Colt Dragoon, firing two shots. One hit the cavalryman, who fell sideways from his saddle into the snow.

The other three swerved away, flanking him, but splitting their forces. Ian could see that they were also carrying short-barrelled musket carbines, which they swapped their sabres for, and it was obvious that they would stand off and shoot him.

Ian knew his pistol was not as accurate as a rifled musket, but as if lightning had struck them, two of the Cossacks fell from their horses, and Ian heard the echo across the plain of the Enfields. Conan and Edwin were not going to allow their officer be cut down by the Russian horsemen.

Ian raised both pistols and charged towards the startled Cossack, who fired wildly at the insane British officer, rapidly closing the gap between them. Ian's hail of bullets slammed into the Russian, who toppled from his horse. Ian grabbed the reins of the rearing horse, and slung himself into the saddle, looking over his shoulder to see the infantry still advancing in the heavy, soft snow. When he turned his attention to the trees, he saw Conan and Edwin providing him covering fire. Ian urged the horse into a gallop, and it forged ahead in the snow until Ian reached the tree line. Ian flung himself from the horse and joined Herbert and the men.

Suddenly, an explosion erupted a hundred yards to their left, and Ian realised that the artillery guns had been brought forward and had entered the unequal battle.

'C'mon boys, time to go home,' Ian said, and they plunged into the rapidly darkening forest of tall trees. Ian made sure that in the dim light, none of the party were separated, and soon the forest was cast into night. They had stumbled, fallen, got up and stumbled on in the dark, until Ian called a halt.

Exhausted, they fell to the snow, hardly feeling its bitter chill. When Ian was satisfied that they were all together, he had the first opportunity to reflect on how they had escaped the jaws of death with his desperate plan. He also suspected that the Russian infantry would have halted at the tree line, knowing that to go any further in the dark would cause only confusion and the possibility of an ambush, should there be British or French troops laying up in the area.

'We did it, thanks to you, Sam.' Herbert gasped through lungs burned by cold and exhaustion.

'We still have to get back to our lines,' Ian cautioned. 'Despite how tired we are, we must march now to make sure the Muscovites don't decide to change their minds and come looking for us with torches. I suspect that they are not going to be pleased losing so many men to such a small force of British soldiers. I doubt that they will consider taking us alive, under the circumstances.'

The exhausted men reluctantly pushed themselves to their feet, and with the use of his compass, Ian led them home. Before sunrise, they could see the plain where they knew their forward trenches were. Smoke rose from campfires beyond, and the distant chatter of British troops could be heard on the chill wind that blew from the east.

Before mid-morning, they stumbled into their own lines.

TWENTY-EIGHT

Ian made his way to the regimental colonel's tent, to report the outcome of the mission that Major Jenkins from brigade HQ, had sent him on. Ian did not voice his suspicion that the mission had been an ambush, but simply said that they had failed to meet with the supposed deserting high-ranking Russian officer.

'Strange,' the colonel said from behind his desk, as Ian stood at-ease in the tent. 'I was not informed of your orders. I suppose brigade felt it was of such a sensitive nature, the less people who knew, the better it was. From your report, Captain Forbes, you have acquitted yourself very well, inflicting losses on the Muscovites, and at the same time using your remarkable ingenuity to make your escape. You are to be commended.'

'Thank you, sir, but it is the high standard of the soldiers we lead that ensured our success,' Ian said, his mind going over the circumstances of Jenkins ordering him to undertake such a risky venture.

'Very good, Captain Forbes. You may return to your company and pass on my congratulations to your brother and the men who accompanied you. You will be mentioned in my despatches.'

Ian saluted the colonel, and stepped outside the tent to return to his company, when he saw Jenkins approaching with four armed soldiers marching behind him.

'Captain Forbes,' Jenkins called, and Ian halted. 'You are under arrest for deserting your post. You are to be placed under guard in your quarters, until a court is convened to hear the charges.'

Ian half-expected that Jenkins would attempt to discredit him in some way, but not his arrest for desertion. His fury rose and, for a moment, he was tempted to reach for the big Colt Dragoon revolver in his waistband.

'Your arms, Captain Forbes,' Jenkins commanded, and Ian obliged by removing his two pistols.

The guard of soldiers stepped forward, taking possession of Ian's weapons and then escorted Ian through the lines to his tent. As they did, soldiers of the company were dumbfounded seeing their commander under close arrest, being marched through their ranks. Men muttered, and the confusion in the ranks was obvious.

When they reached the tent, Ian turned to Jenkins. 'I pray that Mr Forbes is not under arrest,' he said.

'Your brother has been deemed as obeying the orders of a superior officer, and probably not aware of your treachery,' Jenkins replied. 'Nor were the men who followed you beyond our lines.'

'If I was deserting, how do you explain my return?' Ian asked. 'After all, it was you who gave me the mission.'

'I do not remember issuing any orders for you to go beyond our lines,' Jenkins lied, and Ian had the urge to punch the lying superior officer in the face.

'You and I both know, Major Jenkins, that I, and my men, were sent into a trap of your prior knowledge. I expect you did not think we would return alive, and your weak and desperate measure to accuse me of desertion has no basis. My only question is why you would attempt to have me killed.'

Jenkins reddened. He had not expected to see Ian return. He had read a copy of the report sent up to brigade HQ and panicked. This was the only option he thought he had to discredit the bravery of the men he had sent to their probable deaths.

'A guard will be posted outside your tent, and your meals will be brought to you until the time a court martial in the field is convened,' he said. 'As there is nothing else to be discussed, I will leave you.'

Ian did not salute his superior officer, and Jenkins was wise enough to not insist. When he looked into the eyes of the captain, he saw a cold threat of violence.

Ian entered his tent and slumped down on the end of the cot that was his bed. Only minutes earlier, he had been congratulated by his commanding officer for the success of retreating from the enemy under fire. Now he could be found guilty of deserting his post, and possibly stripped of his commission. At least it was not the practice to execute officers for such a military crime. Only lowly soldiers were executed for such crimes.

*

Word of the popular company commander under arrest ran up and down the regimental lines like an out of control wildfire in a conifer forest. Conan was cleaning his rifle by a campfire when Edwin hurried to him from the bell tent they shared.

'That bastard, Major Jenkins, has had Captain Forbes arrested on charges of desertion, Conan,' he said, out of breath. 'What is going on?'

Conan lay his rifle over his knees, and reached for his pipe. Taking a burning twig from the coals, he lit the tobacco, and blew a grey puff of smoke into the frozen air. 'When Jenkins went to water with the company a few months back, he knew that we all saw his cowardice. I think he wants to punish the captain for being the superior officer that day, who saw what he is really like. He will do anything to bring Captain Forbes down, the gutless swine that Jenkins is.'

'What can we do?' Edwin asked, squatting beside the Irishman.

'Not much,' Conan replied, puffing on his pipe. 'This is an officer matter.'

But he picked up his rifle and stared at it. What if a Russian marksman was lurking just outside their lines, and took a shot at Major Jenkins? Conan mused. He knew that under the right conditions, he could just pull off the fatal shot. Maybe then the cowardly brigade officer could not lie to the officers sitting on the court martial board about Ian's supposed desertion from his post. Conan sighed. It was just a dream.

'We have to go and see Mr Forbes about his brother's situation,' Conan said. 'He is an officer, and able to speak with the colonel on Captain Forbes' behalf. That's about all we can do.'

Both soldiers made their way to Herbert's tent and saw their officer in company with Captain Miles Sinclair. Conan saluted, and the two officers turned to him.

'Yes, Corporal Curry?' Herbert said, and Conan could see the expression of worry in his face.

'Sir, Private Williams and I have come to you to see if we can help Captain Forbes.'

'Your intentions are good, Corporal, but there is little you can do at this stage for Captain Forbes. But I thank you for your offer.'

'Captain Forbes is an officer we all respect, sir,' Conan continued. 'Major Jenkins is lying.'

'You know that I cannot listen to criticism of a superior officer, Corporal Curry,' Herbert said, but his face belied his reprimand. 'Captain Sinclair and I will be speaking with the colonel on this matter.'

'Very good, sir,' Conan said, saluted and walked away with Edwin.

'Bloody officers and their ways,' Edwin hissed. 'It's his own brother, and all he can do is rebuke our help.'

'I told you that it is an officer matter,' Conan growled. 'Let's hope they can work it out between the gentlemen they are supposed to be.'

*

Four officers stood stiffly before the colonel's desk. Ian was one, then there was Captain Sinclair, Lieutenant Forbes, and Major Jenkins.

'Sir, I must protest Captain Forbes being brought here,' Jenkins said. 'He is under orders from brigade HQ to be held under close arrest in his quarters.'

'I am sure, Major Jenkins, that the armed guard stationed outside, will protect us from Captain Forbes,' the colonel replied sarcastically. 'It has been brought to my attention that Captain Forbes has been charged with deserting his post in an attempt to communicate with the enemy. A very serious charge, and I feel that I should clear up this matter before it gets out of hand. I ordered Captain Forbes to take a small party of men to carry out a reconnaissance of the area. I am sure my order must have been mislaid somewhere in your brigade HQ.'

'Sir, but it was I . . .' With a red face, Jenkins stopped himself.

'It was you who did what, Major Jenkins?' the colonel asked, leaning forward across the table in front of him. 'Order Captain Forbes to fetch a high-ranking Muscovite deserting from Sebastopol?'

Trapped, Jenkins found his mouth go dry, and he swallowed. 'Sir, I must caution you that this will be brought up with those highest in the staff at brigade.'

'It will be my word as a regimental colonel against your word, in such a case. Who do you think those high-ranking officers at brigade will believe?'

Ian stood at attention, hardly believing what he was hearing from the regimental commander. He was prepared to fabricate a lie to defend one of his officers, and suddenly Ian realised that he was a part of a family whose colours on the battlefield were the true symbol of a family, that protected each other in war and peace.

'Do you have anything else to add, Major Jenkins?' the colonel said, and Ian swore he could see a smirk on the colonel's face. 'If not, Captain Forbes will have his arms returned, and take his post as one of my more capable company commanders.'

Ian had the pleasure of seeing Jenkins squirm, face red with embarrassment, and frustrated rage for being brought to heel by the colonel sitting smugly behind his desk. He saluted, turned on his heel, and stormed out of the tent, leaving them alone.

'I would like to have a word in private with Captain Forbes,' the colonel said, and then both Miles and Herbert saluted before leaving the tent.

'Captain Forbes, I do not like to lie, but I have no time for a fancy upstart interfering in the command of my regiment. After hearing from your brother, and Captain Sinclair, and looking at all the facts, I do not believe in the preposterous story Major Jenkins told me about you deserting your post. You are an officer in my regiment, and not one who works for brigade HQ. Next time a matter of similar circumstances arises, I want to be informed – regardless of its secrecy.'

'Yes, sir. Thank you, sir,' Ian replied. He knew it would not be wise to attempt to explain why he had foolishly trusted the brigade officer. To Ian, it had been an opportunity to break the boredom they were all suffering in this bitter siege of the Russians at the port of Sebastopol. It had been an impulsive act on his behalf that could have got them all killed.

'That is all, Captain Forbes,' the colonel said, and Ian saluted.

Outside the tent, Ian had his side arms reluctantly returned on Jenkins' orders.

'This is not the last of this matter,' Jenkins snarled before marching away to brigade HQ. 'Not even your own family cares for you.'

Ian watched this superior officer who had proved to be just as dangerous as any Russian soldier, and wondered at his parting remark. Surely Jenkins could not be in a conspiracy with Charles? From his short experience, Ian knew that the family ties in the higher levels of British aristocracy ran strong. Ian remembered how Charles had planned an ambush on him and Dr Campbell back in England. Now, it seemed his reach extended even to the Crimea. If so,

Ian knew that Major Jenkins was in a position to put him and his company in grave danger.

Ian marched through the dirty snow, flattened by many army boots, to his tent. As he passed through the company lines, a rousing cheer rose from the throats of his men. The sound was heard all the way over at brigade HQ by Major Jenkins, who uttered curses of frustration.

★

Molly sat by her brother's bed, feeding him a hot broth from a spoon. His recovery had been remarkable, as the doctors attending Owen's wound had predicted infection, but his body had fought the dreaded putrefaction. Molly was not sure if it had been the garlic, the prayers of her friend, Sister Agnes, the older nun who spoke Turkish that had helped in the healing, or simply luck.

'When we get out of the army, we will have enough money to buy a pub in London,' Owen said as Molly spooned the broth.

'No, we will purchase a little shop, and I will make confectionaries we will sell.'

Owen looked at his sister thoughtfully. He remembered how she would scrounge sugar to make a few boiled lollies, which hardly cooled before they were eaten by he and Edwin, when they were young and living in Wales. His sister had a talent for improvising, and he admitted, a good head on her shoulders for business. Even Ikey the Jew had once offered her more money to look after his books, but then he was forced to disappear with the police on his trail for shady dealings in the underworld.

'That sounds like a good proposition,' Owen said. 'A respectable means of employment. But what would Edwin and I do in the business?'

'Do not forget that Conan is a part of our family now,' Molly said, wiping excess broth from around Owen's lips with a clean cloth. 'I would expect you to peddle our wares around the streets. There would be times you would also help in the cooking, and managing in our shop. There is a lot to do running a successful business.'

'Do you think we could make a good go of the business?' Owen asked.

'With hard, honest work, we could make a steady income on our wares,' Molly said.

'Then I am in with my share, Molly,' Owen said and fell into a melancholic state. 'I don't want to go back to the regiment. I will only go back because Edwin and Conan are there.'

Molly had occasionally walked the wards at night with a lamp, following the example of Miss Nightingale. She had heard the sounds of wounded men whimpering, twitching as they relived the trauma of combat. When she had sat by Owen's bed, holding his hand in the dark, she could feel him trembling, sometimes crying out in his troubled sleep. There was something in the heads of soldiers who had experienced the bloodiness of battle that stayed with them, she noted. They did not talk about it, but their bodies continued to tremble during the waking hours.

'I am sure that the war will be over soon,' Molly said, attempting to sound confident.

'Not until we take Sebastopol,' Owen said quietly, remembering the sight of the heavily fortified port town with its artillery and vast numbers of tough Russian infantry. Every soldier knew that eventually the city would have to be taken to force the Tsar to the peace table. Until then, death would remain supreme as lord of their destinies. Until that time, the hopes of a quiet life of prosperity were merely a dream.

TWENTY-NINE

Charles Forbes opened the letter from Crimea. He sat in the billiard room at his London residence, taking in all that was proposed in veiled words in the letter from Major Jenkins.

It appeared that Captain Samuel Forbes led a charmed life and killing him would be much harder than simply dismissing a gambling debt. He proposed for a substantial deposit into his London bank account that could promise Captain Forbes would not be returning from the Crimea, and for a further deposit he could also promise that neither would Herbert.

Charles carefully folded the letter and went in search of his father. Sir Archibald was, as usual, engrossed in reading the articles published from the front by William Russell.

'Damned bad show from what that cad Russell is writing in *The Times*,' Sir Archibald snorted when Charles entered the room. 'A real cock-up if you ask me.'

Charles sat down. 'Father, I have someone well-placed to remove Samuel from the family.'

Archibald laid down his newspaper. 'Who may that be?' he asked.

'It is not someone that you have to know of,' Charles said. 'But I can assure you he is in a position in the Crimea to see that Samuel does not return.'

'I presume that he wants money for services to be rendered,' Sir Archibald said. 'How much?'

Charles mentioned the figure, raising Sir Archibald's brow.

'Are you sure that your source is able to fulfil his promise to rid us of that bastard son of my brother?' Sir Archibald queried again.

'I am sure he is able to manipulate a situation to have Samuel killed. You can then be seen as a father who has personally lost a beloved son fighting for the Queen and Empire. All I need is your authorisation to pay the money.'

Sir Archibald reflected for a moment. From what he had read in the reports from the Eastern front, cholera had killed more British troops than bombs and bullets. But there was no assurance that Samuel would become a victim of the dreaded disease.

'Go ahead and meet your sources financial request,' he finally said, lifting the newspaper from his lap to peruse news on the business sectors of the British Empire's economy.

Charles had been careful not to mention the bonus of eliminating Herbert, as he knew his father would never sanction that. As a matter of fact, Sir Archibald was proud of his youngest son's service to the Queen on the far-off battlefields of the Crimean Peninsula.

But why should Herbert share in the vast estate when it really belonged to him on his father's demise? Alice was not a threat as she was to inherit only a small portion of the estate. The future looked bright – but not for Samuel or Herbert.

*

It was another day of manning the siege trenches facing Sebastopol for Ian's company. Explosive shells fell all around, and one burst in the trench not far from where Ian stood, peering over the lip of the trench. The blast wave threw him off the step, and into the slush of the trench floor. Ian scrambled to his feet as the smoke from the exploding artillery shell cleared in the bitterly cold air.

He could see parts of two soldiers scattered in gruesome meaty chunks about twenty yards away who had taken a direct hit, and heard the pitiful screams of a badly wounded rifleman who had lost his leg and arm. Ian gritted his teeth and tried to block out the noise. Not that it was hard to cut off sound, as the explosion had partially deafened him.

He resumed his position on the lip of the trench, and saw them coming in waves.

'To your posts!' he screamed to the men around him who had been disorganised by the Russian shell.

They scrambled to the forward edge of the trench to see the advancing Russian infantry, levelling their Enfields.

A volley of ragged fire immediately produced gaps in the attacking Russian infantry, and before many could reload, the Russians were on top of the British trenches, firing down into the crowded ranks of men below.

Ian snatched his Colt from the sash around his waist, and unsheathed his sword, just as a Russian soldier leapt into the trench beside him. Ian did not hesitate but fired point blank into the enemy soldier's face, blowing it away. As usual, Conan and Edwin had ensured they were close to Ian, as the Russians poured into their positions.

The hand-to-hand fighting was desperate. Men stabbed, bit, punched, grunted and shot each other in the narrow confines of the trench. Ian lunged with his sword at another Russian, who was raising his musket to club Conan who was occupied fighting off an enemy attempting to bayonet him. The sword strike was true, piercing the Russian's back. The man arched in agony as the blade penetrated through to his sternum. Ian yanked the sword from him, and felt something strike his shoulder. He swung around to see a Russian holding his musket like a club. The distance had been too short to use his bayonet, and he had opted to strike Ian with the butt of his musket. Ian brought up his Colt and fired, hitting the man in the chest. He fell, dropping his musket.

As the rain drizzled on the desperate close-quarter fighting, Ian could sense the Russian assault fizzle out, leaving the trench floor covered in the bodies of dead and wounded British riflemen and Russian infantry. Ian was gasping for breath as he cast around him for any further threats, but the enemy must have decided to retreat from this slit in the ground that was as good as a grave to both sides. Ian fell back against the side of the trench, exhausted by the intense and desperate need to stay alive. His heart was pounding, and he hardly had the strength to hold his weapons because his hands were trembling so badly. He hardly remembered emptying his Colt in the ferocious fighting in the confines of the trench.

'Are you wounded, sir?' a familiar voice asked. Ian glanced up to see the bearded face of Corporal Curry, hovering over him with a concerned expression.

'I don't think I have been wounded,' Ian said, attempting to struggle to his feet. Conan reached down and helped him stand.

'Pass on the word that I want an account of our dead and wounded,' Ian said, standing unsteadily in the trench, staring along it to see the mass of bodies. Some on either side were still moving.

'Organise the litter parties to come down here to remove the dead and wounded.'

'Yes, sir,' Conan replied and moved down the trench to carry out his company commander's orders. Ian took deep breaths to recover but still could not stop his body trembling. He explained to himself that the terrible tremors were a result of the bitterly cold air of the Crimean winter, but knew that was not completely true.

No sooner had Ian raised his head above the parapet than a shot rang out, the musket ball splattering his bloody face with mud. Ian ducked below the forward edge of the trench. It had to be one of the Russian marksmen, concealed in specially constructed pits out in no man's land. They had plagued his company in the trenches for some days, and already, Ian was formulating a plan to rid them of the enemy marksmen, already having taken the lives of three of his company.

Ian's thoughts shifted to the welfare of Herbert's men stationed up the trench, protecting the right flank of the company positions. The wave of attacking Russian infantry had covered the complete front of the company in their assault. Ian stepped over bodies as he made his way along the trench until he came to the section of the line where Herbert's soldiers were manning. The scene was very much like the one he had just left.

To his horror, he saw Colour Sergeant Leslie crouching beside Herbert, who was covered in blood. Ian hurried to Herbert's side and knelt down.

'Mr Forbes took a bayonet in the hip,' the colour sergeant said. 'He needs a surgeon.'

Ian looked down and saw the blood staining the trousers of Herbert in the groin region. Herbert's eyes were half closed, and his mouth open. He made no noise but Ian could see the pain in his face.

'Get the litter bearers to him,' Ian commanded and touched the pain-wracked face of the young man. His fate was now in the hands of their friend, Dr Peter Campbell. In a short time, the men who normally played in the regimental band were carrying Herbert on a stretcher along the trench, to a place where he could be safely evacuated, without the fear of a Russian marksman out in no man's land shooting them.

Ian quickly resumed his duties as company commander, taking toll on their casualties – dead and wounded – before he could stop and take out his tobacco pipe. It was a difficult task to simply plug and light the battered pipe with his trembling hands.

'It was a close one,' Conan said when he sat down next to Ian, his rifle between his knees. 'We lost a lot of good lads. It is always our company that gets hit hardest, as if someone was placing us in the worst part of the line.'

Ian listened to the corporal's remarks and silently agreed. The orders to the regiment from the brigade always seemed to identify Ian's company to hold the most vulnerable section of the siege trenches. The colonel had said to Ian that was so because those in brigade felt his company had the best record for actions against the enemy, but Ian had a nagging suspicion it was because Major Jenkins wanted him dead. That could not be proved when the colonel thought it was an honour to Ian's company to take the brunt of trench assaults. From what Ian had read about warfare in the past, this was a totally different style of war. They had telegraph to send messages in real time. Railroads were being built to bring up supplies and, unlike the ranks that had once stood in lines and squares in the open to face the enemy, they now lived in a static world of trenches where artillery and engineers played a greater role. Tunnels were being constructed by either side to lay explosive charges under the opponent's defences. The tactics for this new kind of war were not even written in military manuals.

'Don't you know, Corporal Curry, it is an honour to be chosen by brigade to face the worst the Muscovites can throw at us,' Ian said facetiously. 'It may be possible that they are depending on us to win the war on our own.'

'I would gladly forgo the honour to be just one more time with my girl,' Conan sighed, reaching for his own tobacco pipe. 'I have received news that she is a nurse at our hospital near Constantinople, and she has written that Owen is recovering very well. He may be back with us in the next couple of weeks.'

'That is good news,' Ian said. 'You terrible three make a formidable team. I am proud to have you in my command.'

Conan fell silent for a moment contemplating the praise. 'How did you and I ever get to this terrible place of carnage?' Conan said. 'It just seems like yesterday – and yet a lifetime ago – we would go to the tavern to get drunk and in the summer, swim in the river. Even now, our friends will be doing just that at home when we find ourselves freezing to death in this bitterly cold hell, living like bloody rabbits in underground burrows, waiting for a musket ball or Muscovite artillery bomb to kill us. Worse, leave us without an arm or leg.'

'Should I remind you, corporal, that you voluntarily signed on for your own reasons, and I am here because I believe it is my destiny to serve the Queen. That is about all I can say about why we are here.'

The conversation was a rare intimate moment between officer and soldier. But it was also a moment when two men from the Great South Land were able to remember their roots beyond the trenches of the Crimea.

'You know, Corporal Curry,' Ian said, puffing on his pipe. 'I think it must be time that we cleared those pesky Muscovite marksmen out of the land between our trenches. How do you think the lads in the company would greet such a mission?'

'Sir, if you lead, they will follow,' Conan replied with a faint smile. 'It is certainly a better option than just sitting on our arses, waiting to be picked off.'

'I will talk to the colonel and get his permission to make a sweep of the ground in front of our part of the line. It will be risky, but it will send a message to the Muscovites that they do not own the land out to our front. We do.'

Ian rose to his feet, tapped his pipe on a piece of timber reinforcing, and strode away, determined to convince his commander of the idea of a sweep of no man's land. He knew it would be a possibility that he would lose men in the attempt, but it was better than just sitting in the trenches at the mercy of the Russian sharpshooters. Ian knew grimly that his plan would be approved by brigade HQ. After all, it was a grand opportunity to get him killed.

*

Dr Peter Campbell had always dreaded this moment. The man laying face up on his operating table in the requisitioned villa was his friend, Lieutenant Herbert Forbes. Peter thought that it was inevitable this moment would occur. Either Samuel or Herbert.

'This is going to hurt,' Peter said, leaning over Herbert whose face was ashen, and his eyes filled with tears of pain.

The trousers had been stripped off, and Peter could see the jagged wound still bleeding, but the Canadian surgeon was pleased to see that the blood was not pumping from a severed artery. Both Peter and the floor were covered in blood from the many amputations he had performed that day. Around him, two other surgeons also worked at a furious rate, removing shattered limbs with saws and tying off ruptured blood vessels. Men screamed in anguish, others bit their lips, sweating in agony. Peter's supply of chloroform was almost exhausted, but he still had a good supply of carbolic acid.

'Hold Mr Forbes down,' Peter ordered two elderly assistants. Peter washed his hands in a bowel of red-tinted liquid, and then pushed his finger into the wound, probing to ensure that it had not been a musket ball that had caused the wound.

Herbert arched as Peter's finger dug around in his flesh. Although Herbert was suffering excruciating pain, he did not cry out. Just a whimper left his lips as he fell back against the table.

'The good news is that from what I can see, it was not a musket ball wound,' Peter said, reaching for a fresh bottle of carbolic acid to wash the wound. 'Herbert, dear boy, I am going to bandage the wound, and recommend that you be sent to our hospital outside Constantinople. The doctors there will monitor your condition, and I am sure that you will be on your feet in no time.'

Herbert nodded his understanding, the pain leaving him speechless. As he was taken by the orderlies to have his wound dressed, Peter prepared his table for another soldier laid out in front of him with a shattered arm. It never ended for the overworked Canadian doctor, whose only respite from the carnage was the constant flow of letters from

Alice. Peter had seen enough of war, and promised himself that when it was over, he would return to London, marry Alice and set up a practice in some quiet part of the British Isles where the scent of flowers pervaded, and he could hopefully forget the acrid stench of blood of the Crimean battlefields.

THIRTY

Ian huddled with the men of his company below the parapet in the darkness that came before the dawn. They shivered in the biting cold, hands trembling as they gripped the stocks of their rifled muskets.

As usual, Conan had placed himself close to Ian, as did Edwin. Ian had ensured that he had the new officer, Lieutenant Sutton, close by, carrying the regimental colours. In the half-light, he could see the fear in the young officer's face. He would be the target of every Russian sharpshooter out to their front.

'Corporal Curry, I want you and Private Williams to keep an eye on Mr Sutton,' Ian said quietly.

'Yes, sir,' Conan replied.

Ian checked his revolvers, and armed himself with an Enfield, bayonet attached. The waiting was the worst part of being in a battle, and Ian tried to take his mind off what lay ahead with thoughts of Jane. Where was she, and why had not she written? Ian calculated that if all had gone well, he was now a father to either a son or daughter.

'Sir, the brigade staff are here,' Conan said, forcing Ian to relinquish his more pleasant thoughts of Jane's beautiful face.

Ian turned his head to see three brigade officers approach his position, including Major Jenkins.

'You have come to join us when we go over the top, sir?' Ian asked, addressing Major Jenkins with an edge of sarcasm.

'No, Captain Forbes,' Jenkins replied. 'We have come to observe the events ahead. I wish you good luck.'

Ian knew that the staff officer did not mean his good wishes, but had come to hopefully observe his death.

'It won't be luck, but speed and surprise, that will carry the day,' Ian said, glancing at the sky taking on the first rays of the bitterly cold day. Ian felt the knot in his stomach tighten, and knew it was time. He turned to a young man, hardly in his teens, and gave the order.

'Bugler, sound the tune.'

The bugler raised his instrument, and played the signal to attack. With a mighty roar, the company soldiers scrambled up ladders to go over the edge of the trench.

Ian ensured he was first over the top, followed closely by the colour party. The young colour officer had stuttered his order to his party guarding the regimental flag, but they were already out of the trench before he could finish his last word.

At first, no shots were fired at the line of infantrymen spread out in a long skirmish line, advancing across the mud and snow slush that lay between the Russian and British trenches. Then a rattle of small arms fire erupted as the

Russian sharpshooters opened fire. They were answered with fire from the advancing British infantry. Already, some of the Russians realised what was happening and made attempts to flee back to their own lines. They were either shot down or bayoneted when the men of Ian's company ran after them.

'Keep the line!' Ian roared, and then noticed that a mass of Russian infantry were pouring over the tops of their trenches to confront Ian's company in no man's land. Ian had been prepared for this to occur, and turned to the bugler close on his heels.

'Sound retreat,' he ordered but the words were hardly out of his mouth when a musket ball cut the young boy down. He fell with an expression of surprise, still holding the bugle to his lips. The blood spread on the front of the young boy's chest, and Ian knew he was dead. Hopefully the men of the company would assess the situation, and retreat on their own accord, as they had been briefed before the mission to clear the sharpshooters. At least the Russians would be forced not to use their artillery, as their infantry were so close to the British enemy.

Off to Ian's right, he could see the colour party stop. The flag fluttered in the cold breeze, and Ian groaned when he saw it had become the prime target of the attacking Russians. Musket balls ripped through the men around the colours, and Ian saw Lieutenant William Sutton suddenly pitch back, still grimly holding the staff of the flag. Ian saw Conan immediately go to Mr Sutton's aid, and once again, raise the standard while covering the wounded officer. Beside Conan was Edwin, firing and reloading as fast as a highly skilled rifleman could. Ian turned to see a small group of Russians coming directly towards him, and fired his rifle, knocking down one of the Russians. He dropped the rifle and pulled out his revolver and his sword, all the time screaming, 'Fall back!'

When Ian levelled his pistol and fired at the small group of Russians, they hesitated in their attempt to kill or capture him. They were aware that the revolver held at least five more balls in the chambers, and stopped to reload their muskets. Ian knew that he was a dead man if they all fired upon him, so he immediately went on the offensive, charging the group with his bayonet-tipped rifle in one hand and revolver in the other. He was on them before they could react, and Ian fired until his revolver was empty. He was able to stab the last remaining threat, fumbling with his ram rod, with a thrust through the Russian's throat, although he had aimed for his chest. The battle had come down to just this few yards surrounding Ian. But he knew his primary role was to command his company, and Ian fell back to quickly assess the situation. He was pleased to see his men were retreating in good order, and would soon fall under the protection of the artillery guns and rifles of his regiment in the trenches behind them.

But no covering fire was observed. Ian and his men fell back under the musket shots of the pursuing Russians. Ian could see Conan and Colour Sergeant Leslie dragging the wounded young officer back, while Conan and Edwin also fended off a small party of Russians attempting to take the regimental colours from them. Ian knew how important it was to save the colours, and fought his way to Conan.

'Get the colours back to the trenches,' he yelled above the din of musket fire. 'Private Williams and I will cover you.'

Ian had his revolver out, and quickly reloaded the chambers while watching the scattered fighting in the field. Why was there no covering fire?

The revolver proved effective in keeping off the Russians,

and the survivors of the company tumbled into the safety of their trenches. Ian could see the colours were also now safely back, and slumped for a moment at the bottom of the trench to gather his thoughts. Then he saw Major Jenkins with the two other staff officers. Ian launched himself to his feet and strode towards the staff officers.

'Sir, was there some reason that my company did not get support fire when we were retreating?' he asked in a cold fury, as he already suspected the despised officer had something to do with the failure for protection.

'I deemed it too dangerous to fire on the Russians, so as to avoid shooting our own men.' Jenkins replied casually. 'I am sure that you understand, Captain Forbes.'

'Sir, the men of my regiment are trained to select their targets carefully before firing. They could easily have provided covering fire for our retreat, and saved the lives of the men of the company, now lying out there dead and wounded. Your decision has cost a lot more lives than was necessary.'

'Are you accusing me of incompetence, Captain Forbes?' Jenkins flared. 'Sir, that is a serious charge that you have made before my fellow officers from the brigade.'

Ian felt his rage rising, and dropped his hand to the handle of his big Colt revolver. A hush had fallen on the soldiers nearby, listening to every word between the arrogant brigade officer and their regimental officer they knew and trusted. Ian fought to control his anger. It was not for himself, but the men who had needlessly been lost because of the decision made by Jenkins.

'Captain Forbes!' Ian recognised the voice of the colonel behind him. 'I am sure you have duties with your company.' Ian turned to see the colonel, and Captain Miles Sinclair standing in the trench.

'Yes, sir,' Ian responded, taking his hand away from the handle of his Colt. 'I will attend to my duties.'

'Good show,' the colonel said, and Ian saluted him as he walked away down the trench to the survivors of his company.

'Well done, sir,' a soldier said as he passed by. When Ian reached his company HQ, he saw Conan attempting to staunch the blood flowing from the young officer lying in the muddy bottom of the trench. Ian could see that he had taken a musket ball in the stomach, and knew that his chances of surviving the agonising wound were about nil. Conan glanced up at Ian, who shook his head before kneeling down beside the stricken young officer.

'You did the regiment proud today, Mr Sutton,' he said gently, taking the hand of the dying man. 'You ensured we did not lose the colours.'

Young William tried to smile his gratitude, but grimaced from the pain instead. 'Thank you, sir,' he gasped, and closed his eyes as if that would make the pain go away.

'Get the litter bearers here now,' Ian said, standing to give his order. He turned to Conan, who he could see had tears in his eyes. His face was blackened by gunpowder stains, as were those of the others who watched the pathetic scene with dead eyes. 'I am going to include your heroic efforts to save Mr Sutton and the colours in my report, Corporal Curry,' he said.

'I was just doing my duty,' Conan replied. 'The lads of Mr Sutton's platoon liked him – for an officer, he cared about his boys. I think it is something he learned from you, sir.'

Ian felt a lump in his throat. He did not consider himself a humane man. He had a commission to lead men in battle, and part of doing that was to care for the men he might have to send to their deaths. Maybe it was the influence of growing up in a place in the British Empire where attitudes were dictated by the egalitarianism that existed between the sons and daughters of convicts. Secretly, he still identified himself with that class of people the aristocracy of England considered disposable in the pursuit of expanding the Empire, and naturally born to serve their interests. But he also knew there were British officers who held the same attitude towards their men as he did, such as Miles Sinclair.

It was time for Ian to return to his tent behind the lines and compose his report. He would have to wait for the butcher's bill before doing so, and prayed that clearing the enemy marksmen from no man's land would save many more lives in the future. It was a terrible scale where the dead were placed on one side, hopefully outweighed by the living on the other. Ian was sure of one thing; Major Jenkins was doing everything in his power to see him killed.

*

Lieutenant Herbert Forbes was taken from the transport ship on a litter, placed on a wagon with other wounded, and transported to the British hospital outside Constantinople.

He was taken by litter into a ward filled with other wounded and sick officers, and placed on a bed with clean sheets. A doctor administered a dose of opium-based medication to help ease his obvious pain. A woman hovered nearby with clean bandages, and the doctor directed her to clean the wound, reapply clean bandages, and sit by the young officer for a short time to ensure that he was settling in.

Herbert could hear the sweet sound of women speaking to his colleagues in the ward that smelled of carbolic acid and cleanliness. When he looked up at the young woman sitting by his bed, he saw that she was pretty. He could also see that she had a curious expression on her face.

'Mr Forbes, are you possibly related to a Miss Alice Forbes of London?' the nurse asked.

'I am. She is my sister,' Herbert answered. 'How may I ask do you know her?'

'My name is Molly Williams, and I have read letters from Corporal Curry that you are his officer. I have had the pleasure and honour of meeting your sister, who was very kind to me,' Molly said with a warm smile. 'It was Miss Alice who spoke to Miss Nightingale to get me this job after I was . . .' Molly cut herself short but Herbert grinned.

'After you were released from prison,' Herbert said. 'My sister wrote to me about you, and what a fine young woman you are. I believe your brother, Owen, was sent here after he was wounded. How is he?'

'He has almost fully recovered from his wound, and has the full use of his arm,' Molly replied but her smile disappeared. 'He has been informed that he will be returning to the regiment in the next couple of days, to rejoin my brother Edwin and Corporal Curry. Were they well when you last saw them? I have not had any correspondence for a long time from Conan . . . Corporal Curry.'

'They were well, the last time I saw them. You should be proud of them. They are brave soldiers.'

'I would rather have all my men home in England,' Molly said. 'The stories I hear from the soldiers I nurse tell me terrible tales of life on the frontlines. When we first arrived at this hospital, men were dying every day from inexcusable neglect, but Miss Nightingale has done a grand job of reducing the death toll. You will be well cared for while you are here, as I will make it my personal duty to be by your side as you recover from your wound.'

'Thank you, Miss Williams,' Herbert said, taking her hand. 'I feel better already.'

Molly held his hand for a short while and said, 'I will tell my brother, Owen, that you are in this ward, as I am sure he would be pleased to visit you.'

'I would like that,' Herbert said. 'We have much to speak about.'

Molly rose from her chair beside Herbert and excused herself to attend other wounded men. Herbert watched her walk away, thinking how ironic that his life was in the hands of a woman once convicted of robbing his sister's fiancé. Forgiveness was as powerful as the strength of love. In many ways, it was a kind of love.

Herbert lay back against the clean sheets, wondering how long it would take him to recover from his wound. He needed to return to the regiment and stand with his brother when they finally attacked the port of Sebastopol.

Within the hour, Molly returned to the officer's ward to see Owen sitting beside Herbert's bed, and she could see that the two men were in deep conversation. Molly had seen similar scenes before in the hospital, where wounded soldiers and officers shared the terrors of the battlefield, which broke down the social barriers between them.

A few days later, Herbert's bed was empty and another officer took his place. Molly asked one of the nuns who had been assigned to the ward what had happened to Lieutenant Forbes, and was informed that the surgeon in charge had signed orders for him to be returned to England to recuperate. Molly was a little saddened to lose her patient, as Owen had already been shipped back to his regiment in Crimea. But she knew that Miss Alice would be overjoyed to have her little brother at home safely by the hearth. Even as she reflected on the situation, the litter bearers entered the hospital with sick and wounded soldiers from the Crimean front. All that Molly could hope for was that she would not look down on the faces of the men she held dearest in her heart. In the meantime, there were so many other men who were brothers, husbands, fathers and lovers to nurse. It never seemed to end, as the casualties continued to flow through the wards.

Part Three

The Redan and Beyond

1855

THIRTY-ONE

The months had passed, and the hot summer was upon the British, French and Turkish armies. Ian felt that his whole life was now war, and as he sat outside his tent, cleaning the popular Beaumont–Adams pistol he had traded his Colt for, he realised that he had been away from England for over a year.

The months had passed monotonously in the siege, with occasional forays against the Russian defences of Sebastopol, but no ground was truly gained.

Ian had noticed that the Russians were more determined to defend the harbour town, and his military mind considered the fact that they should have attacked the port city after the battle of Alma. A captured Russian officer confirmed his suspicions, saying that the city would have fallen, but caution by the British and French generals had lost the opportunity to end the war. Now, the enemy had been able to fortify Sebastopol and the war was at a stalemate.

Truces had been arranged between periods of fighting, to bury the dead and carry away the wounded. On one such truce, Ian had noticed a tall, fine-looking Russian officer smoking a cigar.

They caught each other's eye, and the Russian strolled over to Ian.

'A good day to you, sir,' he said in English. 'Would you like a cigar?'

Ian accepted the offer, and the Russian lit his cigar. Both men stood together observing the truce as if they had been serving soldiers in the same army.

'The weather is unpleasant, no?' the Russian said. He was a fit young man with a handsome face and pleasant smile. Ian guessed his enemy to be about his own age, and could see from the medals he wore on his clean uniform that the man was an experienced soldier.

'Bloody hot again,' Ian said, puffing on the cigar. 'When are you going to give up the port?'

The Russian laughed at Ian's question.

'You will have to come and take it from us,' he replied.

'I guess we will,' Ian said. 'How is the food where you are?'

'Good, we have French champagne captured from your allies,' the Russian officer replied, and Ian felt that under different circumstances, he could be friends with this young officer.

'Captain Samuel Forbes,' Ian said, extending his hand which the Russian officer accepted with a firm grip.

'Count Nikolai Kasatkin,' the Russian responded.

'Well, it seems the time for our truce is almost over so I will thank you for the cigar, and brief but interesting conversation.'

The Russian saluted Ian, who returned the salute.

'Maybe we will meet under better times, and you can share our French champagne,' he said before strolling away, as both armies cleared the killing ground red with blood, human parts and the debris of war.

Ian remembered the meeting, and wondered if the young Russian officer was still alive, after the ferocious bombardments by the allied artillery.

Conditions had improved in the British lines, as fresh food and other essentials were being brought up by the newly constructed railway to the men in the frontlines. Ian had been pleased at his colonel's order that he was not to accept any orders from brigade unless he was first consulted. This meant that Major Jenkins was rarely seen in the regimental lines.

'You have some mail, sir,' the company clerk said.

Ian accepted the letter, recognising Herbert's handwriting. He opened the letter, and read Herbert's complaints of lying around in London with nothing of any importance to do. Herbert wrote that his wound had healed, but left him with a slight limp. More importantly, he could not bear another day of his sister fussing around him, introducing him to the eligible young ladies at balls and afternoon picnics in the park, when he would prefer being back with the regiment. He also addressed Ian's question in a letter he had posted concerning the whereabouts of Jane. Herbert had replied that while at their country estate, he had asked questions of the locals in the nearby village who had said she had disappeared almost overnight many months earlier. None knew of why or where she had travelled. Herbert said he was sorry that he could not be of more help, and the only answer he received was that Charles had said that he had heard a rumour that she had gone to London. Herbert also wrote that his clearance to rejoin the regiment had been approved, and he was counting the days until he could take a transport ship with reinforcements to the Crimea. He concluded his letter saying that he hoped Ian had left some Muscovites alive for him to kill.

Ian frowned, folded the letter and gazed out at the tents of his company. Had Herbert already forgotten the horrors of the campaign? He knew his eagerness to return must be because the young man missed his other family – the regiment. There would be many Russians left to fight, and it seemed that the army would have to face another bitterly cold winter in the trenches. In the meantime, the summer was proving to be just as uncomfortable, as myriad flies infested every nook and cranny within the lines. All the British soldiers could do was traverse the miles of trenches, rifle pits and artillery gun emplacements, to gaze out on the same plan of trenches, rifle pits and gun emplacements of the enemy facing them.

Ian pulled out his pipe, and had hardly lit it when he was joined by Dr Peter Campbell.

'Hello, old chap,' Peter said, pulling up an empty wooden crate to sit on. 'Mind if I join you?'

Ian was pleased to share his boredom with his friend. 'I suppose your work has not been as busy as the past few weeks,' Ian said.

'One would think so, but our medical staff has been given orders to evacuate all our wounded and sick back to Balaclava. I think something is afoot.'

Ian immediately latched onto this little bit of intelligence. To issue such an order could only mean that something big was going to happen. He had hardly puffed on his pipe when the orderly room clerk hurried to him, stopped, saluted and breathlessly said, 'Sir, begging your pardon but the colonel wishes to speak with all his officers within the hour.'

'Thank you, soldier. I will be at the meeting.' The clerk saluted once again, and hurried back to the company HQ tent. Ian rose to his feet.

'It certainly appears that something big is in the offing,' he said.

'Good luck, old chap,' Peter replied. 'Just make sure you keep your head down.'

Ian strapped on his sword belt, tucked his newly acquired pistol in his sash, and scooped up his Enfield rifle. Maybe the waiting was finally over, but Ian felt that same old knot in his stomach. If so, it would mean the death, and mutilation of many of his men if they were about to assault the massive fortifications of the Russian-held seaport.

Later that evening, after Ian returned from the briefing by the colonel, he summoned his officers and issued orders for all men to be under arms and ready for an imminent assault on the Russian port town.

That night, Ian made his way along the regimental lines, speaking with his men, and attempting a joke or two to raise their spirits. Ian stopped at the small fire where the two Williams brothers sat with Conan, smoking their pipes. 'This is it, sir,' Conan said. 'About bloody time we got this war over.'

'You men should try to get some sleep,' Ian said, squatting by the three battle-hardened veterans, and accepting a mug of hot tea Conan passed him. 'Good to see you back with us, Owen,' he added. 'Try not to get yourself sent back to the hospital this time.'

In the distance, Ian could hear the others of the company talking quietly, knowing that this might be the last time they would do so. Horses snorted and stamped their hooves while the eternal stars glittered above, oblivious to the activities of mere mortals.

In the early morning before dawn, and without the sound of drums and trumpets, the formations of cavalry, and infantry began their advance. Ian marched ahead of his company as was his practice, with his rifle slung over his shoulder. As dawn came to the Crimea the massed regiments and squadrons were in formation for the final assault.

They stood waiting, locked in private thoughts and fears, when the order came to withdraw back to the lines.

Confused and frustrated, Ian looked over to the company on his left, where he saw his friend, Captain Sinclair shrug his shoulders. Ian detached himself from his company as they wheeled about to return to their tents.

'What the bloody hell is going on?' he asked Miles.

'No one is sure, but I heard a rumour that General Simpson felt indisposed, and sought relief on one of the ships at Balaclava. He may consider this a rehearsal for the real thing.'

Disgusted, Ian shook his head, and hurried to catch up with his company. It was late summer, and autumn would arrive soon enough. The way things were going, they would have to suffer another winter of siege warfare.

★

It was just another day on the lines when Ian looked up from the reports he was perusing, compiled by his faithful and very competent clerk in his tent, when he saw Herbert limping towards him. Ian immediately rose from his chair to greet the young man.

'Sam!' Herbert exclaimed in his joy. 'Brother, it is so good to see you again.'

Ian took the extended hand of the young officer with a bear-like grip. 'I was informed that you would be joining us again by the adjutant yesterday. Welcome home to hell. How is Alice?'

Herbert sat down on an empty ammunition case in Ian's tent to relieve the pain in his hip. The wound had healed, but left a residue of discomfort. 'Alice sends her best wishes, and the family appears to be profiting well out of the war contracts. Charles has never been happier than poring over the ledgers to see our money piling up.'

'Maybe the family can afford to purchase me a majority, and you a captaincy,' Ian said. 'But not until there is a vacancy in the regiment, as I doubt I would want to serve in any other.'

'I feel the same,' Herbert said. 'The bonds are forged in blood. Do I get my own men back?'

'You do,' Ian said. 'Colour Sergeant Leslie and Mr Sutton did a fine job of looking after your men for your holiday at home. But don't expect to see all the familiar faces as we now have a lot of reinforcements from England.'

'It was no holiday with Alice insisting that she care for me. She would order piles of food to fatten me, because she felt that I was too thin. Had I stayed a day longer, I think I would have been forced to order new uniforms to fit my bulk. She means well, and I know how much she misses Peter. All day, she would ask me how he is faring. Do I still have Corporal Curry and the Williams brothers? I saw Owen when I was sent to our hospital. He said he was being returned to the regiment.'

'You do,' Ian replied. 'They are amongst the few seasoned soldiers we have in the company, but I am pleased to say there are others who have weathered winter, and now this infernal summer.'

'Well, I think it is time to meet the new men under my command and greet the old ones,' Herbert said, rising stiffly from the improvised seat. 'It is good to be back.'

Herbert departed, and Ian made a note to catch up with him that evening. He would send word to Peter that they share a bottle of good rum Ian had stashed away. Ian turned to his desk when his clerk burst in.

'Sir, some news,' he said. 'The Muscovites have overrun the Froggies at some place called Tchernaya. There is to be a briefing now, at the colonel's tent.'

Ian was surprised by the news. It was the Russians initiating the battle, and this did not bode well.

*

From the top of a ridge Ian watched in frustration as the French and Sardinian troops took the brunt of the massive Russian attack across the river. From the heights overlooking the Russian advance, Ian could see the rolling clouds of gun smoke and thicker, billowing smoke of the artillery pieces firing grape shot and high explosive, cutting swathes out of the Russian ranks. As he and his regiment watched, the French were able to first halt the attack, and then push it back. A few enemy units were able to scramble up the heights, but were driven back by the fierce resistance of the French infantry. A couple of Italian battalions of Piedmontese and Bersaglieri counterattacked as if on a parade ground, driving off any Russian riflemen still firing across the river. It was the Allied artillery that had won the day, but Sebastopol still stood defiant, and would have to be taken with rifle and bayonet before this war could end.

*

Alice knew that the invitation had been delivered for Lord Montery's garden party, and it was not an occasion to miss, as members of the royal family were also invited. Alice asked the servants where she might find the much-desired invitation and was informed that it had been delivered to Charles' office. Alice very rarely entered her brother's office in the London house, but decided he would not mind if she was looking for the invitation.

Alice entered the room and looked first to the pile of correspondence on his desk. She flipped through the letters but did not find it. Possibly her brother had seen it and, absent-minded in his heavy workload, had placed it in a drawer. She opened a drawer in his desk, and saw a pile of correspondence. Alice retrieved the letters, and flipped through them. She could not find the invitation, but her attention was drawn to a letter obviously posted from Crimea. Her curiosity piqued she withdrew the letter, and noted that it had been sent by a Major Jenkins. Alice read the letter and was shocked and confused. Alice could not believe her eyes, as her hands trembled while she reread the damning letter and its vague reference to disposing of both her brothers, Herbert and Samuel, for a hefty fee. So engrossed was she that she did not notice Charles enter the room behind her.

'What are you doing?' Charles asked in a cold voice.

Alice's heart skipped a beat as she swung around to confront her brother.

'This letter from a Major Jenkins appears to be an offer to eliminate the problem of Samuel and Herbert,' Alice said in a shaky voice. 'What is your answer to that, Charles?'

Charles frowned, taking a step towards her. Alice shrank away. 'It is not what it seems,' he lied. 'I asked my friend, Major Jenkins, to eliminate the problem of having Samuel and Herbert being exposed on the frontlines, and to have them transferred to Lord Raglan's staff, where they would be safer,' he continued lying and now regretting that he had not destroyed the incriminating letter. 'If you don't mind, I would like my personal correspondence back,' he said, extending his hand.

Alice hesitated but gave him the letter, not convinced that her brother was telling her the truth. She knew how Charles despised Samuel, but wondered why he would include Herbert's name. She had always known that Charles was a man born without any empathy for others, including his own family, had always suspected that Charles would like to see any threats to his total control of the inheritance disappear. The word 'eliminate' had a sinister meaning to her. As if reading her doubts Charles added, 'I ask you, how could a serving staff officer cause the deaths of Samuel and Herbert?'

Alice thought upon her brother's question, and could not see any answer. Her knowledge of military matters was restricted to what she read in *The Times*.

'I suppose you are right,' Alice said carefully. 'Major Jenkins might have chosen a better word to describe how he could help keep Herbert and Samuel safe from the horrors I have read about on the frontlines.'

'I can assure you, dear sister, that the welfare of our brothers is my main concern. I pray that they will return to us whole and hearty very soon.'

Alice did not reply but brushed past him, the invitation forgotten. She was not convinced that her brother had told her the truth.

THIRTY-TWO

It was in early autumn when the gates of hell opened.

Ian wondered how such a wonderful day of mild weather could be disrupted by the constant pounding of artillery from both sides.

From his vantage point, he could see British and French warships floating on a serene sea just outside the entrance to Sebastopol. As he gazed at the city of white buildings, three massive explosions rocked the earth from within the Russian defences. The French had planted their mines after tunnelling towards the city walls. The explosive mines were known as four gases, which exploded and signalled the attack. The mines had been very effective, and Ian watched as a sea of flame ran for three miles in the city with curling, white smoke marking the devastation. Ian knew that the French target had been the heavily fortified section known as the Malakoff on the left flank of the high ground, overlooking the port town.

The bombardment was still relentless as Ian withdrew to his regimental lines. He had seen enough.

The following day, Ian returned, but this time with a handful of infantry regiments at his back to observe the courage of the French troops assaulting the Malakoff position.

Amidst the smoke blowing over the French trenches, the army of France rose up to rush across the short distance between the frontlines. Explosions continued in the Russian defence of Malakoff, blowing men and guns to pieces and cannon continued to blast the stunned Russians. Ian was pleased to see that they had taken the shattered earthworks, but could also see the Russian counterattack against the French infantry.

Ian knew this was also the signal for his regiment to join the attack, focusing on another fortification known as the Redan, while the French provided a force on their right and left flanks in the attack.

Ian glanced around to see his men crouching on one knee, faces grim with fear, rifles ready with bayonets attached. The order was given by their colonel to advance, and Ian roared out the order to his company. 'C'mon, boys. Let's give the Muscovites a taste of our steel!'

They now approached the gates of hell which opened wide, inviting them in to taste death and mutilation while the continuous noise of the artillery guns roared solid shot, high explosive, canister and grape shot into both sides of no man's land. Ian held his sword in one hand and pistol in the other. His rifle was slung over his back. The British force moved forward as one under intense fire, and the first of the Russian landmines exploded only yards from Ian, blowing two of the soldiers into bloody chunks of flesh. The landmines were buried barrels of gunpowder with an attached tin tube. Stepping on the tube caused them to explode a jet of fire into the gunpowder, resulting in the barrel exploding. They were greatly feared by the British soldiers.

On his right, Ian could see Herbert carrying the colours, beside him Colour Sergeant Leslie with Corporal Curry and the Williams brothers surging forward, ignoring the air filled with flying metal death. Beyond the colour party flying the regimental flag, Ian saw Captain Miles Sinclair suddenly throw up his arms and fall as he led his company. It was then that Ian realised officers in the regiment were being selected by Russian sharpshooters. Ian dropped his sword, thrust his pistol in the waist sash, and snatched the rifle from his back. It made him less obvious as an officer.

The carnage of the frontal assault was made worse when Russian artillery opened fire from their flank, enfilading the small force of British soldiers. From their front, the enemy poured in a steady and aimed fire. Ian could feel the fear but knew he must keep going, as their only option left was to overwhelm the defenders and take their positions. There was no going back, and every yard of ground felt like a mile.

A bullet snatched at the sleeve of Ian's uniform, but he ignored the close call. He was panting with physical exhaustion as they reached the outer edge of the Redan fortification. A deep ditch lay before the attacking British companies, and when Ian glanced around him he could see that his company was still with him, but severely reduced in numbers. The men of Ian's company scrambled down the ditch, and up to the parapet above manned by the Russians. With rifle and bayonet, they drove off the defenders, and Ian found himself and his considerably reduced company in the narrow salient of the city walls.

Smoke, noise and the coppery stench of blood filled the tiny area. The British were forced to advance in small groups due to the confinement of the Russian defences. Ian made a quick assessment of their situation, realising from the shouts to their front that the Russians were pushing reinforcements into the Redan in a counterattack. Men from the attacking British regiments were now a mixed force and fell fast from the enemy fire being poured into them by the counterattacking Russians. Blood splattered Ian's face from a soldier hit by a musket ball in the neck, and he tasted the blood in his parched mouth. Through the choking smoke he saw a Russian mere yards away, kneeling to reload his musket. Ian raised his rifle and fired. The soldier toppled forward. Ian knew that they would be engaged fighting hand to hand, and drew his pistol in one hand while trailing his rifle in the other.

For an hour, Ian and his company bit, clubbed, stabbed, fired rifles, punched, kicked and bayoneted the enemy in the close confines. The Russians did the same to the British soldiers, their reinforcements added to the confusion. The British were now outnumbered by at least four to one.

'Withdraw!' Ian roared, recognising the futility of their situation, and those nearest Ian heard the order, falling back slowly with their rifles pointed at the Russians attacking them. It was obvious to Ian that they could not hold the ground they had captured in the initial stages of the attack on the Redan fortification.

When Ian and the survivors of his company reached the ditch, they could see the numerous piles of their dead and wounded at the bottom. The triumphant Russian infantry pressed forward and hand-to-hand fighting continued unabated.

Ian could not see Herbert and the colour party. He

continued to encourage the remainder of the company to follow him into the ditch, and up the other side, in an attempt to find safety in their own trenches. The Russians were hot on their heels, and only the covering fire from the British trenches kept the Russians at bay.

Ian was almost at the top of the ditch when he looked back to see the tattered and blood-soaked regimental colours at the bottom beside the shattered body of Herbert. It appeared that he had been hit by a volley of grape shot that had ripped away his body, but left his face intact. Ian groaned and scrambled back down into the ditch to be beside of what was left of Herbert's body. Herbert's eyes were still open, and he had an expression of utter surprise in his young features. Beside him lay Corporal Curry on his back, covered in blood, and Ian felt tears streak his blackened face, running in rivulets down his cheeks.

But Conan suddenly stirred and made a feeble effort to rise. Ian grabbed the front of Conan's jacket, hauling him into a sitting position. 'Are you wounded?' he yelled above the din of continuing gunfire.

'No, just winded,' Conan slurred. 'Where's the Williams brothers?'

'I don't know,' Ian replied, and Conan scrambled to his feet, immediately recovering the blood-soaked and shredded regimental flag. Ian helped the corporal to the edge of the ditch, and they heard a cheer rise from their trenches as what was left of the flag fluttered in the slight breeze, stirring up the dust, and swirling the smoke. Both men staggered into their lines, holding aloft the standard of their regiment.

As soon as Ian was able to calm his nerves, he glanced around, but could not see the colonel who had led the regiment's attack on the Redan.

'Where is the colonel?' he asked a sergeant from another company, who had passed him a flask of water.

'He was wounded, sir, but we got him back to our lines to the surgeon. The regimental second-in-command has been killed,' the sergeant said. From his uniform, Ian could see that the sergeant had not been involved in the assault on the Redan, but held in reserve with the other battalions.

'We needed more men,' Ian said bitterly. 'They are all dead out there.' Ian found himself staring vacantly at the opposite side of the trench wall, remembering the vicious hand-to-hand fighting in the Redan. How many Russians had he personally killed with his bayonet? Ian could not – or did not want to – remember.

'Sir, Colour Sergeant Leslie is taking a roll call of the company,' Conan's voice drifted to him. 'I am afraid that the butcher's bill is high.'

Ian did not need to be reminded of the heavy toll that had been inflicted on his men in the futile attempt to take and hold the Redan. In the distance, he could hear constant gunfire and artillery shells exploding, guessing that the French were still fighting. Ian closed his eyes.

'I see that you survived the debacle on the Redan,' a familiar and despised voice said. Ian opened his eyes to see Major Jenkins standing over him in his spotless dress uniform.

'You sound disappointed,' Ian said.

'You will address me as sir,' Jenkins said. 'You are an insolent chap.'

'I might have thought about respecting you if I had seen you in our ranks when we went into the attack – seriously undermanned. Was that one of your great ideas . . . sir?'

'Had you the heart, Captain Forbes, your men could have been persuaded to press on against our foe, and carry the day,' Jenkins said, and this time Ian felt the red rage of killing overwhelm him. He reached for the pistol, but discovered that he had lost it on the battlefield. Jenkins saw his motion, and backed away with fear in his face.

'Where is your sword?' Jenkins asked in a frightened voice, realising that he had pushed this officer the men called 'The Colonial' just once too often. But Ian was too exhausted to threaten Jenkins, and he simply sat, staring past him.

'I discarded the sword,' Ian said. 'That is why I am still possibly alive, unlike many other officers of the regiment.'

'You will be reported for discarding your sword, Captain Forbes,' Jenkins said, making ready to beat a hasty retreat. 'It is conduct unbecoming an officer of Her Majesty to do that in front of the men.'

'I don't think they cared,' Ian said with a bitter laugh. 'They were more interested in just staying alive themselves. And if you expect me to stand and salute you, I would think carefully on that right now.'

Jenkins did not reply, but turned on his heel to walk away. Ian stared after him, contemplating the day he would kill the staff officer who had insulted the memory of the men whose smashed bodies lay in the ruins of the Redan and the ditch behind him. It would not be murder, in the eyes of Ian, but an execution.

Ian struggled to his feet and made his way along the trench to Colour Sergeant Leslie who, grim-faced, passed the roll book to him with the words, 'It is not complete, sir. The CSM has the total,' he said. 'We are hoping that one or two of the lads might be wounded, and recovered from the field.'

Ian ran his eyes down the list, and saw another familiar name, Private Edwin Williams.

'Are you sure that Private Edwin Williams is dead?' he asked Leslie.

'Saw it myself, sir,' Colour Sergeant Leslie said sadly. 'He was next to Mr Herbert when our party was hit by Muscovite grape shot. Not much left of him, or Mr Herbert.'

'What about his brother, Owen?' Ian asked, scanning the names on the list of confirmed dead.

'Missing at this stage, sir,' Leslie said. 'It is still early days.'

They were joined by Conan, whose blood-soaked uniform was hardly recognisable as that of a British soldier. Like so many others, it was torn, dirty and covered in blood. 'I've been searching for Owen,' Conan said. 'But no one can remember seeing him after the fight.'

'I am sorry, Corporal,' Ian said.

'I recruited him myself,' Leslie said. 'He was a fine soldier.'

The men fell into a silence, each locked in the screams in their head as the French fought on to overcome the Russians in the town of Sebastopol.

★

The room stank of the coppery smell of blood as the wounded were brought into the factory-like surgery, the doctors waiting with saws and sutures.

Peter Campbell was exhausted. There had been so many and no sign of the supply of patients diminishing. Terrible wounds inflicted by the lead musket balls that shattered bone on impact. Missing limbs from the impact of the canister and grape shot of the enemy artillery guns. Deep bayonet wounds in the stomachs and chests of soldiers. There was no shortage of battle wounds to deal with.

Peter swabbed his forehead with the back of his bloody

hand as the sweat rolled down, stinging his eyes. He felt the amputated arm at his feet and called to an orderly to remove it, lest he trip on it.

Another soldier was placed on his table by two litter bearers. Peter looked down on him through weary eyes, and felt his heart skip a beat. He recognised the shattered face of Private Owen Williams. Owen was semi-conscious and moaning in his distress. Peter quickly diagnosed the wound, and guessed it had been a musket ball that had smashed one side of his face. Skilfully, Peter probed to ensure that the ball was not inside the wound, and Owen hardly noticed the painful examination in his agonised condition. No ball was found, but Peter could feel the fractured cheekbone. Thank God it was not a life-threatening wound, he thought, and reached for the needle and stitches to sew the jagged edges together. There was no time to apply chloroform, and Peter worked quickly to minimise the pain the sewing caused. When he was finished, he turned to an orderly. 'This man is to be shipped to Constantinople for recovery treatment. Take him away.'

No sooner had Owen been lifted off the surgery table than another soldier was placed on the surface slippery with blood. Peter quickly examined the soldier whose leg had been shattered above the knee. This time, he used the chloroform on his patient, and sawed off the leg above the knee. There was no time to think about the fate of Private Owen Williams, but he would ensure the knowledge of his survival was relayed to Sam Forbes.

★

Ian sat at the table in his tent, still wearing the tattered uniform he had fought in. His hand trembled as he recovered a page of writing paper and a pen. This would be the hardest and most sorrowful letter he would ever have to write, and with a trembling hand he began.

My dear Alice,

I regret to inform you . . . .

Ian paused, remembering the oath he had made to her in England; to always protect her beloved little brother. How foolish to say such a thing in a time of war. Only luck decided who lived and died.

Outside his tent, he could hear the distant gunfire of the continuing battle for Sebastopol.

Tears dropped on the letter, and Ian used a sheet of blotting paper to dry them away. He continued writing, forcing his trembling hand to be still.

. . . that on this day our beloved Herbert was killed bravely fighting in the battle for Sebastopol . . .

At this moment in time, Ian knew why Samuel Forbes had hated war so passionately, as Ian did now. But he also knew soldiering was like some terrible addiction. He knew how those who used the opium flower could not rid themselves of the desire to destroy their lives with it. War was Ian's opiate, and he knew that it was destroying his soul.

THIRTY-THREE

It was the French army that finally overcame Russian resistance, and Sebastopol fell at a bloody cost to both sides. The returning French soldiers were cheered, and saluted by the British soldiers as they passed, and Waterloo was forgotten between the two traditional enemies.

Ian received a despatch from the colonel in a British hospital behind the lines that he was to assume temporary command of the regiment as one of the few senior officers left alive. Ian stared at the paper naming him as the temporary regimental commander. He knew that he had very few men left alive to command, and looked to the bloody, tattered flag that so many had died for.

'Sir, what are your orders?' His own company sergeant major was now acting regimental sergeant major, in lieu of the senior regimental NCO now dead on the battlefield.

'Pass the word for the regiment to assemble, sarn't

major,' Ian said in a weary voice. 'I will address them.'

The weary, battle-fatigued men of the regiment fell in, and Ian stood before them.

'I have been commanded to assume command until our colonel is well enough to resume his duties,' Ian said. 'I just want to tell each and every one of you that you have upheld the finest traditions of the British army, and it is an honour to be your commander. We have all lost comrades at the Redan, and their sacrifice was not in vain, although many of you may think we were defeated. Sebastopol has fallen, and the Muscovites are in retreat. We, the Allies, have won a victory.'

Ian scanned the faces of the men standing in ranks, and saw the haunted look of soldiers who had seen too much. He knew that he could not continue with any further words to inspire men who just fought to stay alive.

'Sar'nt major. Fall out the parade,' Ian said.

The men were dismissed to their duties, and Ian returned to his tent, where he had arranged to purchase another revolver from one of the many merchants who followed the army. The Russians might have given up Sebastopol, but the war was far from over.

Not that far away, the smoke rose over a town burning from end to end, marking the bloody victory.

*

The Times correspondent went down to the city to witness, and report on what a victory looked like. He stopped off at a hospital that had been shelled. He entered through a door into a low room supported by square pillars. The windows were shattered, and the ward packed with decomposing corpses, alongside the severely wounded and freshly dead. Some were on trestles, others on the floor in pools of congealed blood. Russell could see a wounded Russian soldier under a bed, glaring at him and the British journalist quickly moved on through the rows of wounded, bones protruding where their limbs had been subjected to gun and artillery fire. It was a pitiful sight and he could hear the cries of those still able to voice their pain calling for water, food and care. The stench was overwhelming, and when he looked into the faces of the soldiers, he saw how young they were. Russell stumbled from the horror into the sunlight. So, this is what victory looked like.

★

Molly sat by the bedside of her brother, Owen, with tears in her eyes. His once handsome face was now disfigured by the terrible wound. 'Edwin and Conan, do you know of their fate?' she asked through her tears.

'Edwin is gone,' Owen answered, hardly able to look his sister in the eye. While being transported on the ship to the British hospital, a fellow wounded soldier recounted how he had seen him blown away by the Russian grape shot, while standing with the colour party. 'I do not know of the Paddy's fate.'

Molly looked around the ward filling each day with the wounded, noticing how so many were from her brother's regiment. Always, she dreaded seeing those she loved amongst the wounded and maimed. The only consolation was that if they were brought in wounded, they were still alive and, thanks to the efforts of Miss Nightingale and her nurses, they had a better chance of remaining alive.

'Edwin had a premonition he would not survive and gave me his share of the bounty we found,' Owen said quietly. 'His share is sewn into my trousers, and I want you to hold it for us.'

Molly nodded her understanding. She would retrieve the cash later that night when she was on her rounds. Molly had previously secured Owen's share safely, sewn into a spare dress she owned. But it was time to make her rounds, knowing that her brother's wound would not stop him returning to his regiment in the future. Molly was a spiritual person, and spent every night off-duty praying that the war would end, and she would not have to hold the hands of dying men, nor hear their cries of pain in the night, as they tossed and turned, reliving the horrors of this modern war of increased technology aimed at killing more efficiently.

*

But the war went on.

Private Owen Williams rejoined the regiment, much to the joy of Conan. Ian was pleased to hear that the Welshman was back in the ranks, and personally greeted him in the lines.

'Sir, I have been told by the lads that you are now the regimental commander,' Owen said as they stood outside the bell tent he and Conan shared.

'Until the colonel is fit enough to return to the regiment,' Ian said, observing the red raw gash along the side of his face. The wound had caused one eye to droop when it was stitched, and it would remain for life as a memento of the disastrous attack on the Redan.

'I have heard talk from the boys that they like having you as the commander,' Owen continued. 'They say you are lucky, and that means a lot in this war.'

Ian thought about that. He had always been in the thick of the fighting, and yet the only substantial wound he had ever received was one he had incurred earlier in the campaign. All he had now was a jagged scar along his arm.

'Do they still call me the colonial?' Ian asked with a smile.

'Er, yes, sir,' Owen answered hesitantly. 'They don't mean any harm by it.'

How ironic that he should have that title from his troops. If only they knew how right they were. 'It is good to have you back, Private Williams,' Ian said. 'Maybe I will be able to put my hands on a good bottle of rum for you and Corporal Curry to celebrate this occasion, and raise a toast to the memories of Mr Forbes and Edwin.'

'Thank you, sir,' Owen said. 'That would be good.'

Ian walked away to return to his duties as the regiment's commanding officer. Secretly, he relished his new title, and with the fading sound of drums and trumpets, was beginning to accept that his boyhood dreams in New South Wales were being realised. The regiment was his family, and he was their father.

Then the war was over.

The Tsar of Russia sued for peace in Paris, and the politicians left their sumptuous lunches to sign the Treaty of Paris in March 1856 in their best clothes that had never been soiled by the blood of their armies.

And Ian's regiment went home.

*

Parades and dinners greeted the regiment when it returned to the streets of London.

Dr Peter Campbell and Captain Samuel Forbes once again took up residence in the Reform Club. Ian did not attempt to seek out Alice, as he still carried the crushing guilt of breaking his impossible promise of ensuring her beloved young brother survived the war. His first priority was to find Jane, and to aid him, he had in his possession what he guessed was a small fortune in precious stones and gold. But first, he would need to find a way of selling his war booty without the government learning of his possession of the generous fortune. He knew that they would insist that he turn over the jewels and gold to the British coffers and be distributed indirectly to the British aristocrats. The first names that came to mind when it came to contacts with the shady figures of London's less scrupulous businessmen were those of Corporal Conan Curry and Private Owen Williams. They had, after all, a background in criminal proceedings in the great city, and the possible contacts to assist him turning the gold, and precious stones into cash.

Ian changed into a suit of civilian dress, and made his way to a hotel he knew was popular with the soldiers from the London barracks. He had heard Conan mention the place as where Colour Sergeant Leslie had recruited him and the Williams brothers.

The day was bleak and cold for spring in London, and rain fell as a drizzle. Ian found the hotel, stepping inside the room thick with tobacco smoke and the sweat of closely packed bodies. It was not hard to find Conan, Owen and a pretty young woman sitting at a table in the corner. Both men were wearing their dress uniforms, and on their uniform jackets each had the two medals issued for the campaign. One was British and had the clasps of the major battles on the riband, whilst the other, a medal issued by a grateful Ottoman Empire to the Allied nations who had defeated the Russian Tsar. In front of the small party were many tankards of ale, and Ian guessed that they were gifts from a few grateful citizens.

Conan rose unsteadily when he saw Ian approach.

'Resume your seat, Conan,' Ian said, pulling up a stool. 'We are not on duty, and I felt a need to join you both for a drink.'

'It is an honour to have you join us, sir,' Owen slurred, half lifting his tankard from the beer-wettened table. 'This is my sister, Molly,' he said, turning his head to her. 'She is a bit keen on the bloody Irishman.'

Molly smiled when Ian caught her eye, and nodded her head in acknowledgement of his presence. Ian returned the smile and could see that she was the only one of them who was sober.

'Molly, fetch Captain Forbes an ale,' Owen said, and she stepped away.

'There is another reason why I sought you two out,' Ian said, leaning towards the two inebriated soldiers. 'I would be grateful for advice on how to go about selling a few trinkets of jewellery I acquired in the Crimea.'

'Ah, I can see why you might want to be discreet,' Conan said, immediately understanding why an officer might need their talents. 'Would the said jewellery perhaps have fallen into your hands when we sacked that Muscovite baggage train?'

'Something like that,' Ian grudgingly admitted, but had come to trust these two men, who had on more than one occasion put themselves in dire peril to keep him alive.

Molly was standing behind Ian with an ale. 'Ikey the Jew would know what to do,' she said, placing the tankard in front of Ian. 'I saw him yesterday in Mayfair. He has returned to London.'

'Ikey the Jew,' Ian echoed. 'Is he a dealer in precious stones and gold?'

The three laughed, and Owen leaned forward as Molly resumed her seat. 'Ikey Solomon deals in everything in these parts, and not a man to be trifled with. But he has a reputation for fairness, and would not do you wrong. Molly used to look after his books, and he is a bit sweet on her.'

'I should consider you on a percentage then, Miss Williams, if you can arrange for me to deal with your former employer,' Ian said.

'No, sir. Conan and Owen have told me what a fine officer and gentleman you are. I would not even think of taking your money.'

'Maybe not a gentleman, if you really knew Captain Forbes,' Conan said with a wink, which Ian ignored.

'Do you think I could meet with this Ikey the Jew tomorrow?' Ian asked Molly, and she said she would try to ensure this could happen after the matter was discussed. Ian then joined the three in a round of toasts to the regiment and the men who had not come home.

That evening, a note was delivered to the club for Ian, and it set out the meeting place and time. Ian read the note before going to join his old friend, Dr Campbell in the dining room. As much as he trusted the fellow colonial, Ian had not told him about the property he had obtained from the fleeing Russians.

The following morning, the rain had cleared, and fluffy white clouds above vied with the odious smog below. Conan and Owen, wearing civilian clothing, and Molly, in a new dress, fell in with Ian wearing his civilian suit, walking the short distance from the Reform Club to the place Molly said her contact had his office. Ian did not know what to expect, but was surprised to see the second-level office in the merchant house was clean and professional. They were greeted at the door by a scarred, heavy-built man who Molly spoke to.

He popped his head around a doorway, and the man they had come to meet called them in.

Ian and his companions stepped into the office, where they saw another heavy-built man sitting behind a desk.

Beside him stood a younger man who bore a resemblance to Ikey. He wore spectacles and was clean-shaven. Ian locked eyes with Ikey and could see an intelligence behind the rugged face. He had a long black beard and rose to extend his hand to Ian.

'Captain Forbes, I presume,' he said with a firm hand-shake. 'Molly has already briefed me about you and some business dealings we may have between us. Please, all take a seat.' Molly, Conan and Owen pulled up chairs before the impressive man's desk. Ian touched the small revolver concealed in his jacket as a precaution and then withdrew the leather pouch containing the jewels and opened it, spilling his cache on the desk. Ian immediately saw the surprised reaction from Ikey at the sight of the small fortune on his desk. The young man standing beside him raised his eyebrows in surprise.

The first stone Ikey picked up was a sapphire the size of an acorn, and passed it to the young man, who had retrieved a small magnifying glass. He studied the stone, and Ian could read his expression. This was a very valuable object. The young man passed it to Ikey, leaning down to whisper in his ear. Ikey nodded.

'My son has told me that the sapphire is worth a Queen's ransom,' he said. 'I do not have the kind of money to pay for it.'

'You can have it,' Ian said. 'All you have to do is find someone for me in London. A lady, whose life is far more precious to me than the value of the stone. Her name is Miss Jane Wilberforce.'

'Your offer is very generous, Captain Forbes,' Ikey said.

'Miss Williams has praised your ability to be able to find anyone in London,' Ian said, retrieving the sapphire from the desk. 'It will be yours when you are able to locate the lady.'

'If she is alive, I promise you, I will find her,' Ikey said. 'And now, let us settle on a price for the rest of your jewellery. I can see it is of Russian origin, but I will not ask you where it came from. I will be generous with you because I have heard that you killed many Russians who forced my family from the Motherland. You have my gratitude.'

The morning went smoothly, with the Jewish merchant giving Ian a generous price. Paper currency was retrieved by Ikey's son, and counted on the desk. Ian was stunned by the amount of money Ikey Solomon was able to retrieve on such short notice. It was indeed a small fortune. Business over, the four left the office.

'I thought that we had done well out of the baggage train,' Conan said, shaking his head as they walked along the busy street.

'I suspected that you had,' Ian smiled. 'I could tell when we returned to our lines that you had a swagger in your step.'

'All our money has gone to Molly, who has invested our shares in purchasing a shop in one of the better London addresses. Molly feels that a confectionary shop will be our retirement fund in a few years' time when we do the service we signed up for.'

Ian glanced at Molly, walking beside Conan with a confident expression. She was a remarkable young lady, he thought, and could see that she was very much smitten with Conan.

'I would presume that Corporal Curry is going to make an honest woman of you, Miss Williams,' Ian said with a warm smile, causing Molly to blush.

'He has not asked me, sir,' she said.

'I will when my enlistment is up,' Conan quickly said. 'I would hope you would be there for the wedding when the time comes, sir,' he added.

'I would be honoured, Conan,' Ian replied. 'But do not wait too long to propose, because from what I can see, Miss Williams is one of the fairest ladies in London.'

Conan beamed at the praise of the lady he loved, and the four decided that they should stop at a tavern to celebrate the business negotiation outcome. After that, Ian would deposit his money in an account at a prestigious London bank, and face the moment he had dreaded since returning to England. He would go to the Forbes residence in London, and meet with Alice.

THIRTY-FOUR

Although it had been months since Herbert was killed in action, the mood in the London house was just as sombre as the day he had died. Ian deliberately did not wear his uniform because the sight of it might upset Alice.

Ian was met by Alice and Peter.

'It is good to see that you have returned to us safely,' Alice said, tears welling in her eyes. 'I cannot afford to lose another brother.'

Peter greeted Ian warmly, and the three sat down in the parlour to partake of tea and sweet cakes.

'Peter has told me that you were present when Herbert was killed,' Alice said. 'Was his death mercifully quick?'

Ian glanced at Peter. 'A musket ball took Herbert's life, and when I found him, it was as if he had simply gone to sleep,' he lied. How could he tell Alice of the terrible mutilation of her beloved brother's body, smashed by the grape shot from a Russian cannon? Peter made a slight nod of agreement, although he also knew the truth. It was better to lie than tell the truth of war to those left behind, who had never been exposed to the harsh realities of modern warfare.

'Peter has confided to me that you blame yourself for Herbert's death,' Alice said. 'It was not right that I should make you promise to keep our brother alive. I do not think that is right, after all Peter has told me of the terrible conditions you all suffered. Peter feels that only sheer luck is the real answer to who lived and died in the Crimea.'

Ian did not want to admit to himself that young Herbert had grown to be like a real brother to him, and forced back the tears when he remembered around the campfires Herbert confessed his terrible fear of dying, or being mutilated. Ian had no answer for him then, nor could simply say that Herbert's luck had simply run out.

'I blame Charles for Herbert's death,' Alice said bitterly, reaching for a dainty handkerchief to wipe the tears from her eyes. 'He and that ghastly Major Jenkins.'

'Jenkins!' Ian exclaimed. 'What do you know of him?'

'I accidentally found a letter addressed to Charles from him,' Alice said, wiping the tears from her eyes. 'It appears that Charles and Major Jenkins were corresponding. In his letter from Major Jenkins, he intimated that he would ensure the problem of you and Herbert would be dealt with. When I questioned Charles on the nature of Major Jenkins' words, he replied that the Major meant keeping an eye on your welfare. I do not believe him.'

Ian looked at Peter. Both men frowned.

'Do you still have that letter?' Ian asked, but Alice shook her head.

'He retrieved it from me, and I believe he may have destroyed it,' she replied.

'In all good faith, I cannot blame Major Jenkins for the death of Herbert, as our regiment took the brunt of the fighting at the Redan, and we almost lost our colonel to wounds that day. But Jenkins is still a man I personally despise as a cowardly and incompetent officer of the Queen,' Ian said.

The tea and cakes arrived, carried by a young servant girl on a silver platter.

Peter attempted to steer the conversation away from the sad reflections on the death of Herbert with news of the up-and-coming wedding between he and Alice. He asked Ian to be the best man, and Ian readily accepted.

When Ian departed after lunch, he did so with the thought that Jenkins was in league with Charles, and that while the major had any dealings with the regiment, Ian would have to watch his back. At least Ian had the consolation that whilst Jenkins remained with brigade HQ, he had little opportunity to interfere with the regiment. For the moment, all Ian could think about was finding Jane.

*

Molly was an astute businesswoman, but accepted that she was gambling with the combined funds to set up a confectionary shop. She had purchased the property in a well-off suburb of London, renovated the premises, and set up the shop to appeal to the senses of sight and smell, stocking such sweets as marshmallow, marzipan, liquorice, toffee, boiled lollies and, of particular speciality, Turkish Delight. Molly had acquired a recipe from the kindly Catholic nun who had lived in Constantinople while they worked together in the British hospital. The business had just about absorbed all the money that she, Conan and Owen had, plus Edwin's share. Before her grand opening, Molly had paid

generously the poverty-stricken children of her old neigh-
bourhood to distribute leaflets advertising her sweet wares,
and on opening day, was rewarded with the more affluent
members of London stopping by to examine and purchase
her confectionaries. Both Conan and Owen, wearing their
dress uniforms with medals on their chests, welcomed the
customers at the door, appealing to their sense of patriotism
upon meeting the two fine examples of England's victory
over the Russian Tsar. The Turkish Delight proved her
bestselling confectionary.

At the end of a very successful day, the three retreated
to the residence above the shop, counting the substantial
earnings, and opened a fine bottle of Scotch to celebrate.
With adoring eyes, Conan gazed at Molly and raised his
glass. 'This is for you, Edwin. I wish you could have been
here today.'

Both Conan and Owen well knew that they had years
to serve before the army would release them from their
service. They could soon easily be facing another of the
Queen's enemies in some far-off, almost unknown part of
the expanding British Empire. For Conan, it was a long
way from the colony of New South Wales and the life he
may have led there if he had continued in his life of crime.

*

It was a windswept day in the Kentish countryside when
Ian stood in the little Anglican church that provided spiritual comfort to the nearby village adjacent to the Forbes
manor. The memorial service for Herbert and the other
men from the county who had been killed in the Crimean
War was over. On a board attached to the wall, Ian could
see Herbert's name engraved with gold paint. Alice, Sir
Archibald and Dr Peter Campbell had attended the service,

but Charles was conspicuously absent. He had apologised but business affairs in London had intervened.

Ian stood wearing his dress uniform and medals, gazing at Herbert's name.

'You have my condolences for the loss of your brother,' a voice said, and Ian turned to see the elderly Anglican priest who had officiated at the service.

'Thank you,' Ian replied. 'You have ministered to your flock for many years in this parish but I am afraid I was not a very attentive parishioner when I was very young.'

'It has proved to be a spiritually rewarding life,' the minister agreed. 'I do remember how you appeared a long way in your thoughts from my sermons.' The minister smiled.

'Was a young woman, Miss Jane Wilberforce, one of your parishioners?' Ian asked, and saw the dark cloud cross the man's face.

'I am afraid that she was not,' the minister answered. 'It was whispered that Miss Wilberforce was more devoted to the old pagan gods of the Druids. I pray that she may one day turn to the one, and only true Lord, our saviour, Jesus Christ.'

'I have been seeking the whereabouts of Miss Wilberforce, and wonder if you may have heard any rumours of her sudden disappearance,' Ian said.

'One of my elderly parishioners did comment that she thinks the stone circle on the hill has spirited her away. Miss Wilberforce is somewhat a little unhinged, and I wonder if the unfounded rumours of her being a witch are nothing more than the echoes around these parts of magic and superstition, leftover from that time when the Druids ruled these parts in pre-history. All that I have heard is that Miss Wilberforce travelled to London.'

'Who told you that?' Ian asked.

'I heard it from your brother, Charles, some time ago, at a church function to raise money for our parish poor.'

'Thank you, reverend,' Ian said and walked outside the medieval church into the sunshine.

'Are you returning to the house?' Alice asked, pushing back her black, gauzy veil. 'It would be of comfort if you did.'

'I will stay the night,' Ian said. 'But I must return to London to attend a regimental dinner at the barracks tomorrow night. The colonel is retiring and we will learn of the identity of our newly appointed colonel of the regiment.'

'It should have been you,' Peter said bluntly. 'After all, you assumed command after the colonel was wounded, and from what the rank and file told me, you were the best commander they ever had.'

Ian was flattered by the compliment. 'Alas, the family funds do not extend to purchasing a colonelcy,' Ian said. 'I will remain a mere captain, but at least I will have my company.'

The three rode in a carriage drawn by two fine horses, and arrived at the country manor. Already, Ian was planning to saddle a horse and ride to the village. He offered money for information concerning the disappearance of Jane, but was unsuccessful. He also noticed the sullen expressions from the local people who distrusted outsiders when he spoke with them in the village streets.

At dusk, Ian mounted his horse to ride back to the manor in the long summer evening when he came close to the copse of trees on the small hill of the stone circle, overlooking the valley and fields of yellowing wheat below. He noticed an expensive, single-horse carriage stopped by the side of a laneway, where a driver sat on his bench seat without his passenger. Curious as to why anyone would be near the hill of the Druids, Ian dismounted a few yards away, secured his horse to graze, and chose to walk to the top of the hill.

He was almost at the top when he saw her. Ian gasped in his shock and for a few seconds, was transfixed.

'Jane!' Ian cried out in his joy, clambering to the top of the hill to join her.

The woman turned to face Ian and he was once again looking into the face of the woman he loved.

'Excuse me, but I am not Jane,' said the woman with the raven hair and green eyes. 'I am Rebecca, Jane's twin sister. I presume that you must be Captain Ian Steele.'

Ian came to a stop a couple of paces away, stunned by the revelation of the existence of the twin sister Jane had never mentioned, and the fact that she knew his real identity. Ian was confused and mystified by the appearance of this woman who was physically identical to his love in every way.

'You know my name,' he said. 'How do you know my real name?'

'Jane would write to me, and she told me how much in love she was with you,' Rebecca said. 'I envied her words of love. She would describe you as one of the ancient warriors of days past, and even told me that she was carrying your baby. From what I can see, I can understand why she loved you so much.'

As Rebecca's words flowed, Ian was overcome by emotion. It was as if the spirit of Jane was speaking to him, from wherever she was. 'Why did not Jane mention you?' Ian asked.

'We were separated at birth, and I was sold to Lord Montegue and his wife, who were unable to have children. I was not aware of my birthright until I was eighteen years old, and my father on his deathbed confessed to who I really was, and that I had a twin sister living in the village. My adoptive mother had died years earlier, and I inherited the family estates when Lord Montegue passed on. Lord Montegue had always been a warm and loving father, and his dying wish was that I knew I was not alone. I was able to find Jane, and from the moment we met, we knew we were true sisters. It was Jane who swore me to secrecy concerning our relationship, lest it be detrimental to my standing in London society.'

There is one other who holds me to this village who I cannot tell you about. Jane's words came to Ian as he listened to Rebecca. So this was her kindred spirit.

'We shared our secrets, and one of them was you,' Rebecca continued. 'But you do not need to be concerned, because your secret is safe with me, as mine was with my sister.'

'Do you know where Jane is?' Ian asked.

'No. The last communication I had with Jane was a week before she just disappeared into thin air. That was over a year past now. I had planned for Jane to leave the village and join me at the family manor and leave that wretched Charles Forbes behind but she said that was not necessary as you had entered her life. I have spent the last months attempting to find her and I confess that I am concerned for her welfare.'

'I was told that she went to London,' Ian said. 'I, too, have people searching for her at any cost.'

'As she was with your child, it does not make sense that she would simply go to London, and not contact you or I,' Rebecca said. 'I fear that harm has come to her.'

'That has crossed my mind,' Ian said, staring at the circle of stones. 'Why did you come to this place?'

'Jane once told me it was a place of peace for her, and was linked to her meeting with you,' Rebecca answered. 'I was curious to see the stones. I feel she is close to me here in a way I do not expect you to understand. It is just something of a strange bond between those born as twins. We were different but, at the same time, joined in life by our souls.'

Ian gazed into the face of Rebecca, and partially understood what she meant. It was as if he was in the actual company of his beloved Jane. 'Do you know who might have wished your sister harm?' he asked. Rebecca's expression darkened.

'There was one man whose name she mentioned as a person she despised – Charles Forbes – your supposed brother.'

The mention of Charles brought back memories of how he had attempted to have he and Dr Peter Campbell killed in an ambush, though neither man could prove his conspiracy in the matter. 'I would support Charles as a person who might be involved in Jane's disappearance,' Ian said. 'But we need proof of his complicity, and I highly doubt that he would confess if confronted. Does he know of your existence?'

'No. We have never met. I have spent most of my life living in Italy and France where my family had estates,' Rebecca said.

Ian could see black clouds rolling in that promised a drenching downpour instead of the current sleeting rain. 'I think it may be wise if we made our way back to your carriage,' he said. 'Otherwise we may be caught in the rain I feel is coming.'

Rebecca agreed, and they walked side by side down the hill to the laneway. They stopped at Rebecca's carriage.

'I would like to meet with you again, Captain Steele,' she said. 'I feel that we have much to talk about.'

'I would like that,' Ian replied.

Ian stood for a moment, watching her being assisted into the carriage by her driver, and thought how much her mannerisms reminded him of Jane. The carriage drove away, and Ian mounted his horse to return to the Forbes estate. As he rode, he thought about the strange circle of stones, and how they seemed to be of great importance in his life. They had at least brought him into contact with the other half of Jane, and he vaguely remembered how Jane had said she had a secret of her own. Now he knew what it was.

The storm broke with a crash of lightning and heavy downpour of rain. Ian was soaked by the time he reached the estate.

*

The dining-in night held at the regimental barracks in London was a grand affair, strictly for the officers and their ladies. The candles along the table flickered, casting gentle shadows and causing the jewellery of the ladies in their best evening dresses to sparkle. Laughter and wine flowed as the different courses of food were delivered to those at the long table, where the colonel presided at one end.

Ian was positioned near the centre, opposite a couple of new lieutenants who looked admiringly upon Ian's medals. They had not served in the Crimea, but had read much about the great battles before purchasing commissions into the regiment that had witnessed so much action. To the newly joined young officers, Ian was already a legend.

Toasts to the Queen were made, the port bottle being passed from one officer to the other along the table, and cigars passed out.

The colonel rose to give his speech, and silence fell in the room thick with cigar smoke.

'Gentlemen and their ladies,' he said. 'This will be my last dining-in night as your colonel. As from the morrow, I will be resigning my commission to retire and write my memoirs. You will have a new colonel to command our glorious regiment.'

Polite protests from the officers of the regiment followed his statement, and died down when he raised his hand. 'But I can assure you that the man to take command is not unknown to you. He served for a time with us in the Crimea, where his courage was of the highest order. I would like to introduce and welcome Colonel Jenkins, and his lady, Lady Montegue.'

All necks strained to see the couple enter the dining room. Ian was stunned when he saw Rebecca on Jenkins' arm, as the officers rose with their glasses of port to toast their new commander. Ian remained sitting. He did not toast the appointment of the man he knew was a coward and despised by those who really knew of his incompetence. But the worst part of the evening was the sight of Rebecca on his arm. She was outstandingly beautiful in her evening dress and sparking jewellery. It had only been the day before they had stood on the hill of the stone circle, and now, here she was on the arm of the man he hated as much as Charles. Jenkins had not honour, but obviously had the money to purchase a colonelcy, and the attention of Rebecca.

Ian did not remain in the mess after the dinner but returned to his club. There, he drank himself into a stupor before one of the staff helped him reach his room.

THIRTY-FIVE

Ian sat in Ikey's office, opposite the imposing man.

'I am sorry, my friend, but my people were not able to find any trace of your lady in London,' he said with genuine sympathy in his voice.

'Molly said that if anyone could find Jane, it would be you,' Ian said. 'I feel that I owe you something for trying to help me.'

'I only expect payment for results,' Ikey said. 'But I would ask a favour of you, Captain Forbes.'

'I think that would be fair,' Ian said.

'Lady Montegue is to have a ball at her estate next week, and my sources tell me you have been invited.'

Ian was surprised at the Jewish man's intelligence, but also considered what he had learned from others at the Reform Club – that he had been successful in accruing a fortune, rivalling even the wealthiest of English aristocrats.

It appeared the immigrant had wisely invested dubious sources of his income into respectable business enterprises. Sitting in the modest office, this was not something Ian could imagine.

'How can my attending the ball be of assistance to you, Mr Solomon?' Ian asked.

'I have a daughter who is both the light of my life and a bane,' Ikey said with a smile. 'My princess, Ella, has come of age, but you may be aware that the English establishment has no love of us Jews. I would ask the favour that you escort my daughter to Lady Montegue's ball. It would make her very happy, and that means it would make me very happy.'

Ian was surprised at the formidable man's request. It was a simple thing to say yes to.

'I will be honoured,' Ian replied.

'You have now made me a very happy man,' Ikey said, standing and extending his hand to Ian. 'I know that my daughter will be respected and treated well, Captain Forbes. You are an honourable man, and I trust you, which is something I rarely say.'

In the crushing handshake, Ian guessed that anything else towards the big man's daughter would mean severe punishment. When Ian looked into Ikey's eyes, he prayed that his daughter looked nothing like him.

When Ian left the office, he had one other task to perform. He took a hansom carriage to his bank, and deposited the single stone he had left in a safe box. It would always be there as insurance against the mean times that may lay ahead.

*

Dressed in his uniform, Ian rode with Peter and Alice in a fine Forbes carriage to Lady Montegue's country manor.

The evening was chilly but clear of rain and when they arrived, the great mansion was lit with lights, making it look like a fairy castle. Many carriages were already in attendance and the cream of London society were dismounting before each carriage was driven away, and another took its place before the grand steps leading to the house.

'Oh, this is exciting.' Alice beamed as they were helped from their carriage by footmen dressed in the attire of eighteenth-century French servants. They could hear the sweet sound of an orchestra drift to them from within the mansion.

'I am to wait until my partner arrives,' Ian said as Peter and Alice prepared to go inside and be announced.

'You said nothing of a partner for the ball,' Alice said in her surprise. 'Is she someone that I may know?'

'I doubt it,' Ian replied, wondering what Ikey's daughter would be like. All he knew was that she was nineteen years old and would be conveyed by one of his carriages to the estate.

'Well, we will go inside,' Peter said. 'I must say, I am curious to meet your mysterious lady.'

'I hope I don't have to wait very long,' Ian said, and Peter escorted Alice into the great house and its huge ballroom.

Ian took a cigar from a silver case and lit it as he waited for the arrival of Ella. He had hardly taken a puff when a very elegant two-horse carriage with matching greys arrived. The driver was dressed in an expensive suit but looked uncomfortable, his brawny build testing the seams of his jacket. He stepped off the driver's seat and opened the door to assist the passenger from within.

Ian stubbed out his cigar, guessing correctly this must be Ella Solomon's carriage.

He blinked when he saw the young lady emerge under

the flickering lights of nearby lanterns and she turned to him. Ella was nothing like her father, he thought. Before him was a truly beautiful young lady with dark eyes and slightly olive skin. She smiled when she saw Ian, who instantly recognised one of the diamond-studded necklaces he had sold to Ikey strung around her slim throat. Her long dark hair was tied behind her head, and she walked towards him as if gliding on the driveway. When she was only a pace from him, she said, 'I am very pleased that you accepted my father's invitation to escort me to Lady Montegue's ball, Captain Forbes.'

'How did you know that it was I who was waiting for you?' Ian almost mumbled, awed by her beauty.

'I must confess that I saw you when you first met my father,' Ella said and Ian could not detect any accent other than that of an educated English aristocrat. She immediately gave the impression of being sweet and charming. 'Shall we make our entrance?' Ella continued and Ian took her arm, walking her up the great stone stairs to the main entrance of the manor house.

'Captain Forbes and Miss Ella Solomon,' the bewigged doorman announced, when Ian gave their names.

Ian escorted Ella into the vast room, where couples swirled around the dance floor. Ian was quick to notice that many heads turned as they passed tables to join Peter and Alice's party, and when they did, he noticed the flicker of interest in all their eyes. On Ian's arm was a truly beautiful young woman, wearing a fortune in diamonds and sapphires.

'Ladies and gentlemen, may I introduce Miss Ella Solomon, of the London Solomons,' Ian said, knowing his introduction would be frowned upon by some at the table. But he did not care.

'Miss Solomon, I am Miss Alice Forbes, please take a seat by me,' Alice said warmly. 'I must learn who your dressmaker is. You are the most elegantly presented lady at this ball.'

Ella blushed at the compliment and sat down beside Alice while Ian took a seat beside Peter.

'Good God, old man, where did you find a beauty like Miss Solomon?' he asked quietly, leaning into Ian. 'She has the certain grace and poise of a true lady.'

'You would not believe my story if I told you,' Ian grinned, noticing the many red uniforms of officers from his regiment watching them with envious eyes. It was then that he saw Rebecca in the company of Jenkins, resplendent in the uniform of a colonel. Rebecca's eyes met his and for a moment, Ian experienced a feeling he could not explain. He was once again reminded of Jane, who he did not want to think was dead but had to face that possibility. And if she was dead, who could have killed her? Alice noticed Ian staring across the floor of the ballroom and gasped. 'That lady looks as though she could be Jane Wilberforce!' Alice said.

'That is Lady Montegue, our hostess,' Ian said.

'Who is Jane Wilberforce?' Peter asked.

'Jane was our playmate at the country estate when we were growing up,' Alice answered. 'But enough of that talk. Samuel, you should request a dance with Miss Solomon before she is swept away by one of those handsome and dashing young officers of your regiment.'

Ian stood and bowed to Ella. 'A dance, Miss Solomon?' he asked, and she extended her hand in acceptance.

The orchestra were warming up to a waltz. Ian had taken lessons while in New South Wales as part of his training for the role of impersonating the real Samuel Forbes. They once again turned heads when they entered upon the floor. The men admiring Ella's beauty, whilst their ladies, her jewellery.

She fitted into Ian's arms as the music flowed, and they floated across the floor. Ian surprised himself with his unpractised expertise with the waltz, and Ella seemed to be a part of his body as they swirled with the music. It was a night of flickering candles, music and romance.

The dance ended, and Ian escorted Ella back to the table.

'You were the most beautiful couple on the floor,' Alice said. 'You look as if you were meant to be together.'

Ian was confused as to why one moment he would be grieving the absence of Jane, and yet this young lady seemed to be able to bring him back from the depths of his despair over her loss. Was it that his exposure to the brutality of war that had made him a realist? It was not that Jane was forgotten, but that she had been a past dream before war had changed him forever.

'Captain Forbes, you are yet to ask me for a dance.' Ian immediately recognised the voice of Rebecca Montegue behind him. He turned, and he could see the smile on her face. Ian stood and introduced Rebecca to his party, seeing how impressed they were meeting this often talked about, mysterious and beautiful woman of London society. Alice frowned at Ian as if to say, *how does Lady Montegue know you?*

Ian excused himself and led Rebecca to the dance floor. It was another waltz and she was very good, folding into Ian's arms as the music took them.

'Miss Solomon is certainly a beauty,' Rebecca said in Ian's ear. 'You do know of her father's rather unsavoury reputation?'

'Not as unsavoury as the man who is courting you,' Ian countered with a growl.

'Colonel Jenkins is a man who has a good pedigree and ambition,' Rebecca said, defensively. 'He has informed me that he despises you but, for the sake of my sister, I can assure you that your secret will always be safe with me. If it was ever revealed that you are in fact a colonial imposter, I am sure it would bring a scandal on the good name of Forbes. Your fate is in my hands, and never forget that, Captain Steele.'

'Why should I be of any interest to a lady of your obvious standing?' Ian asked. 'You have everything any woman alive would envy.'

'I am with Colonel Jenkins because he is a man with an excellent pedigree, befitting my station in life, but I envy my sister because she found true love with you. Love is not a passion one of my social standing entertains, and I often wonder what Jane saw in you. But I have no doubt your position in the regiment will bring us into contact on social occasions. Ah, the dance has ended and I think that I should join the Colonel. You are a superb dancer, Captain Steele, and from what my sister told me, also a magnificent lover.'

Ian caught a glimpse of his new commanding officer with a crystal flute of champagne in hand, glaring at him. Ian ignored him and returned to his table.

'Do you know,' Peter said when Ian sat down, 'Miss Solomon has informed me that she aspires to be a surgeon. Needless to say, I have attempted to discourage her by pointing out that medicine is not a profession really suitable for young ladies – or any ladies, for that matter.'

Ian looked at Ella and read a determination in her face. He had to agree with his Canadian friend – surgery was not a profession suitable for women. It was obvious to Ian that her father could offer his daughter's hand in marriage to a good husband of his choosing. But it would have to be a man who truly appreciated this remarkable young woman of strong opinions and high intelligence.

The evening passed, and Ian had studiously avoided his new commanding officer because he realised how hard it would have been to keep his temper in check. But this did not work, and Ian found himself confronted by a red-faced and inebriated Jenkins.

'Captain Forbes,' he sneered. 'If I could have my way I would have you transferred from my regiment,' he said. 'You have the attitudes of a colonial lout.'

Ian was in a tight spot and glanced around to ensure that they could not be overheard. 'For a short time, I commanded the regiment and that ensured my bond with it can never be broken. I respect your position as the new commanding officer, but that does not mean I have to like or respect the person that I know you are . . . sir.'

'You can thank Lady Montegue for me allowing you to continue service with my regiment, Captain Forbes,' Jenkins said with a bitter tone. 'God knows why she should support you.'

Ian smiled, knowing that Jenkins had seen Rebecca single him out for the waltz earlier that evening. 'Oh, Lady Montegue and I share a secret,' he said quietly. 'One that you are not privy to.'

Jenkins blinked, and Ian could see his words had stung the man he despised as much as Charles and Archibald Forbes. Ian had left him speechless and walked away with a smirk on his face. He wished he could see inside Jenkins' head for the turmoil of thoughts his mysterious statement had caused.

In the early hours of the morning, Ian stood with Ella outside the great house, waiting for her carriage. He admitted to himself that it had been a wonderful and memorable evening in the company of Ella, and secretly thanked Ikey for asking the favour of him.

'Captain Forbes,' Ella said, looking up into his face. 'I cannot thank you enough for being such a gentleman, and such wonderful company. Tonight has been very special for me, and I shall provide an excellent report to my father of your courteous behaviour.'

As Ian gazed into her dark eyes he had an overpowering desire to kiss her but forced the thought out of his mind. She looked so appealing. Her carriage was approaching, and Ella stood on her toes, snatching a kiss on Ian's cheek, surprising him. Before he could respond she had quickly walked to the carriage where the driver assisted her to step inside.

Then the carriage rattled away, leaving him with the lingering feeling on his cheek of the surprise kiss.

'Time to go, old boy,' Peter said from their carriage, and Ian sauntered over to the Forbes grand conveyance. It had certainly proved a night of mixed emotions, brought on by the presence of two remarkable women. But it would be only one of them that Ian would see in the next few weeks, before the gods of war called to him once again.

*

It would be inevitable that Ian would have to confront his new commanding officer, and the call came a week after the ball at Lady Montegue's house.

The regimental sergeant major stopped off at Ian's company HQ office at the London barracks of the regiment to inform him that his presence was required by the colonel.

Ian marched across the parade ground to the colonel's office and was met by the adjutant, a captain.

'The colonel will see you,' he said and Ian marched into his office, standing at attention after saluting. Jenkins was sitting behind a desk with little else than an ink blotter stand with a pen and a paperweight made from half a cannonball. He was signing a report and glanced up when Ian entered.

'Captain Forbes, I feel it is time for you and I to have a talk about my opinion of you remaining with the regiment,' Jenkins said. 'Considering our differences in the past I would like to see you gone but Lady Montegue has, for reasons known unto herself alone, argued that you should remain. I will grudgingly admit that you have proved to be an audacious officer during the past Crimean campaign, and it seems the regiment will be presently sent to Persia to settle a bit of a mess over there. So, you will retain your company but I expect absolute loyalty from a subordinate officer, regardless of personal, unwarranted ill will that I suspect you harbour for me. Am I able to rely on your total loyalty, Captain Forbes?'

'Regardless of my personal feelings, I can swear loyalty to you, and the regiment.'

Jenkins glanced at the page of paper on his desk and then looked up at Ian.

'I accept your word as an officer and gentleman, and hope that we can work together to make this the finest regiment of foot in the Queen's army. That is all, Captain Forbes, you may go.'

Ian stepped back, saluted and marched out of the office with mixed thoughts. It had been easy to swear his allegiance as this was the way of the army and he was an officer. But it did not diminish his personal feelings towards Jenkins. At least he retained his beloved rifle company and it seemed that they were returning to war.

★

The message left at Ian's club mystified him. It was an invitation to meet with Ella at a tea shop not far from the barracks.

When he entered the cosy shop, he noticed her sitting alone at a table, clothed in a simple but smart dress. For a brief moment, he stood staring at her, drinking in how beautiful she was even without all the glamorous attire of the ball. She glanced up and smiled uncertainly.

'I was pleasantly surprised when I received your invitation to meet with you here,' Ian said, sitting down opposite the young woman.

'I just wanted to personally express my thank you for the wonderful evening we spent together at Lady Montegue's ball,' Ella said. 'Would you like to share with me tea and cake?'

'It will be a pleasure, Miss Solomon,' Ian said.

'I would like you to call me Ella. I know that may sound a little forward but I feel comfortable in your presence.'

'Then you must call me Samuel – or Sam,' Ian said with a smile.

Tea was ordered and Ella was at first just a little shy in Ian's company. But he put her at ease, telling funny stories that made her laugh.

'Does your father know that you have come to see me?' Ian asked, and a dark cloud covered Ella's face.

'No, my father would not approve of my coming to see you of my own volition.'

'I can promise that your virtue is safe in my company,' Ian replied.

'I know it is,' Ella said. 'There is something about you, Samuel, that makes you different to all the other men I have met in my life, but I suspect, you have been told that by many other women before. I think my father has also recognised that you are a man of honour to be trusted.'

Impulsively, Ian reached across the table and took her two hands in his own. 'I only wish that I could share my secret with you,' he said. 'But I cannot for now.'

'I would like to meet with you again,' Ella said.

'And I, you,' Ian replied. 'That is our secret then.'

The afternoon passed too quickly for Ian, as Ella shared her life and dreams with him. He listened, occasionally making a comment that made her laugh or smile, and as the day drew to a close, they both realised that they must return to their respective lives.

Ian walked away from the tea shop even more confused about life. He had to face the reality that they were from different walks of life. She was Jewish, and he, a nominal Christian. Ian also suspected that if her father found out about his interest in his one and only princess, Ian might disappear in the Thames River. But that did not deter either of them, and the meetings became more common as he and Ella met to take walks in the park, tea in the shops and even an evening meeting at a theatre to watch a play by Shakespeare.

It was while they were standing under one of the great oak trees in the park that Ella turned to Ian, kissed him passionately on the lips, and broke the kiss by saying with all her heart, 'Samuel Forbes, I love you.'

Ian did not know how to respond. The ghost of Jane's absence in his life still haunted him and there was so much at stake for them both if he answered. He took Ella's hands in his own.

'It is time that you must return home,' he said, aware of the pain in the beautiful young woman's face. The chance of love had once again come into Ian's life but so, too, had the distant sound of drums and trumpets, calling him to the ancient biblical land of Persia. But before he departed with his regiment, he had just one more visit to make.

*

At first, the valet attempted to block Ian from entering the London house of the Forbes family. Ian pushed past his feeble attempt and strode through to the billiard room. Ian was in his uniform and startled both Charles and Sir Archibald, who had been relaxing with a port and cigar. Both men looked up at him as if an ogre had come into their company.

'Samuel, how dare you trespass in this house,' Sir Archibald protested, spilling port wine on his lap. Charles half rose to meet Ian. He still bore a small scar over his eye as a result of the beating Ian had inflicted on him at the Kent country manor.

'I have no intentions of remaining in your despised presence,' Ian growled. 'I have just come to ask one question of Charles.'

Charles was now on his feet and Ian could see real fear in his eyes as he stood uncertainly gripping his port wine. 'Ask and leave,' he said.

Ian turned to him. 'What do you know about the disappearance of Jane Wilberforce?' Ian could see that his question had hit a nerve as Charles paled.

'I do not know what you mean,' he replied. 'As far as I know, she left the village to travel to London.'

'How do you know that?' Ian asked bluntly.

Charles did not immediately reply as Ian stared at him. 'I heard it told to me by a man in the village,' he finally replied. 'But I cannot remember who told me.'

'I and others suspect that Jane has met with foul play, and the only person I can think of who might want to hurt Jane is you, Charles,' Ian said in a steady and threatening tone. 'If I ever find evidence that you may have done her harm, I will kill you.'

'How dare you threaten my son,' Sir Archibald protested from his chair. 'I will have the constables called to arrest you.'

'You won't do that,' Ian said calmly. 'This family has too many skeletons neither of you would want to be exposed – including Charles conspiring with Colonel Jenkins to have me killed. I am sure that you both know of a letter Alice read while Herbert and I were in the Crimea. Charles apparently dictated that he wanted Jenkins to have us both done away with. No doubt your eldest son does not wish to share any of your fortune with any other of your children.'

Ian noticed Sir Archibald cast a questioning look at Charles. Ian knew that, despite all his weaknesses, Sir Archibald had been very fond of his youngest son and had truly mourned his death.

'Is what Samuel is saying true?' Sir Archibald asked Charles. 'Did you request that Jenkins conspire to have Herbert killed?'

Charles looked cornered but quickly regained his composure. 'Samuel is lying,' he responded. 'Alice misread the correspondence I had with Jenkins. Herbert's tragic death was simply the consequence of war, nothing else. It had nothing to do with Jenkins.'

'Well, Sir Archibald,' Ian said. 'You should sometime ask Alice what she thought she read in the letter.' Ian could see that he had put a divide between the two men. 'It may be possible that your eldest son might tire of waiting for his inheritance. I would be very careful if I were you. Accidents can happen, and I won't be around to protect you.'

The stricken expression on Sir Archibald's face told Ian that the patriarch of the Forbes family was accepting some of what Ian had disclosed. At least Ian felt that he had hammered a nail into the coffin he hoped to lay in the ground one day containing Charles' body. Ian felt that Charles did nothing without Sir Archibald's knowledge, and if Jane had been murdered by Charles, Sir Archibald would be aware of how far Charles would go to eliminate anyone who stood in his way.

'I will leave you both,' Ian said and turned his back on them to leave the house. Ian left with a good feeling that he had achieved in a subtle way a division between allies. It was, after all, a military tactic to divide forces. For now, he knew he must steam with his troops to another war but was happy to leave in his wake a very shaky house that might collapse on itself.

EPILOGUE

London

Winter, 1856

The Christmas spirit was on the faces in the snow-swept streets of London.

Wearing a heavy military greatcoat, Ian Steele trudged towards the public house where he knew he would find Conan and Owen. He entered the smoke-filled room, shaking off the bitter cold, and saw the two soldiers sitting at a table. They greeted him with warm smiles as he sat down.

'Well, sir it would be our pleasure to buy you a drink,' Owen said.

'An ale would be fine, Corporal Williams.' Ian said, and Owen paused as he was about to stand.

'Sir, I am Private Williams,' Owen said, correcting his company commander.

'Not anymore, Corporal,' Ian said with a grin. 'I was able to have our former colonel approve your promotion before he left the regiment. As a matter of fact, he also approved Conan to the rank of sergeant,' Ian said, turning to face Conan Curry, who almost dropped his tankard of ale. 'Congratulations to you both.' For a moment both men were speechless. 'I suppose you can view it as an early Christmas present. Sergeant Curry, you can pass on your chevrons to Corporal Williams.'

'Sir, we cannot thank you enough for putting in the good word for Owen and me,' Conan finally said.

'You both proved your worth in the Crimea, and the colonel knew that. All I did was sign the recommendation for your promotions. I believe it is the tradition that you stand drinks for the bar.'

And the two men did.

Ian left them after a couple of rounds and made his way back to his club. Peter Campbell had finally succeeded in his persistent endeavours to marry Alice, and had moved out for modest but comfortable private lodgings not far from Alice's family house in London. Even Sir Archibald and her brother had attended the wedding in London, reluctantly showing faces of pleasure for the union. They had accepted that if they did not agree then Alice would simply elope with the Canadian causing scandal on the Forbes name.

The wedding was a simple affair held before Christmas. The officers of the regiment presented an arch of swords when the married couple left the church in one of London's better suburbs. Alice wore a simple but elegant wedding dress, and at her throat was an extravagant necklace gifted by Ian from jewels he had taken in the Crimea. She was radiant as the snow fell gently on the red-coated officers forming the arch of swords and Peter in his military uniform. He too, beamed with absolute pleasure. Ian had stood in as best man, and the honeymoon was to be taken in India, where Peter's brother, Major Scott Campbell, held a commission with an East India Company cavalry regiment. Alice had always wanted to visit the Crown Jewel of the British Empire, after reading so many stories of its exotic culture and, after all, her own family had made a fortune years earlier, from trade with India.

Christmas Day was spent with Peter and Alice at their apartments, and the day proved to be good for Ian's soul. He returned to the club in the early evening and chose to spend the rest of the evening in his rooms. The regiment was to sail early in the new year and Ian pondered the next campaign. His thoughts were also of Jane's disappearance. He now accepted that she was most probably dead. The pain of confronting the reality of her mysterious disappearance haunted him in his sleeping hours and when he awoke, a new face also haunted him: Ella. But it was too soon as Ian still mourned the loss of Jane, the child they were supposed to have had, and the uncertainty of living through yet another war.

*

Within days, Ian boarded a troop ship to steam to the ancient biblical lands of Persia. It was early evening as the warships built up steam to catch the tide and depart the Thames. Ian stood at the rail of his transport ship, gazing at the docks where only the families and a few friends stood in little clusters to wave their beloved goodbye. It was not the fanfare of the regiment leaving for Crimea, with its parades, bugles and trumpets. This time it was simply a matter of the British army and navy going to a place to settle a local conflict, which did not attract the same attention as when they were off to fight a major European power.

He gazed at the people on the dock, suddenly recognising one face. It was Ella, staring up at him with deep, sad eyes, and a wan smile. Ian's heart beat hard in his chest, and his breathing laboured. He had never expected to see her again, but here she was, waving to him with a dainty hand-kerchief. She was mouthing words but he could not hear her over the tooting of the ship's steam horn, and thump of its engines, as the ship slipped its ropes, and pulled away from the wharf.

Ian wanted to rush to her, embrace her slim body as if never to let her go again in his life. He had realised his dream to be a soldier of the Queen, but it had come at a great cost to him personally. One of his worst enemies was now his commanding officer, and how many campaigns lay ahead until he fulfilled the ten years of military service promised to the real Samuel Forbes?

The waves splashed against the hull as Ian desperately tried to keep Ella in sight. But the ship steamed towards the mouth of the Thames, and yet another military campaign, this time along the banks of the Euphrates River and the adjacent desert land that had seen many armies pass before.

AUTHOR NOTES

Landmines, trench warfare, no man's land, telegraph lines, railways, photographic records, the rifled musket, explosive artillery shells, and the odd war correspondent or two thrown in to the Crimean War, marked it as the first modern war of the nineteenth century before even the American Civil War six years later. It was a geopolitical war as most are today. The French and British helping the Ottoman Empire contain the Russian Empire from expanding to the Black Sea, giving the Russians a sea lane to the Mediterranean for their expanding navy. This was not acceptable to imperial designs by the British and French empires so feeble excuses were found to contain the Russian Tsar, and war was declared, despite the fact that the Russians had been the allies of Britain when facing Napoleon's French and Allied armies years forty years earlier.

Of all the sources I found most useful I must praise Elizabeth Grey's *The Noise of Drums and Trumpets: W.H. Russell Reports from the Crimea*, Longman Group Ltd, London 1971. Russell witnessed all the major battles and reported via telegraph to his readers *The Times* of London almost in real time. He was the father of present day war correspondents and in 1882 he is quoted as saying about his colourful life: *I wonder what would have come of it all had I followed the quiet path . . . instead of those noisy drums and trumpets.* As the author of this fictional novel I am glad that he followed the noisy drums and trumpets.

All the battle scenes are lifted from his eye-witness accounts, and the looting of the Russian baggage train actually happened as portrayed within the pages of this book, with many officers and soldiers acquiring small and large fortunes. That was very convenient for my characters of Captain Ian Steele and his loyal entourage.

To Australian and New Zealand readers the name of Gallipoli Village would mark a name in 1915 that cemented the unbreakable bond between our two nations – except on the rugby and cricket fields – when we go to war with each other.

Naturally this is a book of fiction but the history is real. During the nineteenth century every year the British army found itself fighting colonial wars in so many exotic places from Asia to Africa and beyond. Campaigns today mostly forgotten. Captain Ian Steele will march with his rifle company in the books ahead with Sergeant Conan Curry, VC and Corporal Owen Williams. There will be scores to be settled, and wars to be won in the name of Queen Victoria's empire.

ACKNOWLEDGEMENTS

My thanks go as always to my publisher, Cate Paterson, and all at Pan Macmillan who work indirectly to keep the logistics of publication flowing smoothly. In particular Tracey Cheetham and Lucy Inglis in publicity and the all very important editorial staff of Bec Hamilton, Libby Turner and proofreader, Alex Craig. My thanks are also extended to LeeAnne Walker and Milly Ivanovic.

For the ongoing *Frontier* project I would like to thank Rod Hardy, Paul Currie and Suzanne de Passe. All we have to do is persevere.

Thanks to Kristie Hildebrand who keeps me in contact with readers through Facebook and Peter and Kaye Lowe who maintain the website www.peterwatt.com.

A special thank you to Betty Irons OAM, Bob Mansfield and Dan Grey, who have kept me in contact with readers at the Maclean Community Markets for many years.

To John and June Riggall – John has given his time to help establish the Australian Volunteer Emergency Services Legacy along with members from the Gulmarrad Rural Fire Brigade. To all the men and women of the volunteer emergency services I have worked alongside over the year in flood and fire my thanks.

For those friends in my life, Kevin Jones OAM and family, Mick and Andrea Prowse, John Wong, Jan Dean, Dr Louis Trichard and Christine.

To my family members: my brother Tom Watt and his wonderful family, and my sister Lindy and brother-in-law Jock Barclay. To Tyrone McKee and family. My cousins, Luke and Tim Payne and Virginia Wolfe and their families. My beloved Aunt Joan Payne, a special best wishes. And not forgotten, my cousins of the Duffy clan and their families.

My gratitude to a few of my friends in prose. As always, Dave Sabben MG and his wife, Di. For Simon Higgins, never forgotten, Greg Barron and his latest release, *Whistler's Bones*, Tony Park and his latest release, *Captive*, and introducing Jay Ludowyke's debut novel, *Carpathia*.

As always, my love and thanks to the lady who reviews my work as it progresses, my beloved wife, Naomi.

MORE BESTSELLING FICTION BY PETER WATT

The Duffy/Macintosh Series

Cry of the Curlew

A stark and vivid portrayal of Australia's brutal past.

An epic tale of two families, the Macintoshes and the Duffys, who are locked in a deadly battle from the moment squatter Donald Macintosh commits an act of barbarity on his Queensland property.

Their paths cross in love, death and revenge as both families fight to tame the wild frontier of Australia's north country.

Cry of the Curlew is the first bestselling novel in the compelling Duffy and Macintosh series depicting our turbulent history as never before.

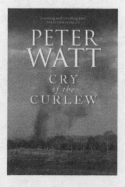

The Duffy/Macintosh Series

Shadow of the Osprey

A riveting tale of love, death and revenge.

Soldier of fortune Michael Duffy returns to colonial
Sydney on a covert mission and with old scores to settle,
still enraged by a bitter feud between his family and the
ruthless Macintoshes.

The Palmer River gold rush lures American prospector
Luke Tracy back to Australia's rugged north country in his
search for elusive riches and the great passion of his life,
Kate O'Keefe.

From the boardrooms and backstreets of Sydney to the
hazardous waters of the Coral Sea, the sequel to *Cry
of the Curlew* confirms the exceptional talent of master
storyteller Peter Watt.

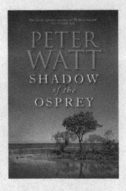

The Duffy/Macintosh Series

Flight of the Eagle

A deadly family curse holds two families in its powerful grip.

Captain Patrick Duffy's passions are inflamed by the mysterious Irishwoman Catherine Fitzgerald, further pitting him against his father, Michael Duffy, and his adoring but scheming grandmother, Lady Enid Macintosh.

On the rugged Queensland frontier, Native Mounted Police trooper Peter Duffy is torn between his loyal bond with Gordon James, the love of his sister, Sarah, and the blood of his mother's people, the Nerambura tribe.

Two men, the women who love them and a dreadful curse that still inextricably links the lives of the Macintoshes and the Duffys culminate in a stunning addition to the series featuring *Cry of the Curlew* and *Shadow of the Osprey*.

The Duffy/Macintosh Series

To Chase the Storm

When Major Patrick Duffy's beautiful wife Catherine leaves him and returns to her native Ireland, Patrick's broken heart propels him out of the Sydney Macintosh home and into yet another bloody war. However, the battlefields of Africa hold more than nightmarish terrors and unspeakable conditions for Patrick – they bring him in contact with one he thought long dead and lost to him.

Back in Australia, the mysterious Michael O'Flynn mentors Patrick's youngest son, Alex, and at his grandmother's request takes him on a journey to their Queensland property, Glen View. But will the terrible curse that has inextricably linked the Duffys and Macintoshes for generations ensure that no true happiness can ever come to them? So much seems to depend on Wallarie, the last warrior of the Nerambura tribe, whose mere name evokes a legend approaching myth.

Through the dawn of a new century in a now federated nation, *To Chase the Storm* charts an explosive tale of love and loss, from South Africa to Palestine, from Townsville to the green hills of Ireland, and to the more sinister politics that lurk behind them. By public demand, master storyteller Peter Watt returns to this much-loved series following on from the bestselling *Cry of the Curlew, Shadow of the Osprey* and *Flight of the Eagle.*

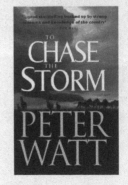

The Duffy/Macintosh Series

To Touch the Clouds

They had all forgotten the curse . . . except one . . . until it touched them. I will tell you of those times when the whitefella touched the clouds and lightning came down on the earth for many years.

In 1914, the storm clouds of war are gathering. Matthew Duffy and his cousin Alexander Macintosh are sent by Colonel Patrick Duffy to conduct reconnaissance on German-controlled New Guinea. At the same time, Alexander's sister, Fenella, is making a name for herself in the burgeoning Australian film industry.

But someone close to them has an agenda of his own – someone who would betray not only his country to satisfy his greed and lust for power. As the world teeters on the brink of conflict, one family is plunged into a nightmare of murder, drugs, treachery and treason.

The Duffy/Macintosh Series

To Ride the Wind

It is 1916, and war rages across Europe and the Middle East. Patrick and Matthew Duffy are both fighting the enemy, Patrick in the fields of France and Matthew in the skies above Egypt.

But there is another, secret foe. George Macintosh is passing information to the Germans, seeking to consolidate his power within the family company. And half a world away from the trenches, one of their own will meet a shocking death.

Meanwhile, a young man is haunted by dreams of a sacred cave, and seeks fiery stars that will help him take back his people's land.

To Ride the Wind continues the story of the Duffys and Macintoshes, following Peter Watt's much-loved characters as they fight to survive one of the most devastating conflicts in history – and each other.

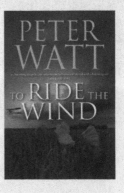

ALSO IN THE DUFFY/MACINTOSH SERIES

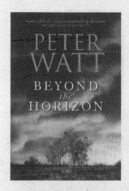

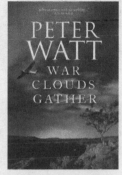

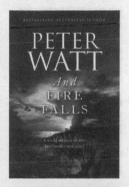

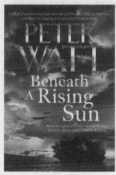

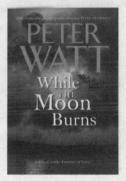

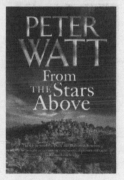

ALSO BY PETER WATT

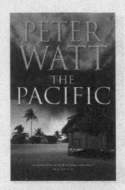

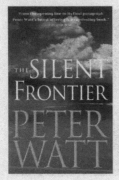

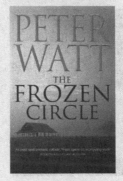